Postcolonial and Postsocialist Dialogues

Through staging dialogues between scholars, activists, and artists from a variety of disciplinary, geographical, and historical specializations, *Postcolonial and Postsocialist Dialogues* explores the possible resonances and dissonances between the postcolonial and the postsocialist in feminist theorizing and practice.

While postcolonial and postsocialist perspectives have been explored in feminist studies, the two analytics tend to be viewed separately. This volume brings together attempts to understand if and how postcolonial and postsocialist dimensions of the human condition – historical, existential, political, and ideological – intersect and correlate in feminist experiences, identities, and struggles. In the three sections that probe the intersections, opacities, and challenges between the two discourses, the authors put under pressure what postcolonialism and postsocialism mean for feminist scholarship and activism.

The contributions address the emergence of new political and cultural formations as well as circuits of bodies and capital in a post-Cold War and postcolonial era in currently re-emerging neo-colonial and imperial conflicts. They engage with issues of gender, sexuality, race, migration, diasporas, indigeneity, and disability, while also developing new analytical tools such as postsocialist precarity, queer postsocialist coloniality, uneventful feminism, feminist opacity, feminist queer crip epistemologies. The collection will be of interest for postcolonial and postsocialist researchers, students of gender studies, feminist activists and scholars.

Redi Koobak is Postdoctoral Research Fellow at the Centre for Women's and Gender Research, University of Bergen, Norway.

Madina Tlostanova is Professor of Postcolonial Feminisms at Linköping University, Sweden.

Suruchi Thapar-Björkert is Docent and Senior Lecturer at the Department of Government, University of Uppsala, Sweden.

Routledge Advances in Feminist Studies and Intersectionality

Routledge Advances in Feminist Studies and Intersectionality is committed to the development of new feminist and pro-feminist perspectives on changing gender relations, with special attention to:

- Intersections between gender and power differentials based on age, class, dis/abilities, ethnicity, nationality, racialisation, sexuality, violence, and other social divisions.
- Intersections of societal dimensions and processes of continuity and change: culture, economy, generativity, polity, sexuality, science and technology;
- Embodiment: Intersections of discourse and materiality, and of sex and gender.
- Transdisciplinarity: intersections of humanities, social sciences, medical, technical and natural sciences.
- Intersections of different branches of feminist theorizing, including: historical materialist feminisms, postcolonial and anti-racist feminisms, radical feminisms, sexual difference feminisms, queer feminisms, cyber feminisms, post-human feminisms, critical studies on men and masculinities.
- A critical analysis of the travelling of ideas, theories and concepts.
- A politics of location, reflexivity and transnational contextualising that reflects the basis of the Series framed within European diversity and transnational power relations.

Core editorial group

Professor Jeff Hearn (managing editor; Örebro University, Sweden; Hanken School of Economics, Finland; University of Huddersfield, UK)
Dr Kathy Davis (Institute for History and Culture, Utrecht, The Netherlands)
Professor Anna G. Jónasdóttir (Örebro University, Sweden)
Professor Nina Lykke (managing editor; Linköping University, Sweden)
Professor Elżbieta H. Oleksy (University of Łódź, Poland)
Dr Andrea Petö (Central European University, Hungary)
Professor Ann Phoenix (Institute of Education, University of London, UK)
Professor Chandra Talpade Mohanty (Syracuse University, USA)

Subaltern Women's Narratives
Strident Voices, Dissenting Bodies
Edited by Samraghni Bonnerjee

Postcolonial and Postsocialist Dialogues
Intersections, Opacities, Challenges in Feminist Theorizing and Practice
Edited by Redi Koobak, Madina Tlostanova and Suruchi Thapar-Björkert

For more information about the series, please visit www.routledge.com/Routledge-Advances-in-Feminist-Studies-and-Intersectionality/book-series/RAIFSAI

"This timely anthology comes together at the generative intersections of the asynchronous and sometimes contradictory struggles of postcolonial and postsocialist feminisms. Boldly confronting the race-blindness of postsocialism, and the overwhelming preoccupation with the capitalist West in postcolonialism, the contributions tackle the delicate challenge of theorizing from non-dominant locations – beyond complicity, and with a sensitive regard for difference. The collection highlights 'uneventful activism' and especially 'opacity' as resources for feminist resistance that confound easy legibility and cooptation by neoliberal recognition and success. The aim here is to safeguard 'spaces of re-existence and change' and a politics of post-colonial/socialist coalitions against racial capitalism."

— **Mahua Sarkar**, *Professor, Binghampton University, SUNY*

"To understand our current complicated and tantalizing geopolitical and corpopolitical situation, feminist scholarship needs to engage with positive meaning making as a way of fine-tuning the researcher's lens. This exemplary and diverse group of authors correlates postcolonial and postsocialist dimensions with feminist experiences in order to offer concepts and enlighten connections, and to combat 'global white ignorance' with much needed innovative politics of knowledge, activism and organizing that may give the world its future dimension back."

— **Andrea Pető,** Professor,
Central European University, Budapest-Vienna

"This collection will be of great interest to researchers, students, and general readers interested in contemporary women and feminist writing across the geopolitical East, West, North and South. It illuminates powerfully how people in different locales theorize, argue and negotiate the meanings of postcolonialism, postsocialism and their own role as intellectuals, educators and activists in the making or unmaking of the oppressive historical systems and relations underlining these phenomena. Yet the volume articulates the contributors' desire for new epistemologies and conceptual constructs that could better capture the complexity and globality especially of postsocialism as a condition, marking important theoretical and political debates about postcoloniality, globalization, political economy, race, and power in transnational feminism, postcolonial studies, and women, gender and sexuality studies."

— **Miglena Todorova**, *Assistant Professor, University of Toronto*

Postcolonial and Postsocialist Dialogues

Intersections, Opacities, Challenges in Feminist Theorizing and Practice

Edited by Redi Koobak, Madina Tlostanova and Suruchi Thapar-Björkert

Routledge
Taylor & Francis Group

LONDON AND NEW YORK

First published 2021
by Routledge
2 Park Square, Milton Park, Abingdon, Oxon OX14 4RN

and by Routledge
52 Vanderbilt Avenue, New York, NY 10017

Routledge is an imprint of the Taylor & Francis Group, an informa business

British Library Cataloguing-in-Publication Data
A catalogue record for this book is available from the British Library

Library of Congress Cataloging-in-Publication Data
Names: Koobak, Redi, editor. | Tlostanova, M. V. (Madina
    Vladimirovna) editor. | Thapar-Björkert, Suruchi, 1966- editor.
Title: Postcolonial and postsocialist dialogues : intersections,
    opacities, challenges in feminist theorizing and practice /
    edited by Redi Koobak, Madina Tlostanova and Suruchi
    Thapar-Björkert.
Description: First Edition. | New York : Routledge, 2021. | Series:
    Routledge advances in feminist studies and intersectionality |
    Includes bibliographical references and index.
Identifiers: LCCN 2020044007 (print) | LCCN 2020044008
    (ebook) | ISBN 9780367434403 (hardback) |
    ISBN 9781003003199 (ebook)
Subjects: LCSH: Feminism—History—21st century. |
    Sex role—History—21st century. | Neoliberalism—History—
    21st century. | Race—Political aspects. | Postcolonialism—Social
    aspects. | Post-communism—Social aspects.
Classification: LCC HQ1155 .P67 2021 (print) | LCC HQ1155
    (ebook) | DDC 305.309—dc23
LC record available at https://lccn.loc.gov/2020044007
LC ebook record available at https://lccn.loc.gov/2020044008

ISBN: 978-0-367-43440-3 (hbk)
ISBN: 978-0-367-72660-7 (pbk)
ISBN: 978-1-003-00319-9 (ebk)

Typeset in Times New Roman
by Apex CoVantage, LLC

Contents

Figures

Contributors

Neda Atanasoski is Professor of Feminist Studies and Director of Critical Race and Ethnic Studies at the University of California, Santa Cruz. Her research interests are in the areas of US and Eastern European media and cultural studies, with a focus on the politics of religion and sexuality, postsocialism, human rights and humanitarianism, and war and nationalism. Her most recent book, *Surrogate Humanity: Race, Robots, and the Politics of Technological Futures* (2019) co-authored with Kalindi Vora, traces the ways in which robots, artificial intelligence, and other technologies serve as surrogates for human workers within a labour system entrenched in racial capitalism and patriarchy.

Catherine Baker is Senior Lecturer in 20th Century History at the University of Hull. Her research has dealt with the linkage of postsocialist and postcolonial perspectives since her doctoral research in the mid-2000s, where representations of "Europe" and "the Balkans" in the narratives of identity surrounding Croatian popular music were an important theme. Her book *Race and the Yugoslav Region: Postsocialist, Post-Conflict, Postcolonial?* (2018) uses a revisiting of these themes through the lens of "race" as a starting point to reveal and account for the contradictory position of the post-Yugoslav region within a racialised global politics.

Petra Bakos is a PhD candidate at CEU's Gender Studies Department, writer, and embodied writing instructor at CEU's Roma Graduate Preparation Program. Her research focuses on decolonial epistemologies in the East Central European borderlands, while as an educator she's been invested in developing teaching practices that integrate as well as serve as laboratories for decolonial methods.

Manuela Boatcă is Professor of Sociology and Head of School of the Global Studies Programme at the University of Freiburg, Germany. Her work deals with world-systems analysis, postcolonial and decolonial perspectives, gender in modernity/coloniality, and the geopolitics of knowledge production in Eastern Europe and Latin America. She is author of *Global Inequalities beyond Occidentalism* (2016), of *Laboratoare ale modernității. Europa de Est și America*

Latină în (co)relație (2020), and the forthcoming book on inter-imperial and transimperial dynamics in 20th century Transylvania (with Anca Parvulescu).

Weiling Deng has a Ph.D. in social sciences and comparative education from UCLA, with a grounding in modern Chinese history of gender, sexuality, women's education and emancipation. While China has been her primary focus, she broadly engages with transpacific Asian histories, American racial capitalism, and critiques of Cold War ideology. Her current research project examines the risks of covid-19 in the United States with respect to catastrophic capitalist governance and racial and ethnic history in the 20th century.

Quinsy Gario and **Jörgen Gario** are performance poets, writers, and workshop facilitators from Curaçao and St. Maarten, currently based in the Netherlands. Jörgen is also a singer songwriter and a music producer, and Quinsy is also an academic specialised in artistic research, postcolonial studies, and gender studies. In their collaborations they focus on the interplay between critical fabulation, decolonial remembering, and genre bending. They have previously performed together at *Salone del Mobile in Milan* (2016), BAK in Utrecht (2017), KVS (2017) and *Kunstenfestivaldesarts* (2018) in Brussels.

Ruthia Jenrbekova is an interdisciplinary post-studio artist and cultural organiser and researcher from Almaty, Kazakhstan, currently a PhD candidate at the Academy of Fine Arts, Vienna. Jenrbekova is a co-founder of krëlex zentre (together with Maria Vilkovisky). Her fields of interest include performance, material semiotics, art-based methodologies.

Tjaša Kancler is an activist, artist, researcher, and associate professor at the Department of Visual Arts and Design – Section for Art and Visual Culture, Faculty of Fine Arts, University of Barcelona, Spain. They are a co-founder of t.i.c.t.a.c. – *Taller de Intervenciones Críticas Transfeministas Antirracistas Combativas* (*www.intervencionesdecoloniales.org*) and a co-editor of the journal *Desde el margen* (*www.desde-elmargen.net*).

Angéla Kóczé is an Assistant Professor, Chair of Romani Studies, and Academic Director of the Roma Graduate Preparation Program at Central European University in Budapest, Hungary. She has published extensively with various international presses on issues of social inclusion, gender equality, social justice, and civil society. She is a co-editor of *The Romani Women's Movement: Struggles and Debates in Central and Eastern Europe* (2019, with Violetta Zentai, Jelena Jovanović, and Enikő Vincze) and *The Roma and Their Struggle for Identity in Contemporary Europe* (2020, with Huub van Baar).

Kateřina Kolářová teaches at the Department of Gender Studies, Charles University, Prague, and is a board member of ATGENDER (The European Association for Gender Research, Education and Documentation). Her work engages intersections of disability, crip, queer, and race theories. Most recently, her manuscript *Rehabilitative Postsocialism: Disability, Race, Gender and Sexuality and the Limits of National Belonging* won the 2019 Tobin Siebers Prize for Disability Studies in Humanities (forthcoming). Together with Martina Winkler, she co-edited *Re/Imaginations of Disability in State Socialism: Visions, Promises, Frustrations* (forthcoming).

Redi Koobak is Postdoctoral Research Fellow at the Centre for Women's and Gender Research, University of Bergen, Norway. Her research interests include feminist visual culture studies; intersections of postcolonialism and postsocialism; cultural representations of gender, war, and nationalism; transnational and local feminisms; and creative writing methodologies. Koobak is the author of the monograph *Whirling Stories: Postsocialist Feminist Imaginaries and the Visual Arts* (2013).

Mithilesh Kumar is Assistant Professor, Tata Institute of Social Sciences, Patna Centre, India. His research interests are in the fields of border studies, migration studies, logistics, and political theory. His recent publications include "Bihar in 1974: Possibilities and Limits of a Popular Movement"; *From Popular Movements to Rebellion: The Naxalite Decade* (2019); and "Migrants and the Neoliberal City" in *The Terra Firma of Sovereignty: Land, Acquisition and Making of Migrant Labour* (2018).

Raili Marling is Professor of English Studies at the University of Tartu, Estonia. Her research interests include gender in modernist and contemporary literature and culture; discourses of neoliberalism in literature and culture; critical affect theory; conceptualization of gender in the postsocialist context; the possibilities of combining affect theory and discourse studies. Her extensive publications include the co-edited volume *Gender Equality in a Global Perspective* (2017) with Anders Örtenblad and Snježana Vasiljević. Marling is the editor of the first Estonian textbook on gender studies and has been one of the acting editors of *Ariadne Lõng*, the only Estonian peer-reviewed gender studies journal.

Maria Mayerchyk holds a position of senior research associate at the Ethnology Institute of the National Academy of Sciences of Ukraine. She teaches at the University of Alberta, Canada, and the National University of Kyiv-Mohyla Academy, Ukraine. Her research interests include sexuality and queer studies; critical folklore studies; Ukrainian culture; diaspora studies; feminist and queer activism; modernity and coloniality. Their co-edited volume *Inventing the Obscene: The Hidden Collections of Fedir Vovk* (2018) got Ukrainian National Book of the Year Award in nomination "Ethnology". She is co-originator and joint editor-in-chief of *Feminist Critique: East European Journal of Feminist and Queer Studies*.

Nivedita Menon is Professor at Jawaharlal Nehru University, Delhi, the author of *Seeing like a Feminist, Recovering Subversion: Feminist Politics Beyond* *the Law* (2004), and co-author of *Power and Contestation: India After 1989* (2007). She is one of the founders and authors of the collective blog on contemporary politics, *kafila.online*, and renowned translator of fiction and non-fiction from Hindi and Malayalam.

Kasia Narkowicz is Lecturer in Sociology and Criminology at the University of Gloucestershire, UK. Her research focuses on the intersections of religion, race, and gender, with a particular focus on Poland and Poles in the UK. Her recent publications include: "Refugees not welcome here: state, church and civil society responses to the refugee crisis in Poland" (*International Journal of Politics, Culture, and Society*), and "Saving and fearing Muslim women in a post-communist context: troubling Catholic and secular anti-Muslim narratives in Poland" (*Gender, Place and Culture*, with Konrad Pedziwiatr).

Lesia Pagulich is a queer feminist activist and researcher from Ukraine. She worked at the Women's International League for Peace and Freedom, All-Ukrainian Network of People Living with HIV/AIDS, and All-Ukrainian Union of Women Affected by HIV. She was an activist of the initiative Feminist Ofenzyva (Kyiv, Ukraine). Currently, she is a PhD student at the Department of Women's, Gender and Sexuality Studies at the Ohio State University. Her research interests lie in the field of postsocialist, decolonial, critical race, and queer studies.

Olga Plakhotnik is the Bayduza Postdoctoral Fellow at the Canadian Institute of Ukrainian Studies, University of Alberta, Canada. Their research interests include feminist epistemologies; gender, sexuality and queer studies; critical citizenship studies; queer diaspora studies; postsocialism studies. Olga is co-originator and joint editor-in-chief of *Feminist Critique: East European Journal of Feminist and Queer Studies*. Their PhD thesis at the Open University, UK titled *Imaginaries of Sexual Citizenship in Post-Maidan Ukraine: A Queer Feminist Discursive Investigation* is being reworked into a book.

Piro Rexhepi holds a PhD in politics from University of Strathclyde, UK. His research focuses on decoloniality, sexuality, and Islam. His recent work on racism and borders along the Balkan Refugee Route has been published in a range of mediums in and out of academia, including the *International Journal of Postcolonial Studies*, *Ethnic and Racial Studies*, *Critical Muslims*, and the *Guardian* among others.

Tatsiana Shchurko is a researcher and feminist activist from Belarus, currently, a PhD student at the Department of Women's, Gender and Sexuality Studies at the Ohio State University. Her research interests include queer feminist art, transnational feminism, postcolonial and decolonial theories, critical race studies, socialist and postsocialist studies, and politics of solidarity.

Jennifer Suchland is an associate professor at Ohio State University jointly appointed in the Department of Slavic and East European Languages and

Cultures and the Department of Women's, Gender and Sexuality Studies. Her research, teaching, and ethical commitments are to a robust study of rights, law, and political discourses as they are culturally and geopolitically entangled. Her book *Economies of Violence* analyses the re-emergence of global anti-trafficking discourse at the end of the Cold War looking in particular at the kinds of anti-violence agendas that gained resonance and power through the figure of the postsocialist trafficking victim "Natasha". She is an ACLS/Mellon Scholars and Society Fellow for 2020–2021 and is working on a book project focused on "modern day slavery".

Suruchi Thapar-Björkert is docent and senior lecturer at the Department of Government, University of Uppsala, Sweden. Her research focuses on gendered discourses of colonialism and nationalism, gendered violence, gender, social capital, and social exclusion and postcolonial epistemologies. Her first book *Unseen Faces: Unheard Voices, Women in the Indian Nationalist Movement* (2006) was reprinted as a *Sage Classic* (2015).

Madina Tlostanova is Professor of Postcolonial Feminisms at Linköping University, Sweden. She focuses on decolonial thought, particularly in its aesthetic, existential and epistemic manifestations, feminisms of the Global South, postsocialist human condition, fiction, and art. Her most recent books include *What Does It Mean to Be Post-Soviet? Decolonial Art from the Ruins of the Soviet Empire* (Duke University Press, 2018) and *A New Political Imagination, Making the Case* (co-authored with Tony Fry, 2020).

Alyosxa Tudor is Associate Professor (Senior Lecturer) at the Centre for Gender Studies at SOAS, University of London, UK. Their work connects trans and queer feminist approaches with transnational feminism and postcolonial studies. Alyosxa's main research interest lies in analysing (knowledge productions on) migrations, diasporas, and borders in relation to critiques of Eurocentrism and to processes of gendering and racialisation. Alyosxa has published extensively on these topics and is the author of the monograph *from [al'manja] with love*.

Maria Vilkovisky is a poetess, artist, and curator from Almaty, Kazakhstan. A graduate of the Kazakh State Conservatory, she was a violinist with the opera house orchestra, then studied at the literary school for writers and Moscow curatorial summer school. Since 2011 she has been running an artistic space in Almaty and is a co-founder of a long-term parainstitutional project called Krëlex Zentre.

Kalindi Vora is Associate Professor of Gender, Sexuality and Women's Studies at the University of California Davis and Director of the Feminist Research Institute. Her research interests are in the interdisciplinary fields of science and technology studies, postcolonial theory, critical race and gender studies, south Asian area and diaspora studies, labour and globalisation, Marxist theory, and cultural studies. Her most recent book *Surrogate Humanity: Race, Robots, and the Politics of Technological Futures* (2019), in collaboration with Neda Atanasoski, examines the racial and gendered politics informing contemporary robotics and artificial intelligence design.

Shana Ye is Assistant Professor in Women and Gender Studies at University of Toronto Scarborough and in the Women and Gender Studies Institute at the University of Toronto. Her research areas include transnational feminism, queer studies, post/socialist studies, and theories of affect and trauma. She examines the ways in which discourses of queer sexualities in post-socialism are intertwined with history of colonialism, Cold War ideology, globalised modalities of neoliberalism, and new forms of empire making.

Lidia Zhigunova holds a PhD from Tulane University (2016) and a master's degree in Comparative Literature from Louisiana State University (2002). Her dissertation "From Harem to Feminocracy: De-Orientalizing the Circassian National Imaginary in Literature and Art From the Early Modern to the Post-Soviet Periods" explores the politics of representation and continuous identity formation of Circassians, the indigenous people of the North Caucasus. Her main areas of academic interest include the study of European modern and post-modern literary and artistic traditions, travel literature, postcolonial and decolonial studies, as well as feminist literary theories and indigenous studies. She has published articles on the politics of memory and identity in the North Caucasus.

Chapter 1

Introduction

Uneasy affinities between the postcolonial and the postsocialist

Redi Koobak, Madina Tlostanova, and Suruchi Thapar-Björkert

We are writing this introduction in the midst of the unprecedented crisis linked to the Covid-19 expansion that has substantially shifted the political agendas locally, nationally, and globally while foregrounding the inadequacy of politics and political institutions. Collectively, we are at crossroads which can lead us either to an ultra-right, nationalist, homophobic, and racist future of biopolitical control and new high-tech slavery, or a rebirth of social equality, solidarity, and largely socialist values that have so far not been implemented in any nation-state forms. We believe that in this historical conjuncture, it is crucial to revisit the socialist and postsocialist feminist trajectories, agendas, concerns, and narratives vis-à-vis the postcolonial and post-Fordist models and conditions. Suddenly, what seemed to be a matter of the past – the shameful and defeated socialist history, the forgotten utopia – calls for realigning with the present and projecting into the future if it is ever to happen. However, the neo-socialist tendencies that are unfolding in these times of corona crisis are very different from the state socialist regimes of the past, but close enough to various anarcha-feminist and autonomous feminist as well as broader social movements that react proactively to the inadequacy of the state and the crisis of legitimacy that neoliberal global "capitalocene" has imposed on us all.

In this volume, we begin from the idea that the postsocialist frame, rejected by many as outdated and obsolete (Müller 2019), should not be discarded yet. Postsocialism is not only about a certain time after socialism and not just about people living in former state socialist spaces. It is also a characteristic of the world in its globality after the end of the Cold War (Suchland 2015; Atanasoski and Vora 2018). As human conditions, postcolonialism and postsocialism are more closely connected than is generally imagined, as they reflect the larger geopolitical shifts that mobilise people to react to the ontological designs imposed by modernity and coloniality. While the whole world has become post/neo-colonial after the massive colonisations of the mid 20th century, it has also been marked by discrediting socialism as the last grand social utopia of a just world, including the welfare state, equal opportunities, social mobility, negative discrimination, and internationalism. Never fully realised in any of the spaces that claimed to be socialist, the state socialist utopia is still crucial as a dream, as an alternative to the capitalist liberal or neoliberal model. In this capacity it has been helpful for the leftist and anti-colonial movements both in the West and in the global South. Thus, exploring the connections between the postcolonial and the postsocialist human experiences (as descriptive terms) becomes all the more urgent. It can create a powerful force of global insurgency because the postcolonial and postsocialist conditions are shared by the majority of the people in the world. This is the rationale from where the volume unfolds.

The emergence of the presently powerful critical theories of modernity, particularly its latest phase, was an immediate response to the end of the global socialist utopia. A good example of this is decolonial thought which can be seen as a bitter reflection on the dismantling of the bipolar system, a reaction to the enforced neoliberal modernity, and a realisation that the state cannot be democratised or decolonised (Walsh and Mignolo 2018). Anibal Quijano's idea of "coloniality" and later Walter Mignolo's concept of "decoloniality" have reframed "decolonisation" as a term from the Cold War era. Coloniality is different from colonialism and decolonisation is different from decoloniality. This rethinking happened at the point when Fukuyama infamously announced the "end of history" (Fukuyama 1992) and the arrival of western neoliberalism as the final destination of humanity. The announcement of the eternal present of the consumer paradise and the cancellation of the course of time launched a chronophobic mechanism (Fry and Tlostanova 2020) whose results are clearly seen today – three decades after the closing of the socialist utopia.

The postsocialist temporality starts with this negation of history and an abrupt historical rupture with the "wrong" socialist modernity. It takes place at the point when the postcolonial model has already been in place for several decades and most importantly, has stayed firmly within the logic of the same western capitalist modernity. Therefore, the postcolonial trajectory is that of a slow successive progress whereas the postsocialist path is a belated break and a start from scratch. The two discourses shared many beliefs and disillusionments but being historically and politically non-synchronous they were not always able to detect these intersections or hear each other's voices. While the early postcolonial discourses were leftist, anti-capitalist, and progressivist, the postsocialist discourses were marked by a visceral rejection of everything socialist and a fascination with Western knowledge. By the early 2000s, however, a more critical stance began to gradually emerge among postsocialist activists and scholars.

In addition, Western thought has interpreted the concept of postsocialism in exclusively temporal terms (as a period after socialism) ignoring its spatial and human dimensions. Furthermore, just like the global North appropriates or ignores the knowledge from the global South, it also tends to dismiss postsocialist epistemologies, seeing them as a part of the local history of a particular region rather than viewing postsocialism as a global human condition. This bias has often been criticised (Tlostanova 2018; Nowicka 1995), yet mainly by scholars from postsocialist countries. At the same time, decolonial thought, even if it started as a response to the end of the Cold War, also ignored – at least in the beginning – both the experience of state socialism and what followed in East Europe, the former

USSR, South East Asia, or Cuba. For decolonial as well as postcolonial think-ers, the postsocialist people have remained a homogenised and opaque group, counted as irrelevant in both of the equations, the post/decolonial and the (neo) liberal. Socialist modernity acted as a trigger for the lighter (end of history) and darker (coloniality) interpretations of the present. Yet the postsocialist countries and people became the proverbial elephant in the room.

As many scholars have emphasised, it makes more sense to regard "post-socialism", like the related term "postcolonialism", as an analytic rather than a fixed time period or locality (Chari and Verdery 2009; Dunn and Verdery 2015; Atanasoski and Vora 2018). For instance, Nina Lykke notes that post-socialism, when "unmoored from a limited geopolitical understanding as spa-tially and temporally linked to former socialist countries in East and Central Europe, can address imaginaries of protest in a broad anti-capitalist sense" (Lykke 2020, 12). As analytical terms, both postcolonialism and postsocialism are concerned with legacies of imperial power, dependence, resistance, and hybridity, therefore pointing to multiple productive convergences between the two. Yet, postcolonialism is commonly equated with the global South, rarely addressed through postsocialist perspectives, while at the same time postso-cialism is often only associated with Central and East Europe, post-Soviet countries in the Caucasus and Central Asia, and China – sites that are always already interwoven with a (post)colonial world order and almost never seen as decolonising. In the context where the false geopolitical universals and ste-reotypes such as West versus East, North versus South, and the reliance on a first-second-third world model continue to operate in full force, we need new models and concepts in order to challenge hegemonic discourses and under-mine the problematic expectation to subscribe to the unifying Euro-American intellectual traditions.

In this volume, even as we attempt to question the attachment of the term to a particular time period or to specific geopolitical places, we often use the term "postsocialist" to refer specifically to the post-Soviet countries, Central and East European countries in the former Soviet sphere of influence, and a number of countries in the global South that for several decades joined the state socialist model, whereas the term "post-Soviet" refers exclusively to the former repub-lics of the USSR. The Cold War era term "second world" is problematic due to its latent ideology of a universal modernisation narrative and its elevation of the "first world" (cf. Chari and Verdery 2009, 18). Moreover, for a number of countries in East Asia the Cold War is still an ongoing experience, and scholars and activists from these countries, referring to a different (from East European) temporality, would be very uneasy about using the term "postsocialist". Their anti-capitalist stance includes a critique of feminism that is largely interpreted as a product of the Cold War logic of knowledge production (Kim 2020). We are aware of this and other important differences between the countries in the East European region, Africa, East Asia, and Central and South America, but we also acknowledge the need for some overarching term to refer to the shared legacy of socialist influence across the world.

The contributors to this volume pick up the term postsocialist in very different ways. On the one hand, some of them regard the term postsocialism as an improved and updated version of socialism, attempting to add critical vigour to it. On the other hand, there are those who see it as a human condition of limitation, enslavement, recolonisation presented as decolonisation and also further, as grounds for racialisation and exclusion. Yet all of them continue to find it useful. Similarly, the term postcolonial is open for discussion. Is it a human condition or a set of beliefs? Are scholars postcolonial because they come from postcolonial countries or because they share the postcolonial theoretical and political agenda?

Positionality and the politics of knowledge production

This volume grows out of conversations that started at a conference we organised in April 2015 at Linköping University, Sweden. These exchanges revealed that the intersections between the postcolonial and the postsocialist surface in feminist studies in a similar way as in many other disciplines. For example, despite the shift of focus towards intersecting differences and the local within feminist studies, Western feminist theorising has remained hegemonic, and entanglements of geopolitical differences are largely understudied.

As feminist scholars from Estonia, non-European Russian/former Soviet colonies, and India, living and working, at the time, in Sweden as "non-Swedes" (Koobak and Thapar-Björkert 2012), we often found ourselves disidentifying with Western feminist academia through our specific overlapping and unfixed postcolonial and postsocialist positions. Our shared experiences as well as our previous and on-going work on the intersections of the postcolonial and the postsocialist (Koobak and Thapar-Björkert 2014; Tlostanova, Thapar-Björkert, and Koobak 2016, 2019), inspired us to open up space for discussions around the overlaps, divergences, and relevance of the postcolonial and the postsocialist sensibilities for feminist theory and praxis.

We are not arguing for or holding on to any kind of fixed positions of postcolonial and postsocialist feminisms because we know from our personal and research experience that there are always overlaps and border spaces between these positionalities. As a feminist scholar from postsocialist Estonia, Redi Koobak grew into feminism through the English language and Western academic contexts where she couldn't quite place herself. Often feeling slightly off or out of sync because her positionality read as similar to the West but not similar enough, while it also registered as different but somehow not different enough, Redi turned to challenging the limits of the "field imaginary" of feminist studies by paying careful attention to the affinities between the postcolonial and the postsocialist. Madina Tlostanova combines post-Soviet and postcolonial sensibilities and originations related to her mixed Circassian (North Caucasus) and Uzbek (Central Asia) ancestry as the two Russian/Soviet colonial spaces that shared many features and experiences with the colonies of the modern Western capitalist empires as they were copied and distorted by the Czarist and later Soviet empires. Madina's internal difference (as a racialised postcolonial other within the Russian Federation) and her external difference (as a foreigner with a Russian passport working in Sweden) merge in a specific invisibilising/hyper-visibilising pattern that erases crucial elements of her dynamic intersectional subjectivity and positionality (which sees her as "black" – in Moscow, or as "Russian" – in Sweden). Suruchi Thapar-Björkert's postcolonial positionality was shaped through the legacy of her parents' anti-colonial activism during the 1940s against British rule in India. The spatial-colonial contexts of academic institutions in the UK, together with the domestic genealogies as a daughter of a nationalist household, gave postcoloniality an emotional and political salience. Our respective academic journeys made us realise that there were important conversations that needed to be forged between feminists who consider themselves as postcolonial and/or postsocialist.

While preparing for the conference, we realised that the topic spoke mostly to scholars from postsocialist Eastern Europe who are often well-versed in postcolonial feminist theory and who engage with it productively to analyse postsocialist contexts. It was a great challenge to find scholars who would fit under the term postcolonial feminist and who would, at the same time, be keen on exploring the convergences and divergences between the postcolonial and the postsocialist discourses. In the course of the conference, we understood that the postcolonial feminist scholars who did attend the event struggled to engage with the particularities of postsocialist contexts. Partly, we thought, this may have been because postcolonialism still tends to be associated with the global South and postsocialism with the former "second world", and in feminist studies much of the focus has been on the relation between the "first world" and the "third world" women and the first and the "second world" women but not so much between the "second" and the "third world" women (see also Suchland 2011). In addition, it could well be that from the perspective of many postcolonial scholars the so-called "second world", with its exaggerated drive for belonging to Europe, including the epistemic one, is perceived as having a trajectory more akin to the "first world", rather than being marginal to it. Nonetheless this idea is misplaced as postcolonial states, since decolonisation, have unapologetically aligned themselves very closely with western epistemological projects. This is a direct result of the continuous epistemic control and dominance of the "first world" whose strategy also includes maintaining vertical models of Western surveillance rather than allowing for direct horizontal relations among the subaltern others. At the conference, we noticed that scholars from postsocialist Eastern Europe were inclined to apply concepts from postcolonial feminism to make sense of their own positionality in relation to Western feminism. Moreover, the participants' interventions revealed that postcolonial feminists form an established part – if not the core – of the global feminist division of labour, whereas postsocialist feminists tend to be seen as lacking a well-defined agenda in the eyes of their postcolonial and/or western counterparts.

Rethinking established concepts, introducing new ones

Addressing the existing and potential resonances and dissonances between post-colonial and postsocialist analytics shifts the established ways of thinking about gender, sexuality, race, migration, diasporas, indigeneity, and disability. In this sense, dialogues between scholars, activists and artists from a variety of discipli-nary, geographical, and historical specialisations put under pressure what post-colonialism and postsocialism mean for feminist scholarship and activism. This volume brings together various attempts to understand if and how postcolonial and postsocialist dimensions of the human condition – historical, existential, political, and ideological – intersect and correlate in feminist experiences, identi-ties, and struggles. The contributors focus on the emergence of new political and cultural formations as well as circuits of bodies and capital in the post-Cold War and postcolonial era in currently re-emerging neo-colonial and imperial conflicts.

Our ambition in this volume is to depart from the conventional mode of aca-demic writing and experiment with different formats such as interviews and conversations, weaving them in between more traditional chapters. To facilitate these dialogues, we create links between them through considering intersections, opacities, and challenges that surface in postcolonial and postsocialist feminist entanglements. The book is thus divided into three sections (see the summaries of each contribution in the section introductions). The first part rethinks intersec-tions in a productive way, as an interaction of cultures, epistemologies, ideologies, and human conditions within modernity/coloniality. The second part disrupts the normative understandings of opacity and relocates its potential for resistance in marginalised imaginaries. The third part grapples with various challenges posed by feminisms' complicity in upholding the racist European imperial project as well as feminisms' co-optation in conservative nationalist frameworks.

In fact, in a larger context, while racial issues have stood at the centre of post-colonial theorising, race as a concept has not been thoroughly analysed in post-socialist thought. The fact that race became one of the recurring themes in this volume demonstrates the need for more complex understandings of race and rac-ism when considering the entanglements of postcolonial and postsocialist his-tories, spaces and epistemologies, particularly in and for postsocialist contexts. For example, in East and Central Europe, discussions on race are often dismissed because the problem of race is seen as belonging to colonialism and its legacies (see Chapter 15). The understanding that racial issues only pertain to those coun-tries that had colonies or those that were colonies allow for race to be displaced elsewhere. Even when some East Europeans try to join modernity through nostal-gically claiming colonial connection as part of their national history (e.g. Latvia, as discussed in Chapter 12), they do not see it in explicitly racial terms.

However, race and racialisation do not refer only to overseas colonies but also to the internal racialisation of populations such as indigenous people (see Chapter 6), Roma people (see Chapter 15), migrants (Chapter 14), and ethnic and religious minorities caught in inter-imperial conflicts (Chapter 13). What binds these groups together is that they do not enjoy full citizenship rights due to the fact that they are racialised. For instance, a closer analysis of European internal indigeneity shows the arbitrariness of racial categories, as exemplified by Lidia Zhigunova's discussion of the ambivalent racial status of Circassians who have become the epitome of "whiteness" in US racial discourse (think of the outdated term "Caucasian" which is still often used in reference to white people) yet who arc branded as "Blacks" in Russia together with other "Caucasians" (i.e. the non-Russians who live in the Caucasus). The gendered, sexualised, and Orientalised Circassian Beauty myth demonstrates "the constructed and highly imaginative nature of racial discourse" and also reveals that "colonialism and imperialism were inseparable from the invention of race in the European and American contexts" (see Chapter 6). Another understanding of internal racialisation is encapsulated in Alyosxa Tudor's concept of "migratism" which seeks to problematise whiteness as a homogeneous category, using the example of East Europeans (see Chapter 14). All these contributions thus challenge the conventional understandings of racial hierarchies.

These racial hierarchies also have an impact on knowledge production in the way feminists from former postsocialist countries are not expected to discuss race and colonisation as this topic is normally reserved for women of colour and black women for whom racism is presumably a more authentic experience. This is a sign of the global feminist academic division of labour that still silently assumes that global North feminists are producers of theory whereas the rest can only describe case studies and act as a more sophisticated version of native informants. To gain visibility and recognition one needs to adopt the academic grammar of the Western world. This visibility is nonetheless contextual with many opting for radically aligning themselves with local histories. The racist division of intellectual labour racialises both postcolonial and postsocialist feminists by assigning them specific topics and areas of expertise as in the case of postcolonial researchers or leaving them without such a subject as in the case of postsocialist feminists who continue to be seen as "ideological, rather than racial, others" (Suchland 2011, 852). Through critical reflections on the existing theoretical and analytical categories, the contributors to this collection seriously disturb and question this feminist division of labour, pointing to new vistas of dynamic transversal research outside the assigned boxes.

Moreover, not only does bringing the critical discourses of the postcolonial and the postsocialist together and examining their intersections as theoretical ground generate new understandings of established concepts, it also enables us to develop entirely new ones. For example, one such concept is Jennifer Suchland's "postsocialist precarity" (see Chapter 2) linked with Eurocentrism and racism which are regarded as hidden epistemologies of socialism and postsocialism. The current racialisation of internal and external borders and the translation of ideological, gender or class differences into racial ones are easier to understand through critically analysing the hidden racist logic of socialism and postsocialism.

Postsocialist precarity helps us to understand the struggles of the former second world to re-join the world system while being perpetually assigned to a peripheral role and having a bitter sense of defeat.

Resonating with "postsocialist precarity", Shana Ye's concept of "queer postsocialist coloniality" (see Chapter 5) emerges at the intersection of postsocialist and postcolonial outlooks, both of which are revised at the same time. In relation to China, this concept troubles the commonplace Western notions of the Chinese trajectory of socialism and its transition to postsocialism. Furthermore, it allows us to think of China as a subaltern empire that does not frame itself in postcolonial or postsocialist terms. "Queer postsocialist coloniality" multiplies understandings of postsocialism in relation to non-Western countries and to the world system at large, bringing back the dimensions of class, ideology, labour, economic inequality, and violence which are often glided over in the discussions of "queer fluidity" in Western queer theory.

Similarly to the analytical potential of "queer postsocialist coloniality", Maria Mayerchyk and Olga Plakhotnik's concept of "uneventful feminism" (see Chapter 9) highlights how postsocialism and postcolonialism become entangled and even clash. The growing militarisation and NGO-isation of mainstream feminism and its complicity with the global North in the recent history of Ukraine has led to a need to articulate alternative forms of resistance termed "uneventful" that combine both anti-nationalist and anti-colonial agendas, including feminist critique of racism, homophobia, transphobia, and cisheterosexism. Here "uneventfulness" refers to anonymity, low visibility, and unsuccessfulness. Stretching Western models of activism and citizenship beyond their boundaries, the activist groups engaged in "uneventful feminism" thus reinvent understandings of protest in an effort to imagine alternative futures in a time of war.

The need for a new analytical language also surfaces when feminist scholars grapple with the challenge of balancing visibility and opacity within the nationalist and neoliberal context. Opacity stands in contradistinction to transparency, an essential universalist principle of enlightenment, which eliminates ambiguity but also difference. Drawing on Édoard Glissant's (1997) understanding of "opacity" which gives the marginalised the right to remain unknowable and reflect on their difference in their own terms, Raili Marling's take on opacity in feminist theorising and activism (see Chapter 7) challenges its possible co-optation with neoliberal agendas that neutralise and tame the critical edge of feminist thinking and agency. Opacity in feminist thinking is then grounded in solidarities and co-relationalities with different others who "write back" from the space of critique in the margins.

In the spirit of building co-relationalities, this volume reaffirms that dialogues between postcolonial and postsocialist feminisms are important as they help us launch "deep coalitions" (Lugones 2003). According to Lugones, "deep coalitions never reduce multiplicity, they span across differences. Aware of particular configurations of oppression, they are not fixed on them, but strive beyond into the world, towards a shared struggle of interrelated others" (Lugones 2003, 98).

Such coalitions require maintaining complexity and heterogeneity rather than homogenous sameness on both universalised global and/or particularised local grounds. Deep coalitions between postcolonial and postsocialist feminisms require keeping the differences between the two in sight while building solidarities against neoliberalism, nationalist populism, and the heteropatriarchal dictate. The multiplicity of voices gathered in this volume thus allows bypassing the Western euromodern centre via horizontal pluriversal multilocal polylogue, dismantling coloniality of knowledge and attempting to give the world its future dimension back.

References

Atanasoski, Neda, and Kalindi Vora. 2018. "Introduction: Postsocialist Politics and the Ends of Revolution." *Social Identities* 24, no. 2: 1–15. https://doi.org/10.1080/1350463 0.2017.1321712.

Chari, Sharad, and Katherine Verdery. 2009. "Thinking Between the Posts: Postcolonialism, Postsocialism, and Ethnography After the Cold War." *Comparative Studies in Society and History* 51, no. 1: 6–34.

Dunn, Elizabeth Cullen, and Katherine Verdery. 2015. "Postsocialism." In *Emerging Trends in the Social and Behavioral Sciences*, edited by Robert A. Scott and Marlis C. Buchmann, 1–9. New York: Wiley. https://doi.org/10.1002/9781118900772.etrds0261.

Fry, Tony, and Madina Tlostanova. 2020. *A New Political Imagination: Making the Case.* London: Routledge.

Fukuyama, Francis. 1992. *The End of History and the Last Man.* New York: Free Press.

Glissant, Édoard. 1997. *Poetics of Relation.* Ann Arbor: University of Michigan Press.

Kim, Suzy. 2020. "Cold War Feminisms in East Asia: Introduction." *Positions* 28, no. 3: 501–516. https://doi.org/10.1215/10679847-8315101.

Koobak, Redi, and Suruchi Thapar-Björkert. 2012. "Becoming Non-Swedish: Locating the Paradoxes of In/visible Identities." *Feminist Review* 102: 125–134. https://doi.org/10.1057/fr.2012.14.

Koobak, Redi, and Suruchi Thapar-Björkert. 2014. "Writing the Place From Which One Speaks." In *Writing Academic Texts Differently: Intersectional Feminist Methodologies and the Playful Art of Writing*, edited by Nina Lykke, 47–61. New York: Routledge.

Lugones, María. 2003. *Pilgrimages/Peregrinajes: Theorizing Coalition Against Multiple Oppression.* New York and Oxford: Rowman and Littlefield Publishers Inc.

Lykke, Nina. 2020. "Transversal Dialogues on Intersectionality, Socialist Feminism and Epistemologies of Ignorance." *NORA: Nordic Journal of Feminist and Gender Research*: 1–14. https://doi.org/10.1080/08038740.2019.1708786.

Müller, Martin. 2019. "Goodbye, Postsocialism!" *Europe-Asia Studies* 71, no. 4: 533–550. https://doi.org/10.1080/09668136.2019.1578337.

Nowicka, W. 1995. "Pekin 1995." In *Federacja na Rzecz Kobiet i Planowania Rodziny: Biulletin*, 2–3. Warsaw: Federacja na Rzecz Kobiet i Planowania Rodziny.

Suchland, Jennifer. 2011. "Is Postsocialism Transnational?" *Signs* 3, no. 4: 837–862. https://doi.org/10.1086/658899.

Suchland, Jennifer. 2015. *Economies of Violence: Transnational Feminism, Postsocialism, and the Politics of Sex Trafficking.* Durham, NC: Duke University Press. https://doi.org/10.1215/9780822375289.

Tlostanova, Madina. 2018. *What Does It Mean To Be Post-Soviet? Decolonial Art From the Ruins of the Soviet Empire*. Durham, NC: Duke University Press.

Tlostanova, Madina, Suruchi Thapar-Björkert, and Redi Koobak. 2016. "Border Thinking and Disidentification: Postcolonial and Postsocialist Feminist Dialogues." *Feminist Theory* 17, no. 2: 211–228. https://doi.org/10.1177/1464700116645878.

Tlostanova, Madina, Suruchi Thapar-Björkert, and Redi Koobak. 2019. "The Postsocialist 'Missing Other' of Transnational Feminism?" *Feminist Review* 121: 81–87. https://doi.org/10.1177/0141778918816946.

Walsh, Catherine, and Walter Mignolo. 2018. *On Decoloniality*. Durham, NC: Duke University Press.

Part I

Intersections

If we were to look at postsocialism and postcolonialism with the help of a traffic analogy that was suggested by Kimberlé Crenshaw in her discussion of intersectionality (Crenshaw 1989, 149), we would see a busy and unregulated intersection with traffic going in all directions and allowing for race, class, language, religion, ethnicity, ideology, geopolitics, gender, sexuality, indigeneity, and other vehicles to enter the scene. Moreover, several traffic systems are merging together and at times, clashing against each other: one consisting of cars, another of trams and trolleys. There are also cyclists and moto-cyclists, a horseman, and a donkey cart as well as many pedestrians who are crossing the street in the wrong places. The streetlight is off due to a major blackout and everyone is trying to push through, avoid a clash, and survive. People come to this intersection from different starting positions and with different privileges. The major force that controls it all is modernity/coloniality which in this limited traffic metaphor can be envisioned through a necessity to move forward faster and faster, to catch up and leave behind, to make sure one is not run over.

Yet it is also possible to look at intersections as a meeting and discussion place of cultures, epistemic models, ideologies, human conditions, dreams of freedom and independence, disillusionments, and hopes for the future. The colonial and imperial dimensions are indivisible from the capitalist and socialist frames complicating and distorting each other in the process of unfolding of modernity/coloniality as an enormous labyrinth rather than a neat intersection. Intersections should not necessarily be seen as a criss-crossing of various forms of discrimination. They can also carry a re-existing meaning as a way of fine-tuning and making relational the researcher's lens, a way of focusing, following E. Glissant, on the texture of the weave of various phenomena rather than on their imagined stable characteristics (Glissant 1997, 190). Intersections then are not about taking one to another or comparing one to another, merely looking for similarities or differences. Rather the postcolonial and postsocialist human and worldly conditions or even analytical paradigms are mutually reflected in each other, simultaneously or with a time lag. It is not an issue of influences or imitations but a result of how modernity/coloniality is manifested in postcolonial and postsocialist trajectories and contexts.

The authors of this section creolise the postcolonial, postsocialist, and decolonial paradigms in their production of powerful concepts such as the postsocialist redoubled precarity theorised by Jennifer Suchland who locates it in the global coloniality and links with Eurocentrism seen as a hidden epistemology of socialism and postsocialism both of which are firmly grounded in racism. Therefore manifesting and disavowing the hidden racist logic of socialism and postsocialism becomes crucial in any effort to understand contemporary geopolitical and corpopolitical situation with its racialisation of internal and external borders and translation of ideological, gender and class difference into a racial one (the whiteness narrative in East Europe and Russia, the agenda of returning to Europe). For one thing, the Russian, Soviet and post-Soviet coloniality systematically hides its complicity in the darker side of modernity and erases the crucial racial dimension that links it to the world system in non-innocent ways. Postsocialist precarity is a lens that allows to make sense of the efforts of the former second world to re-enter the world system, albeit in the prescribed peripheral role that has been economically, structurally and symbolically assigned to it from the beginning of modernity and with a bitter sense of starting from scratch and being defeated before even entering the battle field.

Echoing Jennifer Suchland in her understanding of postsocialism as a global condition, Neda Atanasoski and Kalindi Vora attempt to salvage socialism as a working paradigm for the present and the future, while also looking at it as a fruitful theoretical frame of analysis. In the centre of their attention stands the promising concept of grass roots collectivity which they oppose to top-down state socialist forms, neoliberal corporations, and family institute. Avoiding a clear definition of socialism, Atanasoski and Vora in fact demonstrate a socialist anarchist position placing their hope in the structures of social support and informal economies. The question remains why such forms should necessarily be tagged as or be socialist? And why is it still important to continue using the Euromodern terms and frames such as socialism in defining phenomena of a different order, such as the indigenous, national-liberation, feminist, and environmental movements, that were often hijacked and distorted by the dominant political ideologies including socialism.

In her introspective, ethically charged account at the intersection of critical race studies, transnational feminism, and decolonial thought, Catherine Baker reflects on the postsocialist legacies in the Balkans seen through the prism of orientalism and neo-colonialism with a special focus on race and racism that tends to be overlooked by both postcolonial and postsocialist commentators. Crucially she reinstates race, racism, and whiteness into the discussions of South-East Europe accurately stating that in larger terms, postcolonial and postsocialist feminisms in spite of their seemingly "disparate and contradictory struggles", are in fact "resisting interconnected forces" which should potentially lead to coalitions in protest against racial capitalism. Baker's contribution is important for privileged White scholars who aspire to write on racialised experiences that are not their own history as she confronts the uneasy question of how to make choices in what one writes, who one cites, and who one works with.

Shana Ye's chapter elaborates on yet another analytic concept – the "postsocialist coloniality" that is enacted through "queer postsocialism" in China. Resonating with Suchland, Ye regards this intersection through the revised postsocialist and postcolonial prisms simultaneously. If, in East Europe and the USSR, race was an erased element of coloniality, in China anticolonial and anti-imperial discourses were presented as national/nativist and top down (state supported). Ye's unexpected view of Chinese history as a subaltern empire, free from conventional western stereotypes, opens up unknown contradictory forms of postsocialist coloniality that simultaneously confirm and contradict modernity's logic of linear progress. Decolonising the concept of "queer fluidity" as an elitist western invention, Ye comes up with an intersectional decolonial task of examining queerness from inside the postsocialist coloniality. This allows reintroducing class, ideology, labour, economic inequality, and violence whose trajectories often go back to the socialist past.

Lidia Zhigunova presents one more overlooked intersection in discussions of postsocialism and postcolonialism – that of indigeneity. An awareness of the socialist succession and continuation of the Czarist Empire's colonialist legacy in the treatment of Circassians sheds additional light on the darker colonial side of socialism. Zhigunova's account of long and complex Circassian history is a detailed interplay of colonial and racist discriminatory state policies and a persistent indigenous resistance. This account intersects colonialism, resistant indigeneity, genocide, dislocations, deportations and diasporic dispersions, the forceful imposition of colonialist patriarchal gender models, the ordeals of state socialism, and the neocolonialist present marked by "colonial amnesia". Zhigunova makes it clear that the anticolonial promises of state socialist regimes come to false rhetorical gestures as illustrated by the Circassian narrative. This account is also given with the broader Euromodern racial hierarchies in mind and regarded vis-à-vis the Russian/Soviet contradictory racial constructions that are realised in the "blackness of whiteness" paradox. The positive re-existing and subversive element of Circassian identities, cosmologies, and human rights is represented in contemporary Circassian women's fiction, in decolonial art and social movements, in educational and environmental initiatives.

References

Crenshaw, K. 1989. "Demarginalizing the Intersection of Race and Sex: A Black Feminist Critique of Antidiscrimination Doctrine, Feminist Theory and Antiracist Politics." *University of Chicago Legal Forum*: 139–167.
Glissant, E. 1997. *Poetics of Relation*. Ann Arbor: University of Michigan Press.

Chapter 2

Locating postsocialist precarity in global coloniality

A decolonial frame for 1989?

Jennifer Suchland

Introduction

Decoloniality is a critical worldview born out of the experiences of and resistances to settler colonialism and imperial conquest. While settler and colonial logics are indeed transnational and contemporary, the year 1492 plays a strong gravitational force in theorisations of coloniality and approaches to decoloniality. The timelines of colonialism implied by 1492 appear to be both geographically and ideologically light years away from those that centre 1917 or 1989. The focus of this essay is whether and how postsocialism, in its east Europe and Eurasian contexts, is situated within or in relation to the specific genealogies (and concomitant logics) that are implied with 1492. What are the links, if any, between 1492 and 1989?

I use the idea of postsocialist precarity as a way into thinking across what are treated and assumed to be two different critiques of power – postsocialist and decolonial. Postsocialist precarity captures a critical lens that specifically addresses a variety of geo-historical experiences resulting from the dismantling of state socialist modernity and the (re-)incorporation of relatively closed economies into the capitalist neoliberal order. While that geo-historical experience is wildly heterogeneous and (re)produces many hierarchies within postsocialist Europe and Eurasia, I treat "postsocialist precarity" as a composite category in order to emphasise a point of tension/connection to a decolonial approach. Aware of the provisional nature of such generalisations, I am compelled to explore this question as a way to work through the hidden or recuperated Eurocentrism residing in "critical" postsocialist theorising, including my own. After defining postsocialist precarity and emphasising the role of borders and border-making in its production, I introduce the concept of global coloniality, paying particular attention to the role of Eurocentrism in both obscuring racial epistemologies and constructing temporal plotlines that fix rather than destabilise power relations.

Postsocialist precarity

Precarity is a term used in recent times to critique political and economic policies that promote austerity, defund public services, wager debt and profit over environmental and human well-being, and criminalise social protests against such policies. The wide-reaching protest and cultural movements across Europe and the globe, such as the EuroMayDay annual protest that began in the early 2000s, signal that precarity is brought about by loss – namely the loss of regulated industry, formal labour contracts, and living wages (della Porta et al. 2015). Similarly, the losses brought about by the dismantling of state socialism have given new meaning to precarity. Of course, economic and social vulnerability are not new to east Europe and Eurasia as state socialist economies of scarcity and the myriad informal practices of barter and exchange illustrate. The many internal hierarchies within national economies and across them also suggest that state socialism did not prevent precarity as such. Yet, postsocialist precarity is new in many ways as it captures the loss of previous lifeworlds upon which symbolic and material forms of living were (re)produced.

While emerging out of its own set of specific geo-historical contexts, postsocialist precarity is produced by some of the same neoliberal economic practices riddling other parts of the world, such as flexibilisation, informalisation, and the reduction and transformation of social provisioning. These practices are entangled with the continued political drift towards forms of authoritarianism, neo-traditionalism, and diminished democratic returns. In addition, postsocialist precarity includes a hybrid of neoliberal forms of exploitation and social vulnerability with/in the half-life of state socialist projects, including the abandonment of socialist inspired housing and communal sociality, real estate and urban planning in "smart investments," and the simultaneous disavowal and recategorising of socialist-era histories. While the "post" of post-Fordism is not the same experience as the "post" in postsocialist, they share a similar register of loss. In the case of postsocialist precarity, the loss is of the state socialist social contract that was overwhelmingly rejected in 1989 (Bonfiglioli 2015; Tkach and Hrzenjak 2016). A replacement for that social contract remains contested. In fact, because the adoption of neoliberal capitalist practices coincided with the dismantling of political systems, there is a *doubling* of economic and political loss and uncertainty.

At the same time, already existing internal economic and social hierarchies to state socialism adapted to neoliberal capitalist production and distribution, perpetuating asymmetries while also creating new opportunities and vulnerabilities. The many sexual, gender, ethnic, racial, and class hierarchies concealed by state socialist rhetoric of equality and assurance of employment transformed into "peripheralised" workforces that suited non-standard contract work (Standing 2011). The doubling of precarity and the adaptability of social hierarchy to capitalist production proved the ongoing necessity of informal survival strategies, some of which were practised under state socialism. For example, using informal arrangements to find work, visa documents, or to cross borders or smuggle people and goods was a practice already well known under state socialism. In the case of post-Soviet Russia in the early days of capitalist transformation, these strategies were recycled to manage the rise in non-standard contracts and a workforce at the mercy of private enterprises offering severely reduced pay or operating in arrears

(Walker 2015). The volatility of non-standard contracts and low or no wages for standard labour contracts pushed the need for informal income across former state socialist economies. Some countries have been able to stabilise economically, though even with EU membership there remain economic uncertainties in the context of growing austerity.

Borders and border work

In addition to the register of loss, postsocialist precarity captures shifting (and new) regional power dynamics. Borders play a complex role in producing post-socialist precarity including regarding how "second world" economies are situated as peripheral in both symbolic and structural ways to core economies. I will engage a more critical lens on this spatialisation of power in terms of core and periphery, but for now I want to use it to further illuminate the specificity of postsocialist precarity. Namely, the changing terms of borders and border-making in the wake of the dismantling of state socialism are significant to the production of postsocialist precarity. Two examples illustrate this: one regards the racialised border-making between the Russian Federation and the Soviet ex-colonies of Central Asia and the second regards the border work that ensued from the so-called "return to Europe" discourse.

The Soviet economic model was built on the symbolic centring of the worker. While internal divisions of labour and hierarchies existed as state socialist economic systems changed over time, those practices were either instrumentalised as necessary for socialist modes of production or/and concealed by worker's state rhetoric. The political economy of national borders within state socialism, such as in the USSR, certainly regulated mobility, economic relationships of production and consumption, and internal hierarchies. Yet, the terms of that political economy promoted universal worker's rights and national self-determination. Core-periphery relations within Soviet state socialism were normalised as part of socialist "development" and were institutionalised within the domesticated national borders between Soviet Federated Socialist Republics. Yet, by the time of the collapse of the Soviet Union, great disparities existed between the more developed north-west and the less developed south-east, illustrated by the divide between the Baltic republics and Central Asia. For example, at the close of the Soviet experiment, 69% of the population and almost 74% of the output were tied to Russia and Ukraine, yet the GDP per person ranged from 150% of the Soviet average in Estonia to 42% in Tajikistan (Maddison 1995, 153, quoted in Dunford 1998).

The symbolic and economic terms to the borders between Soviet Central Asia and the republics of the north-west, such as the Baltics, Russia, and Ukraine, shifted with the end to Soviet interdependency. The details of how the hierarchies and relationships transformed are quite complex and certainly ongoing (Khalid 2014). Part of that transformation is that the national borders between Soviet Federated Socialist Republics, while always indeed political, had not been directly understood to be about racialised categories rooted within colonial logics. Rather, the

Soviet Union promoted the idea of a "friendship of peoples" (*druzhba narodov*) – an idea and practice that claimed to be beyond the racism and exploitation created by capitalism and colonialism. While this friendship operated under different terms than western capitalism and colonialism, it too (re)produced racialised and ethnic differences as well as related hierarchies. Indeed, as many now argue, the Soviet "friendship of peoples" was in fact rooted in ethnic and racialised imaginaries even if not overtly (Hirsch 2005; Weitz 2002).[1] Despite an anti-colonial commitment, critiques of American racism and a political commitment to self-determination, the Soviet model of friendship rested on an assumed "white" and ethnically superior Russian norm that claimed political and cultural authority and which implicitly was viewed as "first among equals" (Martin 2001). Thus, the profound changes to borders brought about by the end of the Soviet Union made explicit what was already present – the power of ethnic and racialised hierarchies.

The dissolution of the Soviet Union created international borders between the once domesticated relations between Soviet Federated Socialist Republics. As a result, the terms of core-periphery relations changed, including the removal of the veneer of "friendship". New relations of power between former state socialist states continue to be negotiated and, in many cases, reveal the long-standing colonial logic of those borders and border-making. This is the case regarding both the treatment of labour migrants from Central Asia (and other regions) in Russia and the "migrantisation" of non-ethnic Russians in Russia. As numerous scholars and activists have argued, Russian national discourse has become increasingly nationalistic, xenophobic, and hetero-patriarchal (Arnold and Romanova 2013; Salmenniemi and Adamson 2014; Sperling 2014; Zakharov 2015). The inversion, and indeed subversion, of the Soviet sentiment of friendship is starkly illustrated by vigilante groups such as *Щит Москвы* (Moscow Shield) who hunt down "illegal" migrants in "raids".[2] The daily and structural violence that many labour migrants experience, either due to official or vigilante "raids" is an extreme example of the racialisation of postsocialist precarity (Round and Kuznetsova-Morenko 2016; Salomatin 2013).

While this violence may not be the norm, it is part of a wider discourse that promotes an ethnicised notion of who is Russian (*Российский*) and that increasingly marks any non-ethnic Russian as illegal. Thus, in addition to targeting labour migrants, the racialised "othering" of migrants (as illegal or criminal) has made all non-ethnic Russians suspect.[3] The internationalisation of formerly domesticated borders has contributed to new racial discourses in Russia – one that explicitly defines "Russian" as "white" and in tension to internal and external others, such as "illegal migrants," Chechens, and newly "minoritised" groups (Zanca 2013; Zakharov 2015). At the same time, these new discourses are built on the foundation of the long-standing imperial relations that undergirded even the terms of friendship during the Soviet period.

The shift away from the symbolic language of friendship also is linked to discourses of a "return to Europe" in the former Eastern Bloc. This is the second example of border work that I suggest contributes to postsocialist precarity. As national discourse in Russia has embraced a civilisational and racialised "white" understanding of Russian (*Российский*), so too has the idea the "return to Europe" promoted a civilisational and racialised discourse in different ways in Central and Eastern Europe. At its core, we should consider how the political desire to get out of the Soviet (and Russian) yoke of power, while in many ways also an anti-imperial move, can invoke another colonial turn. That is, the turn in "returning" to Europe cannot be seen outside of the imperial projects of European empires that in fact established global hierarchies and continue to regulate the racialised borders of Europe.

Here it is important to see how the internal borders of Europe that mark former state socialist countries as Europe's periphery are also part of the larger project of *Fortress Europe*. The influx of at least a million Syrian asylum seekers to the EU starting in 2015 illustrates this dynamic. The EU's Dublin Regulation, which gives responsibility for registering and processing asylum applications to the first Schengen country in which a refugee arrives, placed enormous burdens on Greece and Italy (Lehne 2016). Refugees moved through alternative routes, including through the Western Balkans in attempts to reach Hungary and Austria. While some welcomed refugees, many others did not, and governments battled over an "equitable" policy for refugee relocation. The former Communist Bloc countries, Czech Republic, Hungary, Poland, and Slovakia, all rejected this idea and instead militarised their borders and fuelled hostility towards refugees (Gall 2016). The same countries that claimed a "return to Europe", in their gesture of belligerence towards refugees, performed the work of Fortress Europe. For countries at EU's physical and metaphorical periphery and for whom "European" membership challenges forms of nested Orientalisms such as in the Balkans, the internal hierarchies of Europe are revealed as core economies of the EU quibble through bureaucratic dialogue as thousands of people seek refuge at its borders.

These multiple forms of border work produce state power as well as mark certain bodies as mobile and others as not welcome. Policies that enforce Fortress Europe manage the transit of precarious others, including migrants of all kinds, and are tied to the legacies and current entanglements of neoliberal capitalism.[4] Dynamics within the EU also track along a racialised peripheralisation of the Balkans and to a different extent other former Communist bloc countries. The old members of the EU periphery (Portugal, Italy, Ireland, Greece and Spain) are joined with the new (including from the Baltics and Balkans), although those hierarchies are layered rather than consolidated. For example, in 2015 a joint activist/research statement on "Peripheralizing Europe" was made, connecting the ways that the EU "centre" both exploits and depends on its peripheral territories. The statement proclaims that

> The peripheries continue to absorb the most brutal effects of the crisis of Europe. Europe's margins are burning, not just with rapid declassing (PIIGS) and normalized poverty (the East) but also with people trying to cross minefields and seas and jump walls and fences, fleeing from, most often, the effects of western imperial and neo-colonial policies.[5]

The border work of a "return to Europe" both aligns with the ongoing project of Fortress Europe (which produces its own forms of precarity) and has generated new forms of precarity as that "return" produces new zones of periphery.

Global coloniality and (secondary) Eurocentrism

Postsocialist precarity invokes a certain plotline, one that (in part) focuses on the loss of the state socialist project and the effects of neoliberal capitalist transformations. This plotline, with the year 1989 serving as a key moment, obviously centres the political institutionalisation and demise of state socialism. But, what would change if postsocialist precarity were considered within or alongside another plotline, that of global coloniality? I pose this question to open-up a discussion rather than to resolve it. My own intellectual trajectory, and blind spots, are motivation for this (re)thinking. While I still agree with the analysis of precarity and human trafficking I presented in *Economies of Violence* (2015), I also have reflected on the insufficiency of my critical theorising. In particular, I want to think further about the implications of what Madina Tlostanova speaks of as secondary Eurocentrism. While my research unpacked the ongoing operations of east/west power dynamics and theorised how women's rights campaigns are entangled in neoliberal economic practices and repressive state policies regarding mobility and borders, I did not sufficiently consider how Eurocentrism can be recuperated in critical postsocialist approaches. Namely, while neoliberal capitalism is formed out of histories of colonialism, there are important elisions regarding racial thinking in particular that occur when "global coloniality" as such is not integrated into analyses of postsocialist precarity. In this section, I engage these questions in an effort to grapple with the borders of critical theory and the unintended recuperation rather than destabilisation of Eurocentrism.

The idea of global coloniality is not an argument for an origin story. Rather, the concept reveals the "terms of evolutionary time" that European colonialism constructed in its discovery of the "New World" (Lugones 2007, 192). The terms of evolutionary time created such concepts as primitive, civilisation, and culture that even now wield political power in their contemporary guises. Decolonial scholar María Lugones explains, "Europe came to be mythically conceived as pre-existing colonial, global, capitalism and as having achieved a very advanced level in the continuous, linear, unidirectional path" (Lugones 2007, 192). The designation of primitive time or places, then, is a mythical one used to initiate a kind of global thinking that rationalised civilisational missions and conquest. Furthering this idea, Aníbal Quijano and Immanuel Wallerstein argue that the

> modern world system was born in the long sixteenth century. The Américas as a geosocial construct were born in the long sixteenth century. The creation of this geosocial entity was the constitutive act of the modern world-system. The Américas were not incorporated into an already existing capitalist world economy – rather, its construction built the capitalist "world system".
>
> (Quijano and Wallerstein 1992)

Within that world system competing claims to superiority presented different European (and Anglophone) powers as winners or losers. However, competition for the civilisational centre amongst those empires and eventually nations and states who claimed to define or could claim proximity to such notions of civilisation, created a ruse for the (re)production of coloniality. For instance, national narratives that claim to be "innocent" of colonialism because they did not have colonies belies the entangled realities of global coloniality.

What then does this epistemic orientation reveal or alter about postsocialist precarity? While all regional or cultural instances of power may not need to be thread through the eye of global coloniality, it is still important to tend to the various relations and interconnections between empire and colonialism in east Europe and Eurasia and global coloniality. Furthermore, I understand that a turn to this orientation also is a turn to the Americás (including North and South America and the Caribbean) and that may seem like a re-centring of the United States and certain forms of western hegemony. I remain open to such critiques even as I explore how postsocialist precarity is implicated within global coloniality. To be certain, my understanding of the implications of a "decolonial turn" is still in process. It is a process informed by my position as a white scholar within the US academy whose training in "area studies" reproduced rather than challenged the nested hierarchies within that field, including those historically and materially produced in the region and within the US academy itself. My critical orientation to area studies has emphasised the insufficiency of traditional approaches such as Sovietology and its successor democratisation. In contrast, critical postsocialist studies includes approaches that treat "postsocialism" as contested, culturally and politically dynamic, and as globally situated (rather than just or primarily regional). Alongside this critical orientation, global coloniality challenges hidden forms of Eurocentrism that, while seemingly distant from east Europe, are in fact linked. In particular, I consider how Eurocentrism is recuperated in theorisations of postsocialist precarity, especially in the case of some (re)framings of the demise of state socialism as a postcolonial condition.

Ella Shohat and Robert Stam explain that Eurocentrism is a discursive rationale for colonialism and is "the process by which the European powers reached positions of hegemony in much of the world" (Shohat and Stam 1994, 2). Part of that discursive rationale, as Lugones explained, is the "terms of evolutionary time" that parse the globe both spatially and temporally into categories and scales of primitive and civilised. Similarly, Shohat and Stam state:

> Eurocentric thinking attributes to the "West" an almost providential sense of historical destiny. Eurocentrism, like Renaissance perspectives in painting, envisions the world from a single privileged point. It maps the world in a cartography that centralizes and augments Europe while literally "belittling" Africa. The "East" is divided into "Near", "Middle", and "Far", making Europe the arbiter of spatial evaluation, just as the establishment of Greenwich Mean Time produces England as the regulating center of temporal measurement.
>
> (Shohat and Stam 1994, 2)

In both spatial and temporal terms, Eurocentrism attributes to the "West" an inherent progress, elides (and at times appropriates) non-European traditions, and minimises the oppressive practices of civilisation, democracy, and similar rationales/logics of modernity. As Shohat and Stam explain though, this description of Eurocentrism does not also mean that, as a discursive rationale, Eurocentrism is not also complex, contradictory, or historically unstable (Shohat and Stam 1994, 2).

Given that the Soviet Union was made the enemy of the "West" during the Cold War, it may seem odd to position it within Eurocentrism. Yet, as Madina Tlostanova astutely argues, Russian empire enacts a *secondary* status within/to Eurocentrism because it is both inside and outside of the western episteme. As such, she classifies it as subaltern which produces "secondary Eurocentrism" (Tlostanova 2015). She explains,

> For the subaltern Russian Empire, the secondary Eurocentrism and the imperial difference with the more successful capitalist empires of modernity (Great Britain, France, Germany) comes forward in the shaping of subjectivity of both the colonizer and the colonized. On the global scale, this imperial difference mutates into the colonial one, as Russia becomes a country that allows the Western philosophy, knowledge, and culture to colonize itself with no blood shed, the Janus-faced empire that felt itself a colony in the presence of the West and, at the same time, half heartedly played the part of the caricature "civilizer" in its non-European colonies.
>
> (Tlostanova 2015, 272)

I should note that Russia's secondary Eurocentrism is not unique, as Boaventura de Sousa Santos argues that Portugal has figured in the semi periphery of European colonial practice since the 17th century (de Sousa Santos 2002). As Portuguese colonialism moved from the centre to the periphery of Eurocentrism, Portugal reproduced itself "on the basis of the colonial system" (de Sousa Santos 2002, 9). However, the Russian subaltern empire differs from the Portuguese experience because it never was imagined as or in the centre. One consequence of this is that Eurocentrism circulates as a "buried epistemology" of Russian imperial practice. That is, even as political and philosophical traditions distinguish a Russian or Slavic civilisational difference vis-à-vis the west, these traditions are still yoked within the dominant plotline of western hegemony.

For example, Susan Buck-Morss argues that the modern projects of capitalism and socialism, in their east/west oppositional locations, were in fact different approaches to the same project of mass utopia (Buck-Morss 2000). Invoking the idea of dreamworlds (and catastrophe), Buck-Morss convincingly argues that Soviet modernity was imagined, as in capitalist modernity, as a progress narrative. The temporality of revolution, of the *avant-garde*, and of economic planning sets the Soviet dreamworld within "evolutionary time". A key feature of that progress narrative was the anticolonial notion of "friendship of peoples" which, in addition to producing complex material realities in their historical and locational specificity, can also be read as part of what it was projected to be an alternative to, namely racial capitalism. For instance,

Soviet "friendship" was rooted in a paternalism that implicitly privileged an ethnic ranking of peoples and built economic dominance through extractive state socialism. Moreover, the ideological critique of racism and colonialism did not immunise (Soviet) Russian cultural or political thinking from anti-blackness or heterosexism.[6] The point here is *not* that Russian or Soviet political hegemony is the same as western (dominant) forms, but that there are connections and indeed reproductions of those forms in locally and historically specific ways.

Shohat and Stam suggest that Eurocentrism is often a hidden epistemology particularly within political claims that assert to be post-imperial or post-national. For instance, one dimension of Eurocentrism is the construction of (and contestation over) racial categories. While contingent and entirely fabricated, "race" as a system of categories took shape through European colonialism. Yet, as Fatima El-Tayeb argues regarding Europe,

> the geographical and intellectual origin of the very concept of race in Europe, not to mention the explicitly race-based policies that characterized both its fascist regimes and its colonial empires, the continent often is marginal at best in discourses on race or racism, in particular with regard to contemporary configurations that are often closely identified with the United States as a center of both explicit race discourse and of resistance to it.
>
> (El-Tayeb 2011, XV)

Even in "multicultural" Europe, as El-Tayeb argues, there is a disavowal of "race" as an inheritance of European colonialism. This also is the case regarding east Europe and Russia where it is argued by some that "race" is not a relevant classification because different categories (ethnicity and nationality) are more appropriate. But the argument for the specificity of the construction and mobilisation of ethnic and national categories across the different contexts of east Europe (including the Balkans), Russia, and Eurasia need not also be a rejection of "race" as an episteme informing those varied contexts.

While it is true that some western-based scholarship has treated postsocialist east Europe as a homogenous extension of "Europe" and racial whiteness, it also is the case that to different degrees and ways, claims to "Europeanness" (as well as the rejection of it, as in the case of Russia) produces what Anikó Imre calls internalised imperialism (Imre 2014).[7] Similar to Tlostanova's concept of secondary Eurocentrism (though also different), Imre argues that there is a co-dependence between Western and Eastern European nationalisms. This dynamic is "haunted by internalized and rarely acknowledged traces of imperialism on both sides" (Imre 2014, 113). An illustration of this internalised imperialism is the uncritical use of a postcolonial paradigm to explain the (re)mapping of intra-European hierarchies that peripheralise new members and to critique the ongoing political hegemony of Europe. I notice this subtly produced in criticism of postsocialist precarity as well when racialisation practices that are indeed instrumental to new nationalisms in postsocialist contexts are displaced by a primary concern for unequal relations vis-à-vis Europe or the United States.

Some criticism is quick to denounce western hegemony without also critically reflecting on how that work may recuperate intra-European as well as global colonial relations.[8]

A decolonial reading of precarity

To think further about the internal imperialism that can be unaddressed in criticism of postsocialist precarity, I juxtapose two images: one is Ilya Repin's classic painting *Barge Haulers on the Volga* (Figure 2.1) and the other is an image of a post-Soviet sex trafficking victim, similar to the one depicted in the popular film *Lilja 4-Ever* (2002). In juxtaposing these two images, I suggest that the economies of race and labour in global coloniality relate to both of these two very different times and locations. In particular, an internalised imperialism recuperates Eurocentrism in both iterations of what can be understood as two representations of labour exploitation. Repin's painting represents a narrative that casts Russia as exceptional to western imperialism (and immune to its racist pathologies) while the image of Lilja and the film production constructs a narrative about the post-Soviet sex trafficking victim as an exceptional subject of global precarity. I do not question that these two images represent a material reality of exploitation and I am not providing a criticism of the artist or film per se. Rather, I refer to these images to signal the hidden Eurocentrism that can potentially be carried through the narratives that are produced by these images.

Repin was a well-respected painter, having received entrance into the Imperial Academy of Fine Arts as well as a golden medal that allowed him the right to study in Europe. He had spent time on the Volga, making sketches that he would later use to paint the now famous *Barge Haulers on the Volga* between 1870–1873. Known in particular for his participation in the *peredvizhniki* (itinerants) artist collective, the painting is often associated with a realist movement that aimed to expose human suffering and inequality in society. Here, eleven weathered figures

Figure 2.1 Ilya Repin's classic painting *Barge Haulers on the Volga*

strain to pull the distant barge with only their bodies and leather straps. The barge carries Russia's economic interests along the Volga and Don rivers while the *burlaki* earned modest wages.

The term *burlaki* refers to migrant workers, among other ideas relating to being transient. The *burlaki* represented here could symbolise what some in Russian history have called a practice of "internal colonisation". This idea suggests that, with no colonies to dominate, the Russian empire exploited its "own" people. In his analysis of internal colonisation, Alexander Etkind suggests that Russian culture produced categories of caste (*soslovie*) and not race. He states,

> In a society of internal colonization that had annexed, absorbed, and exterminated its others, almost everyone was of one and the same color. To play the function of race, this society created estates, a legal category that was also similar in function to caste.
>
> (Etkind 2012, 93)

Etkind further argues that the elite were subjected to a kind of "orientalizing" when in the late 17th century Peter the Great introduced national legislation that included a beard tax. Etkind writes, "while caste was a substitute for race, the beard was a substitute for skin color" (Etkind 2012, 102). The argument that there were/are cultural substitutes for race does not figure how the racial logics created by Eurocentrism still inform the narrative of a "race-less" empire, not as the same experience but as implicitly and explicitly invested in those logics (Tolz 2019). For example, how does the system of *soslovie* or the beard tax produce notions of Russian national consciousness that are indeed situated within that Eurocentric yoke? When Etkind refers to Alexander Herzen's term "white negroes" or "frozen negroes" to illustrate the absence of "race" in Russia, he misses how this idea is in fact a window into the racial thinking that refers and relies upon the "negro" as a gravitational force. What does it mean to use the category white? Is that not "race" after all? While Russian serfdom was a different enterprise than the trans-Atlantic slave trade, this critique of it reveals an investment in the racial logics of global coloniality.

Furthermore, the notion of "internal" also obscures how those bodies of "the same color" are projected as such. How are the myriad peoples who come to be known as *burlaki* made internal? The fertile cities along the Volga became places of European settlement, as Catherine the Great's manifesto created German colonies. From its basin in the Caspian Sea to the city of Kazan, the river Volga is a route of Russian colonial conquest that defies the race-neutral idea of "internal colonization". The expansion of Russian empire may have relied on the logic of internal (or self) subjugation but it also operated through the idea of what John Richardson calls an "unending frontier" (Richardson 2003). The *terra nullis* of America that Columbus discovered was the "virgin lands" of Russian imperial settlement – the Tatars, Chuvash, Mordvinians, Cheremis, Votiaks, Nogai Tatars, Bashkirs, Kalmyks, Crimean Tatars, Cossacks, Iakuts, Buriats, Koryaks, and Chukchi (for example) are the *terra nullius* of Russian expansion.

The second image of postsocialist sex trafficking was frequently depicted in news and other media. It featured an innocent female victim lacking agency in her decisions to navigate formal and informal economies (Suchland 2015). I suggest there is the potential for internal imperialism (or recuperated Eurocentrism) here as well. The phenomenon of human trafficking, and sex trafficking in particular, shed light on postsocialist precarity unlike any other tragedy from the dismantling of state socialism. Numerous feature films and documentaries depicted the vulnerability and violence that many experienced in an effort to find work abroad. The film *Lilja 4-Ever* is one example and has even been used as an anti-trafficking tool to raise public consciousness about trafficking in hopes of ultimately preventing it. In viewing the precarity and violence experienced by migrants involved (or forced into) sexual commerce there has often been an obscuring of the role of the state in producing that precarity. Elsewhere I have argued that the example of postsocialist trafficking facilitated a view of trafficking that depoliticised the underlying economic arrangements that pushed women and others into dangerous migrant labour. Consequently, approaches to anti-trafficking rarely if ever address the policies of "transition" that produced unemployment, loss of wages, dispossession, and insecurity. A carceral approach to trafficking took precedence, which increased the policing of borders and informal labour, thus adding to the regulation, criminalisation, and surveillance of mobility. This is clearly illustrated by the fact that the United Nations Optional Protocol on Human Trafficking is situated in the UN Convention on Transnational Crime and Corruption.

While the film powerfully represents the violence of postsocialist precarity – particularly in its gendered form – the film also represents a narrative of trafficking that displaces how forced and exploitative labour resulting from the dismantling of state socialism is connected to, rather than exceptional to, gendered and racialised labour within that sphere and globally. For instance, Russian ethnic migration is part of a wider national and international context that includes the value and added mobility that comes from being marked or racialised "white but not quite". This is also important because human trafficking and forced labour in Russia is largely an issue tied to labour migration from Central Asia. The dominant representations of "postsocialist trafficking" tended to separate the systems of exploitation that produce both the "white" victim of trafficking (often in Europe and the US) and the non-ethnic (minoritised) Russians and labour migrants exploited within Russia, including from Central Asia. Thus, it is important to think across these migrations and systems of oppression as I theorise postsocialist precarity as materially produced in the former Soviet sphere and as embedded in global coloniality. Finally, engaging global coloniality as a force in postsocialist precarity reveals the continuities rather than breaks between different geographic and historical forms of imperialism.

Notes

1   The practices of Soviet friendship produced many meanings and outcomes, not all of which are necessarily negative. For instance, many Soviet citizens understood their relationship to each other through that discourse of friendship. In this regard, Jeff Sahadeo's work on intimate interethnic contact, including through intermarriage, is compelling.

Using oral histories, he reveals how individual mentalities and experiences during the Soviet period were shaped by "friendship" and marriage (Sahadeo 2007).

2   The *Vkontake* site for the group shows photographs and videos of raids in which non-ethnic Russians are harassed, intimidated, and violently beaten. https://vk.com/board_of_msk (last accessed January 19, 2017).

3   On the racialisation of labour migrants as illegal, criminal, and diseased see Round and Kuznetsova-Morenko (2016).

4   Raia Apostolova makes the excellent argument that the linguistic emphasis on Syrian migrants as refugees, and thus acceptable subject of empathy, discounts the ways that economic migrants too deserve respect and concern. Furthermore, the distinction between political versus economic migrants is in fact difficult to decipher. https://asaculturesection.org/2015/09/14/of-refugees-and-migrants-stigma-politics-and-boundary-work-at-the-borders-of-europe/ (accessed January 22, 2017).

5   The joint statement is online: https://peripheralizingeurope.wordpress.com/coomon-statement-eng-ro-de-slo-it-cast/ (accessed January 28, 2017).

6   Anti-blackness is a term that refers to a core internal logic of European racial thinking that evolved through colonialism, slavery, and its afterlives. The point I want to make here is that anti-blackness can still be absorbed even if the category of "race" is absent or takes different forms (Law 2012; Sweet 1997). Maria Lugones argues that heterosexualism or sexual dimorphism is constitutive of the colonial/modern gender system. She writes that "sexual fears of colonizers led them to imagine the indigenous of the Americas as hermaphrodites or intersexed, with large penises and breasts with flowing milk" (Lugones 2007, 195). In her formulation of global coloniality, this gender system is central to the operations of coloniality.

7   Miglena Todorova insightfully argues that transnational feminist theorising in the US that has critiqued the domination of white feminism, European colonialism, and racism can problematically extend cultural and political Europeanness and "racial whiteness" to socialist countries and societies in the Balkans, her area of focus. The membership of some formerly state socialist countries to the EU, as well as broader claims to "Europeanness" feed into such views as well. She argues that "these perceptions, however, misunderstand the distinct and very different geopolitical and cultural locations of postsocialist societies in the Balkans often enfolded under homogenising banners such as 'Eastern Europe' or 'the Second World'" (Todorova forthcoming). Reflecting on her analysis, I see how my own thinking has not given sufficient care to the colonial differences between (and legacies of) the ruling empires across the region including Ottoman, Russian, Habsburg, Viking, German, Polish, Swedish, and Mongol.

8   For a helpful summary of some of these tendencies see Navickaité (2014); Rexhepi (2016); Shchurko and Suchland (2021); and Todorova (2018).

References

Arnold, Richard, and Ekaterina Romanova. 2013. "The 'White World's Future?': An Analysis of the Russian Far Right." *Journal for the Study of Radicalism* 7, no. 1: 79–107. https://doi.org/10.14321/jstudradi.7.1.0079.

Bonfiglioli, Chiara. 2015. "Gendered Citizenship in the Global European Periphery: Textile Workers in Post-Yugoslav States." *Women's Studies International Forum* 49: 57–65. https://doi.org/10.1016/j.wsif.2014.07.004.

Buck-Morss, Susan. 2000. *Dreamworld and Catastrophe: The Passing of Mass Utopia in East and West*. Cambridge, MA: Massachusetts Institute of Technology Press. https://doi.org/10.7551/mitpress/2499.001.0001.

de Sousa Santos, Boaventura. 2002. "Between Prospero and Caliban: Colonialism, Postcolonialism, and Inter-Identity." *Luso-Brazilian Review* 39, no. 2: 9–43.

della Porta, Donatella, Sakari Hänninen, Martti Siisiäinen, and Tiina Silvasti. 2015. "The Precarization Effect." In *The New Social Division*, edited by della Porta et al., 1–23. London: Palgrave MacMillan. https://doi.org/10.1057/9781137509352.

Dunford, Michael. 1998. "Differential Development, Institutions, Modes of Regulation and Comparative Transitions to Capitalism: Russia, the Commonwealth of Independent States and the Former German Democratic Republic." In *Theorizing Transition: The Political Economy of Post-Communist Transformations*, edited by John Pickles and Adrian Smith, 72–107. London: Routledge. https://doi.org/10.4324/9780203982907.

El-Tayeb, Fatima. 2011. *European Others: Queering Ethnicity in Postnational Europe*. Minneapolis, MN: University of Minnesota Press. https://doi.org/10.5749/minnesota/9780816670154.001.0001.

Etkind, Alexander. 2012. *Internal Colonization: Russia's Imperial Experience*. Cambridge: Polity Press.

Gall, Lydia. 2016. "Hungary's War on Refugees." *Human Rights Watch*. www.hrw.org/news/2016/09/16/hungarys-war-refugees (accessed January 22, 2017).

Hirsch, Francine. 2005. *Empire of Nations: Ethnographic Knowledge and the Making of the Soviet Union*. Ithaca, NY: Cornell University Press. https://doi.org/10.7591/9780801455940.

Imre, Anikó. 2014. "Postcolonial Media Studies in Postsocialist Europe." *boundary 2* 4, no. 1: 113–134. https://doi.org/10.1215/01903659-2409694.

Khalid, Adeeb. 2014. *Islam After Communism: Religion and Politics in Central Asia*. Berkeley, CA: University of California Press. https://doi.org/10.1525/9780520957862-003.

Law, Ian. 2012. *Red Racisms: Racism in Communist and Post-Communist Contexts*. London: Palgrave.

Lehne, Stefan. 2016. "How the Refugee Crisis Will Reshape the EU." *Carnegie Europe*. http://carnegieeurope.eu/2016/02/04/how-refugee-crisis-will-reshape-eu-pub-62650 (accessed January 22, 2017).

Lugones, María. 2007. "Heterosexualism and the Colonial/Modern Gender System." *Hypatia* 22, no. 1: 186–209. https://doi.org/10.1353/hyp.2006.0067.

Maddison, Angus. 1995. *Monitoring the World Economy, 1820–1992*. Paris: OECD Development Centre. https://doi.org/10.1111/aehr.362br1.

Martin, Terry. 2001. *The Affirmative Action Empire: Nations and Nationalism in the Soviet Union, 1932–1939*. Ithaca, NY: Cornell University Press. https://doi.org/10.7591/9781501713323.

Navickaité, Rasa. 2014. "Postcolonial Queer Critique in Post-communist Europe: Stuck in the Western Progress Narrative?" *Tijdschrift voor Genderstudies* 17, no. 2: 167–185. https://doi.org/10.5117/tvgend2014.2.navi.

Quijano, Aníbal, and Immanuel Wallerstein. 1992. "Americanity as a Concept, or the Americas in the Modern World-System." *International Social Science Journal* no. 134: 549–557.

Rexhepi, Piro. 2016. "From Orientalism to Homonationalism: Queer Politics, Islamophobia and Europeanization in Kosovo." *Southeastern Europe* 40, no. 1: 32–53. https://doi.org/10.1163/18763332-03903014.

Richardson, John. 2003. *The Unending Frontier*. Oakland, CA: University of California Press. https://doi.org/10.1525/9780520939356.

Round, John, and Irina Kuznetsova-Morenko. 2016. "Necropolitics and the Migrant as a Political Subject of Disgust: The Precarious Everyday of Russia's Labour Migrants." *Critical Sociology* 42, nos. 7–8: 1017–1034. https://doi.org/10.1163/9789004329706_011.

Sahadeo, Jeff. 2007. "Druzhba Narodov or Second-Class Citizenship? Soviet Asian Migrants in a Post-Colonial World." *Central Asian Survey* 26, no. 4: 559–579. https://doi.org/10.1080/02634930802018463.

Salmenniemi, Suvi, and Maria Adamson. 2014. "New Heroines of Labour: Domesticating Post-Feminism and Neoliberal Capitalism in Russia." *Sociology* 49, no. 1: 88–105. https://doi.org/10.1177/0038038513516830.

Salomatin, Konstantin. 2013. "Russia: Hunting for Migrants in Moscow," September 23, 2013. www.eurasianet.org/node/67538 (accessed January 17, 2017).

Shchurko, Tatsiana, and Jennifer Suchland. 2021. "Postcoloniality in Central-Eastern Europe and Eurasia." In *Routledge International Handbook to Gender in Central Eastern Europe and Eurasia*, edited by Katalin Fábián, Mara Lazda, and Janet Elise Johnson. London: Routledge.

Shohat, Ella, and Robert Stam. 1994. *Unthinking Eurocentrism: Multiculturalism and the Media*. London: Routledge. https://doi.org/10.4324/9781315002873.

Sperling, Valerie. 2014. *Sex, Politics, and Putin: Political Legitimacy in Russia*. Oxford: Oxford University Press. https://doi.org/10.1093/acprof:oso/9780199324347.001.0001.

Standing, Guy. 2011. *The Precariat: The New Dangerous Class*. London: Bloomsbury Academic.

Suchland, Jennifer. 2015. *Economies of Violence: Transnational Feminism, Postsocialism, and the Politics of Sex Trafficking*. Durham, NC: Duke University Press. https://doi.org/10.1215/9780822375289.

Sweet, James. 1997. "The Iberian Roots of American Racist Thought." *The William and Mary Quarterly* 54, no. 1: 143–166. https://doi.org/10.2307/2953315.

Tkach, Olga, and Majda Hrzenjak. 2016. "Paid Domestic Work in Postsocialist Contexts: Regional Traits of a Global Phenomenon." *Laboratorium* 8, no. 3: 4–14.

Tlostanova, Madina. 2015. "Between the Russian/Soviet Dependencies, Neoliberal Delusions, Dewesternizing Options, and Decolonial Drives." *Cultural Dynamics* 27, no. 2: 267–283. https://doi.org/10.1177/0921374015585230.

Todorova, Miglena. 2018. "Race and Women of Color in Socialist/Postsocialist Transnational Feminisms in Central and Southeastern Europe." *Meridians: Feminism, Race, Transnationalism* 16, no. 1: 114–141. https://doi.org/10.2979/meridians.16.1.11.

Todorava, Miglena. Forthcoming. *Unequal Under Socialism: Race, Women, and Transnationalism in Bulgaria (1930s–2010s)*. Toronto: University of Toronto Press.

Tolz, Vera. 2019. "Constructing Race, Ethnicity, and Nationhood in Imperial Russia: Issues and Misconceptions." In *Ideologies of Race: Imperial Russian and the Soviet Union in Global Context*, edited by David Rainbow, 29–58. Montreal: McGill-Queens University Press. https://doi.org/10.2307/j.ctvqc6kkz.5.

Walker, Charlie. 2015. "Stability and Precarity in the Lives and Narratives of Working-class Men in Putin's Russia." *Social Alternatives* 34, no. 4: 1–24. https://doi.org/10.1163/2451-8921-00301001.

Weitz, Eric. 2002. "Racial Politics Without the Concept of Race: Reevaluating Soviet Ethnic and National Purges." *Slavic Review* 61, no. 1: 1–29. https://doi.org/10.2307/2696978.

Zakharov, Nikolay. 2015. *Race and Racism in Russia*. New York: Palgrave Macmillan. https://doi.org/10.1057/9781137481207.

Zanca, Russell. 2013. "Russia After 'The Friendship Among Peoples'." *Zeitschrift für Ethnologie* 138, no. 2: 285–293.

Chapter 3

A conversation on imperial legacies and postsocialist contexts

Notes from a US-based feminist collaboration

Neda Atanasoski and Kalindi Vora

Introduction

This chapter reflects back our ten-year process of working collaboratively towards developing new directions in feminist research on imperialism and coloniality, race, and (post)socialism. At the start of our collaboration, in 2010, postsocialism was not a term popularly used in the US academy, our intellectual context. However, rather than just demonstrating how postcolonial theory can or cannot be applied to postsocialist contexts, or expanding the range of postcolonial theory to include Central and Eastern Europe, as existing works have attempted to do, we strove to ask how serious conversations between fields that may never be seen as relevant to each other can introduce entirely new sets of questions about geopolitics and, as Madina Tlostanova (2017) puts it, corpopolitics.

Staged as a conversation that took place four years prior to this publication, in this chapter we reflect on the possibilities of a feminist collaborative methodology as a part of a novel sort of field building and conceptual transformation of existing theoretical landscapes. Although we have completed a book manuscript and special issue since this conversation took place, our reflections on collaboration remain valuable as they reveal the process of our co-writing.

In 2010 we were first funded to run a collaborative working group through the University of California Humanities Research Institute titled "Imperial Legacies, Postsocialist Contexts", followed by a ten-week Residential Research Group at UC Irvine in 2012 under the same rubric. Both projects involved ongoing meetings between scholars in quite different geopolitical areas of expertise, including South Africa, China, Turkey, the United States, Germany, Poland, the Former Yugoslavia, Russia, and India. The range of expertise exploded the notion that postsocialism was a theoretically limited term, bound to a post-1989 context and the former Soviet Union and satellite nations.

As postcolonial states and nations in the global North alike liberalise their economies through structural adjustment, and former Eastern Bloc countries re-organise their state structures in the wake of imperialism, and as Russia reactivates border militarism, it is increasingly necessary to examine the intersection of the postcolonial and the postsocialist as theoretical ground. This is a project that requires collaborative and comparative work by scholars specialising in different regions and disciplines, both for practical reasons of data collection and as a response to the challenges of feminist and decolonising methodologies that strive to question the existing knowledge formations.

At the time the conversation took place, we had just completed editing a special issue of *Social Identities* (which was published in 2018) where we provide a definition of postsocialism that developed out of our long collaboration:

> *Postsocialism marks a queer temporality, one that does not reproduce its social order even as its revolutionary antithesis.* Resisting the revolutionary teleology of what was before, postsocialism creates space to work through ongoing legacies of socialisms in the present. [There is also a need] for *pluralizing postsocialisms as a method*, which brings to the fore current practices, imaginaries and actions that insist on political change at a variety of scales, including local, state, and transnational ones. Whereas tethering postsocialism to the post-89 narrative homogenizes what is recognizable as socialism, by queering the temporality of socialism we are able to focus on the inheritances of plural socialisms as an ethos of care for multiple understandings of what is "common," as well as the international movement and body of theory and discipline of state formation and governance. In this way, we seek to develop novel approaches to the temporality and practice of political action. . . . Pluralizing postsocialisms as a method and considering it necessary for analysis of a global postsocialist condition can provide a crucial analytic through which to assess ongoing socialist legacies in new ethical collectivities and networks of dissent opposing state and corporate-based military, economic, and cultural expansionism since the end of the Cold War.[1]

We argue that postsocialist conditions that followed the end of the Soviet project and also that are interlinked with past and ongoing decolonial projects that are not tied to the Soviet empire can be characterised both as *global conditions* and as *contradictory localised formations* troubling the seeming homogenising dominance of liberal democracy rising from the rubble of the so-called three worlds schema. The crisis in both geopolitical and academic imaginaries of protest, particularly those influenced by Marxist critique, calls for a dehomogenising of the "socialism" in postsocialism and for a dialogue between the multiple inheritances of socialism in the present.

The conversation

NA: Will you speak about how our collaboration around the question of postsocialism came about?

KV: As I recall, we were walking to our shared office at UC Berkeley, when we were postdoctoral scholars in 2007–2008, and talking about your dissertation, which you were in the process of rewriting as a book manuscript. We were exchanging writing. One of the interventions you were trying to make was to explain how postsocialism as a theory, as a conversation, and as a way to analyse social and political life was misunderstood when assigned just to a geopolitical region, that is that postsocialism was somehow the same as Eastern Europe. In fact, what your research was doing was showing that postsocialism was a global condition that had a locus in Eastern Europe but that had a lot to say about the rest of the world.

I remember thinking that, in my research in India and South Asia, several different kinds of popular and formal socialist formations were active in politics (including in Bangladesh and Sri Lanka), but these are not places that we would think of as part of the socialist world because they were non-aligned. And then, when I began teaching as an assistant professor at UCSD, in my Marxist theory class I taught readings taking up decolonial theory and Marxist theory, and I remember thinking that the significance of Marxism to decolonial movements often gets erased in the taking up of postsocialism as marking the end of socialism worldwide (whereas it only really marks the demise of the USSR), and only in terms of formal state politics.

NA: Yes, it is interesting. We've been working on this for so many years – since we were postdoctoral fellows in 2007. I remember that when we began, we certainly did not have the theoretical take on postsocialism that we do now. I recall that one of the ways the conversation started was that we were thinking about how there are certain parts of the world that are never researched or analysed in relation to each other, even though similar kinds of issues mark how these regions become visible in the global imaginary. One of the issues we initially talked about was transnational adoption, which has been theorised in relation to China and East Asia, and in relation to Eastern Europe (e.g. Romania or Russia) – but these conversations never come together. So, questions such as, how is Eastern Europe racialised in complex ways through the commodification of bodies? Or, how does such racialisation complicate notions of US racial formations? These questions are left unasked. The issue of cybermarriage raises similar problematics. So, to return to postsocialism, I remember we initially imagined it as a concept that could allow us to highlight the relationality of distinct geopolitical areas. We began asking, what if we put regions that, in the schema of US knowledge formations, would fall under the rubrics of postcolonial theory in conversation with regions that would fall under the rubric of postsocialism? Even if what we meant by the latter, initially, only signified the former Eastern Bloc, from the start we were eager about the possibility that this might shift what we could think of as the contours of postcolonial theory. At the same time, it was exciting to consider what it might mean to think about parts of the world, as you said, that would never be linked to postsocialism, as in fact postsocialist (like India in your example).

KV: That's true. I had forgotten about that original question that we asked, which was, why do we see not only similar political and economic and cultural phenomena happening in the postcolonial world as in the former eastern bloc, but why are there also circulations between them – of markets and commodities circulating between postcolonial nations in Asia, Africa, Latin America, and what is now thought of as Eastern Europe, and what the material conditions leading to that could be. Because of our common training we got excited about this question.

NA: Yes, and I think we saw the potential of postsocialism to work against how scholarship was divided by region in the US academy.

KV: I think that brings us to another important question, which is, why does postsocialism as a concept need collaborative work? As opposed to, say, a more familiar individual scholarly pursuit?

NA: Well, there are a number of answers to that question. Different approaches were important at different stages of the collaboration. Initially, after we were both situated in the UC system, we applied for grants for a project that sought to answer our initial question around the commonalities in the movement of commodities and bodies and ideas across parts of the world never thought of in relation to each other (politically, culturally, racially, and in terms of their imperial histories). So in that sense we were really excited about bringing together people thinking about, OK, what are the contours of postsocialism in China? In Vietnam? In Cuba? The US? Eastern Europe? Or India? Or as our friend, anthropologist Dace Dzenovska, jokingly asked during a meeting of our residential research group at UC Irvine in 2012, what does a postsocialist light switch look like in Latvia vs. in China? I should say that initially we brought together scholars who we thought would bring knowledge of different regions. But we really quickly became dissatisfied with this model. In fact, the scholars we brought together for our 2010 working group, *Imperial Legacies, Postsocialist Contexts*, failed to respond to that call to represent their knowledge about particular parts of the world. And this was a productive failure to respond – a productive rebellion! This is something that was very interesting to me because scholars were not being representatives of their part of the world and then informing on what was the postsocialist condition there, but instead, the collaboration ended up pointing to dissatisfaction with the current theoretical language and its explanatory power.

We quickly went to a second idea on collaboration and postsocialism. So, for example, what would it mean for a scholar of the US and race to take postsocialism seriously as a concept instead of taking neoliberalism as the only concept through which to think about "multiculturalism"? Where would that get us? What is a relationship between postcolonial and postsocialist theory that doesn't just take postcolonial theory and apply it to parts of the world that are postsocialist? And this was important because this was very much the vein of the scholarship at this time (like Verdery and Chari 2009). By the end of our residential group in 2012, we were at a place, then, when we were asking, what does postsocialism offer conceptually as new theoretical ground?

KV: It is also nice to remember those early stages of the project, especially in relation to the later stages of our collaboration. So, one of the things that emerged as we began experimenting with thinking about postsocialism was that it could be a productive alternative to neoliberalism (a concept that we quickly found our-selves and our collaborators to be dissatisfied with. It was too generalising and monolithic, and therefore didn't do much work for anyone). For instance, the disarticulation of economies like India's that were set up to be mercantilist and that had socialist protection. So, neoliberalism would describe the measures taken to liberalise that economy. But it doesn't actually describe or explain the way that society and governmentality are affected by the process. *Now* India has a neoliberal leader, but after 1991 when India took its international loan to invite global trade, neoliberalism didn't adequately describe the transformations under-way. We found that the term painted a false consistency and uniforming of social and economic processes that were everything from the repression and undoing of decolonial national projects of socialisation by international lenders to pro-market financialisation at the hands of national elites. Postsocialisms, as a pluralised con-cept, was more suited to describe those moments of transition.

At the same time, transition is one descriptor of change we've been very criti-cal of in how we've theorised postsocialism. People working on the Eastern Bloc have noted that the term "transition" completely fails to encompass the uneven-ness in the experiences of regime or economic change. Even if describing strictly the privatisation of the economy, transition may be irrelevant in other areas like regional governance.

And this unevenness is not just within nation states. For instance, after the two working groups you described, we started being in conversation with scholars based in North-western Europe, as well – a region we haven't mentioned thus far in our conversation. And we discovered that there too, there was a dissatisfaction with the erasure of legacies of socialism (for instance, in Scandinavia, France, and Germany). This is an unevenness in terms of the post as a marker of time, and also of socialism as standing in for multiplicity, across North-western Europe. Interestingly, then, in Europe people were disbelieving when we told them that postsocialism was considered to be an outdated or irrelevant concept in the US (something we encountered when trying to publish a special issue on this topic over the last few years as we approached several US-based journals).

But, back to this collaboration – it has its own increasing momentum! Wher-ever we go we invite people into this conversation that we initially had with just the two of us. And we learn more and more about these many different ways that postsocialism provokes a dissatisfaction with the notion of transition, the notion of single term single concept descriptions meant to encompass economy and political life (like neoliberalism), but also the sense of injustice that the work currently being done under the rubric of postsocialism provokes against the idea that socialism is – that work continues in many places. For example, we had the pleasure of meeting Victoria Kawesa in Stockholm, a researcher politician who is a member of the anti-racist feminist party that has socialist principles in its platform in Sweden.

NA: You've highlighted some things that are tremendously important to how we've developed our thinking on what postsocialism can do conceptually, epistemologically, and politically. The first is that our expanded definition of post-socialism as a theoretical framework would never have happened if we hadn't from the beginning delved into postsocialism from our collaboration. From the beginning this project has involved bringing different people into a conversation. That's what enabled us to not just say, "OK, postsocialism, we're going to study what it means through the privatisation of factories in, for instance, Serbia". That makes it so bounded in time and place. And this is not at all to say that these local histories of developments do not enable theoretical knowledge because they are localised. It is rather that the potential we saw in postsocialism as an expansive concept was enabled by the initial collaboration that put India and former Yugoslavia in conversation (with your research and my research). So from the start we were open to the idea that postsocialism could have significant impact across areas of knowledge, geopolitical divisions, that each had a different point that could be considered a historical "break" – India's first loan, or the disintegration of Yugoslavia – that brought them into the present day political and economic field. This leaves open the possibility for unlikely alliances (what Grace Hong and Rod Ferguson call "strange affinities") as we imagine movements and action in the present.

The second thing that you spoke about and that I want to underline is that postsocialism in its literal meaning of post-1989 or post-1991 Central and Eastern Europe can't get away from its temporal/economic/social association with "transition" or transitology, which then replicates the inevitability of a teleology of global capitalism, now encompassing the whole world. And I'm really glad that you brought that up because one of the things that has become really important to our current definition of postsocialism is how it allows us to think about the temporality of political action. We see postsocialism as in fact disrupting the notion that global capitalism is the only possible outcome. This is perhaps counterintuitive to how most scholars would understand postsocialism (because the post is only seen as an "after").

In relation to this, I'm wondering if you can expand a little bit on why you think that we've taken a counter-intuitive approach to the "post". Why not just take the "post" as an after?

KV: This is because socialism has so many lives both within and outside of what was the territory and sphere of influence of the USSR! Soviet socialism as a globalising imperial project was just one thing. Also, the legacy of Marx and Lenin as read through the history of Europe is just one life of socialist thought. In *The Anthropology of Marxism*, Cedric Robinson (2001) explains how even to establish that socialism as the one socialism required the stamping out of many local and idiosyncratic socialist practices and beliefs in Europe. Enrique Dussel, and liberation theologists, talk about Latin America's indigenous socialism, for example, where distribution of resources is religious practice and the hoarding of resources is sin.

NA: Yes! And collaboration is the only way to get at the multiple lives of socialism and histories of socialism.

KV: Exactly. So, for me, postsocialism is about the legacies of multiple social-isms – not just what came after.

NA: It is about the emphasis on the socialisms after the post! With the post signalling the legacies.

KV: Yes, but in addition to our ongoing investment in highlighting the lives and afterlives of socialism, we do also have an investment in thinking through the kinds of political projects that have shifted the horizon of political possibility in the present, and how this is tied to legacies of socialism. So many people on the left, at least in the US, saw the only alternative to capitalism in state socialism throughout the Cold War. And we contest this basis of contemporary left melan-cholia in our work. One way to contest that is to insist that Soviet socialism wasn't the only socialism. And socialist potentials didn't necessarily end in any other way other than this formal way.

NA: Post-state socialism is a helpful supplemental concept in that regard, as one of our 2012 group members, Fatima El-Tayeb, suggested. And one thing I want to highlight, in relation to this, is your formulation, Kalindi, which is that socialism itself is always about the collective and what is shared. And so our theorisation of postsocialism enables an analysis or attention to collectivi-ties that aren't recognisable if we just take state socialism as the only way to make legible non-capitalist ways of life. What's interesting to me, to go back to collaboration, is that in this sense we can think of our work as both meth-odologically and conceptually interested in rethinking collective projects. It is the collaborative or shared knowledge project of postsocialism that enabled us to get to this definition that isn't a nostalgic looking back at the socialist project that was in Eastern Europe or Cuba or Vietnam or China, positioned against the capitalist present that has engulfed them all. Instead, we have this articulation of postsocialism as a conceptual tool that enables us to really pay attention to collectivities that are emerging now and still within the contempo-rary condition.

KV: I would put that under the question of how feminist collaboration leads to field building. Collaboration is a process of collective knowledge production. And the process that we've been engaged in for six years on postsocialism has been a part of this kind of feminist methodology that led us to insist on the exist-ence of many forms of collectivity, collective action, and resource sharing. In this sense our formulation of postsocialism points to the unjustness of assuming that socialism ended with the Soviet project. I'm always drawn to research, especially ethnographic research, which pays attention to modes of collectivity that aren't mediated by government or family. Or at least recognisable family forms. And the latter do support people and enact alternative economies. That is why we were originally attracted to those informal circulations of bodies – child bodies, arma-ments, illicit drugs, things that circulate in grey economies or black economies. Because, part of what this understanding of postsocialism, that is the plural ongo-ing lives and legacies of social imaginaries, is about is informal economies and informal structures of social support.

Now why we have to use the post to think beyond something is another question. For me, the post signifies a more than, a beyond, a not yet, or a what is yet to come. And those collectivities, in the US, in the aftermath of the election of Donald Trump, are materialising and utilising themselves in a material way. And I would argue that the lives of those collectivities aren't just starting now, they were there all along, but now there is a reason to materialise themselves in the public eye. They show that we are connected in these ways that aren't mediated by the state or the national government. So, to me what's happening in the US right now [in 2017] could be thought of as postsocialist in that sense, both drawing on legacies of socialisms past, but also imagining and materialising collectivities and redistributing resources from a grassroots level.

But to return to why this is a feminist project: it is one because part of a feminist praxis, as scholars have noted over the years, is to de-individuate, you could say. It is about recognising those contributions that are only possible in our lives because of the care work and contributions of other people. Rather than seeing individuals, we see speakers or actors who are supported by a network of invisible or undervalued time and energy. By shining a light on the collaborative nature of this production of knowledge, we are not doing something new, we are just making it visible. This is a feminist practice. Collaborations are always happening – but it is a feminist necessity to point it out.

NA: And feminist collaborations do lead to field building, in large part because of the revelation that knowledge is never just about the individual genius, but the collective that enables knowledge. It sheds light on all of the conversations and interactions that are needed for asking a different set of questions than those that are familiar and therefore comfortable. I would also add that the common misunderstanding of the feminist project is that it adds difference and stirs the pot, so to speak. If that were true, we would have just added postsocialism to other theoretical frames. Like postcolonialism, or neoliberalism. But that is not actually what a feminist method is at its best. What feminist methodologies actually have the potential to do is to centre on questions of difference in order to completely disrupt the ways in which we already know. In that sense our collaboration is a feminist collaboration because we didn't want to just add postsocialism as another way of theorising a part of the world that was not already included in the postcolonial frame (like Eastern Europe) – even though I think that is the impetus of a lot of the work in postsocialism. This is not to say that this work that emphasises how postcolonial theory can be applied to Central and Eastern Europe doesn't make a contribution. It is just to note that our impetus was really different. We started from the premise that theorising postsocialism could change the frame for how to think difference, how to think collectivity, how to think political action, how to think justice, how to think globalisation. And, so, in that sense, the questions, "how is your theorisation of postsocialism bringing anything new to the table that isn't already theorised by the concept of neoliberalism" or "how is it not a subsidiary of postcolonial theory" are misplaced. We are not saying that postsocialism needs to replace theorisations of neoliberalism or postcolonial theory. We are instead saying that postsocialism brings to light something about sociality and collectivity in ways that are obscured when just one category of analysis is privileged. And, they were also obscured in the Cold War epistemological framework (the three world model). Now we can ask a different set of questions.

KV: Can we expand on that? What would you say was the urgency to think postsocialism/postcolonialism relationally? Where did we start and where have we come?

NA: We wanted to unmoor postsocialism and postcolonialism from their geographic and historical associations, and to instead figure postsocialism as an analytic. This allowed to us consider difference and race relationally. It opened up for us the possibility that Eastern Europe does not fit pre-existing ways of conceptualising difference. This is similar to how I engage Eastern Europe in the US imaginary in my first book, in which I consider the form that US imperialism has taken, particularly humanitarian imperialism, vis à vis the former Yugoslavia. I actually believe that a postsocialist analytic as we have defined it provides a really exciting opportunity to think about the way that difference gets deployed in the enactment of US imperialism, and I'm particularly interested in the reformulation of discourses around race that can are made legible through a postsocialist analytic. So, for instance, in the book, I argue that since the Cold War, the racialisation of ideological difference and belief systems has supplemented the racialisation and categorisation of bodies. This has continued after the Cold War, with the racialisation of Islam, but was enabled by Cold War logics that racialised the illiberal (communist) other.

Similarly, our conversations around postsocialism allowed us to ask what is added to the previous mapping of race in terms of bodies and continents when we now also have the racialisation of ideological formations, the racialisation of religion, or of "anachronistic" belief systems that don't fit the liberal democratic model in which we are all supposed to be now in the postsocialist moment.

KV: Right. In addition to postsocialism as an analytic that allows for places that are often understood to have a shared ethnic history, like some of the nations in Eastern Europe, to be conceived of as sites through which to understand race and racialisation, it also opens up new lines of inquiry for areas already analysed under the rubric of postcolonialism. For instance, whereas India is overdetermined as a site of postcolonial study, we can approach issues of gender, caste, and politics brought up by subaltern studies theorists through a postsocialist analytic that thinks about a new imagination of publics, also of group collective politics and political actions.

What we've continued to work on in relation to the intersections and disjuncture between postcolonial and postsocialist theory is a set of three loosely formulated problems. First is a question of how engaging with temporality as a framework allows us to rethink some of the problems people have had in comparative studies of difference. So how do you talk about racial difference across national contexts? Or even in a national context? Chandan Reddy's book, *Freedom with Violence*, describes how in the US context, juridically, new group identities based on categories of difference (and in his book he is talking about sexuality) get framed as amendments to already existing modes of juridical recognition. So how do we escape this recapitulation of already existing modes of recognition that then enhance the organisation and power of the state as it currently exists. One of the ways that we've been doing that is thinking about temporality, as you pointed out.

Another is thinking about how the so-called failure of Marxist humanism as a governmental model has caused a crisis in various leftist movements around the world in terms of defining the model for political change or revolution. As people will say, there are still revolutions, it is not that there are no existing models of revolution, but there are other important places to look, and modes of looking for, political acts, objects, and subjects. These different sites, as they engage with legacies of socialism and imperialism, produce plural globalisations. These often get overwritten by a logic of neoliberalism. So a theme that has come out is how essential relational analysis and critique is to the project of thinking about these legacies.

A scholar in our 2012 residential group, Dace Dzenovska, was working on the historical relationship between Latvia and USSR, thinking about difference produced by the historical relationship to Soviet imperialism of Latvia. She was writing about an affectively experienced sense of difference, a consequence of having been the object of Soviet imperialism, impacting ways of being in the world. These ways of being constantly announce themselves as difference but don't articulate themselves as race – they aren't particularly to phenotype or ethnicity, but they condition the way people experience themselves as subjects in the face of others who don't share that experience of imperialism. Again, temporality has been an important approach to thinking about difference that can help escape the limits of an amendment way to recognise difference.

NA: A parallel conversation, and one related to our reformulation of postsocialism as an analytic tied to temporality, considers the possibility of figuring multiple postsocialisms. In our 2012 Residential Research Group, we considered what might shift if we think about different moments of when postsocialism begins. How might this reformulation allow us to rethink foreclosed possibilities? We were in this sense also rethinking possibilities for transnational analytics, and as you've mentioned, we were rethinking temporality as one way to re-open historical possibilities that seemed foreclosed after the end of state socialism.

But perhaps we can return to the relationship of race critical theories and postsocialism – a connection we make that may be unexpected to some scholars here in the US. Our conversations about places or subjects that don't fit the existing ways of theorising difference have been an impetus for future work. A lot of friends and interlocutors have been surprised to find out that our project on postsocialism led to our current project, which is a co-authored book manuscript titled *Surrogate Humanity: Race, Robots, and the Politics of Technological Futures [since published by Duke University Press in 2019]*. This book explores the notion of how the 21st century "Revolution" both displaces the ideal or aspiration of socialist revolution and re-creates conditions of racialised and gendered devaluing of human action in the social spheres of industry, militarism, and elsewhere. We see this as emerging from our collaboration because at the same time that we connect colonial and postsocialist legacies and global contexts to the tech "revolution", we also highlight new modes of collectivity or shared feeling that can come out of such technologies when they are not produced for circulation in the global capitalist economy.

KV: Exactly. The book focuses on particular engineering and design projects in artificial intelligence (AI) and robotics, whose imaginaries draw heavily upon the assumed universal nature of the human. That universal human has been the target of the difference-based interventions we've brought together in our collaboration. Even as they reinscribe the erasure of difference, these AI and robotics projects are hailed as the space and site of revolution in our time. So for us, this is an example of the imaginary, or we could say failure of imagination, of revolution following the beginning of the era we describe as postsocialism as a global condition.

Note

1   Neda Atanasoski and Kalindi Vora, "Introduction: Postsocialist Politics and the End of Revolution," *Social Identities* 24, no. 2 (2018): 139–154, DOI:10.1080/13504630.2017. 1321712

References

Robinson, Cedric. 2001. *Anthropology of Marxism*. Burlington, VT: Ashgate.

Tlostanova, Madina. 2017. *Postcolonialism and Postsocialism in Fiction and Art: Resistance and Re-existence*. New York: Palgrave McMillan. https://doi.org/10.1007/978-3-319-48445-7.

Verdery, Katherine, and Sharad Chari. 2009. "Thinking Between the Posts: Postcolonialism, Postsocialism, and Ethnography After the Cold War." *Comparative Studies in Society and History* 51, no. 1: 6–34. https://doi.org/10.1017/S0010417509000024.

Chapter 4

Bridging postcoloniality, postsocialism, and "race" in the age of Brexit

An interview with Catherine Baker

Catherine Baker and Redi Koobak

Redi Koobak: In your recent book *Race and the Yugoslav Region: Postsocialist, Post-Conflict, Postcolonial?* (Manchester University Press, 2018), you connect critical race scholarship, global historical sociologies of race in translation, and south-east European cultural critique to situate the territories and collective identities of former Yugoslavia within the politics of race. How do the intersections between the postcolonial – which is often connected to discussions of race – and the postsocialist – which is usually not – play out in this book?

Catherine Baker: Before I wrote the book (Baker 2018), or rather started the process of reading and listening which led to me writing the book, there were two forms of postsocialist-postcolonial intersections I'd been most concerned with. One was the way that Milica Bakić-Hayden (1995), Maria Todorova (1997), and scholars whom they inspired to write about representations of the Balkans in the 1990s had adapted Edward Said's mode of postcolonial critique into an analytical tool for understanding postsocialist cultural politics in south-east Europe, which had deeply informed my PhD research on popular music and national identity in Croatia, and the other was critiques of international intervention in postsocialist south-east Europe which perceived interventions and the foreign staff who embodied them as keeping the region in a neo-colonial position of dependence on the West and being predisposed to treat the region and its people in similarly neo-colonial ways – this was the main critical perspective I needed to bring to my postdoctoral research on foreign peacekeeping forces and their translators/interpreters in Bosnia-Herzegovina. I have to credit Sharad Chari and Katherine Verdery's call for "thinking between the posts" (Chari and Verdery 2009) with starting to push me to reconsider what postsocialism and therefore postcoloniality stood for: if postsocialism should not be thought of as the condition of countries which used to have state socialist systems but a global condition stemming from the collapse of state socialism in central and eastern Europe and the USSR, then postcoloniality too isn't just a condition of the countries which had overseas empires or were colonised by them but a condition that has implicated the whole of the globe. Had I been coming from different personal and academic starting points than being a white British woman, who entered the academic community via a British "area studies" department (the School of Slavonic and East European Studies at University College London), that might not have taken so long.

It is still very easy, on the other hand, for lenses that fuse the postsocialist and postcolonial to employ a postcoloniality without race – or at least it is if the owner of the lens is already able not to see race. Let's put that more strongly – if the owner of the lens has a position in the structures of global white supremacy and "global white ignorance", as Charles Mills (2015) puts it, that means they have been socialised not to see racism in operation. Obviously, those positions shift, and they're particularly ambiguous and contingent for people from central and eastern Europe, who as they travel often find themselves negotiating very different racial formations. The xeno-racism, to use Liz Fekete's term (Fekete 2009), that has been levelled in the UK against Polish workers and anyone else whose accent makes them legible as "eastern European", all the more so since the Brexit referendum, is a case in point. But the work of translating postcolonial thought into ways of understanding postsocialist cultural politics has largely been done by scholars who would identify themselves as white. That is not to dismiss the marginalisation and belittling that scholars from south-east European backgrounds have faced and still do face in the Anglophone academy. But it does mean there has been a structural politics of knowledge which produces what I *could* call the (until recently) largely unexamined assumption that race is something that happens in the postcolonial West and ethnicity is something that happens in the Balkans. I *won't* call it the largely unexamined assumption because the spaces where that examination was happening were pushed to the margins – it was being examined, in interventions like Anikó Imre's early essays on postcolonial whiteness (Imre 1999, 2005), and in the thoughts of prospective scholars who might have internalised that their research questions or their embodied selves didn't have a home in the field of south-east European studies.

So even the postcolonial is not necessarily always, or even (until recently) often, connected to discussions of race. What I wanted to do when I began the work that led to *Race and the Yugoslav Region* was to make it impossible to conceptualise postcoloniality in south-east Europe *without* race. I needed to overcome the obstacles as much in my own residual worldview as in what we've constructed as "the literature" that were suggesting the structures of racism which had emerged from European colonial violence weren't as relevant for south-east Europe because it hadn't had the same history of empire as Britain – indeed it had been subject to different forms of imperial rule for centuries. Being able to see race, racism, and attachments to whiteness as a global phenomenon through Mills's work started to change that, as did understanding through the work of Ella Shohat, Robert Stam, and Howard Winant and Michael Omi in particular (Winant 2001; Omi and Winant 2015) that it's possible to think of "race in translation" (Stam and Shohat 2012), that is, the same formations of race don't exist everywhere, but the structures that give rise to them do.

One suggestion I make in the book is that perhaps postcoloniality has been quite easy to detach from race in south-east European studies because it has so often been filtered through Said, who didn't really contend with race either. Yet the politics and practices of representation that he critiques, and that scholars of south-east Europe have learned to critique through adaptations of his ideas, are readily applicable to race as well *because those politics were already racialised –* this is how Gloria Wekker, whose book *White Innocence* came out just as I was starting to write up the work that became *Race and the Yugoslav Region*, is able to use Said's idea of the "cultural archive" (Wekker 2016, 2) to expose the many traces of a racialised cultural imagination in a Netherlands where the public of the metropole weren't yet having everyday contact with a large population of people of colour (which seemed to be an immediate answer to the exceptionalist objection that eastern Europe didn't experience postcolonial mass migration and therefore didn't develop racism in a Western sense). Already as a PhD and postdoc, even though I wasn't yet equipped to trace global formations of race in south-east Europe in the ways that are much more possible in our field today, I could read Stuart Hall's essays on representation and cultural identity (Hall 1997) and realise the parallels between his deconstruction of racist stereotypes in British media and the dynamics of representing the Balkans that I knew so well through this critical, postcolonial-inspired approach to SEE. What I was still missing was the framework for understanding Hall's examples such as the British media's hypersexualisation of the black athlete Linford Christie as part of the *same* structures that were also producing the othering of the Dinaric aspects of national cultural heritage in Croatia or the moral panics about turbo-folk.

Fitting those together, where critical race studies and decolonial thought are necessary to provide that extra overarching layer (I feel like I ought to be saying "superstructure" here, though I haven't done so before), allows us and really ought to force us to move from what I call a "mode of analogy" in the book to a "mode of connection". I take the language of connection from Gurminder Bhambra's call for "connected sociologies" and "connected histories" (Bhambra 2014, 151) – that is, to articulate where topics and subjects "we" might not have automatically tied into the global history of coloniality and racism have actually been shaped by it. (Bhambra is the editor of the series that published *Race and the Yugoslav Region* – I proposed it to her because I'd already seen that in the run-up to the Brexit vote she was interested in thinking through things such as how the construction of eastern European national identities fitted into the dynamics of racism and xenophobia in the UK.) I revisit topics I've worked on before – popular music; peacekeeping and peacebuilding; the historiography of ethnicity and nationalism – and outline the main formations of race that have been translated into identity-making in the region. In fact the book uses popular music to establish that racialised cultural imaginations *are* at work in south-east Europe – and that opens up space to examine race, racism, and whiteness in spheres where they might have been easier to dismiss before.

Redi Koobak: As a specialist in post-Cold War history, international relations, and cultural studies, you also draw on and expand on the work of intersectional feminist and queer of colour scholars who have tirelessly worked to decentre Eurocentrism and whiteness. While transnational feminism is generally perceived as attempting to decentre Western epistemologies, it also needs to be interrogated for the assumed relationship between transnational feminist research and postcolonial feminisms, especially when considering how it has positioned the postsocialist feminist tradition. How would you situate your work in relation to transnational feminism?

Catherine Baker: The core of transnational feminism as an idea for me is something that exposes the asymmetries of the politics of knowledge, activism, and organising. More than a way of thinking through feminist lenses about phenomena that need to be explained transnationally – though of course it entails that – it's about the material and embodied labour of how we do that work. In your recent article for *Feminist Review*, which I must tell you once again is one of the most transformational that I've read in years, you relay Jacqui Alexander and Chandra Talpade Mohanty's distinction between "'transnational' as a status quo, and 'transnational' with a radical, decolonising edge" (Tlostanova, Thapar-Björkert, and Koobak 2019, 84). That is (now you and they have put it into words that way) the kind of transnational lens that I want to strive for, though I don't know if I always achieve it. So, on the one hand, it's an approach that I aspire to make my work converse with. The first time I thought about the range of topics that became *Race and the Yugoslav Region*, it was June 2013 when I'd just come from the *International Feminist Journal of Politics conference* at Sussex, surrounded by intersectional analyses that did not let their topics' connections to the historical legacies that have produced coloniality and anti-black racism go unspoken, to a workshop about gender and citizenship in south-east Europe that had been organised at Edinburgh by a research project on citizenship in the former Yugoslav successor states. The questions about historical formations of race in the region that I jotted down on the back of my programme as I listened to Julija Sardelić speak about Romani minorities and post-Yugoslav citizenship owed much to the environment of transnational feminism that I'd just been in: they'd become things it felt necessary to answer in a way they hadn't been before.

Because the way I came into south-east European studies was through this adapted postcolonialism (my PhD supervisor was Wendy Bracewell, who was one of the leaders of a large research project about east European travel writing on "Europe" at the time (Bracewell and Drace-Francis 2009), and interrogating ideas of "eastern" and "western" Europe was and is a major intellectual theme at SSEES), and also because the oversights in transnational feminism towards postsocialist feminism haven't affected me in the way they have you, I think I almost encountered postsocialist feminism as an expression *of* postcolonial feminism – or rather it was a space which posed similar questions to my embodied self as a Western researcher studying the Balkans that postcolonial feminism would pose me as a white Western one. Again that's "analogy" rather than "connection", but noticing analogy is probably a first step *towards* recognising connection. So transnational feminism (or whatever we should call the space of critique and action where postcolonial feminism and postsocialist feminism operate) is also something that holds me accountable, or I aspire for it to be. It forces me to question why I'm the right person to do much of my research and, in particular, to have published a book which has the potential to become a go-to citation for discussing race and postcoloniality in south-east Europe. I'm conscious that I came late to this topic, compared to Imre, Miglena Todorova (2006) whose work on Bulgaria helped me clarify what was distinctive about formations of race in and after Yugoslavia, or someone like Konstantin Kilibarda (2010) who was explicitly writing about whiteness and Yugoslavia's relations with the Non-Aligned Movement in 2010. The map of theories and experiences that made me research and write the book in a particular way is probably what I add to it most originally – particularly the continuum I perceive between popular culture and politics, and the idea of individuals' identifications with collective identities that underpins a lot of how I see the world. I'm more able to say that having heard reactions to the book than I probably was when I was writing it.

But where a transnational feminist ethics also comes in is that it motivates me to pre-empt, and avoid becoming complicit in, the dynamics that could easily lead me as a white Western Anglophone woman working at a university in the Global West/North to become positioned as "the" expert on race in the Yugoslav region. As you know better than I do because you've felt its effects, white Western feminists are socialised to have such a pedagogical, didactic, and paternalistic attitude towards feminists from global peripheries that that structural background is already there whenever I'm speaking and co-operating across difference. As part of negotiating those "transversal politics" (I find Nira Yuval-Davis's way of formulating it a useful way of thinking about these kinds of dialogues [Yuval-Davis 1997, 125]), I need to be very conscious that language or behaviour which might not seem particularly marked to me could actually still be reproducing that. I'm not sure I always get it right. I'm already regretting titling a recent paper "What female pop-folk celebrity in south-east Europe tells postsocialist feminist media studies about global formations of race" – who am I to "tell" postsocialist feminist media studies anything? I also want to be meticulous in crediting the intellectual sources that my own work rests on – for instance the first two people I thank in the acknowledgements to *Race and the Yugoslav Region* are Flavia Dzodan and Zara Bain, whose writing respectively forced me to relate the familiar "Europe" of south-east European cultural studies to the racist and fortified "Europe" of critical race studies and introduced me to Charles Mills whose writing on the *spatialness* of racialised hierarchies of civilisation and modernity was the hinge I needed to suggest how the way I was used to understanding constructions of "Europe" and "the Balkans" could combine with being explicit about the structures of global white supremacy. Without sharing digital spaces with them both in the early and mid 2010s, I almost certainly wouldn't have written the book.

And the third way that transnational feminism informs my ethical stance is that I'm continually questioning how I should be balancing the risks of doing scholarship about race and whiteness in my present place and times. On the one hand the structural privilege that I embody (including the perceived objectivity that whiteness gives me when I talk to colleagues about race, and that my lack of any family heritage from the region gives me in the West when I claim expertise about south-east Europe), and the secure position I currently have in the academy, means I ought to be able to absorb more of the consequences of doing this work in public than scholars who aren't racialised as white and ethnically and linguistically positioned at what the coloniality of knowledge (a term you rightly end on in your *Feminist Review* piece) has made the centre of global academic production. And/or scholars who are in more junior or precarious positions, as marginalised scholars are disproportionately more likely to be. If, fate forbid, I'm targeted for harassment more heavily than some upsetting near-misses I've had, I've got a reasonable expectation that management will believe my side of the story. On the other hand, I have to balance that with the realities of my own psychological and mental resilience as an individual, and I've been wrestling with this a lot at the moment as the context in which I'm personally working has shifted over the last few years.

Redi Koobak: What might postsocialist feminists learn from this book? And postcolonial feminists?

Catherine Baker: My first reaction is that it's hard for me to say – I'm not a postsocialist feminist or a postcolonial one, except in the sense that I'm operating in a world which has been shaped by postsocialism and postcoloniality and my scholarship is continually in dialogue with that of feminists who are responding from more intimately postsocialist and postcolonial positions. I *am* one of those agents of the Western mediation that you rightly say in *Feminist Review* that South-to-semi-periphery coalitions don't need, in fact that they ought to refuse – I can't disavow where that positions me, but I can make choices in what I write, whom I cite, and whom I work with that do as little harm as possible and harness that positionality to have at least some transformative effect. What I think the book has done is given back-up to feminists and other critical scholars and activists working on and in postsocialist spaces who have already recognised how global formations of race have permeated into the semi-periphery – I can say that because from time to time on social media someone will tag me into a photo of a passage from the book that expressed something they found particularly meaningful. The way the book builds its historical and conceptual framework is there to be built on and contested, and I'm sure that experts on particular aspects that I might just have covered in a couple of pages will expose limitations of it (I hope they will – I want to understand those better too). But I think it has established that part of the region's global historical context goes missing when we *don't* ask how the global politics of race have played out there. For postcolonial feminists, maybe it can contribute to demonstrating that "postcolonial Europe" doesn't stop at the rim of the Atlantic and that there are past and present solidarities between south-east

Europe and the Global South that shouldn't be forgotten just because postsocialist nationalisms wanted it to be – but I hope it would lead readers towards more of the postsocialist feminism I draw on if that side of it is new to them.

One thing I don't think I emphasised enough in the book is why it matters to be able to talk about race and racism, rather than just coloniality and Eurocentrism (even though present systems of race and racism exist because of coloniality). Here I'm thinking of an essay by Olivia Umurerwa Rutazibwa (2016, 192) that I hadn't read when I was writing the book – it's very tempting, she notes, for white scholars to strategically avoid "race" in order to make their critiques of "Eurocentrism" more palatable. But Eurocentrism exists in an academy and a world with histories which have already been structured around race. And without having to contend with the vectors of violence and oppression that "race" makes visible, the "postcolonial" as a way of thinking about postsocialist Europe becomes very easy to co-opt in ways that still entrench racist and xenophobic cisheteronormative patriarchy, in the particular ethnocentric form we're seeing in central and eastern Europe which is directed against historic national Others, new migrant minorities, and the targets of anti-gender ideology – the argument that expecting central Europe to accept sexual and gender minorities or Muslim refugees is a colonising act on the part of the West. As well as resisting the kind of far-right and white supremacist co-option of history, language, and culture that colleagues in medieval studies, archaeology, or classics are already contending with, we also have to insulate postsocialist adaptations of the postcolonial from being co-opted in the same sort of way.

Redi Koobak: Does feminism need dialogues between the postcolonial and the postsocialist and why?

Catherine Baker: The short answer: of course it does, and I feel as if I've been part of more spaces than ever this year where they are happening. In the last few months since we exchanged the first round of questions and answers, I joined in a symposium on "Race, Gender, Sexuality and Empire in Southeastern Europe" organised by Christina Novakov-Ritchey, Sunnie Rucker-Chang, Ana Stojanović, and Miglena Todorova in Toronto, Noa Ha and Fatima El-Tayeb's workshop on "East European Cultures of Memory Between Postsocialism and Postcolonialism" at TU Dresden, and a set of panels on postsocialism and racialised borders at the Amsterdam Centre for Globalisation Studies' conference. (I should say that my presence at all but the Amsterdam conference was virtual – rattling off a fast-paced academic travel itinerary isn't a neutral act any more, or rather is much more marked as an act of acquiescence in the climate emergency than it used to be.) Politically, in my home context, these have been several bruising months (the 2019 general election was four weeks ago) for democracy, workers' and migrants' rights, trans rights, and quite possibly reproductive autonomy – one of Boris Johnson's advisers has just been praising Viktor Orbán's "interesting early thinking on the limits of liberalism" and hoping for a "special relationship" with Orbán's Hungary (Walker and Boffey 2020). So the radical connectivities that postsocialist feminists are forging with postcolonialism are happening at a time when our ability to openly name racism, misogyny, and their intersection in public is coming under increasingly sustained attack. (The generations of socialist and postsocialist feminists who lived through the intensification of patriarchal nationalism in the early 1990s after the collapse of state socialism have already lived through such a revanchist reverse of their hopes for social transformation; in the West it is characterising the late 2010s more than any other time in my memory.) This context is on my mind much more than what I could have said about feminism needing dialogues between the postcolonial and the postsocialist in order to arrive at a holistic, globalised understanding of oppression. We need that, but we need that *for a purpose* – once we've understood through those dialogues that struggles we are impelled to see as disparate or even contradictory are actually resisting interconnected forces, what can we then practically do?

In a UK context, which is where I feel most qualified to make suggestions about what feminism "needs", for instance, those dialogues can show us how the postcolonial condition and the postsocialist condition are implicated in our current state of racial capitalism. By racial capitalism, I mean what Gargi Bhattacharyya (2018, x) describes as the racialised (and simultaneously gendered) processes that divide "people . . . from each other in the name of economic survival or in the name of economic well-being" – these politics of entitlement and exclusion stratify the labour market, securitise borders, and regulate everyday space. In London the racial logics of the global city, enforced through urban planning, housing policy, policing, and migration control, are imposed on workers who have arrived via recent postcolonial and postsocialist migrations and the descendants of workers who came to the UK through postcolonial migrations one generation or longer ago (Danewid 2020); those racial logics extend of course also to workers who can state their identity as "white British" without qualification and are offered the nostalgic comfort of identifying with the "white working class". In smaller towns, the workers marginalised through these racial logics may be less numerous or more recently arrived, but the logics themselves remain. Between 2004 and 2016, EU freedom of movement mobilities gave the citizens of some postsocialist countries more access to the UK labour market than the citizens of most countries Britain had colonised, albeit subjecting them to an "institutionalised xenophobia" (Emejulu 2016) which cast them as responsible for conditions designed to immiserate precarious labour; after 2017–2019, they faced negotiating the imprecise "settled status" residency scheme or experiencing what the symbolic Windrush Generation (of black workers who arrived from the Caribbean after 1948) had faced when the ever-expanding UK border met irregularities in their paperwork. It takes a dialogue between postcolonial and postsocialist feminism to reveal the full processes at work here: how minorities have been pitted against each other; the stratifiability of whiteness which has enabled the stigmatisation of "eastern European migrants" (a process that predates the EU enlargements of 2004–2013 and dates back to the Romaphobia hurled against Romani asylum seekers from central Europe and Romania in the late 1990s); the limited "ways out" from discrimination that racial capitalism seems to offer those who can be racialised as white as long as they join in the exclusion of racial Others. Earlier I was tempted to call today's postcolonial/postsocialist feminist dialogues "long overdue", but of course they aren't; as historians such as Chiara Bonfiglioli (2016) have shown, they were already unfolding during the Cold War, in settings where women's activists from postcolonial and state socialist countries came together, such as the UN Decade for Women. In the same way, let me not reduce postcolonial/postsocialist dialogues to the spaces of academic knowledge production where I happen to spend my working life: they are happening already whenever precarious workers from "postcolonial" and "postsocialist" spaces are organising together.

Redi Koobak: How might such dialogues, and perhaps other dialogues that you find important, still be instrumental in looking for some shared agendas or coalitions to fight for a future? To put it simply, can we still save or revamp feminism as a shared agenda or have differences between feminisms grown too enormous?

Catherine Baker: Are feminists even fighting for a future at the moment, or just fighting to hold on to what we fought for in the past? In the UK's current atmosphere, for instance, it feels ever more likely that the government will take the opportunity of Brexit to repeal equalities protections, which for all their limitations still created an important strategic lever for struggling against inequalities in representation and treatment in public institutions in particular. (The booms in queer public history and heritage work this decade, and in more heritage sites being prepared to engage with the colonial legacies of their spaces and collections, would likely not have been so great without the public sector equality duty in the Equalities Act 2010, which required museums and other public institutions in the UK to anticipate the needs of groups the Act defined as protected minorities.) The space that transphobic narratives about children supposedly being misled into believing they are trans have been given to become conservative *and* liberal media common sense has put us only one legislative step away from schools being forbidden to make children and teenagers aware of trans people, just as they were forbidden to promote homosexuality to young people between 1988 and 2000–2003. Part of our immediate future is simply fighting for the recent past not to be erased. And yet I don't think differences between feminisms have "grown" too enormous; rather, they were predestined to *be* enormous because of the way in which racial capitalism stratifies and divides lived communities, nations, and the globe. It exists to preclude the perception of common interests and struggles across hegemonically constructed boundaries of difference, and to separate individuals into socially marked positions from which collective organisation among and between them "ought" to be impossible. It exists to militate against the building of coalitions and encourage people to prefer protection for an entitled few to hope and transformation for the many, at the cost of confronting how they themselves have been implicated in these seductive systems of domination so far.

Redi Koobak: As Neda Atanasoski and Kalindi Vora have argued,

there is still a crisis in both geopolitical and academic imaginaries of protest, particularly those influenced by Marxist critique, which calls for a dehomogenizing of the "socialism" in postsocialism and for a dialogue between the multiple inheritances of socialism in the present.

(Atanasoski and Vora 2018, 14)

In their understanding, and we think you would agree, postsocialism is not a unified phenomenon or experience, and thus, they call for viewing postsocialism, like the related term postcolonialism, as an analytic rather than a fixed time period. How do you think "postsocialism" contributes to current geopolitical and academic imaginaries of protest?

Catherine Baker: Postsocialism as an analytic compels us to ask what happens after socio-economic systems and certainties collapse. What hopes did the old system offer which there are now no longer the conditions to fulfil; what hopes did the new system hold out and then dash? What "alternatives" could be envisioned in the past which are harder to imagine, and might yet still be worth recovering, now? The sociologist Ana Dević (2016) writes of "what nationalism has buried", by which she means the structural and socioeconomic explanations for public discontent and disempowerment during the late Yugoslav crisis that were silenced after the wars began by the rush to explain why ethnic violence had broken out instead – yet a new drive to understand the dislocations of a crumbling socio-economic system surged back up after the global financial crisis of the late 2000s and that moment's own forms of protest. Yet what we have seen more and more since then is how readily the sentiments of losing the likelihood of a future one had felt "entitled" to are convertible into a desire to secure one's metaphorical and literal home against Others who are supposedly responsible for threatening that entitlement – "eastern Europeans" on the Lincolnshire job market; refugees on their way across the border where they will need housing; minorities outbreeding a majority population to the supposed point of "replacement" (a theme both of the anti-Albanian, anti-Muslim rhetoric that Slobodan Milošević took up in during the late Yugoslav crisis, and of rhetoric on today's identitarian and white nationalist right – sections of which even look to the genocidal project of building an ethnically pure Bosnian Serb republic as an inspiration, while the patriarchal and Islamophobic right in central and eastern Europe gains strength from Western preoccupations with "guarding the frontier" against Islam).

Another insight that knowledge from the postsocialist and post-Yugoslav region might have been able to spread wider in better time, if Western academic and policy circles had treated it as able to explain more than the aftermath of the Yugoslav Wars in a narrowly bounded region they constructed as a "post-conflict" space, is understanding that "protest" is not just a thing of progress and the Left. The largest and most organised protests in post-Yugoslav Croatia have been from veterans of the 1991–1995 war of independence protesting against government co-operation with the international criminal justice system, and demanding greater public recognition of their wartime sacrifice – symbolically in post-war Croatian public culture the (male) veteran is sacrosanct as the defender of the homeland, yet the demand for physical and mental health care in the former front-line regions (where successive governments have failed to improve the economy) far outstrips what the state has provided. Yet the most loudly articulated demand, as if to solve these material circumstances, is not to transform the socio-economic structures of post-Yugoslav Croatia but to stop investigating war crimes allegations against Croats, tolerate slogans used by the fascist Ustaše state of 1941–1945 in public, and ban the Serb minority from using Cyrillic script in Vukovar. In the decade just gone, the same networked practices that excited the Left when they saw them being turned against the financial establishment and authoritarian regimes have gone on to empower protest from the Right, perhaps even more successfully. What I've given here is probably quite an empiricist version of postsocialism as an analytic – "what do conditions after the collapse of state socialism reveal about protest?" – which is still quite bound to a specific time and space; but then does postsocialist analysis and critique still have to have some grounding in societies where state socialism collapsed to be recognisably post*socialist*? Where would a deterritorialised postsocialism end and begin?

Redi Koobak: What part might feminist agendas play in refuturing, in imagining new political imaginations?

Catherine Baker: You've asked me this just as I'm struggling with an exhausted *lack* of imagination on my own part, particularly regarding how we use or even exist in the public sphere. The position I'm personally speaking from when I say that is one of grappling with how defensive I've become against the online spaces that used to be where I was able to apply my interdisciplinary and transnational knowledge most: digital platforms always *were* spaces of contention and surveillance, but the spaces they used to contain for speaking and listening with intimacy and vulnerability (against the grain of the profit motives for which they were developed) are being edged out by an ever more continuous networked and automated assault. The creative impulses I used to have feel like they're answering outdated questions, and when it comes to the main form of marginality that's affected me (the subjectivity of having grown up queer and somewhat gender non-conforming in the particular place and time I did), I used to feel a kind of fulfilment at harnessing embodied insights from my own queer experience into an analytical lens, but the more my queer experience is enmeshed with someone else's, the less I want to make it discoverable in a public arena (or at least the public arenas as they currently exist) for the sake of inscribing myself as a theorist. That weighs more on some of my popular culture work than on my work on race, postcoloniality, and postsocialism (where elements of my professional and political life inform my perspective more directly than anything in my private domain – though I recognise the household is one of the spaces where the *most* everyday social reproduction of racialised categories of thought and feeling takes place).

The wider relevance of explaining this unnerving moment in my own "feminist life" (Ahmed 2017) – since, as Sara Ahmed argues, the embodied consequences of our own experiences of doing feminist work are how we start to feel feminist theory – is, I suppose, that speaking about feminist agendas is inseparable from speaking about the conditions under which they are or can be produced: the platforms available to communicate them and put them in transversal dialogue with others; the political economy of how they can be invented, popularised, applied, contested and who is able to do so. The academic platforms where I've personally done much of my work towards a feminist agenda are even less fit for purpose as sites of refuturing than they used to be: they're largely structured not even to give us time to think about the future, even for those among "us" who are allowed in. I *ought* to be offering some kind of answer about how the possibilities that stem from dialogues between postcolonial and postsocialist feminism will breathe life into the kind of feminist and material refuturing we urgently need, but I don't think a Western academic workplace overwhelmed by the audit culture of the neoliberal university is the place from where that answer is most likely to emerge.

References

Ahmed, Sara. 2017. *Living a Feminist Life*. Durham, NC: Duke University Press. https://doi.org/10.1215/9780822373377.

Atanasoski, Neda, and Kalindi Vora. 2018. "Introduction: Postsocialist Politics and the Ends of Revolution." Special issue, *Social Identities* 24, no. 2: 1–15. https://doi.org/10.1080/13504630.2017.1321712.

Baker, Catherine. 2018. *Race and the Yugoslav Region: Postsocialist, Post-Conflict, Postcolonial?* Manchester: Manchester University Press. https://doi.org/10.7765/9781526126610.

Bakić-Hayden, Milica. 1995. "Nesting Orientalisms: The Case of Former Yugoslavia." *Slavic Review* 54, no. 4: 917–931. https://doi.org/10.2307/2501399.

Bhambra, Gurminder K. 2014. *Connected Sociologies*. London: Bloomsbury Academic. https://doi.org/10.5040/9781472544377.

Bhattacharyya, Gargi. 2018. *Rethinking Racial Capitalism: Questions of Reproduction and Survival*. London: Rowman and Littlefield International.

Bonfiglioli, Chiara. 2016. "The First UN World Conference on Women (1975) as a Cold War Encounter: Recovering Anti-Imperialist, Non-Aligned and Socialist Genealogies." *Filozofija i društvo* 27, no. 3: 521–541. https://doi.org/10.2298/FID1603521B.

Bracewell, Wendy, and Alex Drace-Francis, eds. 2009. *Balkan Departures: Travel Writing from Southeastern Europe*. New York: Berghahn.

Chari, Sharad, and Katherine Verdery. 2009. "Thinking Between the Posts: Postcolonialism, Postsocialism, and Ethnography After the Cold War." *Comparative Studies in Society and History* 51, no. 1: 6–34. https://doi.org/10.1017/S001041750900002.

Danewid, Ida. 2020. "The Fire This Time: Grenfell, Racial Capitalism and the Urbanisation of Empire." *European Journal of International Relations* 26, no. 1: 289–313. https://doi.org/10.1177%2F1354066119858388.

Dević, Ana. 2016. "What Nationalism Has Buried: Yugoslav Social Scientists on the Crisis, Grassroots Powerlessness and Yugoslavism." In *Social Inequalities and Discontent in Yugoslav Socialism*, edited by Rory Archer, Igor Duda, and Paul Stubbs, 21–37. London and New York: Routledge. https://doi.org/10.4324/9781315609461.

Emejulu, Akwugo. 2016. "On the Hideous Whiteness of Brexit." *Verso Blog*, June 28, 2016. www.versobooks.com/blogs/2733-on-the-hideous-whiteness-of-brexit-let-us-be-honest-about-our-past-and-our-present-if-we-truly-seek-to-dismantle-white-supremacy (accessed January 14, 2020).

Fekete, Liz. 2009. *A Suitable Enemy: Islamophobia and Xeno-Racism in Europe*. London: Pluto.

Hall, Stuart, ed. 1997. *Representation: Cultural Representations and Signifying Practices.* London: Sage.

Imre, Anikó. 1999. "White Man, White Mask: Mephisto Meets Venus." *Screen* 40, no. 4: 405–422. https://doi.org/10.1093/screen/40.4.405.

Imre, Anikó. 2005. "Whiteness in Post-Socialist Eastern Europe: The Time of the Gypsies, the End of Race." In *Postcolonial Whiteness*, edited by Alfred J. López, 79–102. Albany, NY: State University of New York Press.

Kilibarda, Konstantin. 2010. "Non-Aligned Geographies in the Balkans: Space, Race and Image in the Construction of New 'European' Foreign Policies." In *Security Beyond the Discipline: Emerging Dialogues on Global Politics*, edited by Abhinava Kumar and Derek Maisonville, 27–57. Toronto: York Centre for International and Security Studies.

Mills, Charles W. 2015. "Global White Ignorance." In *The Routledge International Handbook of Ignorance Studies*, edited by Matthias Gross and Linsey McGoey, 217–227. London and New York: Routledge.

Omi, Michael, and Howard Winant. 2015. *Racial Formation in the United States.* 3rd ed. London and New York: Routledge.

Rutazibwa, Olivia Umurerwa. 2016. "From the Everyday to IR: In Defence of the Strategic Use of the R-Word." *Postcolonial Studies* 19, no. 2: 191–200. https://doi.org/10.1080/1 3688790.2016.1254016.

Stam, Robert, and Ella Shohat. 2012. *Race in Translation: Culture Wars Around the Postcolonial Atlantic.* New York: New York University Press.

Tlostanova, Madina, Suruchi Thapar-Björkert, and Redi Koobak. 2019. "The Postsocialist 'Missing Other' of Transnational Feminism?" *Feminist Theory* 121: 81–87. https://doi.org/10.1177%2F0141778918816946.

Todorova, Maria. 1997. *Imagining the Balkans.* Oxford: Oxford University Press.

Todorova, Miglena S. 2006. "Race Travels: Whiteness and Modernity Across National Borders." Ph.D. thesis, University of Minnesota.

Walker, Shaun, and Daniel Boffey. 2020. "Hungary for Brexit: Orbán Praises Johnson and Trump." *The Guardian*, January 9, 2020. www.theguardian.com/world/2020/jan/09/hungary-for-brexit-orban-praises-johnson-and-trump (accessed January 20, 2020).

Wekker, Gloria. 2016. *White Innocence: Paradoxes of Colonialism and Race.* Durham, NC: Duke University Press. https://doi.org/10.1215/9780822374565.

Winant, Howard. 2001. *The World Is a Ghetto: Race and Democracy Since World War II.* New York: Basic Books.

Yuval-Davis, Nira. 1997. *Gender and Nation.* London: Sage.

Chapter 5

Queering "Postsocialist Coloniality"

Decolonising queer fluidity and postsocialist postcolonial China

Shana Ye

Introduction

Queer theorisation and method are conventionally thought of as having originated out of European and American poststructuralist critique of gender, sex, and sexuality in the mid-1980s and expanded globally in the 1990s. This travelling story of the "fluid queer", like many Eurocentric notions, has been disrupted by recent scholarship of queer diaspora, transnationalism, queer of colour critiques, postcolonial studies, and decolonial thought. However, these voluminous interventions have not yet fully engaged with multiple forms of interrelated empires, racialisation, and capitalist accumulation in areas related to "postsocialism". To address this lacuna, this chapter seeks to provincialise US queer knowledge production and to consider how queer's fluidity and mobility are made possible within the material and affective structure of what I call "postsocialist coloniality".

By "postsocialist coloniality", I mean the intertwined nexuses of colonial and imperial formations beyond the coloniser/colonised dichotomy that are reshaped by the political economy of the Cold War and the post-Cold War discourse of transition. As a global socio-historical totality, coloniality has overdetermined social relations of capital accumulation, control over nature, racialised labour, gender and reproduction, struggle for political authority, and subjectivity, knowledge, and being (Quijano 2000). Subsequently, Quijano's genealogy of global coloniality has been expanded through an exploration of the complex histories of imperial and colonial differences and racialisation in non-European empires, such as the Russian/ Soviet empire (Mignolo and Tlostanova 2006, 2012; Mignolo 2011; Tlostanova 2012; Suchland 2012). Similarly, in the studies of East Asian colonial formations, scholars of Chinese diaspora and transnationalism (Chow 1993; Ong 1999), Asian regionalism (Chen 2010), and Sinophone modernity (Shih 2007, 2010; Chiang and Heinrich 2013) have pushed to theorise interrelated colonial, imperial, and nationalist struggles beyond a unifying framework of coloniality.

The concept of "postsocialism" might appear at first glance only to be relevant to the former Soviet Union and Eastern Bloc or existing socialist countries that have hybridised socialism with market economy, such as China and Vietnam (Shih 2012, 28). Yet postsocialism should be perceived as a global condition that restructured neoliberal discourse and practices (Suchland 2015) as well as previous racial and imperial formations (Atanasoski 2013). For example, Neda Atanasoski sees US global humanitarianism and militarism in the late and post-Cold War era as instantiating postsocialist imperialism that allows the United States to displace racial inequality and to solidify liberal racial logic of multiculturalism through racialisation of the Communist world (Atanasoski 2013).

In this chapter, I use China – a historically non-Western, non-White, subaltern empire that achieved anticolonial national independence through third-world socialism, and has emerged as a global hegemon via neoliberal restructuring, as an example to further illustrate the heterogeneity and plurality of global coloniality in relation to the post-Cold War postsocialist conditions. More specifically, I use the cultural, political, and affective economy of queerness in China as a site to examine the local representations and specificity as well as convergence and entanglement of postsocialist coloniality. By "economy of queerness", I mean how the discourse of queerness is produced within the specificities of socio-economic landscapes, which relationalities, institutions, and practices have enabled queer's emergence in particular time/space, how the political presence of "queer" has taken on various meanings in its circulation, and which inclusions and exclusions it reproduces. In other words, instead of assuming "queer" as an unproblematic object of study or lens of analysis, I treat "queer" as an intricate web of power relations and trace its genealogy in hope of understanding the biopolitical and geopolitical operation of postsocialist postcolonial world.

As this chapter will show, the political economy and affective structure of queerness in China have provided global conditions of possibility for the transnational dominance and institutionalisation of US queer knowledge. Contextualising the emergence and circulation of US queer theory in the 1990s within the economy of anti-Marxism and China's market economic reform, I argue that the discourse of queer as fluid and anti-normative, concomitant with the accelerated demand for flexible capital and labour in the 1990s, is promised by the Chinese embrace of western humanist knowledge, cosmopolitan desires, and flexible labour and capital. Yet as the liberal and democratic discourse of queer politics predominantly frames queer precarity in terms of "unfreedom under communism", rather than economic inequality and violence, the blanket anti-communist rhetoric displaces queer inequality as a result of global coloniality and its uneven division of labour onto the orientalist construction of China as the ahistorical "other". While queerness is often thought of as embodying cutting-edge anti-normativity, this chapter shows the collusion of queer as "fluid" and the colonial labour flexibilisation within postsocialist coloniality.

To ground my analysis, I begin with a brief reflection on limited discussions of postsocialism and postcolonialism in China. I use the example of Chinese LGBT advocates' support of US queer organising in the 1990s to reveal the Sino-US queer interdependency in reproducing homonormativity. Moving from the affective structure to knowledge production of "queer", I instantiate the "queer theory versus naturalness of homosexuality debate" to reflect on the logic of capital reproduced in the ahistorical application of Western theories and knowledge. Finally, I unpack different meanings and embodiments of "queer fluidity" in current LGBT activism to show the asymmetrical structure of queer division of labour.

Postsocialist coloniality and China

One of the defining features of postsocialist coloniality I want to focus on in this chapter is its contradiction and ambivalence that often escapes critical reflection. For example, the ripples of colonial history and the question of self-determination that fit well with postcolonial thinking have been expressed mainly through a nationalist agenda of "China dream" and "great restoration of the Chinese nation" (Meinhof, Yan, and Zhu 2017, 3), and therefore often dismissed as state propaganda. On the other hand, "postsocialism" is also a problematic umbrella term that lumps together various economic, political, and social relations pertaining to the end of communist regime, market reform, and transition, which in China's official discourse is described as "socialism with Chinese characteristics". In-depth discussions on the "postsocialist condition" thus far have primarily occurred among the East European scholars, whose insights seldom intersect with scholarship of China. Often, scholars in/of China studies use "postsocialism" interchangeably with terms such as "neoliberal" and "post-Mao" depending on their emphasis and contexts. So far China is an afterthought in both postcolonial and postsocialist theorisation as postcolonialism continues to be associated with the Third World and postsocialism with the Second. This "non-place" of China itself is a result of intertwined colonial knowledge that organises the world along the British, US, and Soviet empires and metageographic mapping of the "three-worlds". Therefore, a brief overview of the discussion on the postcolonial and the postsocialist in China would shed light on the "postsocialist coloniality" and its relation to the studies of queerness.

In a recent special issue of *InterDiscipline* on postcolonialism and China, the contributors emphasise that, despite the fact that postcolonial theory has conventionally been applied to former colonies of European empires, postcolonial concerns are crucial for understanding the Chinese modernity, identities, and the interrelation among Western imperialism, masculinist nationalism, and class struggles in China (Vukovich 2017). Seeking national independence and modernisation on its own terms after its national humiliation, the Chinese communist revolution is a result of anti-colonial anti-imperialist movements. Defying conventional Marxist thought that centres on working class revolution in bourgeois societies and departing from the Soviet model, China's peasantry/worker-led revolution and socialist modernisation was understood as a form of decolonisation opposed to capitalist expansion and reformulation of the history of Chinese empire (Chen 2010, 12) and as a successful example for the Third World reunification of sovereignty, restructuring of economy, nationalisation, and global anti-imperialist alliance. Yet Chinese experience with colonialism and imperialism have also shaped discourses of nativism, self-inflicted othering, and neocolonialism (Meinhof, Yan, and Zhu 2017) as well as concerns of the resurgence of Chinese imperial power in Asia, especially within the Cold War anti-communism-pro-Americanism discourse and China's reopening to the world in the late 1970s with energy for economic prosperity (Chen 2010, 12). These colonial and imperial entanglements are further complicated by China's position within the global postsocialist condition.

Drawing from David Harvey, Jason McGrath (McGrath 2008) traces how the decline of American hegemony in the post-Cold War era (for example, the destructive power of the US military, a decline in manufacturing, the rise of alternative currencies, neoconservatism under the George H.W. Bush administration) presented opportunities for China to rise as the growing market and overconsumption of the latter "fixed" a cyclical problem of previous capitalist overaccumulation and unused surpluses of capital, labour, and commodities (McGrath 2008, 15–17). With the lingering effect of being "othered" as both the "Third World" and the "communist" anomaly, post-reform China sought economic prosperity and globalism through disavowal of socialism, embracing flexibilisation of economy, labour and accumulation, and investment in interdependency with imperial centres such as the United States, forming a symbiosis of what financial historian Niall Ferguson and Moritz Schularick call "Chimerica" (Ferguson and Schularick 2007). The history of Chinese socialism as anti-colonialism (and the romanticisation of it) and the "economic miracle" of postsocialist China have continued to evoke radical hope for and disillusionment of "alternatives", begging the questions of China's position in relation to global postsocialism and coloniality. With this background of China's postsocialist postcolonial ambiguity and ambivalence, I now turn to the analysis of the paradoxes of queerness zooming in on the doublings in queer affective structures, knowledge production, and relations between labour and capital.

Homonormativity, made in China? Symbiosis of queer "Chimerica"

Many critics have observed that the US queer theorising and the social movement in the 1990s departed from a Marxist critique of sexual capitalism and became disinterested in labour politics. Despite the fact that mass LGBTQ political struggles and leftist social movements in the 1950s and 1960s shared a close tie in their battles against racism, imperialism, and war, as historian and queer critic Bogdan Popa shows, this alliance was weakened by an increasing disillusionment of a global communist movement in the 1970s. By the end of the 1980s, socialism, and its higher stage, communism, was regarded as an exhausted global project (Popa 2018, no page number in original). In the Western intellectual sphere and especially the US academy, the waning of Marxist and socialist movement also contributed to the loss of theoretical hope in the egalitarian-oriented ideologies. Many scholars have left Marxist study of colonialism in the wake of Edward Said and Michel Foucault and turned to exploring the discursive practices underlying projects of colonial modernity.

Across the Pacific in China, the emergence of queer studies is also thought of as antithetical to Marxism and socialism (Liu 2015, 1). As the Cultural Revolution (1966–1976) ended with Mao Zedong's death in 1976 and the country transitioned from a socialist planned economy to free market, the previously repressed intellectuals in the 1980s rehabilitated themselves as agents of China's historical developments and turned to Western ideas to repudiate Maoist ideologies (Xu 2009, 198). This "culture fever" (*wenhua re*) characterised by massive translation projects of Western works in the social sciences and humanities also matched the "thought liberation" movement (*jiefang sixiang*) launched by the state that promoted traditions of the Enlightenment and humanism to overturn Maoist project of "class struggle" and sought technocratic means to prepare China for economic reform (Xu 2009, 199). The articulation and studies of (queer) sexuality and gender since the late 1980s were informed by the larger intellectual and political climate that denied the spectre of Marxism and attempted to catch up with Western knowledge for the sake of liberation. Queer studies of China/Sinophone to date have been more concerned with cultural differences, global-local, belonging, "Chineseness", and queer citizenship than labour and class, with the exception of queer sex work.

These resonances of queer emergence in relation to the waning of Marxism and labour politics in different locations could be seen as telling examples of the material and affective entanglements of global postsocialist coloniality. The fall of the socialist states at the end of the Cold War eroded the US war-time nationalism and its military industrial complex dissolved due to the lack of a communally tangible threat. As a result, traditionally western allies have no incentive to seek US leadership or protection (Harvey 2003 in McGrath 2008, 16). To maintain its global hegemony, the United States sought new "alien" enemies, such as religious terrorists, undocumented immigrants, and sexual "deviants", as the enemy *within*, who would soon be selectively incorporated into the racialised discourse and imperialist conquest of what Jasbir Puar terms "homonationalism" (Puar 2007). The AIDS epidemic in the 1980s, wherein homosexuality and sexual non-productivity were cast as threats to national security and the survival of humanity, provided ample opportunities for conservative politics to reduce the budget for public health service, reanimate anti-gay backlash, and promote "traditional family values". These conservative moves of neoliberalisation were largely backed up by the economic symbiosis of "Chimerica" where Chinese overproduction, cheap labour, and vast saving underwrote US debt and overconsumption. It was also under and in response to the resurgence of domestic conservatism in the late 1980s and early 1990s, that US mainstream lesbian and gay political imagination turned to the narrow terrain of rights and citizenship (Duggan 2002) and pursued global recognition and leadership through "gay internationalism" (Massad 2007).

Unlike many post-independent postcolonial countries that were forced into structural adjustment, the discourse of "transition" in China produced both affect and labour to embrace neoliberal restructuring in the realm of culture, politics, and daily life. Coeval with the changes in the US, China sought larger global accept-ance and economic opportunities in its post-1989 *Tian'anmen* era through hosting international events such as the Asian Games in 1990 and the UN's Fourth World Conference on Women in 1995. Instead of aligning with postcolonial positions of anti-imperialism and decolonisation, early Chinese feminists and LGBT queer activists (primarily urban intellectuals and scholar-activists within universities and state research institutes – another legacy of state socialism) turned to Western liberalism and democracy, evidenced in their embrace of the homogenised con-cept of "gender" which itself is a Cold War "biopolitical apparatus" to maintain social and sexual order (Repo 2015, 4) in the United States, replacing critiques of political economy with developmentalist model of rights, equality, and progress defined by the US through "gender mainstreaming" and institutionalised within the UN (Ghodsee 2010). This process is also accompanied by the emergence of a new creative class, as Weiling Deng articulates in this volume, whose cultural, intellectual, and other non-economic forms of capital are utilised to gain recogni-tion, especially in the global feminist realm.

While homonormativity and homonationalism since the 1990s are certainly US devices of sexualised, racialised, and gendered imperialism, we should not lose sight of how these technologies are co-developed, tested, and solidified in dif-ferent locations. Instead of simply seeing the normalisation of LGBT rights and liberalism as US imposition, I want to ask to what extent this universalisation is "made in China" as the Chinese postsocialist postcolonial condition provides both affective labour and the "battlefield" for (its) cross-fertilisation. One example of this "queer Chimerica" can be seen in the coalition between the International Les-bian and Gay Human Rights Commission (ILGHRC) and Chinese lesbian women at the Fourth UN World Conference on Women in Beijing.

In his celebrated work on sexuality and LGBT rights in the Arabic and Muslim world, Joseph Massad identifies the International Lesbian and Gay Association (ILGA) and ILGHRC as key players in imposing Western sexual formations (Mas-sad 2007). But Massad flattens the fact that the institutionalisation of queerness through rights relied on the agency of so-called "native informants" to a Western LGBT movement (Rao 2010, 177). Unlike the ILGA (established in 1978) who ran aggressive campaigns at the UN throughout the 1990s, the ILGHRC (estab-lished in 1991) received little space for its work on behalf of international lesbians and gay men in its early years. The Beijing conference was a crucial moment for the ILGHRC to rise and seek a seat at the human rights table at an international and governmental level, by agitating from outside of the national power frame-work while pressuring governments. At the NGO forum of the summit in Huai-rou, Beijing, the ILGHRC co-organised a Lesbian Tent and successfully collected 6,000 signatures to put sexuality on the agenda of human rights. The Lesbian Tent has been articulated by many Chinese feminist and lesbian activists as an eye-opening and enlightening moment, when lesbian women in China first gained visibility among themselves and recognition by their counterparts in the West/rest of the world. However, this recognition could not be set in motion without the "double bind" of postsocialist postcolonial desire and denial.

During the conference, as the lesbian visibility attracted Western media attention, a Chinese volunteer was interviewed by a Western media outlet and asked about the living conditions of lesbians in China. The volunteer denied the existence of lesbianism and homosexuality in socialist countries and denigrated it as a capitalist corruption. Their response later was also appraised by morality-defending Chinese Communist newspapers. Both the incident and Chinese official response to it were repeatedly cited by Chinese lesbian feminists and Western media as evidence of the backwardness of socialism and as agitator for Chinese lesbian feminism to claim recognition, acceptance, and rights. Replicating a familiar post-Cold War contrast between the "global" represented by the democratic West and the "ignorant" mass isolated in the Chinese socialist regime, Chinese lesbian feminists were able to sever their ties with socialism and step onto the global stage where they were previously excluded as both the "Third World" *and* "socialist" others, while the ILGHRC was able to establish its formal engagement with human rights mechanisms by symbolising the imagined global community of freedom and progress. It was not that the ILGHRC imported "Western" ideas of human rights into China, thereby performing an imperialist role; rather, it was through Chinese feminists' desire for a place in the global community to exercise their agency to combat state erasure, that the hegemony of Western ideology of human rights got consolidated. Unlike many post-independent and democratic liberal states that started to use LGBT rights to butter the imperial and neocolonial bread, it was the postsocialist postcolonial "good queers" located in particular positions with the state and the "globe", who played off against the "bad others" for their version of liberation.

Double-bind of "Fluidity": queer knowledge and postsocialist division of labour

The affective structure of doubling of postsocialist coloniality described in the previous section also needs to be understood in relation to the material condition of postsocialist labour fluidity and flexibility – a crucial formula for global capital accumulation as well as for differentiating population. US queer theory has long celebrated "queer" as an almost infinitely mobile and mutable term whose relevance lies in its rejection to be defined and straitjacketed (Amin 2017, 179). Conceptualised as "a political metaphor without a fixed referent" (Eng, Halberstam, and Muñoz 2005, 1) to intervene various global crisis, such as neoliberalism, collapse of the welfare state, war on terrorism, and militarisation, "queer" however renders itself as ahistorical and embodying universal mobility. As Kaji Amin states, unlike "gay", "lesbian", and "feminist" that are bound to particular identity, historical context, and object of study, "queer" is self-claimed as freed from its own history and could "fly wherever the demands of political urgency might call" (Amin 2017, 178–179). It is this universalised mobility, fluidity, and flexibility and its relation to fluidity of capital that I wish to problematise through a lens of asymmetrical queer division of labour that creates differently conceptualised precarity and disproportionally positioned communities.

Battling for the "Queer"

The word "queer" is translated into Chinese as *ku'er*, the "cool child". It was first vernacularised by Taiwanese scholars trained in the US academy in 1994 and then introduced in mainland China in 1997. In its early years, *ku'er* was predominantly confined to the Chinese academia (because of queer theory's connection to poststructuralism and Chinese academics' interests in Foucault) and cosmopolitan artist-activist communities who adopted the word from (and to discuss) international queer cinema. *Ku'er* started to gain grassroots popularity in LGBT communities in the 2010s as a result of increasing online translation of queer theory by lesbian queer activists and the state shutdown of the annual Beijing Queer Film Festival founded by well-known Chinese queer scholar and director Cui Zi'en.

A landmark event that hyped *ku'er*'s visibility, at least among the younger generation of LGBT identified community, is the so-called *meishaonv zhanshi Lala* ("beautiful young women fighter lesbians") incident. In early 2011, Damien Lu, an influential HIV/AIDS activist and columnist for *Aibai* (one of the earliest gay websites and later the biggest LGBT NGO in China), published a series of online articles that discredit queer theory as "the product of the imagination of those living in an ivory tower" (Lu 2011). As "propagated by Western and Western-educated critics and scholars", Lu contends that queer theory has misled people to believe that sexual orientation is socially constructed, fluid, and thus subjugated to change, therefore it is dangerous as it could be used to induce and justify the harmful public discourse of converting homosexuality. Lu's stance triggered heated debates on and off the Internet. An anonymous user named *meishaonv zhanshi lala* (*meishaonv* for short hereafter) on *Sina Weibo*, a Chinese version of Twitter, posted a series of tweets targeting Lu as well as his organisation *Aibai*. *Meishaonv* started by posting articles and translations of canonical queer theory in order to challenge biologically determined accounts of homosexuality, and soon turned to criticising gay male privilege within the LGBT movements and uneven distribution of resources in activist organising.

Some background knowledge on Chinese LGBT activism would be helpful to understand the significance of this event. Arguably, Chinese LGBT activism began with the HIV/AIDS intervention in the late 1980s, due to both the urgency of tackling the pandemic and the lack of legal status and cultural recognition of LGBT people in China. The early activists were mainly (male) medical doctors, (straight) scholars of sexuality at universities and state research institutes, and *tongzhi* network leaders. During the early years, gay men, not lesbian women, were the main focus of the movements since transnational and state funds were directed to HIV/AIDS organisations. Although lesbians played crucial roles in early organising and community building (such as through leading entertainment activities, salon discussions, and organising dating service and events), for a long time lesbian groups were subjugated under the gay-dominated activism sponsored by both transnational and national capital. Besides the petty cash from gay-focused organising, another funding opportunity for lesbians was/is women's rights and development projects which mushroomed around and after the 1995 Beijing Conference, despite the fact that many women's and feminist NGOs in the 1990s and early 2000s were unaware of lesbian issues at best and homophobic at worst. In the late 2000s, however, lesbian groups started to enhance their solidarity with women's and feminist groups and break reliance from gay organisations, as the transnational HIV/AIDS money started to dry out and be replaced by Chinese governmental funds, and as more and more activists educated in US women's studies or influenced by western intersectional feminism joined the groups as volunteers or for research purposes. Behind the aforementioned *meishaonv* account is a collaborative of several leading feminist, lesbian, and queer activists and young scholars in transitional, diasporic, and Sinophone lesbian queer and feminist communities who sought to challenge gay male privilege, patriarchy, and economic normativity through weaponising queer theory. With their initiatives, concepts such as sex/gender system, gender fluidity, non-binary gender, and anti-normativity are now commonplace terms in the domestic and diasporic young feminist and LGBT activism, especially on digital space.

Instead of siding with either side of the debate, I want to point out that the debate not only exposes conflicts and differences among differently positioned *people* but also reveals the tension among differently positioned *capital* if we think from the vantage point of the doubling of postsocialist coloniality. The ahistorical application of principles, theses, and terms of queer theory to the scientific model of sexuality allows young queer feminists to claim "subaltern" position without taking seriously the relation between the so-called critical position and the mobility mediated by the multitude of global capital within the economy of transnational queer knowledge production. The queer critique of "naturalness of homosexuality" reveals a two-layered inclusion and exclusion that divide people into who can be assimilated into "theory" (read: the most cutting-edge Western theory here): the first layer is a temporal one – queer theory as cutting-edge replacing the "outdated" scientific knowledge of homosexuality, which could be interpreted as colonial, neocolonial, nationalist, and patriarchal; and the second layer is a spatial one – queer critique rooted in high theories but popularised for "grassroots" anti-normativity is in fact inaccessible to the LGBT "masses" due to its abstract language and its limited circulation online. Although the young queer lesbian activists might not necessarily possess economic forms of capitals, they nevertheless belong to what Deng (this volume) calls the "new creative class" – globally connected cosmopolitan elites who present themselves as "cool" and embodying certain "westernized" lifestyles in technological, economic, and cultural transformation. Often utilising their positions, such as marginalised subaltern (third world), dissidents (Cold War anti-communist), and counterculture icons (postmodern cultural signifier in consumer culture), they gain intangible capitals such as visibility, upward mobility, and other social and political currencies – a doubling that begs an intersectional approach beyond conventional Marxist analysis of class. If a materialist approach could be applied to both sides of the debate, what we see is the contrast between a large-scale transnationally organised capital operating through governments, public sectors, and institutions, such as NGOs and research institutes, and more autonomous self-generating "chic" forms of capital in the guise of a non-hierarchal anti-capitalist anti-patriarchy bend. But the latter is more fluid and flexible in current division of queer intellectual labour where queer theory's amorphous political energy of anti-normativity allows young queer feminist activists to render various forms of precarity illegible and inassimilable to queer radicality and anti-normativity. Appearing as oppositional at first, these two groups are both produced by global capitalism's need to make obsolete the "old" for the "new" and to manage the inassimilable "surplus" in its process of "regeneration" and "upgrade". However, we should not criticise LGBT or young queer lesbian activists' complicity with global capital without examining the relation between queer discourse of fluidity and the demand for flexible labour in the postsocialist neoliberal world that is already marked by racialised, geopolitical, gendered, and classed differences, to which I turn in the following section.

Multidimension of fluidity and postsocialist queer division of labour

From the early 2000s, the concept of *duoyuan* (multidimension, plurality, or diversity) started to replace "tolerance" and "acceptance" in Chinese LGBT activism. In the wake of LGBT issues being recognised in the UN agenda, Facebook's announcement of 56 gender expression options and intensified transnational connections through digital technology and social media, *duoyuan* has now shifted to the most cutting-edge concept of *duoyuan xing/bie* (diversity of gender/ sex) in LGBT advocacy to include a broader range of sexual/gender expression and identities. Words such as gender "fluidity," "non-binary," "gender queer," "pansexual," and so forth that are well recognised currency in the global market of queerness, are now populating Chinese queer space (mainly activism and popular online scholarship), transforming the third world queer in first world drag.

While queer fluidity is predominantly conceived in ways similar to picking up a dress and putting on drag, here I want to paint a different scene of "fluidity". In a Beijing gay cruising park, I learned a slang *xijian'er*, meaning "washing the tool". It refers to the practice where a man performs oral sex on another man before the latter penetrates a third man. Although this "backward" unhygienic practice might terrify the 21st century cosmopolitan queer urbanites, it is still quite common among many migrant workers, lower-class, and homeless gay men who have less or no access to safe, sanitary, and private space with warm water, condoms, and other hygienic facilities. Embodying the "dark side" of China's reform as "litter", "failure", and "surplus", these men live in temporary and illegally built housing, squeezing their bodies against one another in small basements, sharing various body fluids, and selling their versatility for low-paying temporary jobs. "Fluidity", "flexibility", and a sense of being "fleeting" are their long-lasting daily norms; but they would never be celebrated as "queer" whose desires mark China's futurity. Bearing the tripartite stigmatisation of men who have sex with other men, rural, and lower-class labour, who perhaps provide sex for money, they might be presented as proof of the "neoliberal vice" here and there by new leftist radical queers who fetishises "alternative resistance" on the ground, but their precarious living condition, "less cultured" mannerism, political incorrectness, lack of recognisable organised political action as well as marvellous skills and tactics for survival in the face of brutal inequalities, do not render them assimilable to the sexy photogenic "subaltern position" claimed by queer radicality nor by urban LGBT respectability. In fact, they are what the new class of liberal LGBT advocates would like to "disappear" through discursive denigration and activist neglect.

The differentially conceptualised queer "fluidity" and the disproportionally dispossessed communities and precarity behind it reveal as much the privilege of LGBT activists and queer theorists as the asymmetrical postsocialist division of labour. China's market reform has brought about growing work insecurity, in which stable jobs and social benefits gained by organised labour have been replaced by precarious, unstable, and casual jobs. Since the late 1970s, the reconfiguration of socialist ideology with neoliberalism in China has produced a massive flow of rural-to-urban migrants and peasant-workers (*nongmin gong*) as domestic cheap labour for national and international capitals, that have powered up the world economy. This dispossession also happened in a period of time when sent-down youths and people in labour camps during high socialism were returning to the cities. The restructuring of the national economy and political changes have also led to lay-offs of over-staffing workers in the former state-run planned economy. Under these conditions, the post-reform state has aggressively promoted labour flexibility by implementing policies and organisations to steer the unemployed to actively seek work. The acceptance and promotion of international NGOs in the 1990s is one of such strategies the Chinese government used to "outsource" its social policy implementation and to limit state guarantee for labour, thus enforcing China's comparative advantage in labour cost (Xu 2012, 202).

It is important to note that the accumulation by dispossession has led to growing unrest and revolts among workers and peasants across China (McGrath 2008, 208), but economic inequality has rarely been addressed in the LGBT agenda, which primarily focuses on advocacy for rights, public representation, and anti-discrimination at workplace (in cooperation settings), nor in Chinese queer theory which makes abstract anti-normative and intersectional claims. On the one hand, as mentioned in previous session, this is due to the fact that queer studies emerged out of the climate of anti-Marxism that discarded analysis of class and labour politics. On the other hand, the current approach to LGBT activism is the result of two intertwined transnational and global phenomena – "Gay Internationalism" (Massad 2007) through "NGO-isation" (Lang 2013).

As Joseph Massad observes in the Arabic context, international LGBT NGOs in the 1990s promoted universalised concept of "gay rights" by reorienting unstable local sexual practices (such as men who have sex with men but do not consider themselves as "homosexuals") into "more enlightened" ideas of westernized sexuality (Massad 2007, 164). This is also the case with China, where certain sexual practices were seen as the pathological leftover of the old feudal society or as closeted non-identity oppressed by state socialism, while others were regarded as a new gay subject embodying celebrated cosmopolitan middle-class sensibilities (Rofel 2007). To defend LGBT rights and obtain protection and sponsorship from the state, there is a need to discover "problems" in local practices – may it be state oppression, societal ignorance, or individual lack of consciousness – and to identify the "violated subject" who deserves expertise and solutions (Thoreson 2011, 14). These issue-focused models are part of the larger process of the professionalisation and globalisation of social movements, as the "non-profit industrial complex" (Incite! 2007) in the North gradually started to expand its global developmental strategies in the 1960s and to institutionalise and bureaucratise in the South through promoting outcome-orientated projects and issue-specific marketable services.

This explains why LGBT issues in China are primarily politicalised in terms of state repression, cultural backwardness, and lack of public representation, rather than in terms of economic inequality and violence. But to suggest that Chinese LGBT advocates simply seek gentrification and assimilation is to dismiss the complex dynamic of global queer division of labour and its impact on LGBT activism. The normalisation of LGBT liberal strategies and models could not be done without the labour of LGBT activists who constantly remake and mould themselves and their organisations to fit the donors' agenda for continuous funding while wrestling with governmental policing caused by ever-changing geopolitical struggles. As Yingyi Wang observes, the labour of Chinese NGO workers is marked by both precarity and flexibility: they are pressured to be efficient, market-oriented, and outcome-driven and to cater to transitional and national donors' needs rather than the needs of the communities, while wrestling with governmental policing caused by ever-changing geopolitical struggles (Wang 2020). This requires various skills, such as versatility in English, keeping up to date with new concepts and theories, making old paradigms and projects obsolete as well as performing transnationally (read "Westernised"). Although they gain upward mobility through social capital, such as connection to the transnational community, benefits of traveling abroad, even gaining access to foreign immigration status and citizenship, they also need to "dispossess" part of their own history and "others and enemies within" in order to render the activism itself viable to fit the demand of a racialised transnational queer world and to also survive in a transnational capital sponsored by NGO-isation. In a sense, their embrace of queer flexibility and fluidity marks their immobility in the postsocialist world where China battles with and redefines previous formations of capitalist modernity and its colonial imperial projects through internalisation, competition, and hegemony. An interesting result of this differentially positioned fluidity is what appears as "passive collusion" with homonationalism. I must point out that unlike many post-independent countries in Africa, Latin America, and Asia, whose economies are largely restructured through Western imperial-led structural adjustment programs by which "LGBT rights" could be used as functional leverage for favourable policies, the strategy of "LGBT conditionality" does not work in pushing China's human rights and LGBT rights issues. What the Cold War discourse does in turning up the volume on LGBT oppression in illiberal China is only to muffle the globally shared condition of precarity and to pre-empt possible transnational resistance and solidarity against economic violence and dispossession.

Conclusion

In this chapter, I have traced the intertwined history and development of queer knowledge and LGBT advocacy across the geopolitical border of China and the United States in order to unpack the multi-layered entanglements of agency and violence, solidarity and divide, and disruption and collusion under postsocialist coloniality. Using the examples of transnational LGBT coalition and the debate on queer theory in China, I have shown that differently conceptualised notions of queer "fluidity" are reflective of the material and affective landscape of postsocialist postcolonial doubling that informs knowledge production, circulation of capital and ways in which communities are glued and divided. To conclude this chapter, I want to pose the question of the relation between queer's political relevance and "decoloniality".

Countering the Eurocentric queer studies that heavily relied on the diaspora model developed out of US-based ethnic studies, current scholarship of queer regionalism and queer Sinophone studies have mapped the complex geography of queerness that does not simply follow the logic of colonial modernity (Chiang and Heinrich 2013; Chiang and Wong 2016, 2017). Exploring "less orderly, bilateral, and horizontal intra-regional traffics of queerness across different countries and regions" (Chiang and Wong 2016, 1645) and "less scripted and more scattered" forms of minor-to-minor transnationalism "without mediation by the center" (Shih and Lionnet 2005, 5), these scholarly works of transcolonial encounters have thus far pivoted on the inter-regional connections of the "frontier" and "borderland" such as Hong Kong, Taiwan, and Southeast Asia. I want to expand this intervention to suggest that early Chinese lesbian feminist scholar-activists, LGBT advocates, and the younger generation of Chinese queer theorists discussed in this chapter also embody the notion of "frontier" as well as the "border" as they are on the verge of transnational transcolonial encounters of knowledge and capital, simultaneously occupying marginalised positions that constantly break apart, transgress, and transform. Queerness in China, structured within postsocialist postcolonial "tearing apart", also demonstrates the epistemology of "border thinking". This "border thinking within" reveals the dark side of the fluidity – those who are stuck and rendered immobile within the normative construction of third world linear development and the Cold War binary of oppression and liberation. It questions the construction of queerness as cutting-edge, anti-normative, and fluid while functioning to "differentiate" people, places, and histories in the transnational circulation. From the "hinterland" of the immobility, we could possibly develop a different decolonial episteme that does not primarily, nor exclusively, privilege the figure of the mobile, the fluid, and the constant crossing and anchor our critique on the temporal and spatial dissonance constructed by specific forms of global coloniality mediated by postsocialist condition. It allows us to acknowledge the continuity of global coloniality without romanticising a utopian alterity outside, a decolonial thinking without idealising a complete escape, possibly to rework concepts, histories, and genealogies which we take for granted, and to redraw connections foreclosed by binary thinking such as dominance and resistance, liberal and Marxist, North and South, and capitalism and socialism.

References

Amin, Kaji. 2017. *Disturbing Attachments: Genet, Modern Pederasty, and Queer History*. Durham, NC: Duke University Press.

Atanasoski, Neda. 2013. *Humanitarian Violence: The U.S. Deployment of Diversity*. Minneapolis, MN: University of Minnesota Press.

Chen, Kuan-Hsing. 2010. *Asia as Method: Toward Deimperialization*. Durham, NC: Duke University Press.

Chiang, Howard, and Ari Larissa Heinrich, eds. 2013. *Queer Sinophone Cultures*. London: Routledge.

Chiang, Howard, and Alvin Wong. 2016. "Queering the Transnational Turn: Regionalism and Queer Asia." *Gender, Place and Culture* 23, no. 11: 1643–1656. https://doi-org. myaccess.library.utoronto.ca/10.1080/0966369X.2015.1136811.

Chiang, Howard, and Alvin Wong. 2017. "Asia Is Burning: Queer Asia as Critique." *Culture, Theory and Critique* 58, no. 2: 121–126. https://doi-org.myaccess.library.utoronto. ca/10.1080/14735784.2017.1294839.

Chow, Rey. 1993. *Writing Diaspora: Tactics of Intervention in Contemporary Cultural Studies*. Bloomington, IN: Indiana University Press.

Duggan, Lisa. 2002. "The New Homonormativity: The Sexual Politics of Neoliberalism". In *Materializing Democracy: Toward a Revitalized Cultural Politics*, edited by Russ Castronovo and Dana Nelson. Durham, NC: Duke University Press. https://doi. org/10.1215/9780822383901-007.

Eng, David, Jack Halberstam, and José Muñoz. 2005. "Introduction: What's Queer About Queer Studies Now?" *Social Text* 23, nos. 3–4: 1–17. https://doi-org.myaccess.library. utoronto.ca/10.2307/40283426.

Ferguson, Niall, and Moritz Schularick. 2007. "Chimerica and the Global Asset Market Boom." *International Finance* 10, no. 3: 215–239. https://doi.org/10.1111/ j.1468-2362.2007.00210.x.

Ghodsee, Kristen. 2010. "Revisiting the United Nations Decade for Women: Brief Reflections on Feminism, Capitalism and Cold War Politics in the Early Years of the

International Women's Movement." *Women's Studies International Forum* 33: 3–12. https://doi.org/10.1016/j.wsif.2009.11.008.

Harvey, David. 2003. *The New Imperialism*. Oxford: Oxford University Press.

Incite! Women of Color Against Violence. 2007. *The Revolution Will Not Be Funded: Beyond the Non-Profit Industrial Complex*. Cambridge, MA: South End Press.

Lang, Sabine. 2013. *NGOs, Civil Society, and the Public Sphere*. Cambridge: Cambridge University Press.

Liu, Petrus. 2015. *Queer Marxism in Two Chinas*. Durham, NC: Duke University Press.

Lu, Damien. 2011. "What Is 'Queer Theory'? What Is Its Relationship with the Tong-zhi Movement?" www.aibai.com/advice_pages.php?linkwords=queer_theory (accessed August 5, 2020).

Massad, Joseph Andoni. 2007. *Desiring Arabs*. Chicago: University of Chicago Press.

McGrath, Jason. 2008. *Postsocialist Modernity: Chinese Cinema, Literature, and Criticism in the Market Age*. Redwood City, CA: Stanford University Press.

Meinhof, Marius, Junchen Yan, and Lili Zhu. 2017. "China and Postcolonialism: Some Introductory Remarks." *InterDisciplines* 1: 1–25. https://doi.org/10.4119/UNIBI/indi-v8-i1-166.

Mignolo, Walter. 2011. "Geopolitics of Sensing and Knowing: On (De)coloniality, Border Thinking and Epistemic Disobedience." *Postcolonial Studies* 14, no. 3: 273–283. https://doi.org/10.1080/13688790.2011.613105.

Mignolo, Walter, and Madina Tlostanova. 2006. "Theorizing from the Borders: Shifting to Geo- and Body-Politics of Knowledge." *European Journal of Social Theory* 9, no. 2: 205–221. https://doi-org.myaccess.library.utoronto.ca/10.1177/1368431006063333.

Mignolo, Walter, and Madina Tlostanova. 2012. *Learning to Unlearn: Decolonial Reflection from Eurasia and the Americas*. Columbus, OH: Ohio State University Press.

Ong, Aihwa. 1999. *Flexible Citizenship: The Cultural Logics of Transnationality*. Durham, NC: Duke University Press.

Popa, Bogdan. 2018. Unpublished Book Manuscript. *What's Queer Communism? Between the Cold War and Gender Theory*.

Puar, Jasbir. 2007. *Terrorist Assemblages: Homonationalism in Queer Times*. Durham, NC: Duke University Press.

Quijano, Anibal. 2000. "Coloniality of Power and Eurocentrism." *International Sociology* 15, no. 2: 215–232. https://doi-org.myaccess.library.utoronto.ca/10.1177/0268580900015002005.

Rao, Rahul. 2010. *Third World Protest: Between Home and the World*. Oxford: Oxford University Press.

Repo, Jemima. 2015. *The Biopolitics of Gender*. Oxford: Oxford University Press.

Rofel, Lisa. 2007. *Desiring China: Experiments in Neoliberalism, Sexuality, and Public Culture*. Durham, NC: Duke University Press.

Shih, Shu-mei. 2007. *Pacific Visuality and Identity: Sinophone Articulations Across the Pacific*. Berkley, CA: University of California Press.

Shih, Shu-mei. 2010. "Theory, Asia, and the Sinophone." *Postcolonial Studies* 13, no. 4: 465–484.

Shih, Shu-mei. 2012. "Is the Post- in Postsocialism the Post- in Posthumanism?" *Social Text* 30, no. 1 (110): 27–50. https://doi.org/10.2307/41479232.

Shih, Shu-mei, and Francoise Lionnet, eds. 2005. *Minor Transnationalism*. Durham, NC: Duke University Press.

Suchland, Jennifer. 2012. "Is There a Postsocialist Critique?" Author's Academia page.

Suchland, Jennifer. 2015. *Economies of Violence: Transnational Feminism, Postsocialism, and the Politics of Sex Trafficking*. Durham, NC: Duke University Press.

Thoreson, Ryan Richard. 2011. "The Queer Paradox of LGBTI Human Rights." *Interalia: A Journal of Queer Studies* 6: 1–27.

Tlostanova, Madina. 2012. "Postsocialist ≠ Postcolonial? On Post-Soviet Imaginary and Global Coloniality." *Journal of Postcolonial Writing* 48, no. 2: 130–142. https://doi.org/10.1080/17449855.2012.658244.

Vukovich, Daniel. 2017. "China and Postcolonialism: Re-orienting All the Fields." *Inter-Disciplines* 1: 145–164. https://doi.org/10.4119/UNIBI/indi-v8-i1-171.

Wang, Yingyi. 2020. Unpublished Draft. "Labor Precarity and Double Erasure: A Discussion of the (De)Valuation of NGO Work in Neoliberal China."

Xu, Feng. 2009. "Chinese Feminisms Encounter International Feminisms: Identity, Power and Knowledge Production." *International Feminist Journal of Politics* 11, no. 2: 196–215. https://doi.org/10.1080/14616740902789567.

Xu, Feng. 2012. *Looking for Work in Post-Socialist China: Governance, Active Job Seekers and the New Chinese Labor Market*. London and New York: Routledge.

Chapter 6

Circassian trajectories between post-Soviet neocolonialism, indigeneity, and diasporic dispersions

A conversation

Lidia Zhigunova and Madina Tlostanova

Madina Tlostanova: In most of the former soviet national republics, the term "postsocialist" is seen negatively, as something to bury in the past. This sentiment marked by a clear realisation that the imposed soviet modernity in these non-Russian locales was a continuation of the Czarist Russian colonising practices which makes the intersection of colonialism and socialism and their aftermaths or revivals a very clear case for the former Soviet "national" subjects. However, this darker colonial side of state socialism is still an internal knowledge hard to communicate to the global North and the global South alike, regardless of their political and ideological preferences and differences. Dramatic Circassian trajectory in the last several centuries seems to be a perfect example of a complex entanglement of colonialism and neocolonialism, resistant indigeneity, diasporic dispersion, the state socialist ordeals, and the post-socialist neocolonial present. This allows us to clearly see the continuity of dehumanising, discriminatory, genocidal policies sustained and gradually increasing throughout modernity. Perhaps the Circassian case is the most clear evidence of modernity's profound neglect for indigenous cosmologies, ethics, knowledges, cultures, languages, lives, no matter which kind of modernity we are speaking about – Western capitalist, Russian czarist, State socialist, or neoliberal state capitalist today. What do you think about the intersection of the postcolonial and the postsocialist in the discussion of gendered and feminist identities, experiences, discourses, and creative works in relation to the Circassian trajectory in modernity? How would you relate to it as a Circassian in both Caucasian and US diasporic contexts and as a rare specialist in Circassian literature, particularly women writers' fiction?

Lidia Zhigunova: Indeed, Circassian case is a vivid example of both the way in which modernity or the "darker side" of modernity treated and continues to treat the indigenous populations all over the world and the way in which these groups are struggling today in their efforts to overcome the present and past injustices, in order to survive, to have a future. Today, the Circassians are unknown to most people with the exception of a handful of historians specialising on the North Caucasus. And, this is not because Circassians suddenly ceased to exist in 1864 after the Russian imperial forces subdued Circassia after long years of resistance – this situation today is a direct result of the damaging effects of colonialism and neo-colonialism that continue to silence and efface this group. It makes me extremely sad, and angry, to realise that today, as a Circassian, I am a non-existent person robbed of my identity, my history, my country, my culture, and my future. Circassian language is on the brink of extinction, and with its disappearance, I will be completely effaced. The question we should ask ourselves is then how come Circassians, who had been a subject of somewhat obsessive attention of the 18th- and 19th-century Western and Russian literature and press, became erased or "omitted" from history? What makes it possible to silence this group, and other groups, who advocate historical justice, freedom, and human rights? This is largely due to the repressive mechanisms put in place by modernity, including the criminal regimes of physical annihilation of the native populations and expropriation of their lands and livelihoods during the colonial period, as well as systematic efforts directed at controlling and manipulating their narratives then and now. During the Soviet period further actions were taken to disperse the remaining Circassian population and to assimilate them by disrupting their traditional ways of life and by replacing their indigenous cosmologies and epistemologies with narratives of civilising missions and with the so-called progressive Socialist ideas of equality and a happy future. Russian imperial and Soviet legacies still haunt many nations, and in many places, elements of the Soviet and even Tsarist legacy are live political issues. The Circassian case clearly demonstrates how colonial history has been transformed into a neocolonial present.

The colonisation of Circassia and the anti-colonial struggle of Circassians lasted more than 100 years (1763–1864) until they exhausted themselves and all their resources. It left a strong imprint on Circassian culture. Circassians have lost most of their territory and population. Tsarist Russia felt it almost impossible to subdue the Circassian tribes during its long military campaign in the Caucasus and used various inhumane tactics to defeat the indigenous population. After Circassians were finally subdued in 1864 in the last battle at Sochi, the majority were forced into exile to the Ottoman Empire, and Russians, Cossacks, and Armenians were immediately sent to the North Caucasus to settle the emptied territories along the Black Sea shore. The remaining Circassian population, which was less than 1% of its previous size, was displaced into the mountainous regions. The majority of Circassians today agree that the exile methods employed by Russian military commanders and colonial administrators amounted to genocide. But the fact that the Russian empire perpetrated genocide against the Circassian population is invisible to most Russians. There are, for instance, no monuments commemorating the victims and the memory of those events on the Black Sea shore and in the Sochi area, but there are many monuments to the Russian imperial generals, who participated in the "conquest" and who were known for their particular cruelty towards the local population. Soon after its success in the Caucasus, the tsarist empire was overthrown by the Bolsheviks in 1917. The Soviet leaders faced new challenges in incorporating this incredibly diverse region into the Soviet state, especially since these people had joined the Russian state through colonisation and imperialism. In fact, the Soviets continued an imperialist agenda by implementing "divide and rule" tactics – they cut off different groups from one another in order to keep the region unstable. As part of the Soviet nationality policy, Circassians were divided into several autonomous units under different names (Circassian, Adyghean, and Kabardian) and separate literary languages were created based on the dialects. Furthermore, the Arabic script was changed to Cyrillic; Circassians along with other Caucasians were forced to form a linguistic bond with the Russian-speaking Soviet administration. Thus, the Soviet state maintained the imperialistic attitude towards its non-Russian population, albeit using different tactics. The strategy was either to alienate and demonise the unfamiliar or to assimilate it. Despite all these events, vocal Circassian national movements emerged during this time, only to be brutally suppressed by Stalinist purges. The national idea and the Circassian national movement that briefly emerged in the beginning of the 20th century did not thrive and did not lead to a true postcolonial situation, as in other places. As a result of Russian and Soviet imperial policies, nowadays more Circassians live outside their homeland: they are widely dispersed in regions as far apart as the Middle East and the United States. The largest Circassian diaspora population is located in Turkey (an estimated 5–6 million). Circassians who remained in their homeland (around 1 million) now live in three small republics of Russia's North Caucasus: Kabardino-Balkaria, Karachaevo-Cherkessia, and Adyghea. The Soviet regime's "divide and rule" approach to the Circassian nation left them divided among four subjects of the Russian Federation.

Most Circassians of my generation who were born in Soviet Russia grew up with the feeling that we do not know who we are, as if we have fallen from the sky or appeared out of nowhere. I was born in the republic of Kabardino-Balkaria, and my official nationality was "Kabardian", which has been separated from Circassians living in the republic of Karachaevo-Cherkessia and from Adygheans in the republic of Adyghea (all of these republics were created artificially from the remaining Circassians who belonged to different tribal groups and refer to themselves Adyghe in their own language). As I later learned, most of the population of Kabarda had been slaughtered by the army of General Aleksey Yermolov in the 1820s, decades earlier, before the fall of Circassia. Unfortunately, the genocide of the Circassian Kabardians remains hidden even from many Circassians themselves (Richmond 2013). The majority of today's Kabardians, including my ancestors, have been relocated there from the western parts of Circassia. There was a sense of rupture and discontinuity in our perceptions of ourselves, but we did not know how to express it or what was it exactly because of the lack of information. Slowly, we started to realise that there is a huge gap between our past and our present and great effort had been made at the official level to erase our past. Despite the fact that the Russian conquest of the Caucasus has been well documented, the Soviet school curriculum hardly touched on any aspects of the history of Circassians before, during, or after the Russian colonisation of their territory. The most tragic events of the conquest – the widespread killings, the heroic resistance of the native population, the mass deportation to the Ottoman Empire – are still conspicuously absent from Russian history books. The historical and literary discourse capitalised instead on the "civilising mission" and the romanticised images of Circassians and other natives of the Caucasus found in 19th-century Russian canonical literature. The Soviet discourse presented the culture of the natives prior to the advent of socialism as something that is not worth mentioning other than in the context of the oppression of the local population by the Tsarist regime and by the local aristocrats. According to the Soviet ideologues, it was the Soviet government that gave Circassians its culture – the alphabet and the literature – and it impressed the feeling of worthlessness and being forever in debt or grateful to the Soviet system into generations of Soviet Circassians. My parents and grandparents, for example, were the victims of such destructive policies. While the generation of my grandparents went through the pains of collectivisation, war, and Stalinist repressions, my parents' generation, who grew up in the '50s–'60s, were thoroughly indoctrinated with this kind of Soviet propaganda and made to believe that their past and their traditions were worthless. I agree with your terms "double-colonisation" and "self-Orientalisation" of the native populations of the Caucasus (Tlostanova 2010), as this was indeed the way several generations of Soviet Circassians have been indoctrinated with lies about their past and their present, effectively stripping them of their future. Due to their forced separation and ignorance of their common history, Circassians became particularly vulnerable to destructive Soviet policies. Their links to the past have been repressed, almost wiped out. Circassians still suffer from the conditions of "homelessness" and memory loss, as well as the lack of positive self-identification, all of which were the products of Russian colonialism and the Soviet imperialist ideology, which on the one hand emphasised "internationalism" and "friendship" among the ethnic groups, but on the other hand marginalised or completely silenced them by falsifying or denying them their history and identity. The physical separation of Soviet Circassians from their compatriots abroad by means of closed borders as well as denied access to the archival documents and to the literary sources in the West made possible this total indoctrination of the population.

Unlike in other parts of the North Caucasus, Russians actively strived to efface the presence and the legacy of Circassians in their homeland. Today, you will find no traces of Circassians in the cities on the Black Sea coast. There is nothing that reminds people of the tragedy that unfolded there 150 years ago. Sochi is one example of this continuous imperial-colonial paradigm which is still in place. In 1872, just eight years after thousands of Circassians died horrible deaths in the refugee camps set up in Sochi area, the Russian imperial administration began preparations to turn Sochi into a holiday resort. During the Soviet period, millions of workers from all over the country were sent to Sochi to take spa-relaxation treatments. None of them, however, had the slightest idea that the area had been home to the Circassians until 1864 when they had been forcefully removed. There is not a single site or a nameplate that reminds visitors of these crimes. But there are memorials commemorating the 1921 Soviet Decree that gave the Black Sea

"Resorts to the Workers", and more disturbingly, openly insulting monuments honouring the Czarist Russian army that colonised the Caucasus and participated in the final genocide of Circassians. Moreover, since the mid-1990s, many monuments commemorating the most notorious and brutal Russian imperial generals who killed and expelled Circassians from their homeland appeared all over the North-West Caucasus. Despite multiple protests by Circassian activists, the authorities inaugurated a monument to the notorious Russian General, Grigory Zass, who was known as the "collector of Circassian skulls". Another Russian general, Aleksei Yermolov, who was responsible for the brutal and deadly campaign against Circassians in Kabarda, in the eastern part of Circassia, was honoured by multiple monuments. Memorials are created for the "Cossacks, who settled and made liveable this wild place" as if there had been no people before the arrival of Russians. The entire coast of the Black Sea in Turkey (Trabzon, Samsun, Sinop, Kefken) and in Russia from Anapa to Sochi, and even in Varna (former Ottoman port in present-day Bulgaria) are scattered with bones of Circassians who perished in the refugee camps there, of people who died by thousands of starvation, cold, and disease, while the whole world was watching indifferently. It painfully reminds us of today's Syrian refugee crisis.

This largely untold Circassian story deserves renewed international attention today because it has been a transnational and trans-regional issue, with various colonial powers seeking to control the region. Unfortunately, in this clashing game of geopolitical concerns, the interests of Circassians were overlooked, and their initiatives and diplomatic appeals were often ignored. Russia, Turkey, Britain, France, and the US have been involved directly or indirectly in the plight of Circassians, and being fully aware of the unfolding human tragedy, they simply watched and easily forgot about the Circassians. Despite many attempts by Circassians to draw attention to these crimes, all parties that had been involved have remained deaf, and Russia still denies the genocide and holds on to old imperialist myths. The only country to recognise the Circassian genocide is Georgia. On 20 May 2011, the eve of Circassian Memorial Day, the Georgian parliament unanimously passed the genocide resolution.

The official attitude of the Russian state towards these events today is characterised by both non-memory (i.e. by the repression of historical facts and cultural memories) and by romanticised reproductions of the past. The repression and falsification of Circassian history is maintained at the highest official levels and is disseminated through the educational institutions – through textbooks that favour the narratives of Circassians "voluntary joining" the Russian state and the rhetoric of the "empty lands" that emphasises how the colonists came to settle the empty territories. The easiest way to forget is to eliminate the traumatic memories with the exception of select memories – Circassians, whose ethnic name is not even mentioned and who for the most part are referred to as "highlanders" or "mountaineers", are represented as a group of savages who attacked Russian military forts (built on the Circassian lands); the sacrifice by Russian soldiers is emphasised, while the atrocities perpetrated against Circassians, such as burning their crops, their livelihood, and their villages, destroying their lives, are deemphasised or never even mentioned. Circassians have been dehumanised, while Russians were made the bearers of progress and civilisation. Thus, the historical narratives never tell a full story of the conquest. Those who were sent to conquer and to kill, the perpetrators, are presented as victims and the real victims have been erased.

In the 1980s, when I was 10 or 11 years old, my father took me to the town of Gelendzhik on the Black Sea coast. It was just an ordinary Soviet-style vacation by the sea. At the time I had no idea that this place once was the homeland of my ancestors and the site of vicious atrocities perpetrated against them. And, I am sure that my Soviet-educated Circassian father knew almost nothing about it as well, since he never mentioned it to me or anyone else. The town was crowded with vacationers from all over the Soviet Union. Crowds, blissfully unaware of the depth and the scope of human tragedy that unfolded here not long ago, were flocking to the beaches and forming long lines to the infamous Soviet cafeterias. As I think of it now, I would be terrified to visit any of these places today after learning the truth. These places, where the Circassian heritage has been completely erased and buried alive, appear to me emptied of their souls. I would not be able to face the people who are devoid of human empathy, compassion, or concern for the people who once called this place their home. And, for me as a Circassian, this is the hardest thing to accept.

MT: You defended your PhD dissertation in Tulane University, which is in Louisiana, with its very conflictual multicultural and racial history: an interesting place to reflect on Circassians under the Russian rule, their resistance and re-existence. And you wrote it on Circassian literature with several chapters devoted to women writers. This is a bold step and you are a true pioneer in many ways. For one thing not many people in the US know anything about Circassians except perhaps in a very superficial exoticising way. So, you have opened a terra incognita for the outside world. Moreover, you are a pioneer in the domestic Circassian context even more so as you bring unknown perspectives into your analysis such as postcolonial theory, feminist literary criticism, critical race and ethnicity studies, which have hardly been reflected upon by researchers in the Caucasus yet. You write about Circassian women's fiction and also gendered identity in such a way that it throws back the persistent canonical schemes, dominant progressivist modes of interpreting creative writing, and naturalised aesthetic regimes. How would you define the fictional works you have analysed? Do they fall under the category of postcolonial novels, indigenous writing, or feminist literary works? Are they comparable with the postcolonial women's fiction created mostly in the anglophone and francophone ex-colonies?

LZ: I think in my case, it was a migration away from home that triggered the process of thorough re-examination of the notions of home and identity. I moved to the United States in 1999, and the first question that you usually get from people after they welcome you is "Where are you from?" Suddenly, I was put in a position to reflect on my origins, and I needed to give straight answers, a seemingly simple act that is regarded so natural by most people, but not me. For the first time I realised how little I knew about myself and my place of origin, and I remember the feeling of being frustrated when people reacted to me as a blank spot when I simply mentioned that I am Circassian. It has been extremely difficult to regain a voice and to speak out. I was often conflicted by my confused sense of identity and by the fact that my parents or other older relatives could not help me out to fill in the gaps in my personal narrative. It seemed that we lived in a perpetual state of amnesia. These are the signs of what Gayatri Spivak calls the "epistemic violence" (Spivak 1988) exhibited by people in marginalised groups who had been continuously silenced. And, Circassians who are still reliving all sorts of trauma associated with Russian/Soviet imperialism are concerned with the issue of how to recover an identity, fragmented, displaced, and discredited by imperialism. The healing process is still ongoing. The colonisation of memory that has produced the condition of memory loss affected generations of Circassians who were denied their history and the sense of national pride. This amnesia has been created and maintained with the help of historical falsifications and the omissions of Russian/ Soviet historiography, as well as by the severe censorship practiced during the Soviet regime that made any effort to expose the truth impossible.

The opening of the borders after the collapse of the Soviet Union relaxed the severe Soviet censorship and made access to information easier. It has also, as Seteney Shami points out, once again set the "Circassian identity in motion" (Shami 2000) making it possible to travel abroad and making the homeland in the Caucasus more accessible to the Circassian diaspora. Only in the post-Soviet period, Circassians started the process of reconnecting, remembering, reimagining, and reconceptualising their identities. But, the struggle for historical truth in the North Caucasus is still ongoing and manifests itself in a clash between the official Soviet/Russian version of history that stubbornly insists on the old imperialist myths and the "counter memory" of Circassians who started to actively object to the ideologically motivated falsifications of their history.

Here in the United States, I have discovered that although Circassians are little-known in the West today, that was not always the case. For the 19th-century Americans and Europeans, "Circassian" was a familiar word, associated with the military prowess of Circassian men and the legendary beauty of Circassian women described in countless works going back to the early modern sources as well as in the texts of the Romantics, most of which were inherently Eurocentric and racist. These works viewed Circassia as a source of exotic culture, and the West was actually able to profit from making a commercial brand out of the Circassian Beauty myth, which was based on the discourse of whiteness. In the Western imagination, Circassian women were also often associated with sexual slavery in the Ottoman harems. These women were believed to welcome that prospect, and in some cases were able to achieve high ranks in the harem hierarchy by becoming the mothers of the Ottoman Sultans. The Circassian Beauty myth in combination with the Orientalist harem fantasy became an important point in the construction of the "Circassian Beauty" exhibit at the American Museum, which was grounded in racial confusion and ambiguity while it mocked, exploited, and appropriated both Circassian and African American culture and identity.

Indeed, I worked on my dissertation in New Orleans, a southern American city with a long history of slavery and white supremacy, which is a rather interesting place to reflect on the Circassian Beauty myth and on "white slavery" that completely intrigued 19th-century Americans who usually associated slavery with African Americans. Not only does this myth demonstrate the constructed and highly imaginative nature of racial discourse, it also shows that colonialism and imperialism were inseparable from the invention of race in the European and American contexts. Racial classifications were used to explain not only biological varieties but the superiority and inferiority of different cultural types. Western Europeans regarded Circassians as a more superior "Caucasian" race, and, therefore, closer to the Europeanised self. The idea of "whiteness", explicitly marked in this context, contributed to the visibility of race by emphasising the more powerful position or status that related to whiteness. In Russia, by the way, Circassians and other "Caucasians" (the non-Russians who live in the Caucasus) were called the "Blacks" of Russia and became the subject of racism and discriminatory policies. Ironically, this neocolonial attitude toward the Caucasians in Russia originated in the Soviet period and has intensified in the post-Soviet period, showing how the Western colonial models were adopted and modified by the Russians.

In my thesis (Zhigunova 2016a), I explore the politics of representation and continuous identity formation of Circassians, with a special focus on the construction of female identities and the sites of their production. The exoticised and racialised images of Circassian women were overtly erotic and were defined mostly in terms of sexuality, sensuality, and submissiveness. Circassian women represented in European Orientalist paintings and literature, as well as the "Circassian Beauty" exhibit at the American Museum are typical manifestations of this rhetoric. These texts demonstrate a symbolic control that is usually enacted through images of the body. Among the damaging effects of these modes of representation is a proliferation of certain images and stereotypes, for example, the notion of femininity that has been exaggerated into social constructions of gender and race and the frozen concepts regarding the feminine and the masculine attributes of Circassians. As these misrepresentations "travelled" through various texts, crossing generic and cultural boundaries, they have acquired a certain power of myths (the Circassian Beauty myth, the Whiteness myth, the harem imagery) that have been internalised by both the West and by Circassians. There is also a tendency in the Circassian nationalistic discourse to uphold these idealised images of women, which strips them of their agency, repeats and further perpetuates the colonial attitude. In other words, with an emphasis on gender and race, I wanted to illuminate the ideological distortions of the indigenous traditions that took place in the Caucasus and demonstrate how imperial narratives – the travelogues, the visual arts, the wildly popular literature of Romanticism as well as the emerging life sciences, physical anthropology, and in particular comparative anatomy – contributed to the invention and circulation of certain myths pertaining to the cultural identity of Circassians. These myths and constructions are being recycled even today without a proper re-examination in contemporary Circassian nationalistic discourses, reinforcing the patriarchal tendencies in Circassian society and erasing the traces of feminocratic traditions.

What was really missing from the picture was the Circassian counter-discourse that would deconstruct the colonial discourse by uncovering the ideological distortions and the layers of imposed constructions in order to unearth the myths and memories hidden beneath the surface of representations. This excavation process of digging down through the layers of memories and representations would interrupt the constant repetition of Orientalised stereotypes. And, this work needs to be done urgently before the remaining traces disappear. I found this kind of subversive counter-discourse that undermines the imperial legacy most strongly pronounced in literature and art of contemporary indigenous women-writers and artists from the Caucasus. In literature, most notable examples are your books, Madina, (both fiction and non-fiction) and Dina Arma's novel *The Road Home* (2009) that I examined in my dissertation and in separate publications elsewhere. *Gender Epistemologies and Eurasian Borderlands* (2010) is a pioneering book that discusses the complex histories of imperialism in the Caucasus and Central Asia through a decolonial feminist lens and addresses the absence of these places in currently constituted postcolonial discourses. And you also published two novels: *V Vashem mire ya prokhozhii* [I Am a Stranger in Your World] (Damian 2006) and *Zalumma Agra* (Tlostanova 2011). Dina Arma is a pseudonym of the Circassian writer and researcher Madina Khakuasheva. Her scholarly works include *Archetypes in the Literary Works of Circassian Writers* (2007) and *Mythological Images and Motifs in Literature and Art* (2014). Released in 2009, *The Road Home* is Arma's first and only literary work.

I set out asking myself the following questions: how do indigenous women-writers frame and articulate their relationship to the gendered and racialised histories of Circassian women? How do they address colonial experience and representation? What are the modes of self-representation and how are colonial language and imagery (re)appropriated, or not, by contemporary Circassian women writers? To what extent do Circassian women resist, revise, or transgress old ideologies and representations, and in what ways do they reinforce such discursive constructs?

Circassian women, as well as other ethnic or native women, have for a long time been objects of study and representations by others, mostly male authors. And the instances in which they did represent themselves – when they told their own stories in their own voices, as part of the oral tradition – have been muted or erased. For them, writing truly becomes an act of resistance, as well as an act of survival and re-existence. It is necessary to note that there is still a glaring absence of indigenous stories and histories in contemporary academia and in educational models, which leads to the ignorance of indigenous issues. Exposure to literature written by indigenous authors existing between multiple epistemologies is crucial, because it makes students think about the issues of identity – what is identity and how identities are formed, controlled, and manipulated by societies and ideologies. Discussing themes such as violence, conflict, and split-cultural and fractured identities present in these works inform students of the dangers of Eurocentric or Russocentric worldviews and colonial/imperial forms of domination and assimilation. Making students aware of the alternative epistemological models, guiding them through multiple worlds and knowledges, as Maria Lugones puts it "traveling into each other's world", should be at the heart of transformative pedagogy. In some places around the globe, the situation is slowly changing, and there are more universities that offer courses on Indigenous Studies. In Russia, however, the situation gets even worse. Russian colonial history in the Caucasus is not a mandatory part of the curriculum in primary and secondary schools. The erasure of colonialism from the national memory affects current discourses of cultural difference in Russia. The process of "othering" or discrimination of the peoples of the Caucasus is manifest in contemporary Russian public political and media discourses. The consequences of Russian colonialism and imperialism are not acknowledged.

In their texts, indigenous women-writers focus on women's agency and authority, re-inscribing and re-signifying representations and experiences of Circassian women. Recovering the self that is buried under multiple layers of distortions and imposed identities is not an easy task. Damian is one of the first authors to break with the Russian literary canon and to address the issues of power, knowledge production, and representation in the 19th-century Russian canonical texts. In *I Am a Stranger in Your World* (2006), she rewrites Mikhail Lermontov's story Bela from his famous novel *A Hero of Our Time* (1839) and produces a counter-narrative, following the example of Jean Rhys' *Wide Sargasso Sea* (1966), a story inspired by *Jane Eyre* (1847), Charlotte Bronte's 19th-century novel, by presenting the other side of the story. Similar to Rhys' idea, Damian retells a familiar story from the perspective of an oppressed character who has been silenced or not given enough of a voice in the original novel. Damian, however, disturbs the stereotypical images and expectations, as she reconfigures hegemonic relations between power, sexuality, culture, and representation. In Damian's interpretation, Bela's imagined voyages and her gender crossings are in many ways a fantasy of freedom, boundary transgression, and self-determination. Damian re-inscribes Bela by building on the standard reading of this character. In a way, she is asserting Bela's right to be so decisive and denying others the power to pass judgment on her. She accomplishes it by giving Bela a strong agency, by re-appropriating her sexuality, and by her refusal to be victimised. Damian subverts and transforms not only the Russian canonical text but also the imperial narrative as well as the larger collective consciousness which exhibits hostility towards females manifesting autonomy and strong physical agency – especially if that female belongs to one of the colonised cultures. One of the taboo topics in Soviet literature was the resistance of the native woman to the imperial power, her active engagement in the process of liberation, not only because of the allusion to the Russian conquest of Circassia but also due to the fact that such an account would inevitably contradict the colonial narrative of the backward, passive Circassian woman who was also victimised by her countrymen. In this regard, Damian's interpretation of Bela simultaneously engender an alternative history of empire as well as of the canon by undermining the whole paradigm of power, cultural authority, and representation. Damian not only challenges the very foundation of Russian literary canon by re-inscribing the native Circassian female subject, but she also writes the postcolonial or decolonial mind as she dislodges the centre from its throne.

Dina Arma's novel *The Road Home* (2009) is a narrative of self-exploration written from the transcultural perspective of a displaced person in search of her identity and her home (Zhigunova 2016b). The preoccupation with loss of one's home, in both a physical and spiritual sense, and the loss of identity shared by many post-colonial writers throughout the world found its particular expression in this novel. This search for self-definition and for the location of a "home" is presented in the novel as a "journey", activating thus a whole range of concepts such as displacement, migrancy, homelessness, border dwelling, and the position of in-betweenness that undermines the fixity of "centres" and "margins" as well as the ideology of a unified natural/cultural norm. By addressing the paradigmatic condition of "uprootedness" and "homelessness" of Circassians, Arma's novel explores the troubled relationship between history, memory, place, and the self. Through rediscovering carefully hidden family archives, Arma's narrative presents a quest for the past, its relation to the present, and the hope it engenders for the future. Memory and history are central themes in the novel whose major task is reclaiming the self and the past by getting rid of omissions, fabrications, and stereotypes created by Russian/Soviet historiography. Other major themes of the novel, such as the concepts of "home" and "homelessness", of memory loss and giving memory a home are closely connected to the process of recovering the self by unearthing the feminine voices. These voices, working from within the parameters of patriarchal/imperialist discourses, destabilise these discourses and end up creating new ways of reimagining the past, the present, and the future as well as new ways of organising knowledge and constructing Circassian identities. Drawing strength from a part of tradition, a part of cultural mythology and native female cosmology, Arma's protagonist makes an effort at decolonising memory. The novel is constructed as an excavation below our conventional sight level to recover the veins of myth and memory that lie beneath the surface. The excavation process begins with the familiar, digging down through layers of memories and representations. The power of Arma's novel lies in its narrative style that harmoniously assimilates oral and literary modes of narration, as much as in its uncompromising messages against colonial injustice. The fact that these literary works, written by indigenous writers, are not widely read and discussed in today's classrooms and in academia in connection to the Russian colonial texts and to the Russian imperialism in the Caucasus suggests the unwillingness to critically engage with the orientalist and imperialist clichés. In contemporary Russia, such revisions of Russian/Soviets imperial legacies would inevitably clash with the "official" version of history currently maintained and cultivated by the Russian state. It perpetuates the spiritual and epistemological colonisation.

MT: Feminist movements, activism, arts, and academic writing have developed quite unevenly in different post-Soviet contexts including the Caucasus. For one thing "feminism" is still an objectionable word and not many Caucasian women would agree to be called feminists even if their views and beliefs are entirely feminist. In many other formerly colonised and otherwise subjugated nations and regions the broader anticolonial, anti-Islamophobic, or anti-neoliberal struggles subsume the gendered and feminist programs even if their claims may be at times mildly or radically different. The present advent of conservative heteropatriarchal forces makes it even more problematic for women's movements and agendas to be properly formulated and put on the stage as a political force. Moreover, it seems that there are too many conflicting forces affecting the construction of Circassian women identities and self-identities and representations (internal and diasporic, coming from the global North and from the (ex)coloniser Russia). As in the case of Chinese women's movements, in the North Caucasus there seems to be a double dictate – external (linked with the global North's colonialist stereotyping) and internal (grounded in local heteropatriarchy) – complicating feminist struggles because women are confined to binary stereotypes of either a reckless warrior or a silent victim. So, women are put in a difficult situation of taking part in two wars at once. Would you agree that something similar can be detected in the Caucasus throughout modernity up to now when the place of the early Bolshevik women activists, who were sent from Moscow to trigger the emancipation of the downtrodden Caucasian women, has been taken by Russian sociologists, who hasten to produce half-baked sensational research, fixed on the negative sides of the Caucasian gender relations in many cases, constructed by these very "researchers" themselves – brides' kidnapping, underage marriages, honour killings, genital mutilation. The modern/colonial intellectual hierarchy in gender studies remains intact so that the voices of the Caucasian women researchers and activists are unheard and erased. What can be done to change this situation?

LZ: Gender remains an important aspect of injustice in the North Caucasus. We will not be able to effectively deal with this issue unless we uncover the ways in which gender hierarchies and the notions of masculinity and femininity have been constructed and maintained in modern (neo)colonial and nationalistic narratives. Here I agree with the works of decolonial thinkers that we need to address the "coloniality of knowledge" that prevents the effective decolonisation of these imposed categories.

The critical mistake made by the Russian sociologists is that they are looking at gender issues in complete isolation from other issues such as the ideological distortions of local histories and the suppression of human rights, including political, economic, and linguistic rights of these communities. They often neglect to talk about these inequalities and power asymmetries of existing social and political relations. Just as their predecessors, the Russian/Soviet scholars have done in the past, these contemporary Russian scholars view the peoples in the Caucasus as socially, culturally, and morally backward and see patriarchy as inherently Caucasian characteristic. Through their constructed discourses on Caucasian gender relations, they continue to exoticise and demonise the region. In addition to treating the Caucasian space as a "void" (Tlostanova 2010), devoid of any local systems of knowledge, they tend to homogenise the region, neglecting the unique local histories and experiences of various ethnic groups in the North Caucasus. Methodologically they usually follow the Western social science and humanities and blindly apply the Western theories in their interpretations of gender dynamics in the North Caucasus, a place that remains a quasi-colony of Russia. This situation also demonstrates that knowledge is still produced and imposed as something normative by the metropolitan centre. This asymmetrical knowledge production is nothing new but a continuation of the Western and Russian/Soviet imperial power and knowledge configuration, in which local histories and voices are ignored. Russian scholars in the humanities and social sciences still maintain this self-proclaimed moderniser and civiliser role in their attitude toward the non-Russian population. They are part of the problem because they perpetuate these gendered identities and reinforce a victimisation discourse. Also, all research on gender in the Caucasus produced without knowing or speaking the native languages or taking into consideration the oral histories and the native cosmologies and epistemologies will be superficial. And, this is exactly the case with the Russian sociologists, who usually come to the region, quickly interview a few people in various republics and make sweeping generalisations about the identities of all Caucasian peoples and ethnicities (Kosterina 2015). To change the situation, these injustices need to be revealed and the constructed histories need to be deconstructed. For example, we need to be more vocal in articulating that the process of the invention of Circassian women went hand in hand with the process of stripping them of power and of their own identity. Through the numerous equations of Circassian women with slavery, passivity, etc. in the imperial/colonial texts, women were deprived of agency and reduced to the level of possessions. We need to restore the links to the indigenous cosmology, where gender roles are defined by non-sexual concepts and based on different factors, for example, on the age or social status of women. The balanced duality of the sexes and the egalitarian traditions that are evident in the oral tradition (e.g. in the Nart Sagas) as well as the nongender-specific attitude reflected in the Circassian language and in some other local forms of social organisation still present in Circassian culture reveal the nearly forgotten layers of alternative gender-relations that were not based strictly on sex. Unfortunately, these layers of memory remain largely inaccessible even to most Circassians in the North Caucasus, which leads to the increase of the patriarchal tendencies in the society. And, this is largely due to educational omissions and the way knowledge is produced and disseminated in Russia.

There is, indeed, a very negative attitude toward the word "feminism" in the North Caucasus, even among women. It is usually associated with radical Western and Soviet movements that sought to impose their gender ideologies and "liberate" or "emancipate" the "repressed" Caucasian women. Feminists are perceived as obnoxious "man-haters" who often talk about sex and engage in promiscuous sexual behaviour. This distorted view of feminism that is prevalent in Russia (not only in the North Caucasus) is due to the lack of or the limited exposure to the global feminist movements and trends. In Russia, for example, various forms of indigenous women's activism are not recognised as such.

As for the Circassians in the North Caucasus, they still remain largely detached from the historical legacies of Circassians in Diaspora, including the history of women's activism. The Russian government hinders trans-diasporic movements and social activism among Circassians to prevent them from developing closer relations to their compatriots abroad and from re-assessing their common past. It is not commonly known, for example, that a vibrant Circassian feminist movement already existed in Circassian diaspora in Istanbul at the beginning of the 20th century. The Circassian Women's Solidarity Association, the first society founded by five Circassian women in the Ottoman Empire, was established in Istanbul in 1918 and existed until 1922. The president of the Association was Hayriye Melek Hunç (1896–1963), the first Circassian novelist in the Ottoman empire. Hayriye Melek Hunç was also the editor of *Diyane* (Our Mother), a women's magazine published in Turkish and in the Circassian language in 1920, and one of the founders of the first Circassian School for both boys and girls. Another example of indigenous feminism is the work of Majida Mufti Hebzhoqwe (1930–2017), an American Circassian activist and defender of the rights of the Circassian nation who worked as a teacher and educator for decades and defended the right of the North Caucasian nations to self-determination at the United Nations in the late 1990s. Recovering the histories of these women and reclaiming their historical and cultural legacy will help Circassians free themselves from self-Orientalising and self-colonising tendencies. Reaching out to other women-activists with the same agenda in the region and worldwide and forming coalitions with them will help in strengthening their voices and consolidating their power.

MT: Could you tell us about your project *Under the Tree*? It radically delinks from the modern/colonial educational models that kill memories and histories and erase languages. *Under the Tree* attempts to heal these colonial wounds. It is an amazing example of indigenous pedagogy, an original and bold community-based project with alternative optics and ethics. Most such projects in the world emerge not from the state (or the state schools and universities as instruments of modernity/coloniality with prescribed agendas, rhetoric, and curricula) but rather from the indigenous communities themselves, as grassroot activities targeted at the younger generation. It seems that in the case of the North Caucasus it is even more so. What kind of actors and activists stand behind such initiatives? What is the role of gender in this project?

LZ: There are several things that I had in mind when I started the *Under the Tree (ЖыгЩӀагъ)* Project, which has been run successfully for three summers in Nalchik (Kabardino-Balkaria, Russia) since 2017. The primary goal of the program was to teach children, aged 7–12, Circassian language with a special focus on the indigenous culture and environmental and gender studies. Firstly, I was very disturbed by the continuous decline of the Circassian language in Russia, and

Figure 6.1 Student-Participants in the *Under the Tree* Project: a Class on Environmental Science (Nalchik, 2017). Eleven children are sitting on the grass
among the trees listening intensely to their teacher. Another instructor
is standing behind them smiling

Source: Lidia Zhigunova, with the permission of the parents

I could not passively watch how my native language with its rich repository of
knowledge disappear, being forced out of public education. Minority languages in
Russia have recently been demoted to "optional" status in schools, which means
they will no longer be a required subject in the school curriculum and will be
taught only with parental consent. Circassian language instruction has been drastically reduced, and a handful of remaining classes are taught very formally in
a traditional Russian school setting. I decided to explore alternative educational
options that would make the learning process in the native language more engaging and fun. My goal was to make education less formal and authoritarian, more
applied and with an emphasis on the development of creative abilities and critical
thinking in children. Secondly, I wanted to empower children with knowledge
about their culture by introducing them to their ancestral heritage, something that
is completely missing in Russia's school curriculum. Russia has been systematically suppressing the Circassian identity and instilling at the same time a feeling
of inferiority subconsciously felt by most Circassians and transmitted to the next

generations. Decolonising knowledge by introducing alternative epistemologies is the only way out of perpetuating this internalised social humiliation. Students in the program felt empowered knowing more about their culture and about their roots. Symbolically speaking, the project aims at unifying the crown and the roots by taking a holistic approach to education. I wanted to encourage children to learn about their natural environment and their culture in a more organic way. I also believe that learning should be project based and community oriented, so students should be able to apply knowledge and skills through an engaging experience with the community. And, thirdly, I wanted to demonstrate that it is possible to move away from the rigid authoritative educational system and practise more creative and subversive ways of teaching and learning. Our classes had been taught as an outdoor summer camp and were accessible to all students in the community who expressed a wish to participate. Most of our classes were held literally under the tree. Some classes were taught by me, others by a group of local artists, researchers, and educators who volunteered their time to share their expertise in their particular fields – indigenous arts and crafts, music and musical instruments, as well as oral history – with children. I received tremendous support from several local women from the community who helped me with organisation and instruction at various stages of the project. Among them are the artist-activist Milana Khalilova, who was my co-instructor during the first summer; Bella Abrokova, a linguist and editor-in-chief of the children's magazine "Nur" published in Circassian language, who developed a unique way of teaching Circassian alphabet and sound system to children and presented her new language teaching methodology as part of the project; Madina Khakuasheva, a senior researcher at the Kabardino-Balkar Research Institute in the humanities, who supported the project at various stages.

Strong gender element of the instruction was also present in the content of classes, in which students were introduced to oral history and to powerful images of female characters found in the Nart epic. The stories in the Nart Sagas present women in possession of exceptional physical and spiritual power, and most importantly, they combine feminine and masculine traits exhibiting fluid rather than fixed gender identities. Reclaiming and passing on this knowledge to the next generation is necessary because it challenges the imposed stereotypes and clichés that tend to simplify Circassian female identities by erasing their agency, diversity, resistance, thinking, and voices. And, since the majority of project participants were girls, it was important to introduce them, and the boys as well, to these images in the format that was more accessible to children.

The name *Under the Tree* originated from my desire to remind children of the ecological wisdom possessed by our ancestors, of the tree cult that existed among the Circassians in the very recent past. Up to the Russian colonisation of Circassia and the devastating Soviet push for industrialisation, Circassia had many sacred groves and sacred trees under which the community would gather for festivals or worship. The most important decisions in the life of the Circassians were made under the sacred trees, and they protected them as they would protect their own homes. Students are usually very excited to learn that their ancestors had such a dynamic relationship with nature and that they knew their environment very well and were able to use its resources skilfully and carefully. It was a shameful act for a person to break the limbs of trees or destroy the healthy trees. The same attitude was exhibited toward the bodies of water and other natural resources. It is necessary to reactivate these layers of memory, in order to move away from the constant recycling of the images of Circassian men as perpetual "warriors" and Circassian women as "submissive beauties".

Unfortunately, this eco-philosophical heritage has been widely neglected, and this knowledge is not transmitted through Russia's educational institutions. One can find it only in specialised literature inaccessible to most students. And this is the case with almost every aspect related to the indigenous heritage of Circassians, which had been either distorted or erased. Thus, the project aims not only to cultivate a harmonious connection to the native language and nature, but also to address the ideological distortions of the indigenous traditions that took place in the Caucasus. Giving people back their ancestral memory empowers them; it reinforces their identities and hopes for the future. And, this is the point where environmental justice and human rights intersect – the rights of the indigenous community to restore this knowledge and to transmit it in their native language to the next generation, and to regain a voice in addressing the environmental issues that became a matter of concern in the region – these are all basic human rights of the indigenous populations that continue to be violated in Russia.

MT: As you have mentioned above, memory is a vulnerable category in Circassian history marked by the waves of devastating wars, genocide, exile, brutal repressions, distortion or loss of indigenous culture, neocolonial dehumanisation, all of which largely remains silenced if not denied in official discourses and memory politics. This makes Circassians extremely precarious as they risk losing forever the links between various temporalities and different generations. It is crucial to do the work on memory, on historical traumas and restless ghosts which continue to consume us, erasing our future. What is your take on memory? What ways of its use as a liberating tool can one potentially find in the Caucasus and what role in this process is played by women (researchers, activists, politicians, artists, writers)?

LZ: The imperial condition, under which Circassians in the Russian Caucasus live today, strips them of their native history and language as the most vital ways of transmitting and regenerating new knowledge. The current Russian anti-Circassian politics destroys the remnants of Circassian culture at home and neglects all appeals of Circassians scattered around the world to support their linguistic rights and their right to return to their homeland making the reunification process impossible. What does the future hold for Circassians and what do they do in the present to fix the historical ruptures?

Seteney Shami has pointed out that there is no homogeneous, unified conception of a Circassian identity today, even in their homeland, due to their political fragmentation in their historical homeland in the Caucasus (with the Soviet artificial divisions still in place) and due to the successive displacements and exile (Shami

1998). The post-Soviet Russian government has made it clear that it will block any efforts to unite the Circassian territories into a common homeland maintaining borders and divisions as an essential political instrument of control. On the other hand, Circassians living both in the Caucasus and in diaspora have gone through painful but ultimately transformational interactions with and adaptation to different cultures. This long history of displacement and migration contributed to the creation of new transnational (multilingual, multi-layered) identities. To be sure, mobility and migration were part of Circassian identity prior to Russian/Soviet modernity. Prior to Russian colonisation, Circassians took an active part in trade, military, and other administration-related affairs, including via slavery and slave trade, in the wider Ottoman/Mediterranean world. Thus, Circassians have a potential for building a *pluriversal* world, in decolonial terms a world in which many worlds could coexist, which is different from assimilationist policies pursued by many states in which Circassians live today, unfortunately, without having much political power to change anything. Since pluriversality is already part of Circassian identities and experiences, if recognised as such, it could become a potential liberating tool for the Circassians, a foundation on which they could build their future. Circassians in Russia, however, are in a precarious situation today, because political persecution of any alternative ways of constructing knowledge and of organising themselves, along with repression of their rights and freedoms, makes the process of retrieving memories and pursuing their aspirations in building any kind of pluriversal models extremely difficult, if not impossible.

Contemporary Circassian artists make an effort at decolonising memory by reconnecting to their cultural mythology and native cosmology. As you discuss in your book *What Does It Mean to Be Post-Soviet* (Tlostanova 2018), the Russian version of socialism radically erased all indigenous ways of life and indigenous knowledge, making it hard to access the native cosmological roots. Since Circassians in the Caucasus did not have strong Christian and Muslim traditions and symbols (they had both religious traditions to some degree, but not in any significant way), today they usually search for their roots in pre-Christian and pre-Islamic traditions, in mythologies, in oral traditions, in folklore, in daily social practices, and in the language itself. These sources became inspirational for many artists and for Circassian socio-political activism which at this point exists only at the grassroots level. Reconstructing Circassian legacy with a focus on gender is difficult, due to the fact that the indigenous spiritual legacy has been distorted, suppressed, and partially erased. Part of this legacy were the indigenous views on gender, sex, and sexuality, which were completely different from the Western fixed dichotomous division into sex and gender. Gender relations were not based on biology, but rather connected with social status, seniority, profession, and so forth. Most importantly, these categories were fluid, not fixed. But, of course, every system, every regime, even the most repressive ones, has its holes and cracks through which alternative knowledges slip, and those slippages helped the process of renewed interest in Circassian past and in reanimating the memory and searching for bits and pieces of lost knowledge. They gave impetus to the emergence of new kind of contemporary Circassian art that through its appeal to the subconscious sought to uncover the deep layers of memory and to heel various colonial traumas.

Oliver Bullough compares Circassian experience to a

> pot that had been smashed, and then tumbled around in a river for a hundred years . . . The shards would still match in color and pattern, but their edges would have knocked about and chipped and scarred and encrusted . . . but, enough of the pattern survived to make the culture recognizable.
>
> (Bullough 2010, 38)

While it would be impossible and unnecessary to recreate the original "pot", contemporary Circassian artists are searching for clues and work with the patterns, symbols, and signs, in order to piece together the shards and fill the vessel with meaning. I think the art that these artists create has a subversive potential because it helps Circassians to heal their traumas and to fix the ruptures in the fabric of their memory, and at the same time these artistic practices are not regarded as a political act of resistance (even though in some ways they are) by the authorities who don't really pay attention to them, because they don't understand them. In the process of designing their contemporary multimedia art works, Circassian artists use natural, more traditional materials such as sand, clay, felt, wood, and grass as well as technological resources such as digital media. And it is not a coincidence that they found these natural, fluid, "borderless" materials more suitable for expressing their feelings toward their culture and their past and present experience.

As an example of a unique mode of self-representation marked by the notion of pluriversality could be cited the post-modern art of Zaina Al-Said, an artist of Circassian origin, born in Jordan. Her eclectic multi-media collage artworks are a combination of painting, photographs, and digital technology – she takes old photographs of her Circassian ancestors and superimposes them with pictures of various spaces and objects cut out from magazines creating unexpected images and compositions. Zaina Al-Said draws inspiration from local stories and knowledge: the history and cosmology of Circassians, Islamic art with its geometric designs, Arabic calligraphy, and the philosophy of Sufism. The artist uses a variety of different materials, combinations of colours and shapes, which at first glance do not fit together but get along in a rather compelling way. She also creates movable collages, in which objects move in space creating a new meaning ("Dreams of Circassia", "Parallel Times"). "Parallel Times" is a series of eight works devoted to Circassian tribes who once inhabited the North-western Caucasus. Yet the artist places them in the interiors and exteriors of various palaces, salons, and theatres of 18th and 19th century Europe. The Circassian ghosts in European colonial palaces bring a memory flashback to the imperialistic war that destroyed Circassia. The "Parallel Times" emphasises the notion of possibility of coexistence of multiple worlds, which as we know it, did not happen in colonial modernity.

Figure 6.2 The artist Milana Khalilova and Lidia Zhigunova at the *Zhyg Guasha* (Tree Goddess) Exhibit in Nalchik, 2017

Source: Lidia Zhigunova (with the permission of the artist Milana Khalilova)

Another Circassian artist from the Caucasus, Milana Khalilova, who designs her art pieces using multimedia sources such as felt, graphic, and animation, draws her inspiration from the Circassian mythology, the Nart epic, particularly from the story of the Tree Goddess (Zhyg Guashe). The Tree Goddess, a female deity who is adored for her beauty, is presented as a personification of wisdom, a repository of knowledge and information. Her roots penetrate deep into the earth, and the crown reaches the infinity of the sky so that she is able to gather all the knowledge and information about the universe and share it with the community. This image plays a vital role in recovering gender-specific knowledge about the role that women played in pre-modern Circassian society undermining the gender categories imposed by the Western and Russian modernity. Milana has authored a series devoted to the Tree Goddess (2017). With this series, Milana also reminded Circassians of the time when they used to have a more harmonious relationship to nature which is evident in Circassians sacred groves and cultivation of the famous forest-gardens. Russian colonisation and Soviet aggressive modernisation damaged the natural resources of Circassia and destroyed the indigenous way of life creating an ongoing ecological disaster. Therefore, recovering this knowledge and recognising the intertwined relationship between the human and natural worlds is vital for the future of the region.

References

Bullough, Oliver. 2010. *Let Our Fame Be Great: Journeys Among the Defiant People of the Caucasus*. New York: Basic Books.

Damian, Dina. 2006. *V Vashem Mire Ya – Prokhozhii* [*I Am a Stranger in Your World*]. Moscow: KomKniga.

Kosterina, Irina. 2015. "Life and Status of Women in the North Caucasus: Report Summary on Survey." *Heinrich Böll Stiftung*, Moscow. https://ru.boell.org/en/2015/08/20/life-and-status-women-north-caucasus-report-summary-survey-irina-kosterina?fbclid=IwAR2sjGSvWhwHsvucqgpjqHr6KMquey8v7pw-EsXKR5fPqdkGKAwUDna8rsU.

Richmond, Walter. 2013. *The Circassian Genocide*. New Brunswick: Rutgers University Press.

Shami, Seteney. 1998. "Circassian Encounters: The Self as Other and the Production of the Homeland in the North Caucasus." *Development and Change* 29, no. 4 (10): 617–646.

Shami, Seteney. 2000. "Prehistories of Globalization: Circassian Identity in Motion." *Public Culture* 12, no. 1: 177–204.

Spivak, Gayatri Chakravorty. 1988. "Can the Subaltern Speak?" In *Marxism and the Interpretation of Culture*, edited by Cary Nelson and Lawrence Grossberg, 24–28. London: Macmillan.

Tlostanova, Madina. 2010. *Gender Epistemologies and Eurasian Borderlands*. New York: Palgrave Macmillan.

Tlostanova, Madina. 2011. *Zalumma Agra*. Moscow: Sputnik+.

Tlostanova, Madina. 2018. *What Does It Mean to Be Post-Soviet? Decolonial Art from the Ruins of the Soviet Empire*. Durham, NC: Duke University Press.

Zhigunova, Lidia. 2016a. "From Harem to Feminocracy: De-Orientalizing the Circassian National Imaginary in Literature and Art from the Early Modern to the Post-Soviet Period." Ph.D. thesis, Tulane University.

Zhigunova, Lidia. 2016b. "Memory, History, and the Construction of Self in Dina Arma's The Road Home." *Journal of Caucasian Studies* 1, no. 2: 75–100.

Part II

Opacities

Theorising postcolonial conditions in Martinique, philosopher and poet Édouard Glissant defined opacity as an alternative to identity and representation, both of which have been central to feminist writings. The socio-ontological discontinuity that accompanies the process of identity (re)construction is deeply inscribed in the "abyssal" (Glissant 1997, 6–7) experience of coloniality in different spheres of social existence. For Glissant, opacity disrupts the "transformation of subjects into categorizable objects of Western knowledge" and inadvertently protects against the erasure of those at the margins of society (1997, 190). In this sense, the politics of opacity could operate as a potential form of resistance that creates an alternate economy and overrides the moralism and assimilative inclinations of the majoritarian public sphere.

Expanding on the concept of opacity and placing it at the intersections of post-socialism and postcolonialism, the contributions in this section evoke opacity as a productive frame, not to resolve paradoxes and ambivalences but to animate methodological and theoretical accounts that are truncated and contradictory. Placing her analysis more generally within the epistemic inequalities in Central and Eastern Europe (CEE) and more specifically the political context of post-Soviet Estonia, Raili Marling explores the usefulness of opacity as a conceptual lever for postsocialist geopolitical contexts. She notes that like neoliberalism, feminism has called for the visibility of women and LGBTQ communities to challenge their exclusion from and marginalisation in their everyday experiences. Nonetheless, visibility also entails the risk of co-opting feminism within neoliberal nationalism, a concern shared by postsocialist and postcolonial scholars alike. While in political decision making, the importance of the Kantian conception of publicity cannot be understated, its twin, visibility, does not unconditionally enhance social justice and democratic polity. In fact, as Marling argues, the strands of Estonian feminism that did retain their critical edge were those that did not enter into public discourse as visibly as academic and state feminism.

Like Michel de Certeau's (1984) notion of a "tactic", opacity insinuates alterity into totalising systems by negotiating the gaps between the "given" and how it can be used and configured, differently. Within these spaces alternative narratives resurface, as the interview with Nivedita Menon demonstrates. Highlighting the historical intersections and disjunctures between anti-colonial nationalism and the current Hindutva regime, Menon points out the homogenising and patriarchal practices of Hindu nationalism, together with its advocacy against the internal "others". This has prompted feminist scholars and activists in India to develop an alternative counter-nationalist discourse while simultaneously acknowledging their own internal fissures. Within this existing domain of constraints, postnationalism "from below", like opacity, embodies a kind of ontological tactic that re(claims) subaltern histories and resists co-optation.

Taking the idea of this limited and limiting understanding of visibility forward, Maria Mayerchyk and Olga Plakhotnik identify a relatively new form of "uneventful" feminist activism in the context of post-Maidan Ukraine. Pursuing both anti-nationalist and anti-colonial agendas, this type of activism troubles mainstream feminist and LGBTQ discourses through its informality and non-engagement with public institutions. Uneventful activism instantiates an alternative form of political engagement that embraces anonymity as a way of acting below the radar of capitalist neoliberal forms of recognisability and success. This underlines the idea that power can also lie in remaining anonymous, unmarked and unseen. In this sense, uneventfulness resonates with opacity as it ruptures notions of the "dominative imposition of transparency" (Brooks 2006, 8) which can be deployed for less than transparent reasons.

In another sense, opacity can help to avoid the normative tropes of identification. This is exactly the strategy of the Krëlex zentr, an imaginary art institution which embodies the poetics and politics of opacity without, conversely, rendering it transparent. In conversation with Lesia Pagulich and Tatsiana Shchurko, Maria Vilkovisky and Ruthia Jenrbekova of the Krëlex zentr explore the possibilities for theorising post-Soviet power relations beyond the Eurocentric imaginary, focusing instead on how creative arts can imagine forms of community and identification within the landscapes of inequality and injustice in Central Asia. Through their poetics, the Krëlex zentr produces postsocialist queer subjectivity that is thoroughly invested in non-homogeneity. This reverberates with opacity as artists generate a space for challenging historically embedded social structures which allow people to imagine alternative realities.

To work with the concept of opacity is not to confound or to diverge from matters of accountability but to create spaces of re-existence and change. Drawing on a decolonial transfeminist critique and placing their analysis within the context of the former Yugoslavia, Tjaša Kancler adopts an "undisciplinary" methodological approach to understand postsocialism as a global condition which is entangled with racial and colonial/imperial formations. Within this context, transfeminism becomes a platform for the struggle against capitalism and heteropatriarchy. Kancler places their ideas in and through artistic projects that explicate the postsocialist void which, as they argue, is reproduced by global coloniality.

Bridging the contributions in this section, opacity thus becomes an affirmative modality for postcolonial and postsocialist subjects because "the right to opacity is a right not to be understood" (Britton 1999, 19), which in some contexts can be empowering.

References

Britton, Celia. 1999. *Édouard Glissant and Postcolonial Theory: Strategies of Language and Resistance*. Charlottesville: University Press of Virginia.

Brooks, Daphne. 2006. *Bodies in Dissent: Spectacular Performances of Race and Freedom, 1850–1910*. Durham, NC: Duke University Press.

de Certeau, Michel. 1984. *The Practice of Everyday Life*. Berkeley and Los Angeles: University of California Press.

Glissant, Édouard. 1997. *Poetics of Relation*. Translated by Betsy Wing. Ann Arbor: University of Michigan Press.

Chapter 7

Opacity as a feminist strategy

Postcolonial and postsocialist entanglements with neoliberalism

Raili Marling

Introduction: gaps in feminist imaginaries

The question of how postsocialist experience can add to transnational feminist knowledge production has been urgent for post-state-socialist Central and Eastern Europe (CEE). CEE scholars have all too often accepted their semi-peripheral status and modelled themselves on the theories produced in the West, dutiful daughters of distant stepmothers who benevolently recognise their presence without treating them as their intellectual equals. The few CEE scholars who have been published in transnational feminist journals have been happy to be noticed, not wondering about their continued semi-peripheral status in knowledge production. Scholars like Madina Tlostanova (2010, 2012) and Jennifer Suchland (2011) have called attention to the former fly-over country between the First and the Third World in transnational feminism not just as a geographical but also an epistemological location. Scholars from CEE feel the gap most acutely, as it renders them largely invisible in the international feminist mind map. There was a brief period of excitement about CEE in the early 1990s, after the fall of state socialism, quickly followed by a series of perplexed reports on the lack of enthusiasm about Western feminisms. CEE has been largely absent from transnational feminism, supposedly for not being academically interesting enough, in its stereotypical interpretation as the blurry copy of the West, uncanny in its interplay of similarity and difference that has been fruitfully theorised by Homi Bhabha (1994) in the postcolonial context.

The "sanctioned ignorances" (Spivak 1988, 287) of Western feminisms, widely cited in transnational feminist texts, have not necessarily been erased when it comes to the understanding of the postsocialist world in its diverse manifestations. Nina Lykke (2010, 55) has argued that a meaningful transnational feminism "requires a self-reflexive stance on global/local locations not only in relation to crude and rather abstract categories such as East – West/North – South". There is little work that builds on concepts of "relationality, complementarity and reciprocity" (Tlostanova, Thapar-Björkert, and Koobak 2019, 85), beyond the reiteration of these words. Although the politics of location has been a feminist commonplace for 35 years, I am not optimistic that this principle is being meaningfully adopted, beyond verbal gestures in academic articles. The type of nuanced comparative work that Inderpal Grewal and Caren Kaplan (1994, 17) envisioned as the replacement of a "relativistic linking of differences" has been slow to emerge.

Turning attention to CEE is not just about arriving at geopolitical representativeness in transnational feminist theory-building. The disregard of the experience of CEE countries like Estonia helps to perpetuate the misunderstanding that postsocialism affects only countries where state socialism was an actual reality and ignore the fact that the fall of socialism impacted the whole world, among other things by aiding the global embrace of neoliberalism (Shih 2012, 27). It is not acknowledged sufficiently that the chronological trajectory of transnational feminism parallels that of the hegemony of neoliberalism, as I have noted in my previous research (Marling and Koobak 2017). In addition, however, the period also saw the rise of postcolonial theory, an important intervention in the feminism-neoliberalism nexus. As Tlostanova, Thapar-Björkert, and Koobak (2019, 81–82) demonstrate, postsocialist scholars have been invigorated by postcolonial thought. Perhaps we can offer our insights to postcolonial theory, for example by creatively re-reading some notions developed on the postcolonial experience in the postsocialist geopolitical context. We will be able to create new knowledge in the spirit of openness and intellectual dialogue. This is what the present chapter also sets out to do.

This chapter is energised by postcolonial thinkers like Édouard Glissant and decolonial theorists, especially Madina Tlostanova. It seeks to provide an example of a dialogue between postcolonial and postsocialist thought through the underutilised concept of opacity developed by Glissant (1997). The utility of opacity is tested in the context of neoliberalism, a challenge to feminisms in all geopolitical locations. There is already a rich feminist literature on neoliberal rationality and economic practices. However, among other things, neoliberalism also relies on a particular definition of agency and visibility. This, in turn, has serious implications for political activism, including feminist one. Feminism has called for visibility of women and LGBTQ people, to undo centuries of invisibility and exclusion. However, visibility also opens up a potential for co-optation, for being rendered part of a world of publicity, not the democratic public (Quieroz 2017). Such visible and publicity-friendly feminism may be submerged in the broader neoliberal rationality and lose its ability to meaningfully challenge hierarchies of power. It is this conundrum that raises the question of whether a politics of opacity might potentially resist panoptic neoliberalism.

I proceed from the specific politics of location in postsocialist Estonia, but believe that this position can be productive more broadly. Re-reading opacity in the context of contemporary surveillance regimes can invigorate a dialogue with our postcolonial colleagues who also grapple with the twin challenges of nationalism and neoliberalism. These two have for long been viewed as conflicting worldviews, but today scholars from different disciplines testify to the rise of neoliberal nationalism (e.g., Harmes 2011; Lueck, Due, and Augoustinos 2015). This is a combination that activists have faced in some CEE countries like Estonia for almost 20 years and this creates the potential for some fresh input into trans-national feminist knowledge creation. My argument moves from the discussion of epistemic inequalities in CEE and its struggle with nationalism and neoliberal-ism to the work of Glissant and its potential for political agency in the context of neoliberal Estonia and more broadly.

What can the postsocialist know?

Regretting epistemic inequalities between the West and the rest is a frequent ges-ture in transnational feminist writing. Theorisation from CEE is certainly a victim of this inequality. In Tlostanova's (2015) scathing wording, it often seems that the post-Soviet is suspected of not being able to think. Even the parallels with the postcolonial world have to be legitimated by Western scholars (David Chioni Moore's 2001 article in *PMLA* recurs in references with greater frequency than that of any CEE scholar). The topic of the absence of the Second World appeared in major English-language feminist publications only in the 2010s, after a decade of authors from CEE pointing out the gaps in Western world-making (e.g., Kasic 2004; Slavova 2006; Blagojevic 2009) and arguing for the need to "bring the second world in" (Grabowska 2012). It seems that the Second World has been brought in through the back door, as we indeed can find more CEE authors in high-impact feminist journals, if perhaps not enough of nuanced analyses that challenge the gatekeepers' epistemic practices.

CEE scholars may be inspired by Western theories but have access to local archives and knowledge that empower them to not just translate but also adapt, deconstruct, and perhaps unlearn. Increased publication in English, the transna-tional feminist lingua franca, also allows scholars from different countries who do not share a common language to exchange experiences and test theoretical conceptualisations outside of the sanctioning gaze of the coveted high-impact journals. Feminist scholarship need not circulate to the periphery through a very limited number of metropolitan centres. In CEE, for decades the important intel-lectual centres have included Belgrade and Budapest, not just Berkeley, Santa Cruz, and London. English-language publications can also move between differ-ent locations in the periphery and semi-periphery where experiences are shared and less is lost in translation.

The post-socialist European countries are frequently and with some justice perceived as "uncritically positioned vis-à-vis the first world" (Suchland 2011, 839), as they seek to return to Europe and the West and distance themselves from the Third World. This, however, by no means suggests an uncritical reception of Western ideas, albeit with a lag, in a form of "temporal drag" (Freeman 2010; Koobak 2013). Just labelling women from CEE countries, in the blunt words of Kornelia Slavova (2006, 248), as "backward, apolitical, full of apathy" is not helping to advance a sustained critique. Perhaps, it is the very lack of vocal cri-tiques of neoliberalism that might make the feminisms of CEE countries like Estonia valuable for transnational feminism, to complicate its assumptions about both neoliberalism and feminist activism (Cerwonka 2008, 822). This is also a context in which a look into the ways in which the postcolonial and postsocialist responses to neoliberalism vary is instructive.

Returns and blind spots in postsocialist Estonia

Tlostanova's (2010) critique of Eurocentrism is a necessary corrective to the conventionally deracialised postsocialist narrative. However, in this chapter, I use the optics suggested by her to discuss those parts of the former Soviet empire that consider themselves the most European. Estonia has stressed its status as an almost foreign country within the Soviet Union, with its easy access to Finnish TV channels and avant-garde culture (cf. Näripea 2015). It quit the Soviet sphere of influence cold turkey and assertively turned itself towards the West, becoming a poster-child of transition and later of economic sobriety in the Euro area (Lindstrom 2015, 62). In this self-narrative, Estonia is not just an undeniable part of the West but also an exemplar of Westernness. However, I believe that it is this very eagerness to deny its actual geo-historical location and deep colonial presences that merits attention as a form of self-colonisation, a perceived ticket out of the global periphery. This should reverberate in other parts of the former Soviet Union that exist in "a strange limbo of the poor North which refuses to be equalized with the poor South" (Tlostanova 2015, 46). Estonia, by stressing its belonging to Europe, is trying to look both to the past and to the future or, more precisely, to move towards the future by looking backward. Such hobbled movement predictably leads to stumbles and self-deceptions that require nimble discursive footwork to maintain the image of progress.

One of the discourses deployed in this paradoxical context is that of return. "Return" overall carries positive connotations in Estonia, with the assumption that the Soviet period cut it off from its natural European home that has now been restored, although the notion of "Europe" continues to be used for very different ideological purposes, as a sort of a floating signifier, especially in the complex interplay of neoliberalism and populism in today's political discourse. Estonia has been called a republic of historians (Tamm 2016) who have sought to fill the "blank spots" of Soviet historiography (Lagerspetz 1999, 382) but have created a series of new ones. As Velmet (2019) shows, the past was mined for a limited understanding of historic continuity, which has notable biopolitical implications for contemporary political debates.

One of the political discourses edited out in this selective historical return discourse is pre-WWII feminist tradition. It is understandable that the socialist legacy might be shunned in the post-Soviet period in a country that wanted to move on, but the forgetfulness has also covered the nationalist-feminist nexus from the otherwise sanctified First Republic. Feminism is not included in the Europe that Estonia returned to. It is, rather, treated as a quasi-imperialist imposition of EU bureaucrats, not an intellectual tradition with local roots and political history. As I have shown elsewhere (Marling 2010), this selective treatment of feminism leaves it as the intimidating other, confronted with a backlash before it could re-emerge. Neoliberalism, conceptually more inimical to the pre-WWII nationalist Estonia than feminism, in contrast, was adopted more or less uncritically, as it was perceived as a direct opposite to the Soviet ideologies that the country was seeking to overcome in the 1990s. Thus, the discourse of return was as selective as the overall process of the travel of ideas in the postsocialist period. Neoliberalism and nationalism were paradoxically fused in order to dispel the spectres of socialism in a way that was rather unique in the CEE, and feminism was a suitable *bête noire* for both.

Historicising these blind spots is not enough. Feminist scholars will need to find a lens to decode what is omitted from this selective vision and also what it makes possible. This requires not just noting the effects of Soviet domination, rehashed in the Estonian public discourse ad nauseam, but the layers of earlier colonising presences. The Baltic crusades have in the post-Soviet period been used by politicians to show Estonia's ancient ties to Europe (Lagerspetz 1999, 388). In the "return discourse" this is seen as integration into the West, not colonisation. This is a symptom of a wider tradition. Similar tendencies can also be seen in the discussion of Baltic-German cultural presence in Estonia, as a means of tying Estonia to the German cultural area, although the German colonial discourse constructed Estonians as the last barbarians of Europe (Plath 2008). We see this tension even in the reception of scholarship. For example, in Epp Annus' (2018) monograph on Soviet postcolonial studies, pre-Soviet colonisations as well as decolonial theories have gone largely unacknowledged in the Estonian reception that has emphasised, first and foremost, the Soviet period.

This is regrettable because the pre-Soviet waves of colonisation nurtured specific biopolitical and gender regimes. For example, the long German colonial presence in Estonia also imprinted itself into the national-romantic self-mythology in the 19th century and its conservative gender ideology (cf. Whelan 1999). Associating Europeanness with the traditional gender order and the Soviet system with gender equality has had deep implications for Estonian public discourse. EU gender equality policies have, at times, been viewed as a sign of the loss of the Western tradition. Velmet (2019) provides a good analysis of how the EU and its "gender ideology" are being demonised by the Estonian nationalists, in alignment with the global Right. This selective reading of gender is tied to a broader attempt to hyper- or proto-Europeanise Estonians, in contrast to the increasingly multicultural Western Europe and neighbouring Russia.

The selective historical narrative of victimisation has blinded many Estonians to the racial nature of its aspiration to achieve the status of what Manuela Boatcă (2015, 220–221) has called "heroic" Northern European nations. German colonisation enables Estonians to name themselves a *Kulturvolk*, even if a secondary one. The colonial roots of this racial thinking are only now starting to get academic attention. For example, Rebeka Põldsam's recent work on Estonian eugenic thinking of the 1920s shows it being rooted in the formerly colonised nation's desire to erase the Asian (then called mongoloid) taint and to "whiten" itself. Predictably, the eugenic path eventually led to purging the national body of other undesirables (including sexual and gender minorities) (Põldsam 2020). Estonian cultural history contains plentiful examples of attempts to make Estonians white, to paraphrase Noel Ignatiev (1995). This, too, is an example of the "ironic compromise" of mimicry, described already by Homi Bhabha (1994, 86), in which Estonia strives to get out of the category of "not quite" and thus to assert Western universalism as its own. However, the West that is claimed, as mentioned above, is not the multicultural Europe of gender equality and LGBTQ rights discourse. Those blind spots are what, in Bhabha's (1994, 86) terms constitute Estonia's "slippage" and difference from the West it so strongly seeks to assimilate into and in the process deny its colonial baggage.

Neoliberal entanglements

The lack of a critical language for analysing layered colonialities is also perhaps one of the reasons why Estonia lacks a mode of dealing with neoliberalism as a form of global colonialism. Since it was chosen deliberately as the fastest antidote to the Soviet legacies in the early 1990s, it has not been easy to view it critically, without acquiring the label of a Soviet nostalgia or economic naiveté.

For my analysis, the most crucial aspect of neoliberalism is its biopolitical leakage into subject formation and the creation of a broader neoliberal rationality that has saturated the social fabric with market-based values, inviting all subjects to self-responsibilisation and entrepreneurship in all spheres of life (Brown 2003, 2015). Dean and Villadsen (2017, 148) believe that the central concern of neoliberal rationality is the "techniques for the shaping of conduct and the formation of subjectivities". The core of the biopolitical pressure is that we all have to take an entrepreneurial attitude towards our careers, subjectivities, bodies, and intimate lives (cf. Foucault 2008, 225–226). The Estonian political sphere has operated on the basis of neoliberal economic ideology, but it has also consistently mainstreamed neoliberal rationality on other areas of life, for example, in academia.

This is very much a concern for feminism as well, as there are quite many uncanny parallels between the language of liberal feminism and neoliberal rationality. In a very simplified form, it can be said that both have talked about individuals needing to take control of their lives and make something of themselves. "You can do it!" and "lean in!" are intended as feminist slogans, but they do not challenge the status quo. In the past ten years, the topic has appeared with some urgency in feminist scholarship. Hester Eisenstein (2010) and Nancy Fraser (2013) have explicitly warned about the co-optation of feminism by neoliberalism. Their arguments are built on a selective reading of the feminist tradition in the US, but they make an important point. The EU's gender policies have also been, first and foremost, built on the market rationale and biopolitical approach to demography, not a pursuit of gender equality (see, e.g. Repo 2015; Lombardo, Meier, and Verloo 2009). As Elomäki (2015) points out, gender equality has been sold to policy-makers with the help of economic language and this, in turn, has sold neoliberalism to women's organisations.

Different authors give different names to this process. Catherine Rottenberg (2018), for example, calls the individual achievement oriented women's empowerment "neoliberal feminism", as it lacks a language for dealing with structural social inequality. If Ivanka Trump claims the title of a "feminist", we need to stop to seriously analyse the reasons why feminism has been so vulnerable to co-optation by people whose politics have done so much to limit the rights of women, people of colour, and LGBTQ folk. This, precisely, is what Chandra Talpade Mohanty (2013, 972) has also warned us against: feminism becoming a mere "privatized politics of representation, disconnected from systematic critique and materialist histories of colonialism, capitalism and heteropatriarchy". As I have argued earlier (Marling and Koobak 2017; Aavik and Marling 2017), Estonian entanglements with neoliberalism have been far from simple and can help to develop more nuanced critiques of neoliberalism's troubled relationship with feminism.

In post-Soviet Estonia, as already argued, neoliberalism has been celebrated as the road from serfdom to freedom. As the seemingly most radical antidote to the Soviet ideologies and practices, neoliberalism was common sense for Estonia in the 1990s and early 2000s. The other political perspectives accommodated to the basic neoliberal rhetoric to the extent that Estonia was a textbook example of really existing neoliberalism, to use the assessment of Aet Annist (2014, 91) until the rise of nationalist populism in the late 2010s, echoing the processes across CEE. Neoliberalism slowed the populist wave in Estonia but could not withstand it, because of its own previous alliances with nationalist rhetoric. Thus, although the neoliberal Reform Party won the 2019 parliamentary elections, it was out-manoeuvred by far-right nationalists and left-wing populists who govern the country at the time of the writing. This has created a hiatus in the otherwise almost uninterrupted neoliberal consensus at the governmental level. The impact of neoliberalism on Estonian social fabric has not shifted (yet), as previous governments had already sutured the seeming contradiction between nationalism and neoliberalism.

Although neoliberalism was a deliberately chosen policy direction in Estonia, the influx of neoliberalist ideas was also aided by outside entities, like in the postcolonial world. Different scholars (e.g. Ghodsee 2004; Horn 2012) have pointed out how in CEE certain approaches to gender and women's rights dominated. Feminist knowledge building had a liberal and cultural, if not explicitly neoliberal face. As a result, questions of class and inequality have been slow to emerge in Estonian gender studies and feminist scholarship. The first gender scholars to take critical interest in inequality and race emerged only in the 2010s. (I have the dubious honour of being the first person to use the term "neoliberal" in the only Estonian academic journal on gender studies – in 2015.) Thus, in a way, Suchland's (2011, 848) summary of the stereotypical vision of the Second World, which is perceived to be pro-Western and hence lacking critique, in contrast to the critically positioned Third World, seems apt at first glance.

However, it is also important to take note of the extent to which this conclusion disregards the complex local process of negotiating with what could be called "neoliberalism with a human face" (cf. Borges 2018). In Estonia, neoliberalism is not a political project that is flanked by well-developed political positions left and right that help to contest neoliberal rationality and practices. In Estonia's case the background influence of neoliberalism on the development of social movements that seek to challenge the status quo has been more acutely articulated than in countries where it exerts its influence in a stealthy manner.

On the one hand, as I have previously suggested, the neoliberal context has created feminisms that have been slow to take up economic and class-based critiques. The most successful types of feminism in Estonia are state feminism and academic feminism: the first because the EU accession process required the integration of Estonian legislation into the EU gender equality paradigm and the latter because in the neoliberal, output-based academic environment what matters is the impact of publications, not the topic or positions taken, allowing feminist scholars to establish themselves without any official support structures (Aavik and Marling 2017). This has, however, meant a certain level of elitism, political compromises, and the muting of the activist impulse. To be comprehensible in the neoliberal discursive space, Estonian mainstream feminisms have relied on the language of neoliberalism and have also been slow to come up with its critiques. On the other hand, even these mainstream feminisms have gradually gained a more radical voice to raise uncomfortable questions about economic inequality and global power relations, especially in the increasingly populist political atmosphere (cf. Marling and Koobak 2017, 2).

This is the context that makes me want to probe the potential of "opacity". If having a voice and participating in the Estonian neoliberal public sphere has encouraged Estonian feminisms to don the mask of achievement, enterprise, and self-responsibilisation, have we perhaps sacrificed too much? Especially in the era of populist resurgence, it is impossible to not think of whether academic insularity, reliance on EU policy narratives, and lack of economic analyses have allowed populist demagogues to place Estonian feminists among the elites who are labelled the enemies of the people. This is a rhetorical simplification, as nationalist populism is by definition inimical to feminism, but the cost of visibility is a topic that feminisms need to tackle in the conditions of neoliberalism. There are, needless to say, different visibilities. I am here primarily looking at the positive coverage that supports acceptance in political/academic deliberation, not social media visibility that can also make one vulnerable to stigmatisation and, in worst cases, trolling. While academic feminism has been chasing visibility by high-impact publication, grant writing, and institutional politics, it has also faced the difficult choice of downplaying activism. The strands of Estonian feminism that did not enter into the public discourse as assertively and visibly as academic and state feminism have retained more of their critical potential.

There are alternatives, however. Redi Koobak has analysed Estonian feminist art as a subversive forum, and it can certainly be asserted that art has been the primary field in which Estonian LGBTQ history has been actively written (see Koobak 2013; Põldsam 2020). The art world's institutional politics are complex and influenced by international attention (like the choice of Jaanus Samma to represent Estonia at the Venice Biennale in 2015 with a LGBTQ project) and will not be addressed here. I will instead focus on online feminist activism. Several analyses, among others Koobak (2017), have already discussed the feminist Facebook group *Virginia Woolf sind ei karda* (Virginia Woolf is Not Afraid of You). I am more interested in the activists gathered around the feminist web magazine *Feministeerium*. It is an independent forum, built on volunteer labour and project-based support from Estonian and international grants. Working outside of government structures has allowed the magazine to retain its independence of opinion and ability to shift public opinion (at a cost, as the present government has also moved to cut their very limited public funding). This is not a precise parallel, but illustrates the costs and benefits of visibility under neoliberal hegemony. *Feministeerium* has enough visibility to make a difference, but the very precariousness of its funding model and existence on the margins of the public sphere also allow it the freedom not to temper its politics.

Opacity as a feminist strategy?

In the neoliberalist context, where the notion of the public sphere is being reconfigured (cf. Quieroz 2017; Dean 2007), we need to return to some of the core notions of the discourse of rights, such as recognition through visibility. Dean Spade (2015) has provocatively challenged the valorisation of individual legal rights within the neoliberal status quo. Spade argues that within the dominant regime, the marginalised "are being offered a limited form of visibility, only to the extent that that visibility can prop up existing norms" (Spade 2015, 20). Spade specifically writes about trans politics, but the idea can be extended to other activist groups. The cost of visibility is labelling, a process that is still marred by epistemic violence, as visibility means being made comprehensible to the legitimising gaze.

This, regrettably, can also be said about some transnational feminist research that traffics in broad generalisations, instead of careful local archaeologies. Perhaps transparency to the Western feminist gaze is one of the signs taken for wonder that Homi Bhabha (1985) writes about? For example, in Estonia all research grant applications also include a bibliometric analysis, and thus the decision what to publish and where is something every academic faces and this makes adapting oneself to the sanctioning gaze of international gatekeepers very attractive. While Bhabha calls for muddying colonial transparency, perhaps it would be possible to argue for opacity as a potential decolonial feminist strategy.

In the following I am delving into the ideas of Martinican writer and philosopher Édouard Glissant, who offered opacity as the opposite of visibility and transparency, which have long been political aims for the marginalised. His intervention is more broadly about Western epistemological practices that demand transparency from the non-Western others that they seek to understand and, through that, to subdue to some externally produced truth (Glissant 1997, 189–190, 194). One possible response is to refuse this visibility. Glissant is not idealising inscrutable local authenticity but challenging the discourses of difference that proliferate in colonial knowledge-making. As thinkers like Edward Said have shown a long time ago, Western epistemic practices have been built around the hierarchy of the knowing centre and the knowable periphery – knowable if subjected to the universalising Western knowledge-making apparatus. This is the gaze that Glissant wants to remain opaque to, not to be placed into a hierarchical relationship but to remain un-transparently specific and yet open to relationality and dialog. Opacity suggests unknowability, "the irreducible density of the other" that we have to grasp to achieve a true relation (cited in Britton 1999, 19). The same type of ambivalence is used by de Villiers (2012). In writing about queer figures who chose to be elusive about their sexuality, he defines opacity "as a tactic to outplay (neutralize) both obligatory confessional speech and closeted silence" (de Villiers 2012, 83). The focus is on ambiguity, refusal of a unitary label.

The right to opacity is thus not "an enclosure within an autarchy but subsistence within an irreducible singularity" (Glissant 1997, 190). Importantly for feminist thought, Glissant's notion of opacity does not exclude solidarity or what he calls "relation" (although he does use the generic masculine): "To feel in solidarity with him or to build with him or to like what he does, it is not necessary for me to grasp him. It is not necessary to try to become the other (to become other) not to 'make' him in my image" (Glissant 1997, 193).

As such, opacity can be seen as "a kind of a radical writing back" (Allar 2015, 43). We should be cautious about easy celebration of resistance, however. This possibility for subversion seems increasingly dubious under neoliberalism, as has been shown by many scholars, due to neoliberalism's ability to channel resistance into commodified identity politics, not solidarity politics. The potential for commodification has been all too vividly demonstrated above in the discussion of the mésalliance between feminism and neoliberalism. The challenge is ever greater in the context of communicative capitalism and the regimes of visibility and surveillance established by social media in what Carrol and his colleagues (2019) have aptly called neoliberalism 3.0.

Allar (2015, 43) believes that opacity "not only protects the subject from the invasive grasp of (neo)colonial thought but also, more affirmatively, invites the reader to join the poet on equal footing in the process of sense-making". Allar refers to Glissant's own poetic practice, but this invitation can also be issued in the context of academic or political dialogue. This, however, could also be evoked as a possibility in a country where most feminisms have remained opaque within the national narrative and thus protected from co-optation either into the nationalist project or the neoliberal one. That space from the margins thus remains a space of critique, of writing back. Because the margins are also in tension with neoliberal academia, they maintain openness for writing that combines careful research and respectful academic dialogue with creative writing practices and are thus able to speak in ways that are not pressed into the predictable epistemic forms. Opacity provides an opportunity for surprise and new forms of relationality needed to nurture grassroots activism and to energise feminist politics.

Conclusion

The usually sharp contrast between the postcolonial and postsocialist conditions may have been exaggerated. Postcolonial theory, like feminisms, has found itself in troubling mésalliances. Several scholars (e.g. Acheraiou 2011) have discussed the co-optation of postcolonial hybridity by neoliberalism. In other words, we can no longer be certain that the postcolonial is automatically more politically engaged than postsocialism. There is reason to believe that in both locations we are seeing the emergence of localised hybrids of nationalism and neoliberalism (cf. Kaul 2019). There is no escaping the complex and time-consuming study of all specific geo-historical localities and their diverse politics of location. The deceptive clarity of large-scale generalisations needs to be challenged in transnational feminist thinking because they introduce potentially colonial imaginaries that control non-Western peoples with a deceptive transparency that is anything but liberating. There are two intertwined reasons why we might want to re-think our fondness for visibility.

As far as I know, Glissant's notion of opacity has yet to be employed within gender studies to discuss epistemic inequalities under neoliberal hyper-visibility. Yet opacity's ability to frustrate knowledge has the potential to "move beyond the instrumentalization of essentialist identity politics and managerial multiculturalism" (Demos 2009, 127). This might be what we need today, both on the over-scrutinised postcolonial and under-scrutinised postsocialist world.

Once postsocialist or postcolonial scholars try to publish in peer-reviewed journals, they step into the field of epistemic inequality in which they have to conform to the expected and well-known references. The unknown postsocialist world is framed by these references in a more recognisable – yet in the process altered – postcolonial universe. Differences blur with distance. My recommendation is not to cease to publish in major English-language journals. The more articles emerge from a diverse range of identity locations, the more nuanced the shared understanding becomes and less space there is for sanctioned ignorance. This is not just for the benefit of the epistemic centre but for scholars in the margins, who might benefit from these optics for self-analyses.

However, side by side with this visibility-based academic economy, feminist scholars also may need to practice opacity by writing in their native languages and in creative arenas where the impositions of the epistemic canon do not iron out idiosyncrasies. Feminist scholars need to quote each other and in languages other than English. They also need to write creatively and on activist blogs like *Feministeerium* to reach the people who need to have feminist principles explained more than do the fellow academics in the West.

Acknowledgements

This work was supported by the Estonian Research Council grant PRG934.

References

Aavik, Kadri, and Raili Marling. 2017. "Gender Studies at the Time of Neo-liberal Trans-formation in Estonian Academia." In *Gender Studies and the New Academic Governance. Global Challenges, Glocal Dynamics, and Local Impacts*, edited by Heike Kahlert, 41–64. Wiesbaden: Springer VS.

Acheraïou, Amar. 2011. *Questioning Hybridity, Postcolonialism and Globalization*. London: Palgrave Macmillan.

Allar, Neal. 2015. "The Case for Incomprehension." *Journal of French and Francophone Philosophy* 23, no. 1: 43–58. https://doi.org/10.5195/jffp.2015.680.

Annist, Aet. 2014. "Losing the Entrepreneurial Self in Post-Soviet Rural Estonia." In *Neoliberalism, Personhood, and Postsocialism: Enterprising Selves in Changing Economies*, edited by Nicolette Makovicky, 89–108. Farnham: Ashgate.

Annus, Epp. 2018. *Soviet Postcolonial Studies: A View from the Western Borderlands*. London and New York: Routledge.

Bhabha, Homi. 1985. "Signs Taken for Wonders: Questions of Ambivalence and Authority Under a Tree Outside Delhi, May 1817." *Critical Inquiry* 12, no. 1: 144–165. https://doi.org/10.1086/448325.

Bhabha, Homi. 1994. *The Location of Culture*. London and New York: Routledge.

Blagojevic, Marina. 2009. *Knowledge Production at the Semiperiphery*. Belgrade: Institut za kriminoloska I socioloska istrazivanja.

Boatcă, Manuela. 2015. *Global Inequalities Beyond Occidentalism*. Farnham: Ashgate.

Borges, Fabian A. 2018. "Neoliberalism with a Human Face? Ideology and the Diffusion of Latin America's Conditional Cash Transfers." *Comparative Politics* 50, no. 2: 147–169. https://doi.org/10.5129/001041518822263647.

Britton, Celia M. 1999. *Édouard Glissant and Postcolonial Theory: Strategies of Language and Resistance*. Charlottesville: University Press of Virginia.

Brown, Wendy. 2003. "Neo-liberalism and the End of Liberal Democracy." *Theory and Event* 7, no. 1: 15–18. doi:10.1353/tae.2003.0020.

Brown, Wendy. 2015. *Undoing the Demos: Neoliberalism's Stealth Revolution*. New York: Zone Books.

Carroll, Toby, Ruben Gonzalez-Vicente, and Darryl S. L. Jarvis. 2019. "Capital, Conflict and Convergence: A Political Understanding of Neoliberalism and Its Relationship to Capitalist Transformation." *Globalizations* 16, no. 6: 778–803. https://doi.org/10.1080/14747731.2018.1560183.

Cerwonka, Allaine. 2008. "Traveling Feminist Thought: Difference and Transculturation in Central and Eastern European Feminism." *Signs* 33, no. 4: 809–832. https://doi.org/10.1086/528852.

Dean, Jodi. 2007. "Feminism, Communicative Capitalism, and the Inadequacies of Radical Democracy." In *Radical Democracy and the Internet*, edited by Lincoln Dahlberg and Eugenia Siapera, 226–245. Houndmills: Palgrave Macmillan.

Dean, Mitchell, and Kaspar Villadsen. 2017. *State Phobia and Civil Society: The Political Legacy of Michel Foucault*. Stanford, CA: Stanford University Press.

Demos, T. J. 2009. "On the Otholith Group's Nervus Rerum." *October* 129: 113–128. https://doi.org/10.1162/octo.2009.129.1.113.

De Villiers, Nicholas. 2012. *Opacity and the Closet: Queer Tactics in Foucault, Barthes, and Warhol*. Minneapolis, MN: University of Minnesota Press.

Eisenstein, Hester. 2010. *Feminism Seduced: How Global Elites Use Women's Labor and Ideas to Exploit the World*. Boulder, CO: Paradigm.

Elomäki, Anna. 2015. "The Economic Case for Gender Equality in the European Union: Selling Gender Equality to Decision-Makers and Neoliberalism to Women's Organizations." *European Journal of Women's Studies* 22, no. 3: 288–302. https://doi.org/10.1177/1350506815571142.

Foucault, Michel. 2008. *The Birth of Biopolitics: Lectures at the Collège de France, 1978–1979*. Translated by Graham Burchell. Basingstoke: Palgrave Macmillan.

Fraser, Nancy. 2013. *Fortunes of Feminism: From State-Managed Capitalism to Neoliberal Crisis*. London: Verso.

Freeman, Elizabeth. 2010. *Time Binds: Queer Temporalities, Queer Histories*. Durham, NC: Duke University Press.

Ghodsee, Kristin. 2004. "Feminism-by-Design: Emerging Capitalisms, Cultural Feminism and Women's Nongovernmental Organizations in Post-Socialist Eastern Europe." *Signs* 29, no. 3: 727–753. https://doi.org/10.1086/380631.

Glissant, Édouard. 1997. *Poetics of Relation*. Translated by Betsy Wing. Ann Arbor: University of Michigan Press.

Grabowska, Magdalena. 2012. "Bringing the Second World in: Conservative Revolution(s), Socialist Legacies, and Transnational Silences in the Trajectories of Polish Feminism." *Signs* 37, no. 2: 385–411. https://doi.org/10.1086/661728.

Grewal, Inderpal, and Caren Kaplan. 1994. "Introduction: Transnational Feminist Practices and Questions of Postmodernity." In *Scattered Hegemonies: Postmodernity and Transnational Feminist Practices*, edited by Inderpal Grewal and Caren Kaplan, 1–36. Minneapolis, MN: Minnesota University Press.

Harmes, Adam. 2011. "The Rise of Neoliberal Nationalism." *Review of International Political Economy* 19, no. 1: 59–86. https://doi.org/10.1080/09692290.2010.507132.

Horn, Denise M. 2012. *Women, Civil Society and the Geopolitics of Democratization*. New York: Routledge.

Ignatiev, Noel. 1995. *How the Irish Became White*. New York and London: Routledge.

Kašić, Bijana. 2004. "Feminist Cross-Mainstreaming Within 'East-West' Mapping: A Postsocialist Perspective." *European Journal of Women's Studies* 11, no. 4: 473–485. https://doi.org/10.1177/1350506804046821.

Kaul, Nitasha. 2019. "The Political Project of Postcolonial Neoliberal Nationalism." *Indian Politics & Policy* 2, no. 1: 3–30. doi:10.18278/inpp.2.1.2.

Koobak, Redi. 2013. *Whirling Stories: Postsocialist Feminist Imaginaries and the Visual Arts*. Linköping: Linköping University Press.

Koobak, Redi. 2017. "Narrating Feminisms: What Do We Talk About When We Talk About Feminism in Estonia." *Gender, Place & Culture* 25, no. 7: 1010–1024. https://doi.org/10.1080/0966369X.2018.1471048.

Lagerspetz, Mikko. 1999. "Postsocialism as Return: Notes on a Discursive Strategy." *East European Politics, Societies and Cultures* 13, no. 2: 377–390. https://doi.org/10.1177/0888325499013002019.

Lindstrom, Nicole. 2015. *The Politics of Europeanization and Post-Socialist Transformations*. Houndmills: Palgrave Macmillan.

Lombardo, Emanuela, Petra Meier, and Mieke Verloo. 2009. "Stretching and Bending Gender Equality: A Discursive Politics Approach." In *The Discursive Politics of Gender Equality: Stretching, Bending and Policymaking*, edited by Emanuela Lombardo, Petra Meier, and Mieke Verloo, 1–18. London and New York: Routledge.

Lueck, Kerstin, Clemence Due, and Martha Augoustinos. 2015. "Neoliberalism and Nationalism: Representations of Asylum Seekers in the Australian Mainstream News Media." *Discourse & Society* 26, no. 5: 608–629. https://doi.org/10.1177/0957926515581159.

Lykke, Nina. 2010. *Feminist Studies: A Guide to Intersectional Theory, Methodology and Writing*. London: Routledge.

Marling, Raili. 2010. "The Intimidating Other: Feminist Critical Discourse Analysis of the Representation of Feminism in Estonian Print Media." *NORA: Nordic Journal of Feminist and Gender Research* 18, no. 1: 7–19. https://doi.org/10.1080/08038741003626767.

Marling, Raili, and Redi Koobak. 2017. "Intersections of Feminisms and Neoliberalism: Post-State-Socialist Estonia in a Transnational Feminist Framework." *Frontiers: A Journal of Women's Studies* 38, no. 3: 1–21. doi:10.5250/fronjwomestud.38.3.0001.

Mohanty, Chandra Talpade. 2013. "Transnational Feminist Crossings: On Neoliberalims and Radical Critique." *Signs* 38, no. 4: 967–991. https://doi.org/10.1086/669576.

Moore, David Chioni. 2001. "Is the Post- in Postcolonial the Post- in Post-Soviet? Towards a Global Postcolonial Critique." *Publications of Modern Language Association of America* 116, no. 1: 111–128. https://doi.org/10.1632/pmla.2001.116.1.111.

Näripea, Eva. 2015. "East Meets West: Tallinn Old Town and Soviet Estonian Pop Music on Screen." In *Relocating Popular Music: Pop Music, Culture and Identity*, edited by Ewa Mazierska and Georgina Gregory, 148–166. Houndmills: Palgrave Macmillan.

Plath, Ulrike. 2008. "'Euroopa viimased metslased': eestlased saksa koloniaaldiskursis 1770–1879." In *Rahvuskultuur ja tema teised*, edited by Rein Undusk, 37–64. Tallinn: Underi ja Tuglase Kirjanduskeskus.

Põldsam, Rebeka. 2020. "Otsides kvääre lugusid sõdadevahelise Eesti ajakirjandusest: Eugeenika rollist homoseksuaalsust ja transsoolisust puudutavates aruteludes." *Mäetagused* 76: 95–124.

Quieroz, Regina. 2017. "From the Exclusion of the People in Neoliberalism to Publicity Without a Public." *Palgrave Communications* 3, no. 1: 1–11. https://doi.org/10.1057/s41599-017-0032-1.

Repo, Jemima. 2015. *The Biopolitics of Gender*. New York: Oxford University Press.

Rottenberg, Catherine. 2018. *The Rise of Neoliberal Feminism*. New York: Oxford University Press.

Shih, Shu-mei. 2012. "Is the Post- in Postsocialism the Post- in Posthumanism?" *Social Text* 30, no. 1 (110): 27–50. https://doi.org/10.1215/01642472-1468308.

Slavova, Kornelia. 2006. "Looking at Western Feminisms Through the Double Lens of Eastern Europe and the Third World." In *Women and Citizenship in Central and Eastern Europe*, edited by Jasmina Lukic, Joanna Regulska, and Darja Zavirsek, 245–263. Aldershot: Ashgate.

Spade, Dean. 2015. *Normal Life: Administrative Violence, Critical Trans Politics and the Limits of Law*. Durham, NC: Duke University Press.

Spivak, Gayatri Chakravorty. 1988. "Can the Subaltern Speak?" In *Marxism and the Interpretation of Culture*, edited by Cary Nelson and Lawrence Grossberg, 271–313. London: Macmillan.

Suchland, Jennifer. 2011. "Is Postsocialism Transnational?" *Signs* 36, no. 4: 837–862. https://doi.org/10.1086/658899.

Tamm, Marek. 2016. "The Republic of Historians: Historians as Nation-Builders in Estonia (Late 1980s – Early 1990s)." *Rethinking History* 20: 154–171. https://doi.org/10.1080/13642529.2016.1153272.

Tlostanova, Madina. 2010. *Gender Epistemologies and Eurasian Borderlands*. Houndmills: Palgrave Macmillan.

Tlostanova, Madina. 2012. "Postsocialist ≠ Postcolonial? On Post-Soviet Imaginary and Global Coloniality." *Journal of Postcolonial Writing* 48, no. 2: 130–142. https://doi.org/10.1080/17449855.2012.658244.

Tlostanova, Madina. 2015. "Can the Post-Soviet Think? On Coloniality of Knowledge, External Imperial and Double Colonial Difference." *Intersections: East-European Journal of Society and Politics* 1, no. 2: 38–58. https://doi.org/10.17356/ieejsp.v1i2.38.

Tlostanova, Madina, Suruchi Thapar-Björkert, and Redi Koobak. 2019. "The Postsocialist 'Missing Other' of Transnational Feminism?" *Feminist Review* 121, no. 1: 81–87. https://doi.org/10.1177/0141778918816946.

Velmet, Aro. 2019. "Sovereignty After Gender Trouble: Language, Reproduction, and Supranatonalism in Estonia, 1980–2017." *Journal of the History of Ideas* 80, no. 3: 455–478. doi:10.1353/jhi.2019.0027.

Whelan, Heide W. 1999. *Adapting to Modernity: Family, Caste and Capitalism Among the Baltic German Nobility*. Cologne: Böhlau Verlag.

Chapter 8

Anti-colonial struggles, postcolonial subversions

An interview with Nivedita Menon

Nivedita Menon, Suruchi Thapar-Björkert and Madina Tlostanova

Suruchi Thapar-Björkert and Madina Tlostanova: You are very well known not only as an academic and analytical journalist, but also as a feminist activist criticising, among other burning issues, Hindu nationalism and the way it is played out at the nation-state level today. The present-day face of this nationalism in contrast with the anticolonial nationalist movement is strikingly conservative, elitist, militarised, and hetero-patriarchal. How would you define the most important nodes in the feminist revision of the nation state as an imagined community in India and globally?

Nivedita Menon: While we do need to mark a break between anti-colonial nationalism in India and Hindu nationalism, we must remember that anti-colonial nationalism consisted of many heterogeneous streams, and so all of the elements you mention (conservative, elitist, militarised, hetero-patriarchal) were always present at some level or the other. Mainstream nationalism (Congress and Gandhi-led) was conservative regarding class politics and actively discouraged trade unionism and anti-landlord protests by peasants. Thus Gandhi and Congress-led anti-imperialist movement was a controlled mass struggle which was never permitted to escape the limits set by the centrist Congress. Furthermore, regarding caste, Gandhi and the Congress were suspicious of B.R. Ambedkar who spoke for the Dalits of India, and at various stages his attempts to place the Dalit agenda on the table were actively thwarted. This is why Ambedkar and non-Brahmin leaders like Periyar E.V. Ramaswamy had no faith in the nationalist leadership and preferred to negotiate directly with the British. Both these leaders welcomed the Simon Commission (1928), sent from Britain to study the possibility of constitutional reform in India, which was massively boycotted by the mainstream nationalist movement. As regards militancy, there were significant political strands that refused non-violence as the method to fight imperialism. The Indian National Army (INA) was set up in South-East Asia by Subhash Chandra Bose, and militarily allied with the Japanese against British forces during the Second World War. There were also underground revolutionary groups that attempted, through assassinations of British officials and armed looting of government treasuries, to bring about an armed overthrow of British rule. As regards Hindu majoritarianism, while Hindu nationalism is explicit about this, there were strong elements of Hindu religious practices, beliefs, and culture within many of these strands of the anti-imperialist struggle. In Bengal for instance, Hindu revivalism and cultural nationalism came together in mainstream nationalism as well as among the revolutionary groups. Mainstream Congress anti-imperialism was often inflected by majoritarianism at local levels. And of course, heteropatriarchy was the default norm of every single one of these strands.

The break that we nevertheless need to mark with Hindu nationalism lies at two levels. One, all of the above trends explicitly accepted "India" to be a nation of many religious communities, while Hindu nationalism claims India to be exclusively Hindu and all other communities are either to be assimilated or rejected. The aim of Hindu nationalism is to consolidate and militarise Hindus against the internal Other. The second level of break with anti-imperialist nationalism lies in the fact that Hindu nationalism is focused on the period of "Muslim" rule preceding British colonialism rather than on the latter, a characterisation popularised by British scholars. In fact, the preceding dynasties that each replaced the other through war and conquest were distinguished by their ethnic identity rather than their religious identity, and each dynasty ruled in close collaboration with local non-Muslim ruling families and elites. But the Rashtriya Swayamsewak Sangh (RSS), which is the root organisation of Hindu nationalism founded in 1925, not only accepted and popularised this periodisation of Indian history, it explicitly opposed its members joining anti-imperialist struggles, urging them rather to keep working on the ground to build the Hindu community. At key moments of nationalist unrest, the RSS came together with the British government to ensure law and order against nationalist disruptions.

Looking at this nationalist history with a feminist perspective, we see that women participated in large numbers in all of the streams except the Hindutva one. The RSS is an exclusively male organisation, although women were eventually permitted to organise separately into a body whose work was to build the Hindu community as "Mothers of the Nation". Despite the mass presence of women in anti-imperialist movement though, feminist issues as such were not visible in the mainstream nor raised centrally until well after independence. Universal adult suffrage was always a mainstream demand, which is characteristic of anti-imperialist struggles across the globe, so feminists did not have to raise it. Issues, including the education of women and abolition of social evils such as *Sati* and child marriage, were raised by male nationalist elites not to establish gender justice, but rather, as a question of modernising Indian communities to demonstrate to British colonialism that India was capable of entering the world stage as a modern nation. Social practices among Hindus were cited by British colonialists to justify colonial rule in India to civilise the natives, and social reform was thus a key response of modernising nationalist elites, although these reforms were strongly resisted by traditionalist sections of nationalist elites. Significant female voices from all communities did raise these issues, too, as anti-patriarchal and anti-caste interventions, and are now invoked as part of the history of feminism in India – Savitribai Phule, Pandita Ramabai, and Fatima Sheikh to cite a few.

After independence, for a few decades, the state continued to have the legitimacy it had acquired during the anti-imperialist struggle, so despite the continuing presence of women in social and political movements, the nation as such was not challenged by feminists.

By the late 1970s, the secular state and its institutions (such as the courts) normalised a conception that permitted *Hindu* to be conflated with *India* especially when it came to religious personal laws that discriminated against women. Furthermore, successive secular governments patronised religious patriarchies over women's citizenship rights. As a result of the recognition of these trends, the women's movement gradually developed a perspective that was counter-nationalist and was suspicious of the homogenising and patriarchal moves that accompany mainstream nationalism as well as Hindu nationalism. The *women's movement* also gradually developed, by the late 1990s, into multiple *queer feminist movements*, which explicitly counter all forms of nationalism that cover up destabilising questions about caste, class, sexuality, gender, and religious community identity. I think this suspicion of claims to a homogeneous nation are characteristic of feminist politics globally. Or rather, I would hesitate to label as feminist any politics that is racist, militarist, nationalist, casteist, heterosexist, or pro-capitalist just because "women" are the ones articulating that politics.

Suruchi Thapar-Björkert and Madina Tlostanova: Your point on Ambedkar reminded us of a conversation that arose among Dalit feminists who suggest mainstream feminism is "savarna", embodying both upper caste and class (Hindu) privileges. This same discussion (re)surfaced on your supposed rejection of intersectionality as a useful tool for feminism (for example, the debate in Arya and Rathore's anthology, *Dalit Feminist Theory* (2020)). Could you say a little bit more about your stance on this?

On the same track do you agree with the claim that the new social movements of the 1970s and 1980s (mainly left-leaning) foregrounded the experiences of middle-class upper-caste groups, as some feminists such as Sharmila Rege, Mary, and Meena Gopal have claimed (Rege 1998; John and Gopal 2020).

Nivedita Menon: Regarding the recent conversation among Dalit scholars as to whether "feminism is Brahminism" or "feminism is Ambedkarism", what has emerged is that just as there is not one "Indian feminism", there is not one Dalit opinion on feminism. The first position, "feminism is Brahminism" offered a critique of feminism itself as being *savarna* on the grounds that feminism necessarily considers only "women" as its base and cannot take on board any other identity, especially caste. For this position, Dalit feminism is a contradiction in terms, and it was critical of all those Dalits who called themselves feminists. This claim was rejected by strongly articulated Dalit feminist arguments, for instance by Anannya G. Madonna (2020), which laid claim to powerful traditions of Dalit and non-Brahmin feminist history that have foregrounded multiple identities of privilege and dis-privilege, including race, class, and caste.

My critique of the easy spread of the term intersectionality was in fact along similar lines – that mainstream elite feminism in India has always been challenged by multiple voices along caste, sexual identity, and class lines, from the 19th century onwards until today. I continue to be puzzled by Mary John and Meena Gopal's response to my argument (reproduced in Arya and Rathore 2020), which suggests that my critique of the term "intersectionality" implies my refusal to recognise that feminism is inflected by multiple identities of privilege and dis-privilege. On the contrary, as John herself acknowledges at the beginning of her response, my argument against the universal use of "intersectionality" was based on the specificity of its original context, to begin with. It was used by Kimberle Crenshaw in the particular context of the law in the US but has become widely applied in "gender mainstreaming" global agendas of governmentality. Another problem is that the term has congealed into non-recognition of multiple axes of identity, seeing race as the primary oppression, thus losing out on the capacity of the term to conceptually capture multiple identities in one location. I tried to address the political and theoretical implications of this loss. Finally, my argument is that we need to be learning from the ways in which feminists of this subcontinent have framed feminism within multiple structures of identity from the 19th century onwards, leading to fierce debates within "the women's movement", and the constant displacement of this movement as new voices of critique continually emerged from marginalised groups – Dalits, trans-people and sex workers being among the more recent ones. To pack this long and complex history into the term "intersectionality" that arose in a different spatio-temporal location at a much later stage, is to flatten all difference, and to accept that theory will always emerge from the West, into which the empirical experience of other parts of the world can be fitted.

The politics of caste insistently poses a question mark over the assumed commonality of female experience, thus challenging the identity of "woman", the supposed subject of feminist politics; while the politics of sexuality throws into disarray the certainty of recognisably gender-coded bodies, the male-female bipolarity, the naturalising of heterosexual desire and its institutionalisation in marriage (Menon 2009a). The discourse that does stabilise the identity of women along one axis is the governmentalising drive of the state, which has attached gender to *development*, so that gender is stabilised and looped right back to become a synonym for women – that is, "women" as they are located in patriarchal society. I argue therefore that the politics of sexuality and caste that *fragment* the identity of "woman" is more productive and rich, from the point of view of feminist ethics, than the latter stabilising trend.

Coming now to Arya and Rathore (2020), their introduction to the volume seems to uncritically accept Mary John's and Meena Gopal's critique of my argument about intersectionality, on which I have already set out my position above. My rejection of the term *conceptually* has been taken with no basis at all, to mean the rejection of the *politics* of caste that fractures the identity of "women" and to that extent complicates feminism. This is a mistaken reading of my argument.

In addition, Arya and Rathore's Introduction conflates any kind of activism by women in politics with "feminism". Thus they term as "Indian feminist" the anti-reservation slogan by women – "We don't want unemployed husbands" (implying both that "meritorious upper-caste" candidates will lose jobs to "undeserving" Dalits and OBCs through caste-based reservations, as well as that women will marry only men of their own castes). There is nothing feminist in this position, nor did these women claim to be feminist. These slogans were part of anti-reservation protests by people of "upper castes". That was the politics of this slogan, and it has been attacked by all feminists as both patriarchal and casteist.

The introduction also refers to my position on "sex-work as work", and rejects this as "problematic from the perspective of Dalit feminism". Their argument is that Dalit women enter sex work as a result of being born into stigmatised castes, and that to take the position that sex work should be understood to be "work" and destigmatised, is to accept the objectification of Dalit women. First, the assumption here is that "Dalit sex workers" and "Dalit feminists" are necessarily two separate identities, based on the presumption that sex-workers cannot be feminist. Second, this is an on-going debate among feminists globally – one position that says *prostitution is violence*, and the other that *sex work is work*. The first wants abolition of prostitution, the other, decriminalisation and destigmatisation of sex work. The debate cannot simply be posited as Dalit feminism versus (implied) *savarna* feminism, for this debate globally cuts across caste and race. The "sex work is work" position is caricatured by Arya and Rathore as "elitist" when in fact it comes into academic feminist discourse *from unionised sex workers*, who organise for their rights, and claim their place in the feminist movement. To claim the "prostitution as violence" position as *the* Dalit feminist position is to silence Dalit feminists who are unionised sex workers. I witnessed this silencing myself at a large convention of women against the Hindu Right held in 2017 in Nagpur, in which participating sex-worker unions were publicly shamed by some Dalit activists from the podium and had to leave.

One of the arguments against sex work as work, made both at Nagpur and by Arya and Rathore (2020) is that B.R. Ambedkar called prostitution a disgraceful occupation. At the Nagpur convention (2017) it was additionally stated from the podium that in 1936, Ambedkar refused to accept financial contributions from Dalit sex workers of Kamatipura (the well-known "red light" area of Mumbai) unless they gave up this life which brought shame to the community. Arya and Rathore present his position on prostitution as coming from an understanding of how it dehumanises women, but their spin on this does not make it *the* Dalit feminist position. For instance, until 1945, Dr Ambedkar argued that Aboriginal Tribes (Adivasis) did not have the "political sense" to use their opportunities wisely and therefore should be excluded from suffrage and administered by a statutory commission (Ambedkar 1945). However, by the 1950s his position had changed. Similarly, in his devastating critique of Gandhi (Ambedkar 2006), he spoke of nature merely as a resource for humans and of humans as superior to nature. But after his conversion to Buddhism, he developed an ecologically sensitive perspective geared towards social justice, in which humans are part of nature themselves (Ravi Kumar 2014). We may wonder therefore, precisely because of his sharp political insight, if he might not have listened to what Dalit sex workers had to say and changed his views on excluding sex workers from mainstream politics? If anything, it is the "prostitution is violence" position that is characteristic of elite non-sex worker feminists. There is no one "Dalit feminist" position here.

Suruchi Thapar-Björkert and Madina Tlostanova: From many encounters with feminist scholars and activists in the global South we have an impression that they are less interested in initiating dialogues with feminists from the former state socialist countries or much less in looking for any parallels in our histories of subversion and resistance, linked respectively with the Socialist and capitalist modernities each with its darker colonial side. In your highly popular book *Seeing like a Feminist* (2012) there is a chapter "Victims or agents" in which you reflect on several problems and categories which are important for feminist struggles locally and globally: among them, commodification, sex work, trafficking versus migration, abortion, pornography, etc. Some of these issues are extremely important for the post-socialist countries as well. Yet you never address or mention Eastern Europe, Central Asia, or Russia either as an example of these tendencies or as a source of distinctly specific voices and perspectives? Why is it so? What do you think are the main reasons for the lack of dialogues between the postsocialist and postcolonial feminisms? Why is that feminist thinkers and activists in the global South today do not seem to be interested in such collaborations?

Nivedita Menon: I would say that perhaps the responsibility for initiating dialogues is always a mutual one, and yes, there have not been many initiatives from either side – feminists from former state socialist countries or from the global South – to bring about such a dialogue. I consider this interview to be such an initiative of course. There have also been interventions in syllabi of women's studies courses in some Indian universities, since the 1990s, to include feminist scholarship analysing the collapse of state socialism in East Europe. So there has been a mutual interest, but perhaps not the resources required to reach out in any substantial sense. The first priority for feminists in India has been to link to feminist politics in other countries of South Asia, in order to counter the militarisation and hyper nationalism of the region. The next level of solidarity and scholarly exchange has been with the global South, say, Africa and Latin America. East Europe is still in many ways seen to have had a very different trajectory from India, a more First World one, and there is no immediate way in which that experience resonates with ours, especially as East Europe from our perspective, is very much the "West" with its post- Enlightenment baggage. At the same time, our access to world literature is marked by the global hegemony of American and Western European theoretical frameworks and publishing industry. We in India need first to see East Europe as marginal to the Europe we imagine when we use the term, only then would such dialogues become possible.

Suruchi Thapar-Björkert and Madina Tlostanova: In several of your texts and speeches you refer to Virginia Woolf's famous quotation that as a woman she has no country. This reminds us of a similar trajectory in a number of the former state Socialist countries with their hardening conservative atmosphere, extreme nationalism, religious revivalism, and patriarchy. A particularly striking case is Yugoslavia where ethnic-national discrimination, conflicts, and civil war atrocities were most powerfully criticised by feminists. With the division of Yugoslavia and the hardening of extreme state nationalism in its successor states, many feminist activists and thinkers were persecuted and accused of collaborating with or being nostalgic about communism (as communism supposedly gave them rights) and even had to leave their countries. In other words, the same mechanism of accusing feminists of betraying the national interests was at work. Why do you think the postsocialist Yugoslavia and the postcolonial India share this pattern almost literally? And what role was played here by the fact that both countries belonged to the so-called non-aligned movement in the Cold War logic?

Nivedita Menon: Feminist politics is not compatible with nationalism which implies internal homogeneity, hyper masculinity, hatred of internal and external others, and the shoring up of the ethnically pure, heterosexual patriarchal family as the guarantor of identity. Similarly, internationalist communist politics implies a refusal to ally within the nation, with class elites, and insists on building cross-border solidarities with anti-capitalist and ecological struggles. So it is not only in postsocialist Yugoslavia and postcolonial India that this pattern is visible, of feminists and communists being considered traitors to the nation. I do not really see any link with the Cold War era's "non-aligned politics" in this; rather, what we have to look at seriously is the ways in which feminism can and should counter the nation.

The reasons why feminists cannot be nationalists are foundational to any feminism committed to radical social transformation. The heterosexual patriarchal family as the cornerstone of the Nation – this is the arrangement that has successfully normalised unjust and unequal forms of identification, property ownership, and access to resources. The story of the nation-state from the 18th century onwards has been told as a heroic saga, of struggle against tyranny, and expanding frontiers of citizenship. That narrative renders unthinkable the closures and fractures, the marginalisations and silencings, that are constitutive of the identity of citizen. Indeed, the "nation" can only represent dominant, majoritarian values – minorities reasserting "their" culture can never claim the legitimacy of representing the nation, whether it is Muslims in India or Native Americans in the US. All nations produce a "national identity" through anti-democratic measures. In the classic case of France, for example, Eugen Weber (1976) has argued that the acculturation process in the 19th century – by which the inhabitants of the area that became France were made "French" – was as overwhelming as colonialism. No project of nationalism is ever "completed" – it is frozen at some point or the other through a coercive apparatus backed by the sanction of violence that prevents the further articulation of other voices and identities with similar aspirations. In addition, in the Indian context, nationalist discourse has been intimately tied to a notion of "development" that is capitalist, unjust, and ecologically unsustainable.

This is why I hold that any radical transformative politics today must be postnational. Here the *post* of postnationalism is to be understood not in the sense of *after* but in the sense of having *passed through* the nation. When I use the term postnational (Menon 2009b) therefore, it is both to build on and depart from scholarship that has problematised the nation-state in various ways. However, in the contemporary moment, it seems only two kinds of reactions to corporate globalisation are possible – either turning to the nation-state to reassert its old authority against Empire, or on the other hand, assuming its demise and celebrating globalisation. The latter trend is of course now on the wane, with the rise of nationalist Right in different parts of the world and the crisis of EU, Brexit, NAFTA, and so on. But the point is that both reactions are entirely misplaced.

Here my insistence on an uncompromising critique of the nation, therefore, is the very obverse of the argument for postnationalism "from above" made from two opposed positions – one, in which the sovereignty of the nation is sought to be bypassed in the interests of global capital, and the other, a Habermasian celebration of global universalism. Rather, the kind of postnationalism I refer to is better described as being "from below". Its politics can be represented by any idea that is counter-hegemonic, whether that hegemony refers to development, sexuality, caste/community, or any other. But equally importantly, it must be seen as having two dimensions – one, "over" the nation, across national borders, and two, "under" the nation, resisting inclusion into the "larger" national identity, insisting on space/time trajectories that do not mesh with progressivist dominant narratives of nation and history.

While the first dimension is comprehensible as "internationalism", the other dimension of postnational politics – "under" the nation – is less obvious as a strategy, because it does not assume the prior existence of the nation. More significantly, its subversive edge may lie in the exact opposite of what animates the politics of "over" the nation – that is, the strategy of exit and *movement* across borders. The interrogation of the nation from under may involve rather, the *refusal* to move, as for example in the struggles against big dams or mining operations that involve massive relocation of populations. From the perspective of counter-heteronormative politics, this dimension may involve claiming histories that run parallel to, that do not intersect with, that of the nation. Or claiming forms of family and kinship that produce identity that are splintered and fluid, that resist inclusion into larger formations. A startling moment, de-normalising the idea of family, is produced when *hijras* contesting elections claim that precisely because they cannot have children, they will be less selfish and corrupt. Sex-workers refusing to shift their work-premises in the face of intimidation by local communities force a recognition of the imbrication of sex-work in everyday life. This *politics of refusal* thus implies the simultaneous transformation, through practices of everyday life, of the place where you insist on staying.

Suruchi Thapar-Björkert and Madina Tlostanova: In the nationalist attacks at your political activism, you are often accused of being a leftist and at times even a communist. How do you define your political allegiances yourself? What is your political and social ideal?

Nivedita Menon: I see myself as part of a queer feminist, anti-caste, ecologically inflected new left. My utopian ideal today is influenced by the massive street protests against governments all over the world since the beginning of this century. In all of this, the possibly irreparable fracture between "the people" and the political elites is what is becoming evident. I don't agree with some analysts who argue that democracy itself is collapsing under its own weight. Rather, what these mass uprisings (mainly nonviolent civil disobedience, but spilling over into violent incidents as well) reveal is the insufficiency of representative democracy. My utopian dream is that some form of localised, decentralised, direct democracy is what may eventually emerge. I think there may be emerging a large-scale rejection of political elites across the board.

Suruchi Thapar-Björkert and Madina Tlostanova: But would you not say that the social protection and public works programmes in India together with the institutions of local governance (Panchayati Raj with reservations for women) brings you closer to the representative model of democracy? Also these programmes may not bring about redistribution of wealth but they definitely enhance the rights of the lower castes.

Nivedita Menon: The welfare state in the global North, too, worked well for three decades, and the Nehruvian socialist state in India also managed a balance between capitalist growth and distribution. The programmes you refer to in India, which ensure right to education, information, employment in rural areas, all do contribute to redistribution and people's control over government and, of course, their own lives. However, these policies were brought about by pressure from powerful people's movements and were able to influence the Congress-led government from 2004 to 2009. This alliance won elections again in 2009, but turned decisively towards neoliberal policies and dismantling of social welfare systems. This process has accelerated unimaginably under the BJP-led government since 2014.

My point is that representative government has revealed its inability to "represent the people" all over the globe since the late 20th century. For instance, hundreds of thousands of Americans marched against war post 9/11, but even under President Obama the wars being conducted by the US did not end. This is because governments are controlled by military industrial complexes and by capital, both global and local. I find the term "populism" not very useful therefore, because it ignores the vast masses who oppose current regimes, which nevertheless continue to win elections through the very structures of representative government, which has ceased to represent "the people". I refer to the indirect system of election in the US, the first-past-the-post system in India, and so on. Here I am not even going into the ways in which elections are subverted (in 2000 in the US when Bush was awarded a controversial election; in May 2019 in India where the Election Commission played a dubious role; and in Bolivia in 2019, when the US-backed coup unseated Evo Morales).

As to the example you cite, Panchayati Raj institutions in India, in fact, the introduction of 33% reservation for women in local representative bodies has been demonstrated by many studies to have increased the power of dominant castes and groups, replacing men of marginalised communities with women of dominant communities. This is why there has been a persistent demand for "quotas within quotas" within women's reservations, so that marginalised castes and groups may be represented within the women's quota.

So it is not an unquestioned fact that, as you put it, "these programmes may not bring about redistribution of wealth but they definitely enhance the rights of the lower castes". They have enhanced the rights of lower castes only where there are powerful parties or movements of lower castes already present, to use the policies to their advantage. Where these are not present, such policies have benefited powerful groups and castes.

The question that we should ask, rather, is what can replace representative government? One answer is local governments, as close to direct democracy as possible. Of course, this would mean greater control by local elites, but the current system also does not protect the powerless from local elites. Nor does the state any longer play the role that was envisaged for it at the time of independence, of preventing the local from remaining dens of ignorance, narrow-mindedness, and communalism, as Ambedkar put it. Nor is it only the village that maintains caste, gender, and community-based discrimination. It is increasingly evident that in India cities too display the same dynamics. And currently under Hindu Rashtra, the state and its institutions directly promote casteism and communalism.

So my point is that we need at least to *start* imagining the kinds of political systems of local, direct democracy that will also challenge class, caste, and gender hierarchies and structures of power.

Suruchi Thapar-Björkert and Madina Tlostanova: In the majority of the postsocialist countries, women's movements today are not in the best shape, experiencing pressure from the nation state, persistent attacks from patriarchal, religious, neoliberal, and other fronts. As an active and articulate fighter with these tendencies in India, you know that one of the remaining contesting spaces until recently was the university which is now going through a shrinking of academic freedoms and closing of the centres of critical thinking. Something very similar we find today not only in Putin's neo-imperial Russia, but also in Orban's Hungary which has recently exiled the Central European University, which has caused a wide protest movement. In your view, how promising are such interventions of the political society to use Partha Chatterjee's term? Can these students, women's, and other social movements or initiatives really change anything in India and in other countries?

Nivedita Menon: To begin with, I see university protests very much as part of civil society in Partha Chatterjee's terms, not political society, because they use the language of citizenship rights and demand access to state resources through the law. The university simultaneously embodies a promise and negates it – it is a promise of a space for knowledge generation and transmission, for critical thought and reflection, for freedom of the mind. But the university also reproduces historical privilege, shores up settled bodies of knowledge, and trains young people to acknowledge authority and to occupy their place in society as it is. That the subversive promise survives despite its negation – this is what marks the university, more than any other modern institution, as a threat to status quo. The public university system in India ensured access to higher education for historically marginalised groups and first-generation learners. It is the coming together of such a diverse student body that produces the space for challenging mainstream hegemony. I think university spaces do have the potential to raise a powerful challenge to authoritarianism, neoliberalism, and ethnocentrism. At the same time a powerful authoritarian state has all the coercive machinery at its command to move brutally against any mass movement. As state power clamps down more brutally though, I believe that resistance will learn to take new forms. Indeed, we have no option but to learn new forms of resistance, for the current regime in India intends to dismantle the public university system altogether, as the New Education Policy indicates. This envisages further reduction of state investment in education and for educational infrastructure to be developed solely through loans to be taken by universities. The entire system is also to lose all autonomy by being brought under the current Hindutva regime.

The threat of the public university to power is very sharp and clear. Those of us who are part of it need to reimagine our work and think of ways of building knowledge commons outside of formal institutions that will bring back in those that have been excluded in the past and who will be further excluded by the new systems that will be put in place.

References

Ambedkar, B. R. 1945. "Communal Deadlock and a Way to Solve It." Address to All India Scheduled Castes Federation, May 6, 1945.

Ambedkar, B. R. 2006. "Gandhism." In *Essential Writings of BR Ambedkar*, edited by Valerian Rodrigues. New Delhi: Oxford University Press.

Arya, Sunaina, and Aakash Singh Rathore, eds. 2020. *Dalit Feminist Theory*. Oxon: Routledge.

John, E. Mary, and Meena Gopal. 2020. "Responses to Indian Feminists' Objections." In *Dalit Feminist Theory*, edited by Sunaina Arya and Aakash Singh Rathore. India: Routledge.

Madonna, Anannya G. 2020. "Ambedkarism Is Feminism: A Response to 'Feminism Is Brahminism'." https://velivada.com/2020/06/18/ambedkarism-is-feminism-a-response-to-feminism-is-brahminism/

Menon, Nivedita. 2009a. "Sexuality, Caste, Governmentality: Contests Over 'Gender' in India." *Feminist Review* no. 91.

Menon, Nivedita. 2009b. "Thinking Through the Postnation." *Economic and Political Weekly* (March 7).

Ravi Kumar, V. M. 2014. "Green Democracy: Relevance of Ambedkar's Ideas for Indian Environmentalism." *Indian Journal of Dalit and Tribal Studies and Action* 2, no. 1 (2) (June).

Rege, Sharmila. 1998. "Dalit Women Talk Differently: A Critique of 'Difference' and Towards a Dalit Feminist Standpoint Position." *Economic and Political Weekly* (October 31): WS39–WS46.

Weber, Eugen. 1976. *Peasants into Frenchmen: The Modernization of Rural France, 1880–1914*. Stanford, CA: Stanford University Press.

Chapter 9

Uneventful feminist protest in post-Maidan Ukraine

Nation and colonialism revisited

Maria Mayerchyk and Olga Plakhotnik

One hot summer day on 18 June 2017, a huge unprecedented scandal broke out in the Ukrainian feminist and LGBT[1] communities and ignited an explosion of debates lasting until now. The reason for the collective anxiety was a hand-written placard at the Kyiv Pride march that day. The text of the placard said, "*Death to the nation, queer to enemies*", mimicking the structure and ridiculing the message of the well-known ultra-right greeting "Glory to the nation! Death to its enemies!" It was drawn in a telling combination of the colours: the first line was red and black – the colours of the Ukrainian far-right flag, while the second line was painted in violet and black reflecting the anarcho-feminist flag and accompanied with hearts of the same colours (Figure 9.1).

Figure 9.1 A handmade placard at the 2017 Kyiv Pride march with a text "Death to the nation, queer to enemies" (in Ukrainian)

Source: Maria Mayerchyk and Olga Plakhotnik

In the following days after Pride, many LGBT organisations and activists fiercely criticised the placard, condemned it for being "a provocation", an expression of disrespect to the Ukrainian nation. (The second part of the placard was seen as a meaningless combination of the words.) The Ukrainian activist community called for identifying and punishing the placard's authors. Some activists went as far as to suggest informing governmental authorities about a threat to national security. Since then, no significant feminist or LGBT street rally in any city of Ukraine has been organised without a new tide of debate as to how to prevent the occurrence of disturbing political messages, whether organisers should censor placards, and what else needs to be done. Closely following and analysing discussions around the placard, we observe that the "Death to the nation" statement hits a nerve, connected to one of the most pressing issues in contemporary post-Maidan Ukraine – the issue of nation and nationalism.

The Maidan (also known as the *#Euromaidan* or the *Revolution of Dignity*) is a Ukrainian revolutionary event that took place in winter 2013–2014 and lasted for more than three months, comprising peaceful and violent phases. The Maidan, subsequent annexation of Crimea, and intervention of the Russian military into the eastern part of Ukraine entailed a sweeping political transformation across the region. Notably, more and more scholars use the term "post-Maidan Ukraine" in order to underline this rupture.

In this chapter, we explore how feminist imaginaries and activist practices have been recalibrated in the rapidly changing political landscape of post-Maidan Ukraine with respect to the language of "nationalism" and "colonialism". Through our examination we have identified a relatively new form of feminist activism – we call it "uneventful" – which pursues both anti-nationalist and anti-colonial agendas. Analysing open-access online data and materials of participant observation, we explore this phenomenon to understand how the new activism challenges the dominant discourses, troubles mainstream forms of feminist and LGBT activism, and reshapes the entire Ukrainian activist scene. Introducing a new social phenomenon, we offer broader theorising of contemporary East European feminisms at the intersection of postsocialism, (post)colonialism, and circuits of global imperial power.

Reflecting on our positionality with respect to this research, we have to acknowledge our insider position as participants of the Maidan and members of the Ukrainian feminist communities during the period under study. This position has opened up certain epistemic possibilities while foreclosing others. Being "materially discursively located" (Lykke 2010, 5) in the marginalised space of postsocialist Eastern Europe in a time of war, in our gendered bodies and non-mainstream feminist activism, we occupy a position that enables problematising some views regarding Ukrainian feminist and LGBT activism, including those prevailing in Western scholarship. Simultaneously, often seen as "academic" outsiders in "non-academic" activist communities, we possess specific privileges and less vulnerability than many grassroots activists in Ukraine. Our recent affiliation with Western universities aggravates this predicament even further.

Ukrainian civic nationalism: the context

Before the early 2000s, feminism existed in Ukraine predominantly in a form of discourse, meaning that it has been developed mostly in an academic context by particular scholars and research centres. The issues of nation and nationalism were at the core of this scholarship, sometimes discussed with reference to the postcolonial framework. Analysing academic debates in the Kyiv Center for Gender Studies launched in 1998 within the Institute of Literary Studies of National Academy of Sciences of Ukraine, Tatiana Zhurzhenko noted that this scholarship:

> identifies itself with some kind of "postcolonial feminism", but the target of the "post-colonial" critique is not so clear. It is not a "Western-centered discourse" as is usual in post-colonial studies, but first of all, Russian (Soviet) cultural influence and dominance – past and present.
>
> (Zhurzhenko 2001, 11)

In the subsequent publications, Zhurzhenko coined the term "national feminism" (2008) to designate the dominant feminist discourse in Ukraine. Whether the adjective "national" refers to a nation-state or ethnicity/culture/language, however, remains unclear: in Ukrainian, unlike English, national has two quite distinct meanings. This semantic ambiguity has been historically determined. While in English, the adjective "national" reflects the context of the established nation-states, Ukrainians, on the contrary, were a stateless subjugated ethnic group in the frame of the multi-ethnic empires and then a republic of the USSR, so "national" never had a state-related meaning. Traditionally national referred to ethnicity/language and started acquiring a new rendition related to the nation-state only after 1991. We assume that in 2008, the adjective *national* in the "national feminism" concept embraced a wide range of meanings from ethnic-centred to state-centred. At that time, the rhetoric of *nationalism* was typically applied to ultra-right ideologies but never to feminist discourse/practices.

After the Maidan and outbreak of the war, more and more activist collectives and individuals in Ukraine started identifying with "*nationalist* feminism" using direct references to postcolonialism. These tendencies can be traced, for example, in *Feminism UA* – the largest Ukrainian feminist community on Facebook:

> We are a postcolonial state, a postcolonial nation, so we can't escape nationalism. . . . It is not nationalism but Bolshevik imperialism that has led Ukrainian feminism to a dead end and has strangled both feminism and nationalism. That is why we should not reject nationalism but claim it back. We must take it back from the right-wing radicals and re-appropriate it. I propose a slogan for the next rally: "Feminism is the Ukrainian national idea".
>
> (Facebook comment in *Feminism UA*, March 2017)[2]

The increasing popularity of the nationalist rhetoric is typical for post-Maidan Ukrainian society and has been reflected upon by the leading Ukrainian scholars and public intellectuals. In their opinion, in a course of the Maidan and the subsequent war, the very meaning of Ukrainian nationalism has been substantially reframed. They argue that the events gave rise to a new form of nationalism which is now "civic" or "political" in contrast to an outdated one, which is "ethnic" or "cultural". New civic nationalism is perceived as all-inclusive "healthy positive nationalism uniting the political nation, regardless of ethnic belonging" (cited after Kulyk 2014, 105). The meaning of nationalism, therefore, has been drifting from being ethnic-centred to becoming (western-like) state-centred. Eventually, in contemporary Ukrainian society, the imaginary of new civic nationalism is widely praised as progressive, gravitating toward Europe, and deemed "nothing more than love for one's people and desire to see one's country free" (Kulyk 2016, 604).

Being driven by the same desire "to see our country free," we cannot, however, celebrate civic nationalism wholeheartedly for two main reasons. Firstly, we see how civic nationalism participates in the construction of new othering that produces a new class of "improper citizens" and "improper Ukrainians". The second reason is the uncritical Eurocentrism of the discourse of civic nationalism. In what follows, we consider both arguments in greater detail.

Notwithstanding its all-inclusive image and wide recognition, civic nationalism is involved in a new massive wave of othering and stigmatisation that split up Ukrainian society yet again. This othering emerged simultaneously with the rise of "civic nationalism", and, apparently, in direct relation to it. While the participants of the Maidan were constructed through "Revolution of Dignity" rhetoric as advanced Euro-oriented citizens who gained/deserve dignity, another part of the population (its scope is unclear and boundaries are shifting but those are typically people from eastern and south regions of Ukraine) is designated as backward and not emancipated enough. These are people who, it was said, are "stuck in Soviet past" and have not developed a proper level of "national consciousness", therefore, are deprived of dignity. The image of indignity has been fostered through a derogative and dehumanising name *vata*, coined during the "Revolution of Dignity". The word *vata* (literally "cotton wool") is derivative from *vatnik* – a cheap cotton wool-padded jacket which was a standard outfit of the working-class Soviet people, peasants, and prisoners.[3] *Vatnik* was also a cliché outfit of Soviet people in the Western imaginary during the Cold War era. Being an invective, *vata* (and *vatnik*) refers to Sovietness equated to poverty and backwardness; recently, it gained an additional meaning of stupidity as these people have "cotton wool instead of the brain" in popular rhetoric. Taking into account that today more than 5 million people from eastern regions of Ukraine are directly affected by the war and considered to be in need of humanitarian aid (in the rhetoric of international institutions (OCHA 2020) and the Ukrainian government), it seems the new wave of othering is aimed at one of the most vulnerable segments of the population.

That is why, in our opinion, it is crucially important to engage with the imaginary of civic nationalism in a more critical way. As Said once suggested, nationalist resistance to imperialism has to be "always critical of itself" (Said 1994, 219).

Colonialism and coloniality: the framework

Before the Maidan, the rhetoric of nationalism had rather negative connotations in the Ukrainian public discourse. After the Maidan, the negative rendition of nationalism started being interpreted as a legacy of the Soviet past:

> Since the early years of independence, this [nationalism] has been one of the most contentious issues in Ukrainian politics and society, as people considering nationalism a driving force of national liberation clashed with those adhering to the Soviet postulate relating nationalism to Nazism.
>
> (Kulyk 2016, 603)

In the cited paper by Volodymyr Kulyk, the negative Soviet attitude to nationalism is opposed to its Western interpretation, which is deemed positive. The author quotes a focus group participant saying: "If you come to America, to any European country, you will see how [strong] their patriotism and nationalism is. Flags are everywhere there. This is normal" (Kulyk 2016, 605). So, Kulyk concludes, "nationalism plays an important positive role in many societies, including those they [people] view as examples for Ukraine" (ibid., 604–605).

In this chapter, we do not argue against any of these statements but want to bring into our discussion a perspective of colonial power which, in turn, is essential in our interpretation of nationalism. The West does indeed praise nationalisms but only the Western nationalisms, whereas anti-colonial non-Western nationalisms, in the Western view, are "essentially condemnable", as Said put it (1994, 216). Paying attention to this nuance, we find it useful to build our perspective upon "coloniality" – a central concept in decolonial thinking. According to Anibal Quijano, coloniality is "still the most general form of domination in the world today, once colonialism as an explicit political order was destroyed" (Quijano 2007, 170). From the perspective of decolonial thinking, coloniality is interpreted as a fundamental matrix of power, which operates through the control of four interrelated domains: economy, authority or governmentality, gender and sexuality, and production of knowledge and subjectivity (cited after Gržinić, Kancler, and Rexhepi 2020). In line with this conceptualisation of coloniality, we develop a critical perspective on two main regimes of colonial power that together create a particular framework for marginalisation and subjugation of Ukraine. Firstly, it is easily recognisable Russian imperialism, which positions Ukraine as its own "little" province. Secondly, it is less recognisable hegemony of Western imperialism that positions Ukraine as a not fully modernised /civilised periphery of Europe, which has been corrupted by the Soviet regime, then "left to the normalizing processes of democratization and Europeanization" (Suchland 2011, 846), and yet remains lagging hopelessly behind. Between these two rival imperial centres, Ukraine, in Maria Sonevytsky's words, appears as

> a quintessential borderland, a buffer, a threshold, the closest "elsewhere" to a European or Russian "here." Its "wild" peoples and territories, observed by so many outsiders, have been tempered by its proximity to those "civilized" observers.
>
> (Sonevytsky 2019, 4)

In economic terms, for both imperial centres, the main value of Ukraine is to provide a cheap labour force for construction, agriculture, care work, and sex service for first-class Western and Russian citizens. As Yuliya Yurchenko aptly interpreted the cause of the crisis and the war, "Ukraine fell victim to the relentless spread of the empire of capital where Russian and Western capitalist geopolitical imperialisms collided" (Yurchenko 2020, n.p.).

Building our study on this framework, we were looking at the contemporary Ukrainian feminist activist scene in search of groups or initiatives that challenge a soothing discourse of civic nationalism justified by postcolonialism. While mainstream feminist discourse in post-Maidan Ukraine mostly seeks to comply with militarised nationalism (Mayerchyk and Plakhotnik 2019), other responses to the post-Maidan political transformations also take place. In the following sections, we scrutinise these alternatives zooming in on a new phenomenon – *uneventful feminist activism* – with particular focus on how the discourses of nationalism and coloniality are in play.

Uneventful feminist activism: positionality and strategy

At the time of our study, several activist collectives shared a critical stance towards nationalist and neoliberal tendencies in Ukrainian feminist and LGBT activism, as well as society as a whole. All of these collectives operated in the modus of uneventfulness, anonymity, and unsuccessfulness (opposing the capitalist meaning of success). We designate this form of activism as "uneventful", borrowing the term from urban activism studies in Central and Eastern Europe by Elżbieta Korolczuk and Kerstin Jacobsson. The authors define uneventful activism as "low-key, small-scale, and initiated by individuals or small, informal groups, and little discussed in the mass media and public discourse" (Jacobsson and Korolczuk 2019, 6). They argue that uneventful activism challenges the narrow understanding of politics and instantiates an alternative way of "political becoming", and thereby call for studying uneventful protest to provide a fair account of the civil society and conceptualise its development in a more nuanced way.

Supporting this appeal, we borrow the concept and partially reframe it with respect to the phenomenon we explore in our study. For us, uneventful activism refers to the particular political activist positionality that shares the ideas and spirit of intersectional solidarities and feminist critique of nationalism, capitalism, racism, homophobia, transphobia, and cisheterosexism. Residing on multiple margins of a variety of activist scenes – namely, feminist, LGBT, leftist, and anarchist – these groups have developed specific strategies and tactics combining different forms of online and offline activism. Political art is of particular importance to the groups' positionalities. For example, famous for sharp political caricatures in online spaces, *FRAU* group positions itself as an *artivist* (i.e., activism + art) collective.[4] Feminist anti-capitalism sewing cooperative *ReSew* claims its adherence to *craftivism*.[5] The *Pva Pva* group used *street art* – graffiti – as their medium.[6] *ZBOKU* describes itself as a *"creative initiative"*.[7] *Grouping Salt* is also a creative collective seeking "to transform art from an empty elitist canon to a political statement" (*Grouping Salt* Manifesto[8]). *Lyeska* channel "resists inequality and erasing" through drawing comics.[9] *Rozmyta povistka* vocal-music band positions itself as a "political project of karaoke . . . that is about a chance to sing when there is no chance to speak" (Rozmyta povistka 2019).

Another significant feature of uneventful feminist groups in Ukraine is their deliberate refusal to become institutionalised and included in the neoliberal grant economy that constantly requires demonstrating "successful cases" and providing quantitative indicators of "success", typically measured by numbers of "events",[10] participants, and "likes". Aiming to meet these requirements and attract as many people as possible, the institutionalised feminist groups (NGOs) are often forced to choose a rather populist agenda while giving up more critical political issues.[11] In contrast, uneventful activist collectives reject the idea of success and mass-influence, so build their digital and offline feminist interventions differently. As the *Grouping Salt* collective states, "being queer anarcho feminists, we don't care about 'mass character' or 'effectiveness.' We are not fighting for a place under the Sun; we create our own place and our own Sun" (*Grouping Salt* Manifesto[12]). Members of the *ReSew* cooperative reflect on their position in a similar way:

> At some point, I decided to stop fighting (for a concept, or the 8 of March rally, or the Kyiv Pride); instead, I stepped aside and do what I believe is the right thing to do. This is my anti-capitalist protest, too. . . . I will not make every effort to prove that my agenda is right while somebody else's is wrong. This reminds me of capitalist rat races. I won't do this because I care about the resources of my own and my comrades.
>
> (ReSew 2019)

The rhetoric of care in the quotation above is not accidental but rather indicative of one more significant feature of uneventful feminisms, namely, prioritising mutual care and support in their political agenda: "self-care as warfare" (Ahmed 2014). Echoing the *ReSew* collective, activists from *Rozmyta povistka* also describe the band as "a project of care about ourselves and our comrades, a way to cope with activist (and not only) burnout" (Rozmyta povistka 2019). Furthermore, all uneventful activist groups mentioned in this paper compose a network for joint activities, sharing resources, mutual support and care.

The search for alternative ways of political engagement has led uneventful activism to develop digital and non-digital practices that embrace *anonymity* as a way to act below the radar of capitalist forms of recognisability and success. This strategy determined the fact that some groups have left Facebook (which was the most popular social media in Ukraine at the time of our study) and moved their online activity to other digital platforms such as Telegram.[13] Such a move enables them to secure anonymity more efficiently and leave a neoliberal online platform with targeted commercials and a strong measurement of one's visibility. It is worth noticing that Telegram channels do not have options for "likes" or reader's comments; the possibility to reach a channel's author is also limited. Importantly, anonymity facilitates a powerful discourse of collective action that is focused on a political message instead of prioritising a publicly visible individual leadership. Rejecting the neoliberal logic of success and progress, uneventful activists turn towards the "queer art" strategies of "failing, losing, forgetting, unmaking, undoing, unbecoming" (Halberstam 2011, 2). A member of *ZBOKU* initiative articulated this as follows:

> When people speak about marginality, they assume the possibility of leaving the marginal space for a better, centrally located one. But what if to imagine that we go somewhere else, to a parallel world, so we don't care about the entire system which put us on the margin? . . . We can break away from the normative system and create a completely new, alternative space.
>
> (Vishnya Vishnya, geo, and Syaivo 2020)

Finally, one more distinctive feature of uneventful activism needs to be explained in detail: the typical usage of the word "queer" in their self-designation. A member of *ReSew* cooperative, for example, proposed the following understanding of the term:

> Looking from the position of the oppressed is crucial for queer critique. I mean, various oppressions – social, economic, also in terms of knowledge, sexuality and ability . . . many of them. Queer theory is a critical method that takes all the oppressions into account . . . that is why this method is appealing to me . . . To some extent, queer and intersectionality have a similar meaning to me.
>
> (ReSew 2019)

This activist interpretation provides an insight into the meaning of "queer", which is quite specific in the Ukrainian context today. Sounding like a loanword from English, in mainstream discourse today, *kvir* stands for a type of identity, such as genderqueer, genderfluid, or non-binary persons within the "LGBTQ" acronym. Another meaning of "queer" circulated in the time of our study to signal a political position of some grassroots initiatives, not a type of identity.[14] The difference from "queer as identity" was also produced through experimenting with the word modifications in the Ukrainian or Russian languages: *kviry, kvirnya, kviryo* which mean "queers" (n., pl.), and *kvirnuti* which means "queered" (adj.). Notably, in the mainstream feminist and LGBT activist discourse, these groups are typically condemned as "enemies from within" that provoke "unnecessary" discussions (as, for example, on nationalism and racism) and "blur" the central agenda.[15] This hostility also applies to queer theorising as an area of knowledge production because it challenges the "born this way" underpinning assumption of LGBT politics[16] or the feminist agenda focused on exclusively interpreted "women's rights". Thus, in the Ukrainian context, where queer theory barely exists in educational institutions, is rather marginalised in academic discourse, and typically rejected by mainstream activism, "queer" self-naming and self-positioning of uneventful collectives is a radical gesture.

At the same time, some groups have gradually developed a critical view on "queer" terminology and started coining new locally rooted concepts. For example, a member of *Rozmyta povistka* band explains such a move as follows:

> Regarding our political/ideological stance, it is rather queer anarchist feminism. But this category is Western-centric, so we prefer to think that we are doing a local variant of the anti-capitalist, anti-heteronormative and antipatriarchal agenda.
>
> (Rozmyta povistka 2019)

Another uneventful initiative – *ZBOKU* – is also a case in point. Its name plays with Ukrainian words *zboku* (meaning "aside", "next to") and *zbochenstvo* ("perversion-ness"): "*Zbochensvo* is the art of living next to the norm", states the group's slogan. Though initially, *ZBOKU* collective identified their activism with "queer art", at a certain point they introduced the concept "*zboku*" as a decolonising gesture towards the word "queer":

> *zbochenstvo* distorts even "queer": turns it over and places a conversation in the east instead of west, in the south instead of north, on the bottom instead of the top. because there are wretchedness and anger in "*zbochenstvo*".
>
> (*ZBOKU* website[17])

Correspondingly, ZBOKU members started calling themselves "*zboch* activist" (instead of "queer activist") and naming the area of their interests as "*zboch* art".[18]

In sum, an uneventful protest is a new form of feminist activism that is substantiated by clear political positionality, non-formality, and refusal to be institutionalised as well as a search for alternative ways of acting online and offline. In the next section, we unpack how political positionality of uneventful activism is produced by and productive of a critical feminist interpretation of nationalist discourse and its material-symbolic outcomes for the vulnerable groups and communities in wartime.

On nation and heroes

The defensive character of the war in the eastern part of Ukraine has made a critical perspective on the growing militarisation of Ukrainian society almost impossible. Even such a classic feminist concern as war-related gender-based violence does not find enough space for discussion or resistance. On the contrary, the alluring heroic figure of the "defender of the nation" is praised and highly protected in public discourse, and the promotion of women's participation in the military has become mainstream in feminist spaces.

In such a context, uneventful activists voice feminist critique of militarisation pointing to the connections between militarism, nationalism, heteropatriarchy, and violence. One of such examples is graffiti by the *Pva Pva* group (Figure 9.2).

This graffiti, placed on the background of the national flag, was produced at night-time in a public space, then photographed and proliferated through the Internet. It says: "My husband was raped by the war. Now he rapes me. Glory to rapists! Glory to heroes!" The accompanying comment on the group's Facebook page (which does not exist anymore) further elaborates the activists' point:

> Let's support our sisters in their fight against rape culture. Be angry and rebellious, smash the institutions and systems of oppression! Wars, states, armies, and churches maintain white hetero-male privileges.

The phrase "Glory to rapists! Glory to heroes!" is of particular interest here because it ironically rephrases a famous greeting "Glory to Ukraine! Glory to heroes!" which has a specific history with respect to the Maidan and feminist activism. The greeting itself was created in the Organization of Ukrainian Nationalists and the Ukrainian Insurgent Army during the 1930s; before the Maidan, it

Figure 9.2 Image of graffiti by the *Pva Pva* group with the text "My husband was raped by the war. Now he rapes me. Glory to rapists! Glory to heroes!" (in Russian), December 2016

Source: reproduced with permission from the *Pva Pva* group

was popular only among far-right groups. During and after the Maidan, however, it has become frequently used by the broadest population in Ukraine. Legitimation of the greeting was completed in 2018 when "Glory to Ukraine! Glory to heroes!" became the official greeting of the Ukrainian military and police.[19] Notably, *Zhinocha Sotnya* ("Women's Squad") – an all-women unit at the Maidan in 2014 – has detected only one problem with the then already popular greeting: its androcentric character. The women suggested replacing "Glory to heroes!" with "Glory to *heroines*!" (Mayerchyk and Plakhotnik 2019). This substitution did not eliminate the dehumanising logic of the greeting that establishes an opposition between the glorified "heroes" of the nation and non-heroic population, "the rest" whose lives do not matter or are less worthy. Neither did it erase the militaristic underpinning of the greeting. When *Pva Pva* ridiculed "Glory to Ukraine! Glory to heroes!" in the graffiti, they expressed their disagreement with the common fascination with the greeting and exposed its violent logic.

Taking a moment, we would like to get back to the "provocative" placard mentioned at the outset of this chapter, which ridiculed another currently popular nationalist greeting "Glory to the nation! Death to enemies!" and addressed the issue of the nation from uneventful positionality. In the context of the specific political meaning of "queer" in Ukraine, delineated earlier, a combination of "queer" wording and nationalist slogan produces an explosive effect. Creating utterance "Death to the nation, queer to enemies", the placard points to the newest social exclusions produced for the sake of the nation. In our reading, it calls to queer (meaning de-construct or de-naturalise) a petrified notion of an enemy, to go beyond "us vs. them" binary thinking about people from occupied territories, to overcome a homogenising notion of nation. The placard's appearance at Kyiv Pride march reminds us that LGBT people are also seen as "enemies" in the imaginary of the nation.

Opposing colonial discourse

While mainstream feminism actively employs postcolonial rhetoric for justification of their nationalist positionality, uneventful activists approach the issue of colonial power differently. A critical stance towards Eurocentric (and, broader Western) hegemony is pertinent to the political positionality of uneventful activism and has been manifested in various ways. In this section, we consider two directions of uneventful feminist critique that discursively align with a decolonial view: coloniality of global capitalism and Western authority in knowledge production.

One of the most telling instances of the anti-capitalist critique that targets both local and global capitalist regime is the "Poverty. War. Eurovision" activist project. It took place in May 2017, when thousands of international visitors crowded Kyiv for the Eurovision Song Contest. Seeking to challenge the glossy media picture of the show, the "Poverty. War. Eurovision" group revealed extensive evidence pointing to pressing issues, such as growing poverty and continuing war, that lay behind the scenes of the "celebrated diversity".[20] In particular, the activists drew attention to the multiple cases of violence that had taken place during the preparation for hosting the Eurovision in Kyiv, such as burning down the Roma settlements,[21] homeless people's displacement, and mass extermination of stray animals.[22] Carefully documenting and publicising these cases online in German, English, Russian, and Ukrainian languages, the activists criticised the neoliberal instrumentalisation of the idea of diversity and Europeanness:

> Homophobia, trans*phobia, lesbophobia, racism, militarism, ableism, ageism and violence against animals are the only "diversity" that we observe both in everyday Ukrainian realities and during the preparations for Eurovision. Racist and homophobic cases that are not investigated become even more significant during Eurovision in Ukraine, contrasting with the postulated highly inclusive agenda of the contest. In the situation of economic crisis, militarization and the right-wing turn, any desire to present Ukraine as a multicultural and inclusive country is an obvious profanation. We do not feel safe during this "celebration of diversity" – neither economically nor physically.
>
> ("Poverty. War. Eurovision" manifesto, May 2017)

Notably, the offline activist action – a massive banner "Poverty. War. Eurovision" that was put on the top of a multi-story building next to the main Eurovision venue – was removed by the state authorities immediately. It seemed to interfere too much with a desire of the powerful to pass a quest for Europeanness, which presumes anything but poverty and war.

There are other uneventful initiatives that pursue the feminist anti-capitalist agenda tackling the issue of environmental justice and resistance to the exploitative capitalist regimes. One such collective, *ReSew* sewing cooperative, articulates their positionality as follows:

> We are concerned about the problems of the sewing industry from the perspective of workers' labor rights and ecological impact, and propose some solutions, such as the use of recycled fabric, repair and renovation. We also call for a fair salary for seamstresses. At the same time, many of our customers continue buying things on the mass-market and, in so doing, become complicit with the over-exploitative cloth industry in the Third World[23] countries or here, in Ukraine. We sincerely don't know how to deal with this knowledge, except for activist interventions.
>
> (Lukianova and Winter 2020)

Activist interventions with respect to such facets of colonial power as control of knowledge production can be also traced within uneventful feminism in Ukraine. The case of debates between resource-rich NGOs and uneventful groups around "The Women's March" in 2018 is particularly illuminative in this regard. As scholarship from Central and Eastern Europe shows, in the context of the growing

NGO-isation of feminist and LGBT activisms, fuelled by the economy of Western donor agencies, NGOs are becoming a part of global Western-centred politics (Butterfield 2014; Kováts 2016). Within this process, NGOs as a whole are used by capitalism and state to "monitor and control social justice movements [and] redirect activist energies into career-based modes of organizing instead of mass-based organizing capable of actually transforming society" (INCITE! 2017, 3). Having much more power and resources, sometimes NGOs dictate a particular agenda while marginalising smaller non-institutionalised initiatives or even hijacking certain of their methods. Something like that had happened in Kyiv during the preparation of a street rally on 8 March 2018: the traditional (since about 2008) *feminist* march had been suddenly monopolised by an NGO and renamed to "The Women's March" following the lead of the famous anti-Trump rallies in the US. Analysing this case, Daria Popova wrote:

> The idea to join the "Global wave of changes" initiative was discussed in the course of the previous [2017] march's preparation but was rejected by queer feminist activists because of producing a *colonial* effect. While we support women's initiatives in the first world, they never support us back, activists explained.
>
> (Popova 2019; emphasis ours)

The queer activists' concern about coloniality had an impact in 2017. A year later, however, a rally had become "The Women's March" organised by a particular NGO without even inviting queer feminist activists to the discussion. Acknowledging the hard work of the organisers and all the risks they take, we also agree with the conclusion made by Popova that already having a several-years tradition of feminist marches, a transition to "women's march" means a step back for feminist struggle in Ukraine. Though "rebranding" had broadened a potential audience, so every next annual women's march gathered more participants, the new conception has evoked massive participant concern about not having "provocative" (meaning anti-nationalist or anti-militarist) placards at the rally. While, to the organisers' credit, they refused to censor placards at the march, a prudent approach has eventually dominated. Recently, a member of *ZBOKU* collective reflected upon the situation as follows:

> It seems the articulation of the anti-militarist agenda in public space had ended with the last feminist march [2017] . . . After that, there were only women's marches organized by some NGOs. In mainstream discourse, only those activisms that gather massive audiences are recognized as such.
>
> (Vishnya Vishnya, geo, and Syaivo 2020)

The activist experiments with the invention of new terms to alter the Anglo-American vocabulary are especially interesting from our perspective. In addition to the concept of *zboku*, outlined earlier on, we would like to introduce another newly coined term: *heteroobrechyonnost* (in Russian) or *heteropryrechenist* (in Ukrainian). The neologism started actively circulating in uneventful and broader feminist discourse after its materialised appearance as graffiti in front of the prestigious University of Kyiv-Mohyla Academy (Figure 9.3).

Being coined by an anonymous activist collective and further popularised through the Telegram channel with the same name, the neologism can be approximately translated into English as "heterofatality" or "heterodoom". It stands for not just a social regime that is grasped analytically (like heteronormativity) but the state of mind that determines people's lives painfully and hopelessly. In our reading, this concept expands the issue of sexuality because of being totally relevant to the broader situation of Ukraine and Eastern Europe, doomed to be an eternal "other" in a global colonial context. Notably, uneventful activists prefer to transliterate, not translate the term for foreign audiences. We also hope to see the new concept recognised in transnational academic discourse and cited according to the context of its appearance, namely: *heteroobrechyonnost* (Anonymous activist collective from Ukraine, 2017).

In mainstream feminist discussions in post-Maidan Ukraine, uneventful feminist activism is often accused of utopianism, a position that allegedly does not lead to "practical changes". In response to this we can say that, in Rita Raley's words, "small actions may have unforeseeable large consequences" and assert "the value of the ordinary, the seemingly *uneventful*, on its own terms" (Raley 2015, 270; emphasis ours). At the same time, the significance of

Figure 9.3 Image of graffiti in front of the main building of the National University of Kyiv-Mohyla Academy with a text *heteroobrechyonnost* (a made-up word that translates as "heterofatality" or "heterodoom"), September 2017

Source: reproduced with permission from Galka Yarmanova

uneventful activism in post-Maidan Ukraine goes far beyond its contribution to "enacting citizenship based on small acts" (Jacobsson & Korolczuk 2019, 15). Reinventing feminist protest beyond the institutionalised scripts, neoliberal agenda of "women's rights", and Western models of activism and citizenship, uneventful activism sketches pathways for alternative futures – for the future that can avoid pitfalls of nationalism, capitalism, and colonialism, even in a troubling time of war.

Acknowledgements

We owe our sincere gratitude to uneventful activist groups for permission to use their materials. Our special thanks go to *ZBOKU* collective for creating and maintaining a unique open-access archival collection of contemporary Ukrainian activism and political arts. We are also grateful to Redi Koobak, Madina Tlostanova, and Suruchi Thapar-Björkert for the incredible editorial support and valuable comments on this manuscript, and to Jessica Zychowicz and Vita Yakovleva for thinking together and feminist solidarity.

Notes

1 We use the abbreviation LGBT as a conventional term and self-designation in reference to the majority of corresponding organisations. We refuse to add other letters or "+" because of our critical perspective on identity politics which underpin the acronym and the neoliberal idea of inclusivity. Along with this, Ukrainian intersex activists fight against folding inclusion into the acronym and queer feminist groups (which are the focus of this chapter) develop their naming in opposition to identity-based LGBT politics.
2 www.facebook.com/groups/feminism.ua/permalink/1429672707063764/ Since all quotations from empirical materials are in Ukrainian or Russian, all the translations into English are ours. Only open-access sources are quoted in this chapter.
3 We are thankful to Madina Tlostanova for drawing our attention to these details.
4 www.facebook.com/fraugroup/
5 www.facebook.com/ReSewKyiv/
6 The group has acted online since 2016 via Facebook. Today their works and an interview are available in *ZBOKU* online archive: https://zbokuart.wordpress.com/people/ukraine/pva/?fbclid=IwAR2XXCsdEFt2nxfSUkeOqZKxRU0RLmoFe_tT3CX5zf1mg9-QrZKZ1ixqwQ4
7 https://zbokuart.wordpress.com/about/
8 www.facebook.com/queerfemsalt/photos/a.567906250281661/567905733615046/?type=3&theater
9 https://t.me/llyeska
10 Interestingly, under the influence of the Western-centred grant economy, the word "event" that can be easily translated into Ukrainian, started being increasingly used in the NGO-based activism without translation, that is in its English form. The spread of this notable calque is another reason why we have found the concept of *uneventfulness* so appealing.
11 While we critically expose the complicity of the growing NGO-isation of feminism with interests of the global grant economy, it is also important to admit the multiple possibilities for NGOs to resist the capitalist rules. There is evidence that some NGOs

in Ukraine shared their resources with uneventful groups to support the subversive anti-militarist feminist agenda without de-anonymisation of activists.
12 www.facebook.com/queerfemsalt/photos/a.567906250281661/567905733615046/?type=3&theater
13 Telegram is a cloud-based instant messaging and voice-over IP service. Since Telegram messages are heavily encrypted and can self-destruct, this messenger is the most popular amongst activists concerned with security protection and anonymity.
14 This positionality is close to what Leticia Sabsay called "politically queer" (2013).
15 One of the uneventful groups plays with this accusation in their name: *Rozmyta povistka* means "blurred agenda".
16 It is the same situation as Susanne Walters concluded about the US: "in our present political context, gay volition is like Voldemort – dangerous even to be uttered. Biological determinism is the new normal" (Walters 2014, 115).
17 The original version: "збоченство збочує навіть 'квір' – перевертає його і повертає розмову з заходу на схід, з півночі на південь, згори донизу. адже у 'збоченстві' – злиденність і злість" (https://zbokuart.wordpress.com).
18 Interdisciplinary Symposium, "'*V teme*': Sex, Politics and LGBT Life in Central Asia," Bishkek, 22 March 2019.
19 The law amendment was adopted on 4 October 2018 (https://zakon.rada.gov.ua/laws/show/2587-19)
20 "Celebrate diversity!" was an official motto of Eurovision 2017.
21 It is worth noticing that solidarity with Roma people and protest against Romaphobia was actively expressed by other uneventful activist groups, for example, by means of the slogan "Yes to Roma, no to pogroms" shouted out-loud by the Queer Anarcho Feminist Block at the 2017 Kyiv Pride march.
22 www.facebook.com/poverty.war.eurovision
23 Although this term might sound problematic today, it was used in the original quotation.

References

Ahmed, Sara. 2014. "Selfcare as Warfare." *Feministkilljoys* (blog), August 25, 2014. https://feministkilljoys.com/2014/08/25/selfcare-as-warfare/.
Butterfield, Nicole Ann. 2014. "LGBTIQ Advocacy at the Intersection of Transnational and Local Discourses on Human Rights and Citizenship in Croatia." Ph.D. dissertation, Central European University, Budapest.
Gržinić, Marina, Tjaša Kancler, and Piro Rexhepi. 2020. "Decolonial Encounters and the Geopolitics of Racial Capitalism." *Feminist Critique: East European Journal of Feminist and Queer Studies* 3: 13–38.
Halberstam, Judith. 2011. *The Queer Art of Failure*. Durham, NC: Duke University Press.
INCITE! 2017. *The Revolution Will Not Be Funded: Beyond the Non-Profit Industrial Complex*. Reprint edition. Durham, NC: Duke University Press.
Jacobsson, Kerstin, and Elżbieta Korolczuk. 2019. "Mobilizing Grassroots in the City: Lessons for Civil Society Research in Central and Eastern Europe." *International Journal of Politics, Culture, and Society* (May): 1–18. https://doi.org/10.1007/s10767-019-9320-7.
Kováts, Eszter, ed. 2016. *Solidarity in Struggle – Feminist Perspectives on Neoliberalism in East-Central Europe*. Budapest: Friedich-Ebert-Stiftung.
Kulyk, Volodymyr. 2014. "Ukrainian Nationalism Since the Outbreak of Euromaidan." *Ab Imperio* 3: 94–122. https://doi.org/10.1353/imp.2014.0064.
Kulyk, Volodymyr. 2016. "National Identity in Ukraine: Impact of Euromaidan and the War." *Europe-Asia Studies* 68, no. 4: 588–608. https://doi.org/10.1080/09668136.2016.1174980.

Lukianova, Mariia, and Rita Winter. 2020. "Strochki iz zhizni shvey" [Lines from Seamstresses' Life]. *Feminist Critique: East European Journal of Feminist and Queer Studies* 3: 125–134.

Lykke, Nina. 2010. *Feminist Studies: A Guide to Intersectional Theory, Methodology and Writing*. New York and London: Routledge.

Mayerchyk, Maria, and Olga Plakhotnik. 2019. "Between Time of Nation and Feminist Time: Genealogies of Feminist Protest in Ukraine." In *Feminist Circulations Between East and West/Feministische Zirkulationen Zwischen Ost Und West*, edited by Annette Bühler-Dietrich, 47–70. Berlin: Frank & Timme Verlag.

OCHA. 2020. "Humanitarian Needs Overview: Ukraine." https://reliefweb.int/report/ukraine/ukraine-humanitarian-needs-overview-2020-january-2020 (accessed July 1, 2020).

Popova, Daria. 2019. "Zhinochyi chy feministychnyi? Chsho trapylos' z marshem do 8 Bereznya" [Women's or Feminist Event: What Happened to the March on 8 March 2018]. *Feminist Critique: East European Journal of Feminist and Queer Studies* 2: 85–88.

Quijano, Anibal. 2007. "Coloniality and Modernity/ Rationality." *Cultural Studies* 21, nos. 2–3: 168–178. https://doi.org/10.1080/09502380601164353.

Raley, Rita. 2015. "The Ordinary Arts of Political Activism." In *Global Activism*, edited by Peter Weibel, 289–297. Cambridge, MA and London: Massachusetts Institute of Technology Press.

ReSew. 2019. "Dovga rozmova z ReSew teplogo litnyogo vechora" [A Long Conversation with the ReSew in a Warm Summer Evening]. *ZBOKU* (blog), February 10, 2019. https://zbokuart.wordpress.com/2019/02/10/resew/.

Rozmyta povistka. 2019. "Rozmyvaty, tak z musykoyu!" [Gotta Blur – Blur with Music!]. *ZBOKU* (blog), July 22, 2019. https://zbokuart.wordpress.com/2019/07/22/blurred-agenda/.

Sabsay, Leticia. 2013. "Queering the Politics of Global Sexual Rights?" *Studies in Ethnicity & Nationalism* 13, no. 1: 80–90. https://doi.org/10.1111/sena.12019.

Said, Edward W. 1994. *Culture and Imperialism*. New York: Vintage Books.

Sonevytsky, Maria. 2019. *Wild Music: Sound and Sovereignty in Ukraine*. Middletown: Wesleyan University Press.

Suchland, Jennifer. 2011. "Is Postsocialism Transnational?" *Signs: Journal of Women in Culture and Society* 36, no. 4: 837–862.

Vishnya Vishnya, geo, and Syaivo. 2020. "Tomu Shcho My Govorymo z Uzbichchia" [Because We Speak from the Side of the Road]. *Feminist Critique: East European Journal of Feminist and Queer Studies*. https://feminist.krytyka.com/ua/articles/tomu-shcho-my-hovorymo-z-uzbichchya (accessed July 1, 2020).

Walters, Suzanna Danuta. 2014. *The Tolerance Trap: How God, Genes, and Good Intentions Are Sabotaging Gay Equality*. New York: New York University Press.

Yurchenko, Yuliya. 2020. "Ukraine and the (Dis)Integrating Empire of Capital." *Lefteast* (blog), January 9, 2020. www.criticatac.ro/lefteast/ukraine-disintegrating-empire-of-capital/.

Zhurzhenko, Tatiana. 2001. "Ukrainian Feminism(s): Between Nationalist Myth and Anti-Nationalist Critique." *Vienne: IWM Working Paper 4*. https://cdn.atria.nl/epublications/2001/UkrainianFeminism.pdf.

Zhurzhenko, Tatiana. 2008. "Vpisyvayas v Diskurs Natsionalnogo: Ukrainskiy Feminism Ili Feminism v Ukraine?" [Inscribing to the Nationalist Discourse: Ukrainian Feminism or Feminism in Ukraine?]. In *Gendernye Rynki Ukrainy: Politicheskaya Economiya Natsionalnogo Stroitelstva [Gendered Markets of Ukraine: Political Economy of Nation-Building]*, 38–72. Vilnius: European Humanities University Press.

Chapter 10

Postsocialist poetics

Interview with *Krëlex zentr*[1]

*Krëlex zentr, Lesia Pagulich and
Tatsiana Shchurko*

Introduction

The dissolution of the USSR produced a new global order in its "globally homogenized neoliberal consumer-driven cum politically liberal-democratic modality", in Sylvia Wynter's apt terminology (Wynter and McKittrick 2015, 43). This post-Soviet global modality facilitates the enactment of new social, economic, and cultural relations that generate new forms of recognition and agency (Atanasoski 2013). Importantly, much scholarship on gender and sexuality politics in the post-Soviet region has not interrogated the complex interplay of ethnicity, racialisation, class, gender, and sexuality in imperial and colonial power relations (for similar critique see Gržinić and Tatlić 2014; Koobak and Marling 2014; Tlostanova 2010). Furthermore, privileging the "catching up with the West" mode forecloses possibilities for many scholars and activists to challenge Eurocentric perspectives on gender and sexuality.

In turn, we grapple with possibilities for theorising post-Soviet power relations in a different register beyond Eurocentric imaginary. This focus necessarily involves crafting a language that may alter understandings of power in the region. For many, poetics is a way to emancipate thinking from the Eurocentric constructions (Tlostanova 2017). Poetics unfolds the language that bases on the rules, forms, and expressions that can be flexible, fluid, and more attentive to the experiences of pain, devastation, intimacy, and corporeality. Poetics addresses bodily experience as a register of knowledge production when to think is also to feel, consider, touch, imagine, move, and breath. Poetics provides ways to express subjectivity, not through the rational markers of identity politics invented by the western epistemology, but through the experiences, geographies, temporalities, feelings, and ruminations.

In conversation with *Krëlex zentr*, we explore how creative practitioners have imagined forms of community and identification within the landscapes of inequality and injustice in the post-Soviet region. In 2013, two artists Ruthia Jenrbekova and Maria Vilkovisky from Almaty (Kazakhstan) presented *Krëlex zentr*, an imaginary art-institution not existing in reality. The artists deliberately turned to the idea of *créolisation* and wrote a manifesto titled "Apology for creoleness: The case of Central Asia" emphasising their intention in the following way:

> We look for advantages in this half-life in the hinterlands, in new uninhabited places where silence reigns, because a language in which we could talk about ourselves has not yet been invented here. We wonder how this finally happens. A voice emerges amidst silence? Sense congeals from nonsense? Identity is born of imitation?
>
> (kreolex zentre 2012)

The artists denote that they are inspired by the poetics of Édouard Glissant who states that *créolisation* is "new and original dimension allowing each person to be there and elsewhere, rooted and open, lost in the mountains and free beneath the sea, in harmony and in errantry" (Glissant 1997, 34). For *Krëlex zentr*, the concept of *créolisation* uncovers marginalised locations and "the histories of the Souths, Easts, Far Norths, and all the other points we see on the horizon through the kaleidoscope, points without number" (kreolex zentre 2012). We suggest that their poetics produces postsocialist queer subjectivity that invests in the local and the particular as well as the momentary, the ephemeral, the transitory, and the non-homogenous in order to avoid normative tropes of identification: "Like all newcomers, we have no names, so we refer to ourselves like those who resort to tricks on the long journey home: we are Nobody. Bogeys, half-men, Creoleaks, the devil knows what, experimental creatures busy mapping the non-existent" (kreolex zentre 2012).

Krëlex zentr's poetics mixes forms and tropes of narration through creation of texts, images, maps, gestures, songs, and performances. Their poetics is full of ruptures, discrepancies, and transformations. Through self-irony and absence of strict articulations, the artists explore the grey zone between speech and mumble, amateur and professional. The artists actively use grotesque, subversion, and self-irony. In the following interview, in conversation with the artists, we would like to contemplate on radical possibilities of poetics and créolisation in the post-Soviet context. We have conducted this interview in Russian, and then translated it into English.

Lesia Pagulich and Tatsiana Shchurko: To get us started, tell us what thoughts cross your mind when you think about "postsocialism" as a concept?

Ruthia Jenrbekova and Maria Vilkovisky: We have a feeling that "postsocialism" can be rethought not in a sense of a reflection directed towards the past and focused on the disappeared socialist camp. But in a sense of multiple diffraction within the socialist (Barad 2007). Such diffraction spreads out beyond the local past of the former socialist countries and gravitates towards other times: the planetary, subjunctive present, perfect future. Therefore, the "reflective model" of cognition seems too constraining for us. It only reflects what "objectively exists in reality", while the "diffraction model" describes something that has not been yet but will be or could have been under certain conditions. Any "post-" seems to be connected with re-flection and re-action, while we are more likely interested in "-flections" and "-actions". Perhaps we need new prefixes and new terms. What about "trans-socialism", for example? "Trans-" is our favourite prefix, which miraculously conveys the meaning of such optical phenomena as diffraction or refraction. These phenomena are associated not with the reflection of an "objectively existing" barrier but with the passage of light through the boundaries and beyond the obstacles. Thinking as a process of passive reflection and thinking as a process of passage through and beyond are completely different cognitive strategies. Thus, we just want to note that we are most likely interested not in the reflection on the differences between various "post" prefixes but in the diffraction on the "trans" prefix, which implies the continuation, incompleteness, and indeterminacy of the outcome.

LP and TS: Créolisation is a central concept in your work. Why have you decided to use créolisation, and how do you connect it to decolonial or anticolonial projects in Central Asia?

RJ and MV: Since the idea of créolisation has become popular, there has been a discussion about the applicability of this concept outside the Caribbean. Édouard Glissant (1997) believes that the term créolité should remain specific to the Antilles, while créolisation is more or less ubiquitous and rather refers to a general model of colonial "cultural clash", a model that is not tied to a specific content. Being descendants of marriages of the autochtones with the transmigrators who arrived in Central Asia in the 20th century, we are unable to determine whether it's ok or not to appropriate a foreign term, but it is precisely indeterminacy that constitutes an integral part of the concept of "créolisation". Caribbean theorists constantly point out this fact as if pre-empting a possible stabilisation of what is fundamentally versatile. So, one of the poetic definitions of this word that can be found in the famous manifesto "Éloge de la Créolité" is "the world diffracted but recomposed" (Bernabé, Chamoiseau, and Raphaël 1997). The three authors of this essay claim that to define créolisation would be an "act of taxidermy", and therefore, "it seems that, for the moment, full knowledge of Creoleness will be reserved for Art, for Art absolutely" (893). It seems that the main concern is to preserve a certain conceptual openness, which allows avoiding the "freezing" of créolisation and turning it into another local identity. We just take up this intention to leave open the possibility for recontextualising créolisation while understanding that some misuse of this word may have taken place, for example, in the works of the anthropologists (e.g. see Kirndörfer 2014). We wrote about this "problem of transferring" a concept from one context to another, referring to Stuart Hall's essay "Creolité and the Process of Creolization" (2015) and to the compilation of articles *The Creolization of Theory* (Lionnet and Shih 2011). The latter is particularly remarkable. This publication makes a much bolder attempt to expand the concept of créolisation not so much in terms of other geographical locations but in terms of theory itself, which despite its seemingly western origin, from the very beginning was creolised by the concept and image of the Other. We do not know how justifiable the application of this terminology for Central Asia can be. Rather than talking about francophone term "creolité" as a signifier for our local heterogeneity, we prefer to talk about "krëling" as a political choice not to identify ourselves in terms of nationality/ethnicity. In the process of transfer and re-contextualisation, the word "creolité" has turned for us into krëling and krëlex, yet further mutations are also very likely (such mutations and localisations are characteristics of creole languages all over the world). In fact, we had no choice but to start a conversation about mixing: after all, we are from mixed families, our friends are from mixed families, Almaty is an incredibly mixed city, and our entire former Turkestan region has always been a culturally and ethnically heterogeneous region. Just as the Caribbean is a crossroads between Africa, the Americas, and Europe, our Transoxiana is a meeting place for Buddhist, Islamic, and Christian civilisations. Located in the very centre of a gigantic continent, we are at the same time a distant periphery for any metropolitan centre, roaming around our deserts, like Arawaks across their seas. As for decolonisation, we always emphasise that it is not about returning to what supposedly took place before colonisation but making an effort of self-invention. What enchants in the Caribbean discourse is precisely the promise of a new, unforeseen, "third". We see this discourse as a variant of constructivist, anti-essentialist, and therapeutic decolonisation. Créolisation is a kind of creative synthesis, and therefore, it has much in common with art. Créolisation is precisely the poetics of Relation in every sense of the word. As workers of culture, which is as synthetic and experimental as if it has never existed before, we have to invent a lot in the process. So, for example, we invented Transoxiana taking the name from antiquity and attaching it to a nebulous society of the future, in which there will be no nations, genders, classes, and probably there will be no people in the traditional sense. Thinking about this society of the future, we created the project "Transoxiana. A Tour for Newcomers" subtitled "Futuristic tour of the history of Central Asia in the 21st century". In this project, we tried to tell the story of the cyber-feminist revolution and the radical social and anthropological transformation that took place in Central Asia in the second half of the 21st century. The project exists in the form of video and text (Krëlex Radio 2018). This is a kind of popular guide for alternative history, commissioned by Krëlex zentr in the 22nd century. The guide tells in a concise form an improbable story of the five post-Soviet Central Asian states that transformed over the course of several decades into a single political entity of an unprecedented type: a democratic confederation that unites several thousand autonomous digital tribes. This revolution became one of the first symptoms of the so-called "technological singularity" and was a part of a sort of créolisation (cyborgisation) of consciousness, the material basis of which consisted not only of the Homo sapiens nervous system but also of some hybrid neural-digital network. By analogy with peripatric speciation, our future technological singularity manifests itself for the first time in the peripheral region, which outstripped the western democracies in development over a super-short period and presumably gave rise to a new cyborganic species. Such miracles happen precisely as a result of créolisation. No wonder, the famous Guyanese writer Wilson Harris (1999), for instance, considers créolisation as an analogue of the alchemical process. Specifically, Harris explains that in this process, after the *nigredo* and *albedo* stages, the rainbow stage of *cauda pavonis* or the "peacock tail" emerges, "which may be equated with all the variable possibilities or colours of fulfilment we can never totally realize" (cit. Burns 2008, 6).

LP and TS: Decolonial and postcolonial conceptualisations pay a lot of attention to rethinking the dichotomies, such as global and local, universal and particular, time and space. To this point, in one of your writings, you envision the locality of Central Asia not through the prism of national identity, but as "the mixed uncategorized post-national creole diaspora" ("Creoleak Centr" n.d.). How does this understanding of "creole diaspora" allow reconsidering the relationships between such dichotomies?

RJ and MV: Rethinking dichotomies is our main theme. The intellectual trend, with which we would like to associate ourselves, can be conditionally defined as a "queer-feminist critique of Modernity". Here, the word "queer-" could be replaced by "cyber-" or "krëlex-". In any case, it will be a reference to the paradigmatic shift that took place in the late 20th century and which is often associated with the influence of Gilles Deleuze and Félix Guattari (1987). This is a shift from being to becoming, from Cartesian dualism to Spinozian monism, from the hierarchical thinking of Identity and Other to the horizontal entanglements of rhizome, which Glissant (1997, 18) calls the "thinking of errantry":

We will agree that this thinking of errantry, this errant thought, silently emerges from the destructuring of compact national entities that yesterday were still triumphant and, at the same time, from difficult, uncertain births of new forms of identity that call to us.

A critical rethinking of the basic assumptions of Modernity is at the heart of our attempt to see processes instead of states. Indeed, it's difficult to understand our state/condition because it depends on the chosen framework: our femininity, skin colour, social status, belonging to the sphere of art, all depend on against what background and in relation to whom we are considered. We feel more of belonging to a trajectory rather than to a territory. Therefore, rather than thinking about a border, we are thinking about a gradient, potentially endless series of differences (in the logic of intensities and parameters, rather than identities and facts). The ambivalence in the concept of créolisation overtakes us everywhere, because the creoles were originally those who had double origin, were simultaneously from one country and from another, thereby confusing the imperial table of ranks, undermining the very reality of a territorial divide. Hence, this is the paradox of a creolised "glocality". We are always attached to a particular place, but this attachment is like a road sign, it points to another place, and thus works as a marker of planetary translocality, as a symptom of cosmopolitan consciousness. We are Almatinians, local women artists, but this is only one side of the matter. Another side is that we are actually "newcomers" and "strangers" and not quite women here – for example, according to more patriarchal and heteronormative local communities. Hence, this is the fundamentally relational nature: in Austria, I am a Kazakh, in Kazakhstan, I am not. Turning a dichotomy into a spectrum inside our Kazakh-non-Kazakh, female-non-female bodies, we seem to experience a Deleuzian multiplicity in action: sex is not one (as we know from Luce Irigaray (1985)), and the body itself is not one (as we know from Annemarie Mol (2003)). This bodily multiplicity is not a predetermined fact of nature or biography. It is rather a kind of existential and political choice – not to reject those parts of ourselves that have been "othered", not to expel "illegal" internal migrants in the name of "legal" migrants, but to include in the "human" everything that wants to be included. Otherwise, we will never come closer to understanding what we are, or what we can be. We call this tactic of radical inclusion an "internal democracy". Since the subject has left his central place, splitting into an unknown number of parts, is it possible to convene a parliament out of these parts? Each fraction of this parliament envisions itself as a kind of "diaspora". But unlike the actual diasporas, ours is not united around the myth of the lost homeland. Instead, our translocal diaspora is united around the myth of the shared planet, which can be lost in case we continue to divide and exploit it. So, instead of looking into the past, we look into the future, approximately in the same direction in which José Vasconcelos (1925) looked a hundred years ago when he spoke of the imminent coming of new people, *La raza cósmica*, the cosmic race.

LP and TS: Following Glissant, you understand créolisation as a "netting multiplicity of relations" (Creoleak Centr 2016, 77). Could you tell more about this understanding of créolisation?

RJ and MV: When we were in the art-residence in Bishkek in 2012, we were invited to the local television, to a morning talk show. The two of us were telling our "creolized tales": where the creoles came from, how they "came" to Central Asia, and why it is important to talk about it. We received quite a powerful feedback; the audience called, asked questions, as if recognising themselves in this story of créolisation. After that, we had an artist talk in the School of Theory and Activism, Bishkek (STAB). And we had a similar feeling there. After that, Georgy Mamedov, one of the curators of the residence, told us that it seemed as if in Bishkek and Almaty there was some kind of social request for myths about mixed identities, that it seemed that we touched some important string. Shortly afterward, in January 2013, we first held a presentation of Krëlex zentr in Almaty. And again, to our surprise, we saw quite a lot of interest among people. For example, a girl came up to us to thank us, and she said,

I'm a Kazakh, and I love my Kazakh culture. But I always felt somehow constrained in the boundaries of our traditions. And you suddenly opened the window, and the wind blew. And I realized that there were other options, that I didn't have to fit myself into the boundaries established by someone.

These and other instances made us think that even a simple popularisation of the word "créolisation" makes sense in a situation where ethnic nationalism is an official doctrine of the state, when all citizens – especially women! – are obliged to obey the requirements of the "nation", performing rituals and following the rules established by our patriarchs. The idea that nationality is an eternal naturally predetermined fact, which means that no one has a choice how to live, what clothes to wear, whom to love, etc., is so widespread that the very idea of the possibility of redefining identities is perceived as revolutionary and liberating, especially for women. It is for this reason that we called our imaginary art-institute Krëlex. Because even a simple acquaintance with the meaning of this word may turn out to be inspirational or perhaps even therapeutic. Not without reason, créolisation, understood in line with Wilson Harris's creative synthesis of opposites, has common traits with Jungian therapy. In our context, the word "creolised" looks a bit strange and unusual. People sometimes ask us why we don't use a local Central Asian term, which could be employed instead of borrowing words from other languages. Yes, we could recall such forbidden words as "Sarts"; it would sound much more authentic, but the fact is that we are not going to create identities and social movements. We are just artists; our specialisation is imaginary and unreal. In any case, we must expand our vocabulary to find a way to tell about our experience of colonisation and Sovietisation. The former Soviet republics have an experience, which is in many ways similar and in many ways different from the experience of the former colonies of the West. This experience could become the basis of our archives of the future if we find a way to comprehend and articulate this experience. Probably, this is what we are learning now by reading the Caribbean writers: how we can think and interpret our histories falling neither into the narcissism of a "sovereign nation" saturated with postcolonial resentment nor into scepticism about the failed attempts to build a democratic state with certain social guarantees. The problem is that the current cultural policy in Kazakhstan is based on the idea that culture can only be national, and that it cannot happen otherwise. All institutions that used to be called state institutions are now renamed as national. Our entire cultural infrastructure is based on the idea that people are endowed with nationalities by nature, and that each nationality has for centuries preserved and protected its cultural traditions. It is not surprising that, in such a picture of the world, there is simply no place for critical, experimental, and politically engaged forms of art.

LP and TS: We think about poetics as one of the important methods for creating new knowledges and decolonising the western construction of thinking and being. For example, Boaventura de Sousa Santos (2014) writes that the Global North is not capable of producing transformative knowledges, and "genuine radicalism seems no longer possible in the global North" (3). Santos sees potential only in the epistemologies of the anti-imperial South, which mix different forms and logics, interrupt the flow of narrative and time, oppose linearity, and expansively recapture space and time. Santos (2018) defines the South as "an epistemological, nongeographical South, composed of many epistemological souths having in common the fact that they are all knowledges born in struggle against capitalism, colonialism, and patriarchy" (1). In your works, we see many forms and expressions that produce a transformative space for thinking and feeling (for example, the performances "Subaltern Mumble" (2014) and "Stage Performance" at the festival "Between the Lines" (2016)). What do you think about your poetics in the context of the decolonisation of thinking and being?

RJ and MV: Our krëlex perspective is a kind of poetics or even the poetics of cognition if we may say so. We draw on Glissant's concept of relation that is simultaneously an attitude, knowledge, and a story. As intersectional queer femmes, we build our poetics on the concept of openness and the question "how is radical inclusiveness possible?" This is a difficult question for every art institution that is aimed to foreground the ability to distinguish the best from the worst. Therefore, we are talking about openness in terms of Umberto Eco's "open work" (1989) as well as about a new cultural politics, which would imply a revision of the criteria for evaluation and selection. For our art institution, albeit imaginary, two aspects – openness as the aesthetics of work and as a policy – are closely interconnected. Precisely this inseparability of an artistic and political made us turn to the genre of fake institutions. For example, we were inspired by Harald Szeemann's *Agentur für Geistige Gastarbeit*, Marcel Broodthaers's *Department of Eagles*, and Iain and Ingrid Baxter's *N.E. Thing Co.* In a desire to collect all the available art genres under one "art centre" without distinguishing between low and high, local and imported, "authentic" and "fake" art, one can see a desire to explore almost unknown territory of post-mediality, a kind of creative nomadism, when an artist wanders from one means of expression to another without stopping anywhere for a long time and avoiding excessive professionalisation in any narrow sphere. Such a strategy resists the logic of a single discipline that generates experts and professionals. Instead, this strategy undermines the elitism of the art sphere and offers access to the means of cultural production for those who reputedly "do not under-stand" or "do not know how" to draw/dance/write poetry, etc. Therefore, the main point for the krëlex and trans feminist agendas is the view that to have access implies having the means of production of identities. Following this strategy, in our performances, we put together interchangeable parts according to the principle of multi-genre cabaret. In this sense, our performances repre-sent a sequence of short sketches, quite heterogeneous, each of which may be completely different from the previous one. Performing on stage as an artist without her own role is a rather risky occupation, and we are aware that we can look like a bad amateur theatre, confirming the stereotypical opinion that only amateurs, who do not have professional skills, produce contemporary art. However, often our viewers are well aware that they are dealing with an attempt to subvert conventional wisdom about how to distinguish a good theatre from a bad one. Sometimes we even directly discuss these issues with the audience. For instance, after the successful presentation of Krëlex zentr in Bishkek and Almaty, we made on the basis of this presentation a two-hour theatrical perfor-mance "Intermedia", which was an experiment of mixing genres within one performance (shown in Moscow and Berlin in 2016, Bishkek and Kazan in 2017). The title refers as to the Russian term "intermedia," which means an intermediate performance between the main theatrical performances, so to the English word that Fluxus artists used (e.g. Dick Higgins, Alison Knowles, and Anna Higgins) in order to indicate their own inter-genre-al positionality. The performance has a subtitle "How to organize artistic production on your own". As cultural workers in Walter Benjamin's sense, first and foremost, we turn to our colleagues, workers of so-called creative industries, suggesting that they think collectively about what and for whom is our work. For example, at some point during the performance, one of us starts a dance improvisation on stage, and the other one asks whether an amateur without special choreographic skills can perform any dance improvisation. In response to this question, the dancer states that the criteria for assessing professionalism are set by the large institu-tions, and we, as a counterinstitution, can challenge these criteria. We are try-ing to involve the audience in this discussion, for whom such a "dance" is probably a new experience because it is not often when one can see people dancing on the stage who do not know how to dance. The revision of quality criteria in art is an important topic, but very few people take it up as the repu-tational risks are too high. However, just as the cognitive experience can be either contemplative and theoretical or active and practical, so the aesthetic experience can imply not only contemplation but also intervention. The audience cannot co-participate in the art process as long as our criteria are based on the traditional concept of mastery. Therefore, we are interested in approaches of deskilling that imply technological art production. It seems interesting to create situations when people in the audience feel that the stage is within their reach, and they are not doomed to just watch how the artist-master demonstrates his "natural" talents. It is no coincidence that the word "master" acquires colonial connotations because this figure is always mythic and traditional for colonial times. Our theatre is trying to abandon this paradigm as we are interested in affective experiences that arise in a result of identification not with a character of the scene, as in the case of colonial theatre, but with a more real person, a performer, who does not play anyone, speaks on her own behalf, and just like anyone in the audience, feels vulnerable, confused, not good enough, etc. In addition, the krëlex aesthetics problematises the classical European opposition between harmony and disorder because chaos is our high-level order. In this sense, we are quite Deleuzians as we follow the postmodernist tradition with its dialectic of form and openness, contingency and intentionality. Importantly, the critical attitude towards the Euro- and androcentric assumptions of modernity is in line with postmodernist criticism. In general, the contraposition between the "rationality" of the West/North and the "sensuality" of the East/South does not seem to us so justified. We know such dichotomies from the history of Négritude, for example, that are based on the vision that if Europe relies on science and rationality, Africa will rely on magic and sensuality. However, the capitalist exploitation of a living planet, for instance, is ultimately irrational, while ecological co-existence without competition and economic growth seems to be more rational. The definitions of rationality and its antithesis, "rationality" and "irrationality", depend on the paradigm of argumentation. For example, the current interest in affective, poetic, and magical is quite rational, though such understanding might not necessarily coincide with the traditional European definitions of rationality. Besides, from the very beginning, the innovations of western modernity drew inspiration from non-European sources. There must be much written about the exploitation of these sources in early Modernism (e.g. Coutts-Smith 1991). The cultural systems of the global South have always been in the focus of white European artists, at least since Romanticism (e.g. Said 1993). They have served and continue serving as sources of modern and postmodern innovations in the "first world". In this sense, little has changed over the past 100 years, with the exception that the moment of appropriation is finally gaining recognition, and the question of restitution is becoming more acute. For instance, Eduardo Viveiros de Castro, in their book *Cannibal Metaphysics* (2014), proposes to consider anthropology as a kind of native knowledge. Possibly this argument can work for other areas of science and theory as the "knowledge-power" of the modern era was produced with silent, invisible, and indispensable participation of non-European cultures and societies (see Buck-Morss 2009). These cultures are the Aladdin's

Cave of Wonders both for art and for theory with their fascination with the images of the Other. Perhaps the 21st century is different in the sense that there is no Other in traditional understanding. Exoticism has disappeared, and today it would be unethical to envision someone's culture as strange or exotic. The planet in our century once again managed to greatly decrease and the character, which Victor Segalen (2002) called "Exot" and which, according to Segalen, was the source of our ability to change and perceive otherwise, remained in the past. Possibly, in this situation, decolonial thinking should become more futuristic than passeist, more socialist and internationalist than liberal and multicultural. In the field of cultural production, obviously, the exploitation of "exotic" local features is a commercial tactic that leads to a kind of stereotyping or self-orientalisation and runs against the needs of the groups and communities. A vivid example of such liberal market-driven approach is a project of British photographer Jimmy Nelson titled "Before They Pass Away", representing among the other "exotic" natives, a group of Kazakhs, wearing theatrical outfits on the top of the mountain, apparently in an attempt to earn some money from a western entrepreneur with camera. Riding horsebacks with eagles in hands they look exactly the way as if playing in a fake costume show that fuels the imagination of our far-right nationalists. The ideology behind this type of artistic production is the one of global extractivist capitalism; it aims at keeping us, the poor peoples, locked in our cultural otherness, offering the ridiculous western fantasy of "authenticity" in exchange for proper education, health care, and democratic institutes. Therefore, the krëlex tactic would go, on the contrary, for appropriating universalist discourses falsely marked as western, abandoning the idea of building collective identities "in opposition" and focusing on emancipation, technology, and new institutions. In the post-Soviet space, contemporary art often turns to the pre-modernist past to oppose Sovietisation. However, this turn is not creole/ krëlex at all but a completely traditional "national" way of self-construction. Our approach is trickster-like, it is imbued with leftist and secular ideas, which are no less our own than they are European. This approach rather destabilises borders than draws them and therefore does not seem to fit into the usual picture of decolonial struggle. For those who are interested in Central Asian art, we are not part of it. For example, at the festival of contemporary poetry "Between the lines" in Almaty, organised with the support of the US Embassy, many people perceived our performance as a provocation. Our screams, crawling around the stage, punk mini-scenes were in sharp contrast with the high romantic (ostensibly, decolonial) aesthetics of those who spoke before us and set a tone for the whole event by praising "the land of our fathers and mothers" and suchlike. Two times during the performance, the organisers tried to remove us from the stage, apparently fearing a possible scandal. The first time, when we were asked to finish, happened immediately after playing a slightly changed song by The Doors, which we called "Oil Is Almost Gone". The second time, the organisers interrupted us during our performance of an even more ironic and "childish" pamphlet "Jesus, Jesus Go Away! (Devil Loves Me)". It seemed to us that these performances were perceived as politically incorrect and dangerous for the image of the US-Kazakh friendship. The audience actively rejected not so much the content of our texts as the aesthetics of the Dadaist cabaret, which is not very common for our region.

LP and TS: We also would like to ask about the relation between créolisation, queer, and trans politics. In the context of the Americas and the Caribbean, créolisation enriches the understanding of queer with sensibilities to racism and colonialism. What role does créolisation play in your understanding of queer and trans feminism?

RJ and MV: Yes, these concepts seem to be reflected in each other or rather refract through each other. We understand that many queer people of colour consider the word "queer" to be a symbol of white hegemony, just as representatives of non-binary traditional cultures (for example, in South Asia and Oceania) may refuse to apply words beginning with trans* to themselves. For our imagined cosmopolis, such a position would be too isolationist and ultimately essentialist. The openness and lack of foundation (homelessness?) of créolised journey are important to us, because our créolisation is a kind of transcultural nomadism. The rejection of a fixed identity means, in fact, nothing else than unmooring from the anchor and the beginning of the path in an unknown direction. This is one of the strong points of Glissant's poetics, which he calls thinking of errantry or thought of errantry. Créolisation begins with a journey from which it is impossible to return, just as it is impossible to return to the past. It is these wanderings, metaphorical and not, that make us understand that those non-European societies have their own answers to questions about gender, sexuality, equality, and fluidity of identities. If homonormativity is possible within the framework of national ideologies, then queer and trans* communities do not fit into these ideologies in any way. Queer, like créolisation, we read as a sign of translocality, a sign of a new "vernacular cosmopolitanism", which is always significantly wider and much narrower than the nation. To us, it seems useful to shift the framework, not to forget that we are not only people but also animals, spirits, creatures, part of the biosphere, and inhabitants of the Galaxy. Perhaps trans feminism can be understood also as a trans-human, trans-species ideology. When we discussed what could hypothetically be called "queer", we came up with a story about the movement of oviparous people, abbreviated ovi. In this story, the main character was a queer person from Kazakhstan, who, due to her physical characteristics, had to lay eggs (about the size of a chicken-egg) every month. She would talk about how strong the prejudices against egg-laying people in society are. She would also talk about her ovi-activism, about how she and her partner were making colourful nests in parks as a sign of interspecies solidarity with different oviparous creatures. We've made "Layer", an amateur

budget-free mocumentary film based on this plot, in which, of course, we ourselves played the main roles. This film was shown at the Flaherty film seminar
in New York, at the Bratislava International Film Festival, and private shows.
This is quite a science fiction story, because there are egg-laying mammals.
Therefore, the existence of such people does not contradict any laws of nature,
and the eggs of humans, platypuses, reptiles, and birds do not differ too much.
However, in a human-made culture, some traits are considered decisive (e.g.
skin colour or genital form) while others may be ignored (e.g. finger length).
Are we ready to deal with "facts of nature" for which cultural interpretations
have not yet been made? Créolised identities emerged as a result of colonial
conquests and in this sense constitute "new kinds" of people. Trans* people are also often perceived as such a new kind. And although in both cases
nothing new emerged in the "nature" of human, the change of focus itself,
the emergence of an interest in interpreting this particular reality (for example, the reality of gender and sexuality) brings the question into the political
sphere: Who has the right to assign identities to beings? Is there a possibility
for self-determination? Do we have to accept those versions of reality that are
designated by the authorities as mandatory?

LP and TS: What is the significance of collectivity for the decolonial project of
    Krëlex zentr?

RJ and MV: Our decision to speak on behalf of the collective, that is, to sign
    our work not with surnames, but with the collective signature "Krëlex zentr"
    indicates our interest in experiments with collective subjectivities. This deci-
    sion was made at a time when the intellectual environment of Almaty was
    extremely atomised. And in general, in our individualistic society, artists
    were considered the most radical individualists. Many saw the artist's mis-
    sion in confronting institutions and collectives. For us, it was obvious that the
    main problem was precisely in the absence of collective forms of life – insti-
    tutions, organisations, and self- organisations. We became interested in these
    mysterious and often very powerful entities whose bodies are composed of
    individuals. Following Marie Douglas, we ask ourselves, how do institutions
    think (Douglas 1986)? Does the collective have its own mind? What hap-
    pens to the agency of individuals when they form a collective, for example,
    a family, an enterprise, or a creative association? We think of the ecology
    of institutions as a method of studying practices, agencies, and networks,
    because the difficulties of decolonisation in Kazakhstan ultimately rest on
    the numerous institutional failures. However speculative it may sound, for us
    the main problem with decolonisation in Kazakhstan is that people are often
    afraid and do not trust institutions, especially state (i.e. national) ones. We
    don't sue, because the courts are unfair; we don't go to hospitals, because we
    don't believe in the competence of doctors; we don't go to educational insti-
    tutions, because they are simply terrible; we don't call the police, because
    we are sure that the police will only aggravate the troubles. The only sphere

where there is a ray of light is the sphere of cultural and activist initiatives, that is, grassroots and art organisations. Recently, there are more and more of them. Artists are starting to form some kind of associations, discuss and criticise the decisions and actions of state institutions on social media. These are all very important changes. We use Krëlex zentr not only as an alternative supra-individual subjectivity producing events and texts but also as an experimental model for a possible institution, somewhere in the post-national future. Therefore, we open different departments, as in any institution, draw diagrams of this imaginary organisation, sometimes announce vacancies, in general, mimic and depict a certain bureaucratic structure in order to better understand how it all works or could work. Perhaps our interest in institutions is simply the interest of hungry people in food because we have spent most of our lives outside any institutions (for example, for Ruthia, it's simply unrealistic to get into any kind of organisation for any position in Kazakhstan). Therefore, we had to invent such an institution where we could work, albeit pretend. Many of our projects are in themselves collaborations. So, the exact number of full-time and part-time employees of Krëlex zentr is never known, especially if we take into account all our subpersonalities and more subtle psychic entities, for which the doors of our paranormal institution (parainstitution) are also open. In 2018, we received job applications from two other Kazakhstani artists. Their names are Maria Nef and Ramil Niyazov. So gradually we are becoming more people. We received the applications during our performance-exhibition "Phantom Office", which was held in Almaty on the premises of one friendly semi-underground techno club. This three-day event was planned as a temporary office of Krëlex zentr. It was announced as follows:

Krëlex zentr is a paranormal art institution (parainstitution) engaging with a cultural exchange with the otherworldly and non-existent. From time to time, very briefly, our office opens its doors to the so-called reality. For something to actually exist, official recognition is required. In other words, the reality is always institutionalized, and everything that is not confirmed by certificates and seals is considered invalid: imagined, fictional, unreal. Not all of us get a pass into reality. Creatures expelled from this planet by searchlights of enlightenment, capital, and colonial expansion still continue to appear at dusk, recalling that nonexistent in its own way exists and sometimes produces effects in the reality whose legitimacy is confirmed by the social institutions of modernity. Everything marked as abnormal or undesirable, inferior or excessive, subject to devaluation, denial, or crowding out, however, continues to seek opportunities for communication; as psychoanalysts say, what was repressed always returns. Krëlex zentr, being a ghostly institution, is interested in the practices of social exclusion, covert violence, and silencing, as a result of which phantoms appear. How does anything that is not visible manifest itself in the world? What forms can absence take? How and when does it become noticeable?

Within three days, two departments were opened at the exhibition: "Feminine Counseling" (department head Maria V.) and "Information Bureau" (department head Ruthia J.). We must say that our approach to collective work also involves troubling the differences between art and curatorial activity: we "hire" ourselves, but we can "hire" someone else, and many of our works have a remark "commissioned by Krëlex zentr". Total installations like the Phantom Office serve as an example of the intermediate format between the exhibition and the collective artwork. The "curatorial installation" shown in St. Petersburg in the Rose Center was a similar hybrid. The installation was titled the *Central Asian Mental Map*. We asked our fellow artists to send us instructions on what and how to draw/sculpt/create in the exhibition space to symbolise a concept that was important for them. Using the instructions and pictures sent to us, we made an exposition, something like a mental map of Central Asian art concepts. We must say that, in the contemporary art of our region, the "Central Asian" identification has always been more important than national ones. This has been the case since our artists started participating in the Venice Biennale, which during 2005–2013 had a Central Asian Pavilion, one of the few at this Biennale that infringed the framework of national representation. So, we tend to believe that if any new forms of collectivity can arise under the extremely individualistic neoliberal regimes of post-Soviet nation-states, then contemporary art is able to provide a space where these forms can be tested and cultivated.

Note

1   The spelling Krëlex zentr has been changing over time. In this interview, you will see different spellings of the title depending on the time period and the source cited.

References

Atanasoski, Neda. 2013. *Humanitarian Violence: The U.S. Deployment of Diversity*. Minneapolis and London: University of Minnesota Press.

Barad, Karen Michelle. 2007. *Meeting the Universe Halfway: Quantum Physics and the Entanglement of Matter and Meaning*. Durham and London: Duke University Press. https://doi.org/10.1215/9780822388128.

Bernabé, Jean, Patrick Chamoiseau, and Confiant Raphaël. 1997. "Éloge De La Créolité." In *Praise of Creoleness*, Édition bilingue francais/anglais, texte traduit par M. B. Taleb-Khyar ed. Paris: Gallimard.

Buck-Morss, Susan. 2009. *Hegel, Haiti and Universal History*. Pittsburgh, PA: University of Pittsburgh Press. https://doi.org/10.2307/j.ctt7zwbgz.

Burns, Lorna M. 2008. "Creolization and the Collective Unconscious: Locating the Originality of Art in Wilson Harris' Jonestown, The Mask of the Beggar and The Ghost of Memory." *Postcolonial Text* 4, no. 2: 1–18.

Castro, Eduardo Batalha Viveiros de. 2014. *Cannibal Metaphysics: For a Post-Structural Anthropology*. Translated by Peter Skafish. Minneapolis, MN: Univocal.

Coutts-Smith, Kenneth. 1991. "Some General Observations of the Problem of Cultural Colonialism." In *The Myth of Primitivism*, edited by Susan Hiller, 15–16. London and New York: Routledge.

"Creoleak Centr." n.d. *BodyPolitix.* https://bodypolitix.me/the-team%D0%BA%D0%BE %D0%BC%D0%B0%D0%BD%D0%B4%D0%B0/creoleak-centr/ (accessed February 1, 2020).

Creoleak Centr. 2016. "Istorii Transoksiany: kreol'nost', kompozitsionizm, transfeminizm." V *Poniatia o Sovetskom v T͡sentral'noĭ Azii: Al'manakh Shtaba № 2*, pod redakt͡sieĭ Georgii͡a Mamedova i Oksany Shatalovoĭ, 76–128. Bishkek: SHTAB Press.

Deleuze, Gilles, and Guattari Félix. 1987. *A Thousand Plateaus. Capitalism and Schizophrenia*. Translation and foreword by Brian Massumi. Minneapolis, MN: University of Minnesota Press. https://doi.org/10.5040/9781472547989.

Douglas, Mary. 1986. *How Institutions Think*. Syracuse, NY: Syracuse University Press.

Eco, Umberto. 1989. *The Open Work*. Translated by Anna Cancogni, with an introduction by David Robey. Cambridge, MA: Harvard University Press.

Glissant, Édouard. 1997. *Poetics of Relation*. Translated by Betsy Wing. Ann Arbor: University of Michigan Press. https://doi.org/10.3998/mpub.10257.

Gržinić, Marina, and Šefik Tatlić. 2014. *Necropolitics, Racialization, and Global Capitalism: Historicization of Biopolitics and Forensics of Politics, Art, and Life*. Lanham, MD: Lexington Books.

Hall, Stuart. 2015. "Creolité and the Process of Creolization." In *Creolizing Europe: Legacies and Transformations*, edited by Encarnación Gutiérrez Rodríguez and Shirley Anne Tate, 12–25. Liverpool: Liverpool University Press. https://doi.org/10.2307/j.ctt1gn6d5h.6.

Harris, Wilson. 1999. *Selected Essays of Wilson Harris: The Unfinished Genesis of the Imagination*. Edited by Andrew Bundy. London: Routledge. https://doi.org/10.4324/9780203981832.

Irigaray, Luce. 1985. *This Sex Which Is Not One*. Translated by Carolyn Burke. Ithaca, NY: Cornell University Press.

Kirndörfer, Elisabeth. 2014. "Analysis and Discussion of the Concept of 'Creolization' with Focus on Édouard Glissant – Between Local 'Rootedness' and Global Application." https://eu.bilgi.edu.tr/media/uploads/2014/06/30/AnalysisAndDiscussionOfThe ConceptOfCreolizationWithFocusOnEdouardGlissantBetweenLocalRootednessAnd GlobalApplicationByElizabethKirndorfer.pdf. (accessed February 18, 2020).

Koobak, Redi, and Raili Marling. 2014. "The Decolonial Challenge: Framing Post-socialist Central and Eastern Europe Within Transnational Feminist Studies." *European Journal of Women's Studies* 21, no. 4: 330–343. https://doi.org/10.1177/1350506814542882.

Krëlex Radio. 2018. "Transoxiana: A Tour for Newcomers." *YouTube video*, 17:41, June 19, 2018. www.youtube.com/watch?v=3HHFpqfSv9k&t=486s.

kreolex zentre. 2012. "Apology of Creoleness: The Case of Central Asia." *Kreolex Zentre* (official website). http://kreolex.center/texts/apology-for-creoleness-the-case-of-central-asia/.

Lionnet, Françoise, and Shumei Shih, eds. 2011. *The Creolization of Theory*. Durham, NC: Duke University Press. https://doi.org/10.1215/9780822393320.

Mol, Annemarie. 2003. *The Body Multiple: Ontology in Medical Practice*. Durham, NC: Duke University Press.

Said, Edward W. 1993. *Culture and Imperialism*. New York: Knopf.

Santos, Boaventura de Sousa. 2014. *Epistemologies of the South Justice Against Epistemicide*. London and New York: Routledge. https://doi.org/10.4324/9781315634876.

Santos, Boaventura de Sousa. 2018. *The End of the Cognitive Empire: The Coming of Age of Epistemologies of the South*. Durham and London: Duke University Press. https://doi.org/10.1215/9781478002000.

Segalen, Victor. 2002. *Essay on Exoticism: An Aesthetics of Diversity: Post-Contemporary Interventions*. Translated and edited by Yaël Rachel Schlick, foreword by Harry Harootunian. Durham, NC: Duke University Press. https://doi.org/10.1215/9780822383727.

"Stage Performance," at "Between the Lines" Poetry Festival, Almaty, Artpoint, August 5, 2016. http://kreolex.center/live/between-the-lines/.

"Subaltern Mumble," stage performance with half live music and hardly spoken word, at "kvir_feminist_actziya" D.I.Y. festival, Vienna, 2014. http://kreolex.center/projects/8-subaltern-mumble-stage-performance-with-half-live-music-and-hardly-spoken-word-kvir_feminist_actziya-d-i-y-festival-vienna-2014/.

Tlostanova, Madina. 2010. *Gender Epistemologies and Eurasian Borderlands*. New York: Palgrave Macmillan. https://doi.org/10.1057/9780230113923.

Tlostanova, Madina. 2017. *Postcolonialism and Postsocialism in Fiction and Art: Resistance and Re-Existence*. Cham, Switzerland: Palgrave Macmillan. https://doi.org/10.1007/978-3-319-48445-7.

Vasconcelos, José. 1925. *La Raza Cósmica: Misión de la Raza Iberoamericana: Notas de Viajes a la América del Sur*. Madrid: Agencia Mundial de Librería.

Wynter, Sylvia, and Katherine McKittrick. 2015. "Unparalleled Catastrophe for Our Species? Or, to Give Humanness a Different Future: Conversations." In *Sylvia Wynter: On Being Human as Praxis*, edited by Katherine McKittrick, 9–89. Durham, NC: Duke University Press. https://doi.org/10.1215/9780822375852-002.

Chapter 11

Speaking against the void

Decolonial transfeminist relations and radical potentialities

Tjaša Kancler

When thinking about postsocialism today, we cannot avoid the complexities that arise from this term and the risk of falling into generalisation and homogenisation of the (post)socialist experience. Locating historical and present feminist struggles there complicates the analysis further. Considering the need to address the specificities of local contexts and their differences within the geopolitical space labelled former Eastern Europe, I delineate some points to re-think the relations between the postcolonial and the postsocialist and contextualise decolonial and transfeminist politics of positioning, its challenges as well as radical potentialities within that. To alert against the reproduction of whiteness and the colonial gender binary, I refer to the "coloniality of gender" (Lugones 2008) as one of the central problems to address when re-thinking resistance, imagining and acting for economic, political and social change.

The main idea underlying my un-disciplinary approach is that there are a number of multiple, heterogeneous, entangled, and complex processes within one single colonial capitalist historical reality. As a former Eastern European, from the former Yugoslavia (Slovenia), who migrated to Italy and then to Spain before Slovenia joined the European Union, not quite white and not quite trans*[1] and still inhabiting this symbolic space called the East because of a continuous reproduction of racialisation, I think it is necessary to search for decolonial ruptures, modulations and interferences which metamorphose the grid, its point system, coordinates, pre-established channels and threads, moving in new directions.

Referring to Somerville (2000) and Puar (2007), I will engage in "reading sideways". As they write, this means linking together seemingly unrelated and often disjunctively situated moments and their effects in ways that attend to the interconnected histories of racial, gender, sexual, and other bio-necro-political formations and regulations. By questioning postsocialism and challenging the colonial epistemology of the gender binary, I search for ways that the sex-gender dissident pre/post/socialist subjects put forward to unleash the binds that produce the modern/colonial terms of recognition and to resist the regulation of bodies, labour, and space.

Situating postsocialism

By drawing attention to geo-politics, I begin from the necessity to disrupt the linear narrative of the expansion of neoliberalism after the fall of the Berlin Wall to emphasise the relational processes of colonial/imperial differentiation and subjectification across Eastern Europe and the global South, as well as practices of resistance. Capitalism must be analysed in relation to coloniality, gender, and racism which are profoundly linked to class and sexuality.

The concept of postsocialism should be analysed as a global condition, entangled in the European colonial/imperial and Cold War legacy, that is, built on its racial and colonial/imperial formations, rather than as a historically and regionally bound concept to describe the economic and political state of countries that were formally socialist during the Cold War. As Neda Atanasoski (2013, 26) argues, what is crucial here is that "if postsocialism is relegated to periodizing a particular moment of regional transition that at once affirms the death of socialism and consigns it to an ideological formation inferior to Western modernity and universality, it particularises what is actually a global condition in which the West situates the universal claims of human rights, freedom, democracy, that underwrite its global violence." Postsocialism thus becomes a dynamic concept, allowing for a much more complex engagement with and recontextualisation of hegemonic historical narratives as well as other modes of geopolitical restructuring beyond governmental and structural reforms in former socialist countries that occurred after 1989.

From this perspective, rather than celebrate embracing "democracy" and "freedom", the "post" of postsocialism speaks of further processes of colonisation which allow the West to suppress the materiality of our history, knowledge, and memory. The reconfiguration of the former socialist states through the deregulation of economy, the privatisation of public institutions, and their integration into the global market, erased their anti-fascist, anti-colonial, feminist, and sex-gender dissident histories, theories, and practices. In this political context, nationalism became a predominant mode of organising social and political life, presented as "liberation" from what was supposedly suppressed during communism/socialism. Fascist, racist, sexist, and homo-transphobic politics fit perfectly into this matrix and contribute to its efficacy. While the condition of loss and erasure is further characterised by the absence of any credible global emancipatory project or horizon of hope, the former Eastern Europe has actually become a void in the new world order (Tlostanova 2012).

Remembering the Bandung conference of 1955 is not only crucial to alter the understanding of the expansion of capitalism and its consequences, but also to think about the possibilities for resistance on molecular, bodily and geo-political level. At the conference, 29 countries from Asia and Africa participated and represented at that moment one third of the world, people of colour, and non-Christians, pointing to the colonial history and the problem of racism in its religious and secular manifestations. This summit was important because of its aim to find new ways of imagining and formulating a common vision for the future which would de-link from two main macro narratives: capitalism and "communism" as well as modernity and Eurocentric legacy (Mignolo 2007). At that moment, the historical bases for decolonisation were set down. Drawing on the principles agreed upon at the Bandung conference, the Non-Aligned Movement started in 1961 in Belgrade, Yugoslavia. After the fall of the Berlin Wall, Aníbal Quijano (1992), one of the founding members of the research group Modernity/Coloniality/Decoloniality, linked the colonial history to capitalism on the basis of José C. Mariategui's work and Black Marxism, in order to emphasise that colonialism is not a question of the past and colonial formulations still operate, mutate, and extend through globalisation into our present time.

By introducing the concept of coloniality as an indispensable underside of modernity from the 16th century onwards, Quijano conceptualised the intersectionality of multiple, heterogeneous, global hierarchies and forms of domination and exploitation: racial, sexual, political, economic, linguistic, and spiritual, where the racial/ethnic hierarchy reconfigures transversally all global structures of power. Emphasising its structural, constitutive, and non-derivative relations by claiming intersectionality, these are in fact the analytical methods introduced previously by Black feminists (Combahee River Collective, Kimberlé Crenshaw, Audre Lorde, Patricia Hill Collins among others) and developed further together with women of colour feminists (Chela Sandoval, Chandra Mohanty, Gloria Anzaldúa, Cherie Moraga) to point to their historical, theoretical, and practical exclusions and take action. From the 1990s onwards, the intersectional method is placed in relation to the concept of coloniality which allows for new analytical scopes through which to examine, as Tlostanova (2013) argues, how the West determined one single norm of humanity, the legitimate knowledge of economic and social system, spatial and temporal models, values and cultural norms.

Quijano's concept of coloniality logically invoked the concept of decoloniality as an emancipatory project. Decoloniality means working towards liberation from coloniality, but also to articulate social relations, locally and globally, in ways not controllable by the colonial matrix of power. This also implies epistemic disobedience, or in reference to Gloria Anzaldúa (1967), a border epistemology. It means questioning the common universal basis of modernity's self-narrative, its logics of racialisation(s) and systems of annihilation, its construction of difference as "Other(s)" and its operations to categorise and classify human beings as dispensable.

If postsocialism in such framework of analysis is not at all postcolonial, we have to modify the basis of our analysis in order to understand the former Eastern Europe through coloniality in relation to the former West. This implies taking into account its imitation of Western modernity with racism at its core. Within these processes the colonial history of European colour-blindness is inscribed, although the concept "race" has its geographic and intellectual origins in Europe. While there are all kinds of negations around racism or it is silenced or presented as a marginal problem (also by the white left), we have to emphasise that racialisation prevails as the main logic of global capitalism today, which regulates and differentiates the social, political, and economic space (Goldberg 2009; El-Tayeb 2011; Gržinić and Tatlić 2012; Essed and Hoving 2014). Understanding racialisation as contextual and racism as fluid shows that freedom and opportunity for some people is generally acquired at the expense of "Others". This is also related to the processes of zonification. The European politics of segregation transformed the former Eastern Europe into a buffer zone to control and block migrations from Africa and Asia, while migrants from the former Eastern European countries became in turn subjected to control, discrimination, violence, and processes of deportation from the "former" Western Europe.

By claiming that the division West/East is "obsolete" after the fall of the Berlin Wall, the repetition of Occident/Orient division as a part of colonial history and its continuity is intensified. Far from ending the friend/enemy logics, succeeding the socialist states, the "invisible terrorist network" called Al Qaeda became a new enemy (today's ISIS) needed to re-enforce Western hegemony and neoliberal values worldwide. With the "war on terror" announced after the September 11 attacks in 2001, a new shift in global political relations took place with its consequences still resonating in the present crisis. As Gayatri Spivak (2006, 169) explains, "terror in this guise is not a monopoly of some Muslim fundamentalists. It is the preserve of whatever entity – including our democracies – convinced that its enemy is by definition the enemy of "humanity", "civilization", even "God" himself – a theological enemy". While Islamophobia as a form of structural, cultural, and epistemic racism is linked to the coloniality of power, knowledge, and being, intrinsic to the modern/colonial world system, it is necessary to state that we are trapped in the epistemological-existential, spatial-temporal, and aesthetic prison (Adlbi Sibai 2017, 33).

Whole countries have been destroyed (Yugoslavia, Afghanistan, Iraq, Libya, Syria, Ukraine) and reinvented through further Western intervention and wars, the economic stimulus needed to maintain its supremacy, to compensate the deficiencies provoked by globalisation and the expectative placed in "new economy". The postsocialist transformation of modes of production and fast expansion of capitalism is sustained mainly in the realm of financialisation and immaterial labour as a new paradigm, linked to the development of new technologies. In this situation the "politics of security" is turned into an active mechanism to persistently re-enforce the global order. In this sense, the process of disappearance of certain borders after 1989 implies its simultaneous multiplication and conversion into zones, border regions, or territories. The postsocialist Eastern Europe operates as one of them. Such a notion of security was imposed to justify a constant activity, on national as well as international level, which can be read as a form of bio-necro power (Mbembe 2003; Gržinić 2009) that assumes the task of producing, controlling, transforming, and destroying social life all over the globe.

In 2008, the world experienced a moment when the proper concept of crisis entered in crisis and witnessed a phenomenon where capital is beyond its limit. Nowadays the valorisation of capital operates independently of real production which creates "bubbles" because it produces an immense accumulation of fictitious capital through financial mechanisms, without the necessity of real production. The "bubbles" are no more an aberration, but rather a permanent character of financial accumulation regime (López Petit 2009). In this context, the relation capital/work as opposed to political force is equivalent to the relation capital/debt, which acquired unprecedented role, almost eclipsing the theory of work-value (Vishmidt 2010). By extending debt in general over whole societies, this became a mechanism of subjection, bio- and necro-control of lives. The extortion of public debt interests, depredation, expropriation of goods, and common wealth operate through the process of accumulation by dispossession and simultaneous negation and violation of human rights. The accumulation is now possible without real inversions, and while it works simultaneously through and across different scales of "race", the principal consequences are material and existential precarity, or dispensability of populations (Mbembe 2012; Butler 2011). These recent transformations, according to Paul B. Preciado (2013), point to the articulation of a set of new micro-prosthetic devices for the control of subjectivity with new molecular biological techniques and media networks. As he writes, we are faced with a new kind of capitalism that is hot, psychotropic, and punk, but we have to add: in the "zones of being", while it is cold, bureaucratic, necrotoxic, and heavy metal in the "zones of non-being" (Fanon 1963).

Rethinking the economic and financial crisis cannot do away with but demands addressing with a grave concern the racism and fascism that are increasing sharply. Thousands of people are dying as they cross the militarised borders of Fortress Europe, which is multiplying its walls, while undertaking negotiations about its externalisation to intensify the control of the EU external borders and cut the possibility of crossing borders in the south and east to Europe. The militarised borders, immigration detention centres or identification and expulsion centres, NATO, Frontex, the coast and border patrols, Dublin III, and other criminal conventions and the sophisticated biometric control systems go hand in hand with how the situation of refugees and migrants is "managed", with the imposition of hierarchies through the status of citizenship and the multiplication of internal borders that are constitutive of the global division of labour. These brutal processes of selection of people in terms of racial, class, gender, sexual, religious categories are embedded in western capitalist colonial history and present, and are at the same time repeated in former Eastern Europe and the Global South through externalisation of borders and local political servitude to colonial imperial centres. This is how those who are labelled as "Other(s)" are constructed as differentiated subhuman(s) through different processes of dehumanisation.

With the suspension of democracy in the name of global oligarchy's investments and the international financial industry that are politically inexpungable, through individual debt, public deficit, and public debt, lives of entire populations are mortgaged and expropriated (Mbembe 2012). All of this points to the fact that the crisis, which is not only economic but at the same time political, existential, institutional, spiritual, environmental, and so on, does not describe anymore an exceptional period, something temporal or episodic, but has rather become a norm, the fabric of postsocialist life, existence, and death. This necropolitical mode of life means pure abandonment. The surplus value of capital today is based and generated from (the worlds of) death (Gržinić 2009).

Transfeminism(s) and decolonial feminism(s): limits and challenges

Contemporary western global politics is a continuation of the modern/colonial capitalist matrix from which it has developed. These processes are also related to postsocialism as one of the outcomes of coloniality which is why any emancipatory struggle today should be thought of as part of a decolonial process embedded in historical and current relations with Black, postcolonial, lesbian, pro-sex feminist, queer of colour, and trans* politics and struggles. These struggles have brought about "new" terms in theory and activism in recent years, such as transfeminism(s) and decolonial feminism(s), both of which are barely present in feminist debates in former communist/socialist countries due to the colonial capitalist erasures.

Re-thinking postcolonial and postsocialist relations, where we should contextualise body-politics, transfeminist and decolonial politics, their limits, challenges and radical potentialities for former Eastern European space and beyond, requires tackling the reproduction of Eurocentrism, whiteness and whitening. Entangled in western modern/colonial system, Eurocentrism was produced in the last five centuries through a set of colonial capitalist values and a system of knowledge that became universalised through erasing, silencing, and disqualifying socialist gender trajectories and the pre-socialist local genealogies of women and feminist struggles as well as the multiplicity of sex-gender dissident expressions and experiences. These erasures operate through the mind-colonisation through the intensified circulation of white western feminism and queer theory, supported by grants and accompanied by particular ideological demands. At the same time, the coloniality generates difficulties for a proper production of knowledge and articulation of struggles that would take into account a specific pre-, post-, and socialist practices (Tlostanova 2013).

Transfeminism takes us back to the conflicts around the ticklish subject of feminist struggle in the western context, in reference to Sylvia Rivera and Marsha P. Johnson's antiracist trans* activism from the 1970s on, Leslie Feinberg's and Sandy Stone's work in the 1990s, which afterwards made it possible for Diana Couvant and Emy Koyama to coin the term, first at Yale University and afterwards in the "The Transfeminist Manifesto" (2003). They spoke about transfeminism as a movement for and by trans women who understand their liberation as entangled with women's liberation, antiracism and anticapitalism, a movement which has also started to gain visibility in Russia, for example (see Kirey-Sitnikova 2014, 2016).

In Spain, the activist group Guerrilla Travolaka and other autonomous trans* and lesbian feminists have pushed for a pro-depathologisation movement as a political project based on a radical feminist critique and struggles since 2006. The activists challenged the problems in feminism in relation to trans* issues, and trans* movement in relation to feminism, in order to make trans* demands for depathologisation a common issue. Understanding sex and gender in the sense of technological interventions (technologies of gender), Preciado introduced the term "technogender", stating that "man" and "woman" exist as a social norm that is maintained by means of control: pharmacological and audio-visual techniques that constantly distort the reality that surrounds us. As he claims, "sex", "heterosexuality", and "race" are three violent somatic fictions, produced by the western capitalist colonial system and continue to persist nowadays (Preciado 2008, 58). During the state feminist conference in Granada in 2009, *Manifesto for a Transfeminist Insurrection* was written collectively to expose the problems of binary thinking and reduction of feminist struggle to abortion rights, sexism, violence, precarity, and access to labour market. In order to broaden the scope of issues depathologisation of transsexuality, HIV, postpornography, sex work, critique of institutional feminism, mercantilisation, and depoliticisation of LGBT movement, immigration laws and regulations, transmigrations, and so on took place in further debates (Solá and Urko 2013). Arising after queer critique and activism, which has been exposed to the accelerated process of mercantilisation and recodification by dominant discourses and thus lost some of its political potential, transfeminism became the position of those who experiment with multiplicity by deconstructing the political fiction of the binary categories man/woman, while stressing the fact that capitalism and heteropatriarchy remain our shared basis of oppression.

Even though in the Spanish context it is recognised that race, gender, sexuality are powerful western colonial fictions, the problems of amnesia, displacing, or neglecting the analysis of racialisation, whitewashing of intersectionality, appropriation, and Eurocentrism continue to be reproduced. That is why the potentials of "sudaca/euraca/norteca transfeminism", to use Sayak Valencia's (2014) expression, were discussed in the Latin American context in relation to coloniality in order to point to a different genealogy, where the following four lines cross the transfeminist debates:

> US women of color third world feminism (by Black, Chicanas, Native American and Asian American feminists); sexual dissidence and its geopolitical displacement to South: from Queer to Cuir; movement for depathologization of trans identities (Stop Trans Pathologization) and *pro-puta* movement for de-stigmatization and legalization of sex work; minoritized becomings, migrations and economic precarity.
>
> (Valencia 2014)

Queer theory and activism, transfeminism as well as trans* activism have for a long time been criticised by decolonial theoreticians and activists. The decolonial critique continuously exposes the reproduction of Eurocentrism, whitewashing, and racism within feminisms, those that marginalise or silence the concerns around racialisation processes which are central to the colonial capitalist gender system and its logics of oppression. Re-thinking emancipatory potentials by confronting coloniality and racialisation in relation to becoming a migrant and related movements in which many different practices, voices and discourses, embodiments and mobilities are inscribed, brings us to the decolonial erotic turn (Rodríguez Moreno 2018) and positionality.

For radical potentialities within postcolonial and postsocialist debates and the current crisis, I claim that the theorising of Maria Lugones (2008, 2010) poses crucial challenges for both transfeminism and decolonial option. On the one hand, as Espinosa, Gómez, and Ochoa (2014) write, she developed a critique of the central idea of "race" from which the modern configuration of power and exploitation, as elaborated by Quijano, emerges. She questions his understanding of sex as biological as well as his failure to see that within the concept of gender the idea of sexual or biological dimorphism (man-woman dichotomy), heteronormativity, and the patriarchal distribution of power are inscribed. On the other hand, Lugones poses important challenges for transfeminism from the decolonial perspective by inscribing her analysis of gender within coloniality (the colonial matrix of power) in order to dismantle the universal notion of "women", the colonial formulation of gender classification, to question its history, and to point towards decolonial feminism.

Along these lines, Lugones argues that "the gender system is not just hierarchically but also racially differentiated and this differentiation negates the humanity and gender to colonized peoples" (2010, 748). Her main claim is that sexual difference, which in itself is a colonial invention (fiction), is not a social category as such. The enslaved and racialised workers, as she states, were bestialised. In many societies and locales before the Western colonisation gender categorisations did not exist in the Western sense, while categories of seniority, professional, and other principles were more important than biologised gender. With her analysis, she shows how gender and sexual diversity are filtered through a colonising, binary gaze into naturalised ideas of "sex" and "gender", both operating as a Eurocentric category, thus the fixed gender binarism is far from being the only possible way of human social relations. Instead, as she writes, its meaning must be understood within the particular cosmology/metaphysics. The traces of these histories of removal and dispossession remain, as do their entanglements in global sexual and gender politics today. Through such an analysis, Lugones' postulates are related to the re-empowered critique and work previously developed by counter-hegemonic, anti-racist feminisms, which at the same time have an important influence on the development of decolonial option (Espinosa, Gómez, and Ochoa 2014).

Decolonial feminist and activist contributions highlight the need to shift the "geography of reason" (Gordon 2005) and disrupt the Western progress narrative. It becomes clear that through the European colonial expansion, which started with conquest of the Americas, the first regulations and punishment laws, prohibition of homosexuality, and multiplicity of sexual and gender expressions were steadily introduced. Thus, in decolonial discourses, coloniality of gender which assumes that the whole world must operate according to modern/colonial gender binary model is constantly questioned and deconstructed.

While a discourse that would capture systems of knowledge that exceed the categorisations of gender, sexuality, and even transgender is still poorly or not at all conceptualised in the former Eastern Europe, our condition should be regarded in its complexity and dynamics with today's dispersion of postsocialist subjects in different directions (Tlostanova 2013). Hence, we need to push for a radical approach to developing an analysis that leaves behind Western-derived meanings of gender altogether or at least problematising them (Chiang 2012). It is necessary to insist on unsettling the existing conceptual frameworks from the multiplicity of pre-, post-, and socialist sex-gender dissident expressions, experiences, and practices, trans*migrations, becomings, and movements, while questioning the complicity of feminist and LGBT*IQ+ struggles in the very classist and racist oppressions they claim to oppose. This means asking at the same time how we might better engage materially with dismantling white supremacy, heteropatriarchy, gender binary, and coloniality in all their forms.

Radical imaginaries, politics, and potentialities

To the extent that the body is a culturally intelligible construct, and the modern/colonial techniques in and through which bodies are positioned and transformed are in fact inextricably related, it is important to discuss its relations to the visual – the production of images and imaginaries. Entangled in the capitalist colonial system to stimulate desire and reconfigure the everyday, physical, political, and sensible conditions of embodiment, the modern/colonial visual techniques of mind-colonisation shape subjectivities for the hyper machine of capitalist production. This phenomenon could be called "image capitalism" (Mbembe 2013), or "the coloniality of seeing" (Barriendos 2010). Therefore, the production of radical critical imaginaries to oppose mainstream visual codes challenges the colonial binary gender system by conceptualising political interventions from multiple local interrelated positionalities, thus disrupting the logics of colonial visual orders and make these visible beyond what we can already see. Directing critical attention towards the questions of embodiment, situated thinking, and the visual means taking into consideration a much more complex system of colonial power relations that also points to the need to break down the body politics in a molar sense (a whole, integrated body with one identity) in the name of multiplicity, affective, and sensibility, its resistant and transformative political potentials.

When thinking about historical traces of decolonial transfeminist critique and current debates, imaginaries, and struggles in (post)socialist Eastern Europe, and more specifically the former Yugoslavia and the Balkans today, I want to mention two important artistic projects that bring further together a set of key references. The first one is the "Transvestite Museum of Peru", a project developed by the philosopher and drag activist Giuseppe Campuzano (2003–2013), which confronts the colonial epistemology by questioning the relations between the state and the Western modern/colonial body's disciplining, the politics of representation, memory, and disidentifications as a transvestite revolutionary practice. The second one is the "East Art Map" (1999–2005), a project and a book edited by the group IRWIN (2006) to (re)construct the missing history of contemporary art, art networks, and art conditions from an Eastern European perspective. These references are important to think about as the potentials of engaging in postcolonial and postsocialist dialogues as well as for re-reading the postsocialist space by making sex-gender dissident practices, traversed by the processes of racialisation, a central political question for a construction of counter-history, memory, imaginaries, and articulation of our struggles.

In my attempt to gather the traces of decolonial transfeminist critique, I will begin by emphasising the theoretical, artistic, and activist work by Marina Gržinić and Aina Šmid, done during the last three decades in the context of former Yugoslavia, initially as members of the group Borders of Control N.4. The artists produced some of the first videos in the former Eastern Europe during socialism, entitled "Icons of Glamour, Echoes of Death" (1982) and "The Threat of the Future" (1983) in which they tackle the core by conceptually and politically dismantling the biological understanding of sex and sexual difference, gender binary, and heteronormativity through performative drag practices from a lesbian and feminist positionality. Staging a performance in front of the camera, they speak about sexual and gender politics, female pleasure, sadomasochism, and pornography. Gržinić further developed a theoretical research on dissident feminist practices, artistic performances, and spaces in her texts "Former Yugoslavia, Queer and Class Struggle"(2008), "Europe: Gender, Class, Race" (2012) and "Dissident feminisms, anti-racist politics and artistic interventionist practices" (2014). In her work, she continuously questions the western capitalist colonial processes of racialisation, necropolitics, image capitalism, and construction of a feminist genealogy, by articulating a counter-history of dissident antiracist feminist struggles and thought from (the former) Eastern Europe.

In their video "Relations: 25 Years of Lesbian group ŠKUC-LL" (Gržinić, Šmid and Simčič 2012), the artists elaborate a testimony of counter-power of lesbian movement and its struggles for visibility. From the dissolution of socialism at the end of the 1980s, through war and transition in the 1990s, up to the present time of global capitalism, the video brings together critical discourses, artistic potentialities, and political interventions in relation to politics, economy, law, culture, arts, and institutions. Since the 1980s onwards, ŠKUC-LL and its founding members Nataša Sukič, Susana Tratnik, Tatjana Greif, Nataša Velikonja (2012) produced the most important analysis and political interventions in the form of texts, books, performances, events and manifestations, redefining the very point of struggle to end discrimination in Slovenia. The need for a persistent redefinition of the subject of feminist movement in Slovenia expressed itself first as a lesbian political stance. As Gržinić stated in the radio program "Lezbomanija", which was hosted by Nataša Sukič and more recently by Urška Sterle on Radio Študent Ljubljana: "Before being feminists, we were lesbians". Lesbians who took the position through re-reading of history, language, and performativity, developed a sharp critique of western LGBT activism and established alliances across the (post)Yugoslav space, not only among lesbian activists but also among Roma, trans*, sex workers, the disabled, and other minoritarised groups.

Among many publications, documents, and an ongoing self-organised struggle by the Erased since the 1990s, Dražena Perić's documentary "The Caravan of the Erased" (2007) shows that the state itself with its repressive apparatuses and collaborationists is the most illegal. In Slovenia, this is exposed paradigmatically through the erasure, continuous expulsion and discrimination of migrants, refugees, LGBTQI+ and sex workers. Slovenia was constituted as a sovereign racist state on the basis of the erasure of more than 20,000 Yugoslav citizens, who were deleted from the register of permanent residency on 26 February 1992. The question of erasure, as committed in the Republic of Slovenia, still remains unsolved. What this documentary tells us is that we also need to put the concept of the state at the centre of analysis: the process of constitution of a new state on the basis of organised administrative genocide, the need to transform the concept of citizenship and stand in opposition to colonial capitalism, EU's criminal migration politics and control, zonification processes, as well as precarious conditions of labour, related to history and present racism, anti-Semitism, Islamophobia, sexism, and homo-transphobia.

Among these critical audio-visual works that go back to the Yugoslav Black Wave, it is necessary to also point to Želimir Žilnik's film "Marble Ass" (1994), which is the only fiction film depicting trans* practice, and the subversive power of transvestites to challenge nationalism at its core by sabotaging the very idea of natural, essential, and identity. Furthermore, more recently developed critique by a younger generation of theoreticians and activists is put forward in the book entitled *LGBT Activism and Europeanisation in Post-Yugoslav Space* (2016) where the authors interrogate a link between "Europeanisation" and "gay emancipation" that elevates certain forms of gay activist engagement to a measure of democracy, progress, and modernity while at the same time relegates homo-transphobic attacks to the status of non-European "Other(s)", who are inevitably positioned in the patriarchal past that should be left behind. This separation serves the purpose of creating and strengthening a local liberal European-oriented elite whose number then act as local interlocutors who, in advocating Europeanisation as the solution to violence directed towards queer communities, become vehicles of EU expansionism (Rexhepi 2016). In this sense, inviting-in, disidentifications, imperceptibility, and invisibility, as Rexhepi argues, may be just some of the living strategies sex-gender dissidents use to confront the normative liberal politics of coming-out and visibility, to avoid being absorbed into neoliberal governmental technologies.

Another crucial book for further debates is *Džuvljarke. Roma Lesbian Existence*, written by Vera Kurtić and published in 2013. Džuvljarke is a term used among the Roma living in Serbia, and together with its Serbian-influenced suffix, refers to lesbians implying a negative connotation within the heteronormative patriarchal social matrix. Kurtić's work shows that Romani lesbian existence and its visibility cannot remain issues separate from the challenges that are encountered by non-Romani LGBT community in Serbia, former Yugoslavia, and beyond, and the challenges within the larger Roma community. As she writes, "Romani lesbian existence needs to be on the shared agenda, just as yesterday's impossible is tomorrow's inevitable" (2013, 17). Kurtić's crucial analysis points to the whiteness and racism being reproduced within former Eastern European space, feminist, and LGBT*IQ+ theory and activism which is not an outcome of postsocialism but has much deeper historical roots. As Rexhepi (2018, 13) asks:

> What does it mean, that while Roma, Black and Muslim people were (in socialism) and are racialized in Eastern Europe – their racialization is subsumed and levelled out under broader critique of coloniality or Orientalization of former socialist subjects? What does this erasure through levelling achieve? More importantly, who speaks in the name of the post-socialist subject? These questions are very important because they also highlight a frequently ignored racialized hierarchies during socialism (as a result of the imitation of Western modernity) by anchoring the contemporary rise of racism as a simple outcome of post-socialist Europeanization (Dzenovska 2013; Böröcz and Sarkar 2017).

All these references and questions set the basis for engaging in postcolonial and postsocialist dialogues by undoing the foundational myths, ideological fantasies, and political fictions that lay "hidden" under the capitalist colonial, socialist, and postsocialist binary gender system, and to further elaborate on decolonial transfeminist relations and radical potentialities for transformation. It is not about uncovering the lost truth from the past, but instead becomes a creative process that minds the gaps through the attempt at a decolonial counter-reading, intersectional thinking of history and present, and by inventing new truths which are coming from the past.

Against the postsocialist void in which we are trapped and global coloniality that (re)produces it, our further feminist theorising and practice should address the contemporary condition which is the result of a relational processes of colonial/imperial differentiation and subjectification. This involves both resisting the process of reproduction of colonial taxonomies and reclaiming radical multiplicity as the basis of decolonial transfeminist politics and any imagination of the social. Thus, from our double consciousness we have to elaborate a double critique of the West and of the former Eastern Europe. The question is not only how to create a negative resistance but also a re-existence (Alban Achinte 2018), a non-hierarchic proliferation of (re)existential becomings. It is important to show that today's decolonial consciousness is based on and takes from previous flows of resistance to western domination; to insist on the history, memory, and contribution of those voices and experiences which made a political shift, a change in perspective, fractures in the existing system, or revolution. In order to dismantle the colonial matrix of power and to work on our critical alliances transversally, the imaginary and affective dimension has to be taken into account as one of the key sites for radical political interventions today.

Note

1   To quote Marina Gržinić, Marissa Lôbo, and Ivana Marjanović (2013, 117):

> In relation to "former" Western Europe, its hegemony (supremacy) and construction of deficient "other", someone coming from former Eastern Europe is always part of process of discrimination; because there is always implemented the so-called principle of the "deficiency" of a certain geographical region called former Eastern Europe, where it is seen as such by its Western counterpart. But when the color of the skin is a border, then within the discrimination processes, we have to recontextualize ourselves, so to speak, every moment, both while entering the public as well in the private context, because it is not the same, – we can still hide ourselves within a system of mimicry.

> The term "trans*" with an asterisk has recently been used as an umbrella concept to include many different gender expressions and identities, such as trans, transexual, transgender, gender queer, etc. The asterisk emphasises the heterogeneity of bodies, identities, and experiences, which goes beyond the imposed gender binary social norms. Trans* is a concept introduced by its protagonists out of rejection of the terms coming from the pathologising medical discourse. It also points out that while we share a common struggle, we recognise that there is not just one interpretation of what it means to be trans, transexual, or transgender. Both queer and trans* have to be re-thought from decolonial positionality.

References

Adlbi Sibai, Sirin. 2017. *La cárcel de feminismo: Hacia un pensamiento islámico decolonial*. Madrid: Akal.

Alban Achinte, Adolfo. 2018. *Prácticas creativas de re-existencia: Más allá del arte . . . el mundo de lo sensible*. Buenos Aires: Ediciones del Signo.

Anazaldúa, Gloria. 1967. *Borderlands/La Frontera: The New Mestiza*. San Francisco, CA: Aunt Lute.

Atanasoski, Neda. 2013. *Humanitarian Violence: The U.S. Deployment of Diversity*. Minneapolis, MN: University of Minnesota Press.

Barriendos, Joaquín. 2010. "La colonialidad del ver: Visualidad, capitalismo y racismo epistemológico." In *Desenganche: Visualidades y sonoridades otras*. Quito: La Tronkal.

Bilić, Bojan, ed. 2016. *LGBT Activism and Europeanisation in Post-Yugoslav Space*. London: Palgrave Macmillan.

Böröcz, József, and Mahua Sarkar. 2017. "The Unbearable Whiteness of the Polish Plumber and the Hungarian Peacock Dance Around 'Race'." *Slavic Review* 76, no. 2: 307–314. doi.org/10.1017/slr.2017.79.

Butler, Judith. 2011. "Fiscal Crisis or the Neo-liberal Assault on Democracy?" *Critical Legal Thinking*. https://criticallegalthinking.com/2011/11/14/fiscal-crisis-or-the-neo-liberal-assault-on-democracy/.

Campuzano, Giuseppe. 2003–2013. *Museo Travesti de Perú*. http://hemisphericinstitute.org/hemi/es/campuzano-presentacion.

Chiang, Howard. 2012. *Transgender China*. New York: Palgrave Macmillan.

Dzenovska, Dace. 2013. "Historical Agency and the Coloniality of Power in Postsocialist Europe." *Anthropological Theory* 13, no. 4: 394–416. doi.org/10.1177/1463499613502185.

El-Tayeb, Fatima. 2011. *European Others: Queering Ethnicity in Postnational Europe*. Minneapolis, MN: University of Minnesota Press.

Espinosa Miñoso, Yuderkys, Diana Gómez Correal, and Karina Ochoa Muñoz, eds. 2014. *Tejiendo de otro modo: Feminismo, epistemología y apuestas descoloniales en Abya Yala*. Popayán: Universidad del Cauca.

Essed, Philomena, and Isabel Hoving, eds. 2014. *Dutch Racism*. Amsterdam: Rodopi.

Fanon, Frantz. 1963. *The Wretched of the Earth*. New York: Grove Press.

Goldberg, David T. 2009. *The Threat of Race: Reflections on Racial Neoliberalism*. Singapore: Utopia Press.

Gordon, Lewis. "African-American Philosophy, Race, and the Geography of Reason," In *Not Only the Master's Tools: African-American Studies in Theory and Practice*, edited by Lewis R. Gordon and Jane Anna Gordon, 3–51. Boulder, CO: Paradigm Publishers.

Gržinić, Marina. 2008. "Former Yugoslavia, Queer and Class Struggle." In *New Feminism: Worlds of Feminism, Queer and Networking Conditions*, edited by Marina Gržinić and Rosa Reitsamer. Vienna: Löcker Verlag.

Gržinić, Marina. 2009. "Subjectivation, Biopolitics and Necropolitics: Where Do We Stand?" *Reartikulacija* no. 6. http://grzinic-smid.si/?p=893.

Gržinić, Marina. 2012. "Europe: Gender, Class, Race." *The Scholar and Feminist Online* 10, no. 3. http://sfonline.barnard.edu/feminist-media-theory/%20europe-gender-class-race/.

Gržinić, Marina. 2014. "Dissident Feminisms, Anti-Racist Politics and Artistic Interventionist Practices." *p/art/icipate – Kultur aktiv gestalten #04*. www.p-art-icipate.net/cms/dissident-feminisms-anti-racist-politics-and-artistic-interventionist-practices/.

Gržinić, Marina, Marissa Lôbo, and Ivana Marjanović. 2013. "The System of Racism/White Supremacy: A Conversation Between Jude Sentongo Kafeero and Sheri Avraham." In *Utopia of Alliances, Conditions of Impossibilities and the Vocabulary of Decoloniality*, edited by the Editorial Group for Writing Insurgent Genealogies (Carolina Agredo, Sheri Avraham, Annalisa Cannito, Miltiadis Gerothanasis, Marina Gržinić, Marissa Lôbo, and Ivana Marjanović), 117. Vienna: Löcker Verlag.

Gržinić, Marina, and Šefik Tatlić. 2012. "Global Capitalism's Racializations." *Deartikulacija* part 2: 11–15. http://grzinic-smid.si/?p=806.

IRWIN, ed. 2006. *East Art Map: Contemporary Art and Eastern Europe*. London: Afterall Books.

Kirey-Sitnikova, Yana. 2014. "Transgender Activism in Russia." www.academia.edu/5886543/Transgender_activism_in_Russia.

Kirey-Sitnikova, Yana. 2016. "The Emergence of Transfeminism in Russia: Opposition from Cisnormative Feminists and Trans* People." *TSQ: Transgender Studies Quarterly* 3, nos. 1–2: 167–176. doi.org/10.1215/23289252-3334343.

Koyama, Emy. 2003. "The Transfeminist Manifesto." In *Catching a Wave: Reclaiming Feminism for the Twenty-First Century*, edited by Rory Dicker and Alison Piepmeier. Boston, MA: Northeastern University Press.

Kurtić, Vera. 2013. *Džuvljarke: Roma Lesbian Existence*. Nis: European Roma Rights Centre.

López Petit, Santiago. 2009. *La movilización global: Breve tratado para atacar la realidad*. Madrid: Traficantes de sueños. www.traficantes.net/libros/la-movilizacion-global.

Lugones, María. 2008. "The Coloniality of Gender." *Worlds and Knowledges Otherwise*: 1–17.

Lugones, María. 2010. "Toward a Decolonial Feminism." *Hypatia* 25, no. 4: 742–759.

Mbembe, Achille. 2003. *Necropolítica*. Barcelona: Melusina.

Mbembe, Achille. 2012. "Theory from the Antipodes: Notes on Jean and John Comaroffs' TFS." *The Johannesburg Salon* 5: 18–25. https://jwtc.org.za/resources/docs/salon-volume-5/JWTC_Vol5_FINAL.pdf.

Mbembe, Achille. 2013. "Lectures to 'African Future Cities." Lectures presented at Harvard University, Cambridge, September-December 2013.

Mignolo, Walter. 2007. "Introduction: Coloniality of Power and De-colonial Thinking." *Cultural Studies* 21, no. 2, 155–167.

Preciado, Beatriz. 2008. *Testo Yonqui*. Madrid: Espasa.

Preciado, B. Paul. 2013. "Pharmaco-Pornographic Capitalism Postporn Politics and the Decolonization of Sexual Representations." In *Utopia of Alliances, Conditions of Impossibilities and the Vocabulary of Decoloniality*, edited by the Editorial Group for Writing Insurgent Genealogies (Carolina Agredo, Sheri Avraham, Annalisa Cannito, Miltiadis Gerothanasis, Marina Gržinić, Marissa Lôbo and Ivana Marjanović), 245–255. Vienna: Löcker Verlag.

Puar, Jasbir. 2007. *Terrorist Assamblages: Homonationalism in Queer Times*. Durham, NC: Duke University Press.

Quijano, Aníbal. 1992. "Raza, Etnia y Nación en Mariátegui: cuestiones abiertas." In *José Carlos Mariátegui y Europa: el otro aspecto del descubrimiento*, 167–188. Lima: Editorial Amauta.

Rexhepi, Piro. 2016. "From Orientalism to Homonationalism: Queer Politics, Islamophobia and Europeanization in Kosovo." In *LGBT Activism and Europeanisation in Post-Yugoslav space*, edited by Bojan Bilić, 179–203. London: Palgrave Macmillan.

Rexhepi, Piro. 2018. "Prologue." In *Arte-Política-Resistencia*, edited by Tjaša Kancler, 13. Barcelona: Ediciones t.i.c.t.a.c.

Rodríguez Moreno, Celénis. 2018. "Andar erótico decolonial." *Desde el margen* no. 1. http://desde-elmargen.net/resena-andar-erotico-decolonial/.

Solá, Miriam, and Elena Urko, eds. 2013. *Transfeminismos: Espistemes, fricciones y flujos*. Bilbao: Tafalla, Txalaparta. https://transfeminismos.wordpress.com/.

Somerville, Siobhan. 2000. *Queering the Color Line: Race and the Invention of Homosexuality in American Culture*. Durham, NC: Duke University Press.

Spivak, Gayatri. 2006. "Religion, Politics, Theology: A Conversation with Achille Mbembe." Humanities Research Institute at the University of California, Irvine. https://read.dukeupress.edu/boundary-2/article-abstract/34/2/149/6293/Religion-Politics-Theology-A-Conversation-with?redirectedFrom=fulltext

Tlostanova, Madina. 2012. "Postsocialist ≠ postcolonial? On Post-Soviet Imaginary and Global Coloniality." *Journal of Postcolonial Writing* 48, no. 2: 130–142. doi.org/10.1080/17449855.2012.658244.

Tlostanova, Madina. 2013. "Post-Soviet Imaginary and Global Coloniality: A Gendered Perspective." An interview with Madina Tlostanova by *kronotop.org*. www.kronotop.org/ftexts/interview-with-madina-tlostanova/.

Valencia, Sayak. 2014. "Interferencias transfeministas y pospornográficas a la colonialidad del ver." *E-misferica 11.1: Decolonial Gesture*. https://hemisphericinstitute.org/es/emisferica-11-1-decolonial-gesture/11-1-essays/interferencias-transfeministas-y-pospornograficas-a-la-colonialidad-del-ver.html.

Velikonja, Nataša, and Tatjana Greif. 2012. *Lezbična sekcija LL: kronologija 1987–2012 s predzgodovino*. Ljubljana: Škuc – Vizibilija.

Vishmidt, Marina. 2010. "Human Capital or Toxic Asset: After the Wage". *Reartikulacija* no. 10–13, http://grzinic-smid.si/?p=920.

Audiovisual references

Borders of Control N.4. 1982. "Icons of Glamour, Echoes of Death." http://grzinic-smid.si/?p=170.

Borders of Control N.4. 1983. "The Threat of the Future." http://grzinic-smid.si/?p=290.

Gržinić, Marina, Aina Šmid, and Zvonka Simčič T. 2012. "Relations: 25 Years of the Lesbian Group ŠKUC-LL." http://grzinic-smid.si/?p=276.

Perić, Dražena. 2007. "The Caravan of the Erased." https://archive.org/details/Karavana_izbrisanih_-_The_Caravan_of_the_Erased.

Žilnik, Želimir. 1994. "Marble Ass." www.zilnikzelimir.net/marble-ass.

Part III

Challenges

While it is clear that the postcolonial and the postsocialist discourses diverge as much as they converge, it is worth holding space for the challenges that the affinities between the two pose to feminist thought and practice. One of the challenges that emerges as central in this section is complicity; the way in which we are implicated in systems, structures, and institutions that carry harm. In line with feminist theorists who argue for the importance of accountability in knowledge production, Gayatri Chakravorty Spivak makes a case for acknowledging our complicities in order to be able to act (1999, 370 n. 79). Moving past the commonplace negative valence of the term, this section thus explores how centring on acknowledging complicity might carry the potential to take discussions forward.

Etymologically, complicity derives from the Latin word *complicare*, meaning *to fold together*, and shares a root with the modern-day terms *complicate* and *complex*. We are complicit when we are folded into a larger system of complex relations, be it a particular society, an environment, or a history that is marred by colonialism and/or state socialism, the consequences of which extend to this day. In myriad ways, then, the spread of global capitalism and its aftermath demands that we do the work of thinking through individual and collective responsibility and guilt in relation to racist and colonial practices.

In an interview, artists Quincy Gario and Jörgen Gario invite us to reflect on the recognition of complicity as grounds for political engagement and action. Their performance *How to See the Spots of the Leopard* in Kuldīga, Latvia (August 2020), explores the relationships between difficult pasts, colonial as well as state socialist, and their influences in the Baltic States today through the perspective of shared histories. Reflecting on their Dutch Caribbean heritage, the artists pick up on Latvia's connection to European colonialism, more specifically the Baltic German-dominated Duchy of Courland's involvement in the colonial endeavours in Tobago which has been presented uncritically to the general Latvian public particularly since the end of the Cold War. Their attempt to critique and trouble Latvian colonial complicity opens up new ways of thinking about how the colonial mode of power still endures in Europe and beyond.

Manuela Boatcă warns us of the dangers of reproducing one regional and historical focus to the detriment of others when thinking of the terms "postcolonial" and "postsocialist" together, thus remaining implicated in a colonialist framework. She draws attention to the ways in which feminist thinking has been "uneasily postcolonial" and maybe also "uneasily postsocialist" because "it is rooted in more than one political tradition and goes back to more than the experience of state socialism". Boatcă claims that the postcolonial "duress", complete with a set of racial, religious, and other taxonomies, is to be found in both former colonial and imperial nations as well as countries that never had colonies, such as some of the former socialist states, or those whom she addresses, following Laura Doyle, as "inter-imperial" since they have been situated at the intersection of several imperial influences and interests.

In their conversation on connecting the "posts" to confront racial capitalism's coloniality, Alyosxa Tudor and Piro Rexhepi examine the contradictions and challenges of the postsocialist position within transnational anti-racist solidarity in the face of emboldened structural and situational forms of violence that have come to dominate formerly socialist spaces. Moving through queer, trans, and decolonial interventions, they explore how the temporality of the "post" prefix not only conceals the connections and continuities between colonial and Cold War projects and contemporary racial capitalism but also advances a colour-blind narrative of Europeanness that seeks to recruit the postsocialist subject in the ongoing racial, classed, and gendered (geo)politics of EU border politics. Importantly, not only do they raise critical questions about the racist politics of the far right, they also point to the necessity to challenge the complicity of the postsocialist left in perpetuating racism through their silence and continued use of Eurocentric epistemologies.

In conversation with Petra Bakos, cultural and community organiser Angéla Kóczé reflects upon her investment in developing a critical race feminist agenda sensitive to the specific characteristics and needs of Eastern European Roma communities. She sheds light on what is it like for an Eastern European Roma woman scholar to navigate the largely Roma-blind US American academia in parallel with the anti-Roma Hungarian academic context. Juggling various preconceptions and reflexes within academia when attempting to introduce an intersectional, transnational agenda, especially in face of the recent rekindling of old colonial racist discourses, she questions if and how critical race studies, developed primarily in the United States, might be useful for Eastern European Roma communities, thus challenging academia's complicity in producing knowledge that erases certain histories.

In a conversation on feminist queer crip epistemologies, Kateřina Kolářová explores the ways in which a dialogue between postsocialist and postcolonial theories can be enriched and expanded through intersectional crip theory and, in particular, through thinking crip and racialised chronicity. She lays out the concept of "rehabilitative citizenship" that defines the social imaginary in the postsocialist Czech Republic and explains how national efforts of "rehabilitation" utilise disabled people as well as Roma and racialised communities for its own legitimisation. Her proposal to "crip postsocialist chronicity" enables us to acknowledge how promoting the postsocialist curative "transition" narrative in fact makes us complicit in perpetuating certain forms of protracted and invisible violence against bodies and lives that cannot be embraced by the rehabilitative, affirmative, and positive promises of the future. The conversation also probes the limits of postsocialist scholarship in relation to race and the failures of transnational feminism vis-à-vis postsocialist experiences.

Spatialising diasporic Chinese feminism in North American academia in relation to the new social divisions in postsocialist societies, Weiling Deng theorises the formation of the Chinese feminist diaspora as inherently related to two historical integrations that are usually examined separately: Asian immigrants into North American social and political mainstream and socialist history into capitalist economy. In doing so, she complicates the agency of translation and the politics of visibility and mobility, which both trouble and animate diasporic feminisms in North America. With a special background in the transpacific context marked by both postcolonial/racial policies and Cold War ideology, Chinese feminist diaspora articulates the impasse and potential breakthroughs of feminist interrogation framed in the "three-worlds" human rights discourse that is symbolised by the "China crisis".

Complicity also surfaces as an important theme in feminist discussions of gendered nationalism and the so-called femonationalism. In their detailed analysis of recent anti-Muslim sentiments in India and Poland, Mithilesh Kumar and Kasia Narkowicz delineate the complicity of conservative patriarchal nation-states in (re)producing a discourse which underlines the protection of "their" women from the Muslim "other". Through a critical analysis of media coverage as well as both policy and public documents discussing the Indian Citizenship (Amendment) Act and the Polish migration policy, the authors explore contemporary expressions of gendered nationalism/femonationalism and point to the conjunctural nature of postcolonial and postsocialist conditions. Through tracing the genealogy of right-wing populist thinking and evolution of national identity that excludes undesirable bodies, the chapter brings forth the dilemmas of decolonial politics in the two countries.

Importantly, an acknowledgement of complicity should never result in a new "moral confidence" or a mere acceptance of *the way things are* but rather in understanding that such an acknowledgement "can never be complete" (Keenan 2002, 192). In this sense, "[c]omplicity can be a starting point: if we are *on it*, we are *in it*. We are implicated in the processes we identify; we can identify processes because we are implicated in them" (Ahmed 2020). As the world is still grappling with how to connect across the vast array of issues that divide us as people variously positioned in relation to histories of colonialism and state socialism, the contributions in this section welcome challenges, such as complicity, by thinking of them as enabling and constructive rather than as disabling and destructive.

References

Ahmed, Sara. 2020. "Feminists at Work." https://feministkilljoys.com/2020/01/10/feminists-at-work.

Keenan, Thomas. 2002. "The Push and Pull of Rights and Responsibilities." *Interventions* 4, no. 2: 191–204.

Spivak, Gayatri Chakravorty. 1999. *A Critique of Postcolonial Reason: Toward a History of the Vanishing Present.* Cambridge, MA and London: Harvard University Press.

Chapter 12

How to See the Spots of the Leopard

An interview with Quinsy Gario and Jörgen Gario

Quinsy Gario, Jörgen Gario and Redi Koobak

Redi Koobak: Your performance *How to See the Spots of the Leopard* (August 2020) in Kuldīga, Latvia, explores the relationships between difficult pasts, colonial as well as state socialist, and their influences in the Baltic States today through the perspective of shared histories. Reflecting on your Dutch Caribbean heritage, you pick up on Latvia's connection to European colonialism, more specifically the Baltic German-dominated Duchy of Courland's involvement in the colonial endeavours in Tobago which has been presented uncritically to the general Latvian public, particularly since the end of the Cold War. How did the project come about and what was the performance like?

Quinsy Gario: A couple of years ago I met Rotterdam-based Estonian curator Margaret Tali, and in 2019 she and curator Ieva Astahovska from the Latvian Center for Contemporary Art (LCCA) invited me to be part of their summer school in Kuldīga. The summer schools that the LCCA puts together are connected to upcoming exhibitions. At the time, they were organising an exhibition called "Communicating Difficult Pasts" which looks at the uneasy relations between the present and the past and their entanglements in the 20th and 21st centuries. Unfortunately, I couldn't take part in it then – I was in Curaçao and Sint Maarten with our mother working on another project. So they invited me to give a guest lecture at the Art Academy in Riga and participate in an exhibition forthcoming this year. In November 2019, I came to Latvia and together with Ieva went to Kuldīga to see the town, visit the museum about its history and the monument established in 2013 to the Baltic-German Duke Jacob Kettler (1610–1682) of the Duchy of Courland and Semigallia, under whose rule the duchy reached its peak in wealth and engaged in colonisation attempts in Gambia and Tobago. Surprisingly, Tobago isn't a far away, abstract idea in Latvia. It's actively remembered. For instance, when I got off the plane and the taxi driver asked me where I was from. I have gotten into this mode of saying I am from the Netherlands because I don't want to have another drawn out conversation but this time I said: "I'm from Sint Maarten". He was surprised: "Sint Maarten? Where is that?" I explained: "In the Caribbean". And he lit up: "Oh yeah! We used to have Tobago!" By that time, I had already done some research about Latvian history and it was really elucidating. This is something that is widely felt and widely disseminated. It's not a backward story that nobody knows, it centralised in certain types of conversations. In that sense it was very revealing to read Dace Dzenovska's article "Historical Agency and the Coloniality of Power in Postsocialist Europe" (2013) where she criticises the Western writers and the way they look at Latvia's remembrance of colonial pursuits. She is spot on in her critique of the Portuguese journalist and the American writer whose comments she discusses who seem to forget their own positioning in terms of the colonial past. Their supposed neutral position to observe and critique is anything but. In our work we think about Latvia's attempt to relate to European coloniality from our position as people who are from the Caribbean, which also brings these complications with it. Yes, we are from the West, but we are also involuntarily implicated because our subjugation, our oppression was used to establish the West as a political and economic power. In our performance we stand next to the monument of Duke Jacob Kettler in Kuldīga, draw an image of Tobago on the ground with a shiny black duct tape, and play the musical instruments *steelpan* and *kokle* as we ask the audience to think about the effects that colonial nostalgia produces. The title of the performance is a reference to the slave ship *Der Leopard* that in April 1653 sailed from Courland to Amsterdam to Guinee to Martinique and back to Amsterdam. It was commissioned by Duke Jacob to forcibly migrate abducted Africans to then be enslaved and sold in Martinique. They could have been our ancestors. It's about thinking through what our implication as both from the West and rejected by the West does to this particular nationalist reading of coloniality as a means of determining its development and placement within the Western world. This necessity to be implicated in Western European colonial history. I asked my brother Jörgen if he wanted to do something together for the exhibition. Jörgen and I have been working together for at least a decade now on our performance lectures that we put together based on our research. One of the first things that I sent to Jörgen for this project was a link to the 2002 musical "Tobago!" by the renowned Latvian poet Māra Zālīte and the Dailes Theatre. It's amazing! For us this insistence on using music and thinking about music as a way of pushing a different type of conversation on the past was important. This link to music is also why I wanted Jörgen to be involved – his finetuned way of merging different sounds and musical forms together became pivotal for the performance.

Jörgen Gario: During my flight over from Amsterdam to Riga, I was by myself and with this facemask on, realising that I was making a journey I have never made before – it felt as if I was stepping into a story. This story that Quinsy was telling me about this man who has a statue, this Duke of Courland, how this story was connected to me hearing the voice announcing where I was going, how it connected different places. But I also made a connection to the static noise of the plane – not knowing what to expect, not necessarily knowing what it is going to hold and finding the music in that. Finding the music in uncertainty, of trying to connect two places that have a shared history. A shared history that kind of lays under the surface became a very important element for me in the performance: to be able to use the sound itself, the sound of the travel, to bridge the gap between the two places through music.

Figure 12.1 Two men are engaged in doing a performance. One man is standing and facing the crowd with a tape in his hand and the other man is sitting and picking up a musical instrument. They are on a street in front of a monument of Duke Jacob Kettler, with passers-by and onlookers in the background.

Source: Reproduced with permission from Annemarija Gulbe

QG: I am also reminded about the Dutch airport Schiphol and the fact that before the terraforming and the airport, it was the sea and it used to be called "scheepshol" – ships' hole – because this is where all ships were sent that couldn't be fixed anymore. It used to be a ship graveyard. So to have the pilot saying "we are now going from Amsterdam to Riga" is in a sense a reiteration of these traces. It gave me goosebumps during the performance.

RK: In the performance you use a synthesizer, a *steelpan*, a *kokle*, the static from the plane, the announcements and field recordings in Kuldīga. How did the sounds come together in the performance?

JG: The static of the plane was used as a basis because in modern music, what we don't know, even in pop music, there are sounds that are there that we can feel but we cannot hear. They are called filler sounds. Different types of producers use them in their own way to convey a message that is not necessarily meant to be heard but it is meant to be felt. These sounds also create a texture which you can hear, which blends into the other sounds. This is a way to merge the different identities of the sounds together. They basically have the same foundation. So the sounds of my travelling are a foundation for the introduction of the *steelpan* from Tobago and the *kokle* from Latvia and creating a way for them to come together.

QG: I think one of the interesting similarities between the *steelpan* and the *kokle* is that they were both banned by occupying forces. During the Soviet times, the *kokle* was actually banned by the Soviets and the British banned the *steelpan* for a period of time before the independence of the island.

JG: All of the colonial powers in the Caribbean outlawed percussion instruments because they were afraid that these could incite rebellion. So, for example, drums were banned. But the enslaved never forget the rhythms and they started making new instruments. The predecessor to the *steelpan* on Trinidad and Tobago (the islands were joined into one political body by the British in 1888) was a percussion instrument made out of long bamboo sticks. Since it was found to be used to relay information and rebellious messages, this item was also outlawed. So people went in search of something new and because of the then recent discovery of oil in the region there was an abundance of oil drums around. This instrument was thus created from the leftover economic spoils of the oil industry which was established on the island. Musicians started playing around with the sounds that were coming from these barrels. It started to take shape very slowly from there just being one sound that the drum made to finding out that there was a whole way of tuning it. Different masters arose from this idea of being able to tune a *steelpan*, the literal making of it. *Steelpan* music became an artform and that development really interests me. Where music is not just a series of calculations, but where it becomes an artform that only certain people can practise. In the beginning also every one of these *steelpans* was handmade. That again links to the *kokle*. Each instrument was preferably made out of a single piece of wood and hand carved. Another connection between these two instruments is also that there are shapes and forms of the *kokle* that have less strings and that produce different sounds. It was very interesting for me to bring these two very different items together because they differ a lot in sound. The *steelpan* as a rhythmic instrument that can create melody and rhythm and the *kokle* as a string instrument which is solely focused on melody. The *kokle* is also considered more of a solo instrument, at least how I have seen it, whereas the *steelpan* is usually played in large groups in Tobago.

QG: One of the things I always keep thinking about is that you have these families, these sailors going on these ships travelling to faraway places, these Latvian peasants. One of the things that is clear in the archival work of Latvian historian Edgar Andersons from the 1950s and his publication in 1970 is that only the Baltic-Germans were mentioned, and a lot of the other names were Germanised and changed. We don't know if ethnic Latvians were actually present. But if we presupposed that they were, they had to be the ones scrubbing the decks, they had to be the ones thinking of ways to escape feudalism. They would have brought along instruments for entertainment. They would have brought along an instrument such as *kokle*. A *kokle* would have been on the island. So even these different types of traces are, I think, interesting. You have stories of violins that are 400–500 years

Figure 12.2 Two men are engaged in doing a performance. One man is standing
and reading animatedly from a notebook and the other man is crouch-
ing next to him. They are on a street in front of a monument of Duke
Jacob Kettler and in front of them, the contours of Tobago have been
taped on the pavement with black tape. There are passers-by and
onlookers in the background.

Source: Reproduced with permission from Annemarija Gulbe

old – so there could be a *kokle* somewhere out there that has seen all this history.
In Tobago, or already back, or in someone's home. For instance, one of the traces
of Suriname, a former Dutch colony with a monoculture plantation system that
gained independence in 1975, in Latvia was pointed out to me by Iļja Ļenskis, the
director of the museum "Jews in Latvia" in Riga. When I was there last year, he
gave me a personal tour of the museum and told me about their research on the
archives of a Jewish soldier whose surname was Surinamer. He wrote letters in the
1920s trying to get compensation for the loss of his family stocks in a plantation in
the then Dutch colony. When you think about this in the context of the 1920s, lots
of historical moments come together: the economic crash is near, the First World
War has just ended, fascism and anti-Semitism are rearing their heads and people
are trying to find ways to escape. And then there is this person who has stocks in a
Surinamese plantation, whose name is literally the name of the country, trying to
get them back, maybe in an attempt to flee the country. All of these different types
of connections come together in this performance and they also connect back to
our previous work. We did a performance piece together looking at Curaçao in

the 20th century and connecting it to three different incidents which seemed like they only pertained to the island but actually had international implications. We also did a performance together about Italian colonialism and created a monument between two olive trees, with tape and hemp string. We looked at the Belgium student uprising and the way in which it was connected to the civil-rights movement in the United States and the decolonisation movement in Africa. Our practice so far involves trying to disentangle different knots. Importantly, we disentangle them not to make it seem as if they are separate incidents but to tease out the connections between them and to show their inseparability.

RK: In the Latvian case then it's also thought-provoking to think about how postsocialism comes into play. Earlier you referred to Dace Dzenovska's analysis of Latvian attempts, particularly during the national re-awakening of the postsocialist 1990s when Latvia became independent from the Soviet Union, to "establish historical presence in European modernity through appropriation of 17th century colonial pursuits of the Duchy of Courland into Latvian national history" (Dzenovska 2013, 394). This would thereby bolster their sense of belonging to Europe and their fledgling national narrative that would show them as agents in history rather than simply indentured serfs ruled by the Duchy or later a labour force occupied and controlled by the Soviets. So there is that troubling connection of how the postsocialist and the colonial/postcolonial merge that needs to be challenged – which your performance is wonderfully doing, critiquing our complicity in continuously upholding the colonial mode of power in Europe and beyond. How do you view postsocialism as a framework or a concept, also in relation to postcolonialism? Has the project shifted your perspectives?

QG: I think what is important not to see postsocialism as a timeframe but as an analytic to think through all these different modalities, this notion of not yet being European or never actually being able to become European. The postsocialist condition also brings up the ways in which capitalism itself can be constantly questioned and seen as reproducing a certain type of order. The postsocialist order is different because it places a different emphasis on different understandings of collectivity, trauma, memories of the trauma, and notions of belonging. And I think coming from the Caribbean, for us, postsocialist spaces also resonate with this understanding of being on the periphery of Europe but having been necessary for Europe to develop itself. The postsocialist condition is in that sense this necessity for Europe to be able to develop itself against the aftermaths of the Second World, these different understandings of means of production and collectivities. When looking at resistance and labour movements in the Caribbean in the 20th century, a lot of them were socialist and Marxist. So there is inherently a postsocialist framework here which is really provocative to think about – the ways in which the Caribbean as this mode, as this theatre for the creation of Europe as we know it today relates to and compares to the Baltic states and other postsocialist countries as we call them.

RK: Exactly, kind of expanding the term's capacity in a sense. It is habitually used to denote the former Soviet bloc and the aligned countries, and we rarely think about, for instance, the Caribbean as postsocialist. Moreover, in a way, for Eastern Europe and the former Soviet Union, postsocialism has come to denote some kind of disillusionment with socialism as this grand utopia that can combat racial capitalism. So everything becomes entangled once you start unpacking these terms and what they might mean, and what they might mean if you are not attaching them to certain areas of the world – like the global South is postcolonial and Eastern Europe is postsocialist.

QG: Exactly. And even I mean in terms of thinking through the idea of socialism itself as a means of fighting against oppression. The way in which attempts have been made to geographically locate it, also is a way to defang it, to make it seem less potent than it actually is. If you look at Fidel Castro and what he did in Cuba, Maurice Bishop in Grenada, if you look at the whole left wave in South America, Thomas Sankara in Burkina Faso – if you look at their writings, you will see that all of them connect to this idea of socialism. Thus, the postsocialist analytic enables us to see how capitalism has wreaked havoc in all of the peripheries of the capitalist world which has seen them as resources to be blundered for the imperial and the colonial centre. In that sense then it is also really interesting to use that postsocialist analytic to analyse how Soviet Russia thought about socialism or tried to present socialism and how it morphed and differed and changed. For instance, the fight between Russia and Cuba at one point reveals how those types of ideologies then move because of the proximity to modes of production and histories of exploitation.

RK: Coming back to the performance, how was it received by the audience?

JG: I must say I had my head in the instruments. We definitely drew a crowd. Many came and stayed, they watched and some of them filmed. I can also recall a man who was just walking his dog straight into the performance as if we were invisible. He did see the statue, but he didn't see us. However, we did notice that the man who was selling fruits next to the monument treated us with a gesture which you could interpret as some kind of respect which had grown between us in the two days that we were there. The first day when we rehearsed, he had a kind of a question mark expression on his face and the day after our performance when we walked past him again, there was an acknowledgement that we had created something in which he saw something. What it was, I don't know, but he did want to give us acknowledgement. Like a nod and a smile. There was no interruption from him even though he was there, and he had his business. I think we had his full attention.

QG: There was a great question to you by Iļja Ļenskis of the Museum "Jews in Latvia" about the way in which the *kokle* being played by a Black Caribbean man could be interpreted.

JG: Yeah, I think he questioned whether people who couldn't understand English would think I was some kind of prodigal son from Tobago returning to show his coloniser that he had picked up the language or that he had understood the culture. Or that I was in a sense returning home to something which I had never met but had been in contact with or more like a person who was left behind, coming home to claim his right by embracing the instrument of this other culture as his own. He wondered if people saw me as a statement. He asked me if I had thought about my performance as a statement.

QG: We started the performance by asking if people were nostalgic. And that is like a continuing mantra to our piece: are you nostalgic? This question carries a statement behind it, like these bucolic scenes, and then at one point in turns severe because the question is really: are you nostalgic for the divisions of the past, the knowledge of the past, the separations, and the horrific things such as slavery and subjugation? At the beginning everyone said: "Yeah, yeah, we are nostalgic. We love the past!" But once they figured out what sort of a past we were referring to, the question itself became a trap that they couldn't escape. We were suggesting that no, that's not the nostalgia we should be thinking of, or these types of attempts to reframe the past as this warm blanket that is going to absolve everything that is going wrong in the present. That's just not the way to do it. That's when the realisation comes in. Jörgen had a pretty neutral face as he was playing but I smiled, I laughed at certain points, and I just watched people's reactions when asked: are you nostalgic? I saw them get involved and at a certain point shift to: "No, I should have answered no". One of the interesting things about the way we set it up was that people could just join in and be part of it. We tried to make it as inclusive as possible. The whole performance was in English so we are not sure how many of the local kids who were standing around, the teenagers, could understand. For sure they must have been intrigued and that is why they stayed and watched. The funny thing is, the notion of sound kept coming back and this insistence on thinking through what it means to communicate differently and how sound carries heritages that we might not be able to decipher but that we can feel.

RK: Like the background static noise from the plane.

JG: Also, this idea of trying to bring it to the future. Like the statue of Duke Jacob, which is literally him walking through a time portal where the past is dark and rusty, and the future is bright and silvery. It's the involvement of the synthesiser, sounds that can be defined by anybody who hears them or can be created by technology. It's another layer which crosses borders and brings people into contact so electronic music has actually less of a nostalgic heritage that points to violence and colonialism.

QG: The electronic music and static also has a feminist aspect to it, when considering the development of electronic music. Thinking through positions and positionalities of the foremothers who stood at the forefront of figuring out that the wave machines could do something revolutionary for music. I think the way we approached it was to constantly think through the production of sound outside of gendered norms while thinking through the fact that we were presenting it as two Black men who identify with certain type of Blackness – Caribbean Blackness – and thinking through what that means in the context where we were presenting it.

RK: To pick up on this point, since you, Quinsy, have studied gender studies, how has feminist theory informed your art practice and thinking, particularly in this project?

Figure 12.3 Two men are engaged in doing a performance. One man is playing a musical instrument, the other is listening. They are on a street near the monument of Duke Jacob Kettler and in front them, the contours of Tobago have been taped on the pavement with black tape. The onlookers in the background are watching and taking photos or videos

Source: Reproduced with permission from Annemarija Gulbe

QG: One of the ways in which I have been able to work now for the last two-three years is thinking through the solitary single artist, the male genius idea. I have been trying to subvert it and sabotage it through collaborations with my family members: Jörgen, my mother, my uncle and aunt, and my cousins. And then creating also a different type of genealogy of artistic production which is outside this dominant white male canon, trying to think through what it means to have a canon when the word itself refers to violence and a projection of steel balls. If we take that away, what do we have left? We have these relationships, these understandings and behaviours which are coded. Saidiya Hartman says it beautifully when she talks about speculative non-fiction, or "critical fabulation" (2007) as she calls her method of writing against the archive, when she is trying to fill in the gaps where information about what used to be there is gone, where relationships that used to be there are severed. What does that mean? Or like Christina Sharpe (2016) says: how do we mourn that which we have never known? All of these different things. The reason why I like working with Jörgen is how his musical practice, his singing, song writing is also involved with this deep pathos in a certain way. It's not about trying to get to an exploitative core but to these feelings that we have, that we feel, but that are not communicated, that sometimes are incomprehensible even to ourselves. How do we present these situations that push these different types of conversations? And I think what is funny in terms of how we work is that we are just trying stuff out, improvising. So the evening before the performance we did a small try-out for Vala T. Foltyn, one of the teachers at the summer school, and with her ideas about witchcraft, she started calling us warlocks. I thought that was pretty cool. This understanding of how we talk and communicate and present invites people into the conversations that Jörgen and I are having. I think a friend of mine once said – Lucie Vítková who is a Czech composer – she said it's like me and Jörgen are having a conversation on stage. I'm talking and he is talking as well, but he is talking differently and it is sometimes a response and sometimes an opposition, sometimes in contention with me so it becomes a conflict. We try to get to a resolution. Sometimes it works and we get to a resolution and sometimes it doesn't and that is also part of the work. At least, that is how I see it.

JG: Yes, I like this idea about moving away from the male genius thing. It's also about being vulnerable. I don't know why, when Quinsy said about this deep pathos, but there was a definite necessity for me to also connect with Latvia and play this *kokle* even though I had it physically in my hands only two days before the performance. To sit with it and to go through the process of presenting it to a group of people during this performance – this connection had to be made. A logical explanation is that there isn't any connection. But there is a story there, like Quinsy says, and we must fill in the gaps, you know. We must think who has played this instrument before – people whom we have never seen or heard of. We have no stories about them and there is no documentation of them. Who else created or tried to create this sonic alchemy with this instrument before? Who tried to convey a feeling with the instrument? Who tried to tell a story? Who tried to be in resistance?

References

Dzenovska, Dace. 2013. "Historical Agency and the Coloniality of Power in Postsocialist Europe." *Anthropological Theory* 13, no. 4: 394–416.

Hartman, Saidiya. 2007. *Lose Your Mother: A Journey Along the Atlantic Slave Route.* New York: Farrar, Straus and Giroux.

Sharpe, Christina. 2016. *In the Wake: On Blackness and Being.* Durham, NC: Duke University Press.

Chapter 13

Uneasy "posts" and unmarked categories

Politics of positionality between and beyond the Global South and the European East. An interview with Manuela Boatcă

Manuela Boatcă and Madina Tlostanova

Madina Tlostanova: As an extremely versatile scholar of critical global studies, world-systems analysis, postsocialist semi-peripheries, decolonial option, transnational gender studies, and also as someone who has been part of this project directly or indirectly for a number of years from its inception at a conference in 2015 where you were one of the keynotes to this present volume in which we strive to launch a dialogue among the transnational postcolonial and postsocialist feminists, how do you understand these very terms and do you find them relevant for contemporary feminist critical thinking and agency?

Manuela Boatcă: Thank you for initiating this as a conversation and for involving me in it – I think it is important to multiply the formats in which we engage in these types of debates in order to draw attention to what is at stake. Your question already points to the complexities of the terms involved and to the challenges of having a shared understanding of them. I think a shared understanding – or at least considerable overlaps in our definition of these terms – is what should be at stake in establishing a dialogue among transnational postcolonial and postsocialist feminists. As you know, I have long been sceptical of both "postcolonial" and "postsocialist" as adequate analytical lenses for grasping the issues in which I was most interested. A lot has already been written about the ambivalences of the "postcolonial" and the extent to which its "post" is a temporal one or not. But, given its emergence in the context of administrative decolonisation at the end of World War II, the label "postcolonial" has created an at least ambiguous timeline that has excluded many parts of the world from its purview. Among them were regions that had achieved independence long before the end of World War II and had therefore been postcolonial *avant la lettre*, such as Latin America; territories that were occupied in the immediate aftermath of World War II, but were not perceived as Western colonial outposts because of a long history of ideological legitimation of Western control, such as Palestine; countries that participated in the Western colonial enterprise, yet only after having been themselves colonised, such as Ireland; and areas that continue to function as colonies today, such as

Puerto Rico, the British Virgin Islands, and the French Antilles. For someone interested in the history and present of the Caribbean like myself, all of these were instances within which the label of the postcolonial sits awkwardly – I therefore called them "uneasy postcolonialisms". At the same time, as a Romanian scholar living in Germany, I have long been thinking and writing from the border between Western Europe and one of its other Europes – the one that, at different moments in its history, has been defined as Eastern Europe and is often still reduced to being an Other within. Its inter-imperial history – between the Habsburg, the Ottoman, and the Russian Empires – did not warrant its inclusion into the postcolonial, either – so this was an uneasy postcolonialism, too, that, although internal to Europe, made the very Europeanness of this area questionable. All the more so after 1989, when this became the part of the world to which the label of "postsocialism" was supposed to apply, and which was to gradually "return" to Europe (where else had it been before that, one wonders). But the term "postsocialist" itself quickly became an empty signifier, holding in place a category for which there was no other name. If it was a credible label for a transitional phase following state socialist rule and rightly indicated a break with the past, it revealed little about the present. Thirty years after its emergence, it is even less clear how long the transition is supposed to last or what the content of the category is – beyond the break with the past and maybe the 180-degree shift from centrally planned to neoliberal market economies.

So, the terms "postcolonial" and "postsocialist" are in my view of little individual analytical value. When used by themselves, they mostly end up reproducing one regional or historical focus to the detriment of others – for a long time, only former British colonies were the focus of postcolonialism; and African countries with former state socialist regimes are never considered "postsocialist". What makes these terms interesting, though, is using them in order to frame a dialogue in the context of transnational critical thinking and mobilisation, as you do in this project. Drawing the necessary transnational connections between what are generally the disconnected fields of postcolonialism and postsocialism not only allows you to unearth the common ground between them, but to show how feminist thinking and agency crisscrossed, straddled, and undercut regional and academic borders; how it was itself uneasily postcolonial, for instance in initiating conversations about Black feminism from Europe as a way to destabilise understandings of both white feminism and Europeanness, as Afro-German women did in the '70s and '80s; how feminist thinking is maybe also uneasily postsocialist, because it is rooted in more than one political tradition and goes back to more than the experience of state socialism; and how this means it was born transnational, which cannot be said for many of the phenomena analysed as transnational today (migration, for instance, was there before there were nation-states to be transcended, which makes it transregional, or, in the case of the trade in enslaved people, transcontinental – but that is another topic).

MT: Indeed, a shared understanding of postcolonialism and postsocialism is precisely what is lacking and the question remains, as you suggest, what can act as a ground for "overlaps in our definition of these terms"? In this volume we deliberately did not wish for any homogeneity in the understanding of postsocialism and postcolonialism and the authors represent an incommensurable and flexible spectre of various possible interpretations which is easier to be defined negatively as non-temporal, non-geopolitical, and non-economic. What could be its positive definition remains an open question as we are not interested in merely looking for postcolonial elements in the postsocialist or the other way a round, but rather attempt to reflect on an alternative transversal discourse beyond euromodernity in which various post/neo-dependence human conditions (including postcolonial and postsocialist ones) intersect both in being discarded from modernity/coloniality and in building re-existential shared positionalities. Could you comment on this?

MB: Yes, looking for the postcolonial in the postsocialist and vice versa would only end up reifying both – which could well be a project in its own right, first claiming ownership of or at least originality in the definitions of the terms, while ultimately seeking institutional validation and the creation of academic positions or departments that correspond to these reifications. But it would not be a critical project, let alone a decolonial one. A transversal discourse in which these conditions intersect is by far more interesting to me as well, precisely because it allows for the postcolonial to striate the postsocialist as well as to vie or intersect with it. In this sense, it helps to make sense of the wider notion that not only former colonies are postcolonial today, but so are the former colonial powers and – surprise! – so are countries that never had colonies. This is the case for several postsocialist states, which were at an advantage – at times symbolical, at times economic, and often with regard to their position in the racial hierarchies on which coloniality was grounded – vis-à-vis colonised countries. We see this relative advantage particularly in the way Eastern Europeans' claims to both Christianity and whiteness are back with a vengeance after a state socialist period during which religion was suppressed and racial allegiance was downplayed in the service of internationalist solidarity. This brings me to another reason why I think a transversal discourse in which what you aptly call post/neo-dependence human conditions intersect is crucial – the fact that it includes, but is not limited to, the postcolonial and the postsocialist. This transversality leaves room for less explored, but not less significant positionalities, such as the inter-imperial that I briefly mentioned before. My current work with Anca Parvulescu focuses on the inter-imperial positionality shaping one of Europe's most undertheorised regions, Transylvania, as the object – and much more rarely subject – of the constant tension between Habsburg, Ottoman, Austro-Hungarian, and Russian empires. We draw on Laura Doyle's concept of inter-imperiality (Doyle 2015) – which rejects the assumption implicit in most postcolonial or world-systems theorising that a region is either a postcolony of the West or it has not been colonised – and instead highlights the dialectical role of vying empires before as well as after Western European hegemony. Transylvania's inter-imperial history suggests that the coloniality that gradually engulfed the world after 1492 constituted a late moment in a larger inter-imperial configuration of power that predated the emergence of Western Atlantic expansion and vied with it. Just as coloniality represents the carry-over of colonial hierarchies into post-independence times and thereby both parallels and outlives colonialism, inter-imperiality both precedes coloniality and coexists with it, while outlasting imperialism (Boatcă and Parvulescu 2020). At the same time, this history casts a long shadow, that is, its impact is felt far beyond what most academic literature considered as the decline of pre-modern European empires in the face of the Atlantic colonial project. Accordingly, inter-imperial histories such as Transylvania's also inform a region's postsocialist or postcolonial positionality and it is important to take them into account in a transversal discourse that aims at building shared positionalities of re-existence.

MT: What triggered our initial interest to reflect on the postcolonial and postsocialist feminist dialogues and opacities was the fact that, with the end of the Cold War, feminists of the former state socialist world were left with no voice and no problematic of their own (Suchland 2015). Soon the discriminated Eastern European part of the former state socialist world usurped the symbolically understood postcolonial discourse to describe its situation of the internal other of expanded Europe. While doing it, as you correctly pointed out, this new subalternised postsocialist feminist subject, in its turn, discarded many past and present socialist phenomena, events, and voices that were coming from outside euro-modernity. We are trying to somewhat restore the balance in this volume and include the voices of non-European feminists from former and present socialist countries. Although this has proven to be the main challenge as feminists from the global south are seldom interested in or ready to discuss the socialist and postsocialist dimensions in their agendas and experiences or much less, reflect on manifestations of coloniality in state socialist modernity. This asymmetry and uneasiness of the feminists of the global south in engaging in critical discussion of socialism, has become clear in preparation to the conference in 2015 and intensified in working on this volume. We see it as a core element in the postcolonial-postsocialist feminist puzzle. What is your explanation of this asymmetry and uneasiness?

MB: I agree that this uneasiness is a core element of the puzzle, and it is certainly not limited to postcolonial and postsocialist feminism alone. While it could easily be dismissed as lack of global solidarity, I think it is rather a clear proof of how coloniality works – in this case, the coloniality of knowledge that relegates certain experiences to certain spaces and assigns them a category – like when postcolonialism emerged after World War II as an issue *of* the recently created "Third World", making socialism the hallmark of the Second. Categories like the Second or the Third World, "Eastern" Europe, "Latin" America, "transformation societies" or "postconflict societies" then become the terrain over which competing political interests fight. They tend to be internalised as frames of self-reference even by critical scholars and subsequently reproduced in the dialogue – or confrontation – with their equally constructed counterparts. This makes it easy to gloss over the fact that, as I mentioned earlier, there were several African socialisms in the 20th century – even if they did not translate into an African socialist block. This would warrant an analysis of socialist experiences by African feminists without the need of European state socialism as a frame of reference, but rather as a connecting thread, the potential of which has only recently started being explored (yet, as far as I know, not in relation to feminism, so your project is pioneering in this respect). The same coloniality of knowledge makes us gloss over the fact that being racialised as non-European also happened and is currently happening in Europe – which is not to equate histories and experiences of racialisation, as they certainly differed widely, and at times dramatically. But these multiple forms of racialisation include experiences as diverse as those of Black Europeans, Eastern Europeans, or European Muslims (and sometimes one person could be all of the above), infamously involved those of European Jews, as well as the even more complex and understudied enslavement, segregation, and racialisation of the European Roma. So, a great deal of what constitutes the remit of postcolonialism would benefit from an awareness, acknowledgment, and analysis of the interconnections between the Global South and the European East. Of course, a structurally unequal world-system such as global capitalism will always be premised on the fragmentation of political interests in order to prevent system-wide change – or, plainly put, divide and rule so as to prevent a world revolution. When white feminists disregarded Black experiences, Third World feminism arose in response. Conversely, Second World feminism is associated with and often acts as white feminism alone and is thus considered European – ironically, at the same time as full Europeanness is being denied to the European East and its whiteness remains questionable and is subjected to scrutiny. Dismantling the constructed categories of the coloniality of knowledge is therefore indispensable for the emergence of transversal coalitions. This does not only refer to rather recent constructions such as First, Second, and Third Worlds, which have already fallen into disrepute, but also to notions of Europe as an unmarked category, of Europe's colonial history as a thing of the past, and of a white Christian European identity as the norm.

MT: In your insightful problematising of the postcolonial and postsocialist through the signifier of "uneasiness", what role is given to feminism? How does it enter the equation? Is there some specificity of particularly feminist optics related to postcolonial and postsocialist existential experience?

MB: That is a great question. Indeed, how does feminism enter any equation? We know that the relationship feminism(s) had with both colonialism and socialism was already uneasy, starting with the fact that the very category of gender was denied to the enslaved, because their humanity was negated in the racial colonial matrix to begin with. How deeply ingrained this denial of humanity-as-womanhood remained in modernity/coloniality resonated as late as the mid-19th century in Sojourner Truth's speech *Ain't I a Woman?* at the Women's Rights Convention in Ohio in 1851. White feminists like Olympe de Gouges and Mary Wollstonecraft, arguing from within the self-appointed humanity of Western Europeanness, had already denounced the male dividend of the human rights and citizenship discourse in the wake of the French Revolution. Nevertheless,

19th-century socialism famously relegated both the issue of nationality and that of gender to side contradictions (*Nebenwidersprüche*, in Marxian terms) with respect to the international class struggle. Anti-colonial and anti-imperial discourses and politics, which often made nationality a key focus, likewise forfeited gender as secondary or even irrelevant. Cutting across these divides is the modern/colonial reshuffling of gender relations, or what Maria Lugones has captured with the notion of the "coloniality of gender". Thus, 1492 was not only the year in which Jews were expulsed from the Iberian Peninsula and Columbus landed in the Caribbean, thus paving the way for the incorporation of the Americas into a modern/colonial world-system fuelled by plantation economies in which dehumanised African men and women laboured. It was also the year in which the first ordinance forbidding women under the age of 50 to live alone and stipulating that they instead go into service until they were married was passed in Coventry, England – soon to be followed by stricter ones all over Western Europe. That is to say, European socialism's disregard of gender was a late manifestation of an already colonially inflected gendering of economic, social, political, and epistemic spheres. Both postcolonial and postsocialist feminisms grapple with realities shaped by the reorganisation of the various gender relations on the European continent into a comprehensive gender hierarchy that pivoted on the creation of a racial hierarchy in the Occident and imposed it on its colonies. The answer to your question about whether there is any "specificity of particularly feminist optics related to the postcolonial and postsocialist existential experience" is thus both "yes" and "no". To explain why, I think we need to go back to feminist subsistence theorist Claudia von Werlhof's (1988) formulation that, when applied to the entire world-economy, "the women's question is the most general, not the most particular, of all social questions, because it contains all others". So, on the one hand, yes, there is a specificity of feminist optics, but this specificity is not the same as particularity, it is the opposite. The "women's question" is the most general social question only in a system premised on the logic of gendering, as in the case of the modern/colonial world-system infused with the coloniality of gender. On the other hand, my answer as to whether the specificity of feminist optics is related to the postcolonial and postsocialist experience in particular would be "no". One reason is precisely because gender divisions have permeated the entire system since the beginning and are constantly reproduced throughout all layers of existential experiences. Another reason is that arguing for a direct relation to these experiences rather than others would mean to reify the postcolonial and the postsocialist as distinct rather than interrelated, both with each other and with anti-colonialism, anti-imperialism, and inter-imperiality. That doesn't mean, however, that feminist optics cannot connect postcolonial and postsocialist existential experiences in unique ways, for instance by infusing politics with a different, historically informed notion of the role of the state in mitigating inequalities through redistribution – as long as such redistribution doesn't have a racial dividend, a male dividend, or both.

MT: When you refer to White feminism, could you please elaborate a bit more on what this concept might mean, particularly in the context of this volume on intersections, opacities, and challenges of postcolonial and postsocialist feminisms, and also, more broadly, the way White feminism is evoked in current critical discussions?

MB: This is a crucial point, thank you for asking me to clarify it. Your own tiptoeing around the meaning of the term says it all, because indeed, White feminism *might* mean different things – but the conversations about it are rarely as open-ended as the one we are having here. What is commonly subsumed under White feminism notoriously started out as Western feminism centred around the experiences of white, middle-class women. The movements arisen in response to the multiple exclusions of this type of feminism mobilised around the regional or racial categories whose experiences were not on its agenda – despite its claims to universality. They accordingly self-designated as Third World feminism, Chicana feminism, womanism, African or Black feminism. So, while there was an overlap between the interests which these counter-movements championed and their self-identification, this was not the case for Western feminism, which was only revealed as White (and thus as partial and partisan, instead of universal) through the prism of those who it left out. White feminism thus is seldom, if ever, a self-designation, but is instead a denunciation of the lack of all other experiences from the overarching category of feminism.

Now, this is a familiar story. We know from scholarship on Orientalism, racism, and critical whiteness that prevailing norms – whether it is the West, Europe, heterosexuality, or whiteness – feature as "unmarked categories", as I briefly mentioned above using Maria Todorova's term (Todorova 2005). Their normativity is apparent in the fact that they require a negative counterpart – the Orient as the non-West, Eastern Europe as lesser Europe, homosexuality as non-heterosexuality, or blackness as non-whiteness. While the categories thereby constructed as deviant need qualifying labels, the unmarked norm(al) remains unnamed, unqualified, or unlabelled. Thus, feminism *tout court* was the prevailing norm – although it had itself started as deviance from the norm of male suffrage – and only appeared as *White* feminism through confrontation with Third World, Chicana, African feminism. The "white" in White feminism is therefore a political positionality – whether or not its proponents assume it. It is not the equivalent of "Western", not the same as "European" and most certainly not a phenotypical description. These meanings get easily conflated when postcolonial feminists accuse postsocialist feminists in Europe of championing White feminism. But it is indeed not always easy to tell. While the label of "Europe" always includes both Western Europe and its white populations, Eastern Europe needs to be specifically mentioned in order to be included in the term, while Black Europe needs to be argued, defended, and explained. Where does this leave postsocialist European feminists? That depends on which side of the political positionality of Whiteness they find themselves – not on their geographical location, their class, or their physical appearance. The post-1989 rhetoric of the postsocialist world's "return to Europe" did frame Europeanness as whiteness, to be achieved by a thorough break with and disavowal of Easternness, the Orient, the Ottoman, and Soviet legacies. Postsocialist feminists invested in "becoming Europeans" in this way are politically "whiter" than Western European feminists (this being the feminist version of being more Catholic than the Pope; I'm only half-joking). But there is also a committed, globally-minded, historically informed, politically active – and yes, younger – generation of postsocialist feminists, many of them artists and activists, rather than (only) academics that is deeply aware of the coloniality of gender and its inflections in the Global South and the European East and is invested in building precisely the transversal dialogues for which your volume advocates. This potential would be wasted if the label of White feminism were used literally or allowed to conflate race and geography.

References

Boatcă, Manuela, and Anca Parvulescu. 2020. "Creolizing Transylvania: Notes on Coloniality and Inter-Imperiality." *History of the Present* 10, no. 1: 9–27. doi:10.1215/21599785-8221398.

Doyle, Laura. 2015. "Inter-Imperiality and Literary Studies in the Longer Durée." *Publications of Modern Language Associations of America* 130, no. 2: 336–347. doi:10.1632/pmla.2015.130.2.336.

Suchland, Jennifer. 2015. *Economies of Violence: Transnational Feminism, Postsocialism, and the Politics of Sex Trafficking.* Durham, NC: Duke University Press. doi:10.1215/9780822375289.

Todorova, Maria. 2005. "Spacing Europe: What Is a Historical Region?" *East Central Europe* 32, nos. 1–2: 59–78. doi:10.1163/18763308-90001032.

von Werlhof, Claudia. 1988. "The Proletarian Is Dead: Long Live the Housewife." In *Women the Last Colony*, edited by Maria Mies, Veronika Bennholdt-Thomsen, and Claudia von Werlhof, 168–179. Atlantic Highlands, NJ: Zed Books.

Chapter 14

Connecting the "posts" to confront racial capitalism's coloniality

Alyosxa Tudor and Piro Rexhepi

Alyosxa Tudor: A decade ago, I first suggested differentiating between racism and what I call "migratism" to analyse the complex nexus of racialisation and migration in postcolonial Europe. Since then, I have published quite a bit on the topic (e.g. Tudor 2017a, 2017b, 2018). My insistence that not all migration-based discrimination can be called racism but that whiteness – semi-peripheral East European whiteness for that matter – needs to be reflected upon critically, has been met with vehement critique. People often bemoan that I would take away "racism" as a word to name the discrimination against East Europeans (who implicitly or explicitly are imagined as racially homogenous = white in these accounts). It is the affective anxiety that is bewildering to me – the idea that harm is done to white East Europeans when the discrimination against them/us is not called "racism", the idea that it was Black feminism or Critical Whiteness Studies that had taken something away. Floya Anthias and Nira Yuval Davis in an article published as early as 1983 claim: "The notion of 'black women' as delineating the boundaries of the alternative feminist movement to white feminism leaves non-British non-black women (like us – a Greek-Cypriot and an Israeli-Jew) unaccounted for politically" (Anthias and Yuval-Davis 1983, 63). These approaches alternate in their argumentation between calling for inclusion of white migratised women into the group of people discriminated against by racism (Rzepnikowska 2019, 74; Anthias and Yuval-Davis 1983, 63) and between claiming that migration-based discrimination produces racialisation through de-whitening (Rzepnikowska 2019, 64). Those who believe in keeping racism as a universal signifier want their exclusion from the nation state to be transformed into racism-experiencing inclusion in anti-racist scholarship. What is striking to me is that in these accounts that fight for the inclusion of – in my words – white migratised positions into the definitions of racism, the frustration and the feelings of being left out are not mainly directed against the dominant group but come with envying the perceived recognition of Black and anti-racist interventions. In Alina Rzepnikowska's case it is "non-white ethnic minorities" who get all the space in anti-racist scholarship and in Anthias/ Yuval-Davis's case it is "black women" who get to be recognised as the "alternative feminist movement to white feminism". Gabriele Griffin and Rosi Braidotti

(2002, 225) even fear the "obliteration within European feminist race politics of the reality of racialized issues faced by women in Europe" when the discrimination against East European women is not named with the blanket term "racism". It is a language of loss (Before this new focus on racism that centres Black people and people of colour, we were able to name the discrimination against white migrants) and even obliteration (White migrants are being undone by Black people and people of colour who define racism as "white supremacy" and therefore as not directed against white migrants).

This brings me to the relations of postcolonialism and postsocialism as it is important to revisit the epistemologies of the "posts-". What is the work of the "post-" in *post*colonialism and *post*socialism? The two certainly have in common the attempt to grasp the complexity of present geopolitics and reflect on the blurry spatial-temporality of histories, borders, boundaries, and modes of becoming. Learning from critical (feminist) scholarship on the intersections of postcolonialism and postsocialism (see for example Cervinkova 2012; Chari and Verdery 2009; Koobak 2013; Suchland 2011; Tlostanova 2012), I want to ask: how do we not deplore the seemingly peripheral role of postsocialism compared to postcolonialism in gender and feminist studies based in the West (as this assumes the postcolonial cannot be postsocialist and as it replicates the laments towards postcolonial and Black feminism mentioned above) or avoid equating postsocialism with Eastern Europe (as state socialism is not an exclusively European phenomenon)? Moreover, I am concerned with the question: in which ways can postsocialist whiteness be held accountable for its role in the modern white supremacist project?

Similarly to my reflections on the "post" in "postcolonial Europe" (Tudor 2017a) and in line with Neda Atanasoski and Kalindi Vora (2018), I suggest here that the prefix "post-" provides odd, contradictory, and productive spatial-temporal dimensions not only in relation to the term it is attached to (see Shohat's 1992 theoretisation of the "post" in "postcolonial"), but also in interrelation between different terms that are prefixed with the syllabus "post" (see Appiah's 1991 question "Is the Post- in Postmodernism the Post- in Postcolonial?" and various adaptations of the question). Based on the idea that the prefix "post" means continuities and ruptures in relation to the term it specifies and not a simple "after" (Shohat 1992) but a non-linear, queer temporality that cannot even be fully explained in exclusively temporal dimensions, one could also ask how the terms which are specified by the prefix "post" interrelate and how they are put into context to each other through being prefixed in the same way. Is for example the *socialism* in postsocialism the *colonialism* in postcolonialism? Why is this equation problematic and what insights, challenges, and potentials would a focus on the role of revolutionary socialism in decolonial struggles provide?

I consider myself an epistemologist. That's why I see my work as exploring the potentials of the "queer" temporalities of the prefix "post" and resisting attempts to erase contradictions. Indeed, I am rather interested in the (messy and contradictory) relatedness of the "posts" than in their equation. One of the things that is important to me, especially in my role as a teacher and researcher in the field of migration and diaspora studies, is to identify Europe as postcolonial: as shaped through European colonialism (Bhambra 2009; Tudor 2017a). Therefore, my work privileges postcolonial understandings of racialisation as central for critical analysis. Following Brah (1996) this also means understanding Europe as diasporic space – as the product of migrations and diasporas. A queer perspective in my work is more than a focus on sexuality, although it is not not-about-sexuality. For me analysing the "queer" temporalities and trajectories (histories, wanderings, stayings and strayings, productive failures to belong to the nation state, etc.) of queer and trans migrant presents and presences is a queer undertaking. Most notably scholars in the field of queer and trans of colour critique use "queering" as critical practice that is not only connected to non-heterosexuality (e.g. El-Tayeb 2011; Tinsley 2008). Building on their knowledge productions, I conceptualise "queering" and "transing" as critical moves with histories in different (but at times converging) political movements. While "transing" can mean "going beyond a category", "queering" can mean disrupting normative orders. "Transing" the nation and "transing gender" (Tudor 2017b, 2019) could be thought as critical moves for a radical deconstruction of gendered and national belonging. Coming back to a point raised already, I find that speaking about postcolonialism and postsocialism in the same breath always carries the danger to equate either the "posts" or the two terms that are prefixed in the same way. This makes me feel uneasy, because certainly there must be ways to acknowledge that colonialism was and has always been bad, and socialism is at its core what? Good? In theory, a disruption of colonial/racial capitalism, in practice partly used as the driving force of Russian colonial modernity (Tlostanova 2012). Even in this formulation, both terms are not on the same level, as socialism seems to be used as colonising (as the case for Russia/the USSR) or as decolonial tool (e.g. the Black Panther Party in the US or African decolonial socialisms; see for example Césaire 2001 for a meta-reflection).

In a turn towards resignification, Atanasoski and Vora (2018) suggest: *"Postsocialism marks a queer temporality, one that does not reproduce its social order even as its revolutionary antithesis*. Resisting the revolutionary teleology of what was before, postsocialism creates space to work through ongoing legacies of socialisms in the present". Bogdan Popa (2018) speaks of "queer postsocialism" as a way to disrupt straight linear time that understands socialism as heading towards revolution, but also as a queer temporality that does not cede socialism to the ash heap of history, defeated by Anglo-American liberal capitalism. In this vein, queering postsocialism is not just about queers in postsocialist countries or the diaspora. It is more a critical reflection on what socialism means when queered (and transed?). I think it is necessary to apply this insight to the scholarship that addresses the intersections of postsocialism and postcolonialism and with this put in plain sight the asymmetry of the terms. There is no such thing as queered and transed colonialism, of course. On the contrary postcolonial/

decolonial intervention is about decolonising queer and trans and gender studies – making them accountable to critical analysis of racism and colonialism.

Piro Rexhepi: I think your point about postsocialist whiteness is an urgent one because when you say, "I am concerned with the question: in which ways can post-socialist whiteness be held accountable for its role in the modern white suprema-cist project?" What you are calling into question is not just the colour blindness that often governs postsocialist studies but also the "political racelessness" to quote Fatima El-Tayeb (2011), that dominates post-socialist politics today. This is a conversation that we have both engaged in for some time now. I remember a few years ago at the *Sexuality and Borders*[1] conference we discussed what Charles W. Mills (2007) work on the epistemology of ignorance and "white ignorance" reveals about postsocialist whiteness. I want to start with a small story from the student protests in Albania in 2019 that I think best illustrates how racism and anti-Blackness continue to be erased and silenced in political debates through deployments of amnesia and ambiguity on the one hand and ignorance and inno-cence on the other.

Halfway through news coverage on the student protests in Albania in 2019, the camera zoomed in and focused on a sign that one of the students in the city of Elbasan carried that read "European prices, African Salaries, Arian Race, Tali-ban Standards, Miserable Albania". The news commentator read the sign that had become popular since the protests had started in 2018[2] during a live report to sug-gest the strength and sentiment of rage and disappointment that the students were delivering home. In other words, how can an Arian race be given African salaries, Taliban standards, and yet pay European prices while not being part of the Euro-pean market? Or in short, why are Albanians being robbed of their "Arian" race privilege? While the protests are far more complex and merit a more thorough analysis that I am committing to here, I draw on this slogan to illustrate some of the ways in which race functions as capital that the post-socialist subject can claim, trade, and negotiate in the racial capitalist marketplace of the European Union. On the one hand, the sign illustrates the geopolitical imaginaries that gov-ern racial capitalism's hierarchies and come to inform the post-socialist position in relation to them, while also exposing the racist premises of privileged relations promised by the politics of EU "integration".

In *Humanitarian Violence* (2013), Neda Atanasoski points out that in 1990s, "one crucial task of U.S. nationalist, liberal multiculturalism was to distinguish normative modes of inhabiting and representing diversity from aberrant ones, which could lead to "tribalism" and separatism of the kind witnessed in the former Yugoslavia, Chechnya, and Rwanda" (2013, 34). Atanasoski's work that exam-ines these dynamics in the 1990s is extremely important for the present political moment as it points out how Euro-American interventions in, and integration of, post-socialist spaces, came at a price of underplaying the rise of the incarcera-tion of communities of colour in the US and intensification of police violence on migrant communities in Europe and at its borders. Nowhere is this perhaps more obvious that in the first post-Cold War decades when while the EU and US were promoting racial capitalism as "Euro-Atlantic integration" and "democratisation", they were simultaneously busy building carceral regimes at home as the work of Ruth Wilson Gilmore (2007) shows. The reason it is timely to return to this point is because it now brings up a new set of questions about what those post-Cold War politics of "Euro-American progress" did to solidify the far-right regimes across post-socialist spaces whose primary targets have been Roma people, refugees, trans, and queer communities with Islamophobia underwriting all those projects of EUnification.

But I also worry that if we think of racism in Eastern Europe as a purely post-socialist phenomenon, we risk obscuring the durability of pre-socialist racial hier-archies in their continuation and collusion with socialism and post-socialist racial capitalism or to go back to Charles W. Mills (2015) again, a "global white igno-rance". Moreover, these temporal brakes of pre-socialist/socialist/post-socialist can sometimes construct a nostalgic colour-blind and colonial-less image of socialist progress in between reactionary and racial times. Examining the deeper forms of whiteness in postsocialist spaces today can allow us to confront both the more protracted forms of racism in the region as well as their re-deployment in the post-socialist realignment with racial capitalism and coloniality. To do this, we have to always start from the position of racialised people across postsocialist spaces.

I want to think through some of those more protracted forms of whiteness and racism in the postsocialist spaces through the work of Selma Selman because I think her confrontation of Roma racism in the Balkan region unsettles not just the politics of the far right but also the silence and compliance with racism in left-ist movements. One of the best commentaries on this intersection of racial capi-talism, class, gender, and coloniality in postsocialism is her performance piece "Self-Portrait".[3] In it, Selma, who is a Roma artist from Bosnia takes the elec-tronic waste that people deposit in Roma neighbourhoods across the peripheries of postsocialist cities to demolish them into their city centres. In my conversations with Selma, she has described the process of the performance as wanting to spare no one from what the noise of capitalist violence sounds like,

> you can't deposit your waste in the periphery and return to the comfort of the centre making abstract noise about 'rights,' . . . for instance, I chose to demolish a washing machine because I was trying to point out how the work of waste recycling that takes places in Roma neighbourhoods forces us to reckon with the racist, gendered and environmental violence that result from capitalism.

Selman's work is important because, in confronting the post-socialist left and liberal peripheralisation of questions of racism and refugees, it also exposes their comfortable collusion with the EU and its captive and carceral border regimes in the region. Selma comes from Bihać, the site of refugees where the space once used for refugees from the Bosnian genocide now serve as EU-sponsored camps for migrant detention. Connecting her own racialised reality in Bosnia to the refugees that are being pursued along the Balkan Route to prevent them from "entering" Europe, in a virtual reality performance called "No Space",[4] where she says that "There is no space here for you" she echoes the term that the Roma people encounter in the Balkans when looking for jobs or housing that is not disconnected from the same message being given to refugees when they are told that "there is no space for you here".

I want to return to your question of "What is the work of the 'post-' in *post*colonialism and *post*socialism?" because I think Selma's work illustrates the kind of political projects and questions that emerge from connecting "posts" to confront racial capitalism's coloniality. This requires as you say, a "queer undertaking" which would mean not only thinking "against the dominant arrangement of time and history" as Elizabeth Freeman (2010, XI-XIV) puts it, but also taking apart the epistemology of the closet of racial capitalism's coloniality. Clare Hemmings (2020) recent re-reading of Eve Kosofsky Sedgwick's *Epistemology of the Closet* (1990) aptly reminds us that the closet still retains its interpretative tensions to think through the current constellation of racial capitalism in as much as it "is the open secret through which difference and inequality are both obscured and played out in front of our eyes in plain sight".

AT: Yes, it is exactly those questions around identifying whiteness, nationalism, and borders "hidden in plain sight" in discourses on Eastern Europe or the diaspora that makes our work resonate with each other. As an East European diasporic queer/trans subject, I am very much aware of the fact that belonging to the nation, to "proper" rather than peripheral Europeanness and to normative gender and sexuality is neither possible nor desirable. The melancholia of non-belonging is based on a loss that cannot be recovered – maybe it is the queer/trans migrant who knows that and who embraces rather than fights that melancholia?

Resonating with the example you mention in which student protestors pose the question "why are Albanians being robbed of their 'Arian' race privilege?", in the diaspora these feelings of dispossession are reproduced in nationalist and racist ways. In a recent piece on anti-Polish discrimination in the UK, Rzepnikowska (2019, 73) mentions that her interviewees complain about "unfairness . . . about being victims of racism and xenophobia despite being white and European" as seen in questions they pose in the interviews with her, like "[W]hy can't [the British] focus more on blacks and Asians?" What really makes me uneasy here is that the academic scholarship that aims to point out anti-East-European discrimination in Western Europe and calls this "racism", does not seem to have the tools to intervene or theorise the actual racism uttered by white migrants that follows the logics of claiming proper, white, racist Europeanness – wanting to be a part of racist Europe as the "Euro-American progress" story promises.

This normative understanding of belonging and progress very often comes as heterosexist and gender-normative nationalism (Tudor 2017b). For example, in 2013 the Romanian newspaper *Gandul* ran an ad campaign in response to growing anti-Romanian hostility in the UK that used slogans like "Half of our women look like Kate [Middleton]. The other half, like her sister" (see Morse 2013).

National white femininity as property of both Romanian men and the nation gets invoked by the use of the possessive pronoun in "our women". Examples of this kind that try to "educate" the West on the whiteness and Europeanness of Romanians are countless, both in academic and public media debates (see also Tudor 2017b for discussing a far-right example). In 2015, Channel 4 aired a documentary series that can be watched on YouTube with the title "The Romanians are coming"[5] that follows Florin and others, recent migrants from Romania to the UK, on their journey. While the title of the series already plays with stereotypical phobia against Romanians invading the UK used widely in the run-up to the Brexit referendum, the comment section is bursting from contributions by outraged white Romanians who denounce Florin, the protagonist of the first episode as being Roma, not Romanian. "G[-] are migratory tribes from India, Romanians are an (sic) European Latin nation. There is a HUGE difference and every European citizen should know this."[6] (For an analysis of this topos see also Oprea 2012.)

All of these examples show that is important for scholarship, art, and activism to connect, as you say, "the 'posts' to confront racial capitalism's coloniality". This is especially necessary in order not to fall into the trap of another progressive narrative: the one that assumes anti-racism is situated in the West and Eastern Europe lagging behind once more, being "more racist" than the West, needing to learn from Western critical race theory. Confronting the idea that a specific East European racism was imported into the UK by Polish migrants, Magdalena Nowicka (2018) calls the racism she encountered in the conversations with her white Polish interviewees "European racism". This relates to El-Tayeb's (2011, XIV) warning that "[a]ll parts of Europe are arguably invested in 'whiteness' as a norm against which ethnicization is read as a tool of differentiation between insiders and outsiders". Therefore, as I want to stress, a transnational analysis of racism, nationalism, and white supremacy is necessary to make sense of the multiple layers of power relations that are often played against each other. For example, in the *Black Lives Matter* statement that protestors read out in Bucharest on 7 June 2020, they draw connections between police violence against people of colour, anti-Roma violence, and power relations like classism, misogyny, queer/transphobia, and discrimination against sex workers and underline the need for a transnational frame.[7] Even though the initial moment of the intervention was George Floyd's death and subsequent protests in the US and therefore had nothing to do with a communist past, the trolls on YouTube accuse the protestors of "communism", one of them going as far as suggesting they should die like Ceaușescu died (a.k.a. be shot by the Romanian military). While the postcolonial moment of the radically intersectional analysis the protestors offer is clear through both the anti-racism of the protest and the racist backlash in the comments, the postsocialist moment is more blurry: we have queer/trans-feminist anti-fascist anti-racist protestors and we have a Romanian social media public consisting mainly of fascists and racists accusing the protestors of communism. This is very much in line with UK far-right politician's Nigel Farage polemics that all migrants "coming from these communist countries" are uncivilised: the idea that due to their communist past, Romanians have not learned how to be proper members of society.[8] As Cristian Cercel (2020) puts it, Romania is seen as having "[n]o politics, no society". Both rhetorics, the one of the Western anti-East-European far-right and the one of the Romanian far-right, are anti-communist, but they ascribe communism to different actors. Western Europe sees all Romanians as tainted by communism; the European East sees itself as having put communism against the wall together with Ceauşescu. In this narrative, anti-racist, anti-fascist queer-, and transfeminist activists get equated to the past, they have not moved on to the "post" in postsocialism which in this grim understanding is the solidification of fascism/far-right regimes, as you point out. Of course, I am not following this use of the term. If we want to make "postsocialist" work as an adjective that describes a current moment in states that were socialist during the Cold War, the postsocialist aspect of the example above both makes opposing white supremacy, nationalism, and racism possible *as* post/socialist anti-racism, makes the postsocialist moment into a postcolonial one. In other words, opposing white supremacy, nationalism, and racism does not work in the example as either anti-socialist or socialist.

PR: There are similar politics in Bulgaria and Macedonia too – but there, in a bizarre twist, the far-right folds together post-socialist liberalism with communism even though anti-communism has been a prominent feature of all post-socialist far right and liberal platforms. In Macedonia for instance the casual terminology for liberal civil society organisations is now *sorosoidi* deployed as attacks on George Soros and the Open Society Foundation, whereas in Bulgaria the term *liberasti* is meant to synchronise liberal with *pederasti*, the latter being term used across the Balkans to interchangeably mean both faggot and a turncoat. These terminologies are deployed not only by the far right but also by "socialists" who frequently merge with nationalists on political questions regarding refugees and particularly racism against Roma communities.

In 2017 for instance when I was doing research in Bulgaria on the racist protests on "Roma aggression" that accompanied the state-organised destruction of Roma houses and communities across the country, I remember how the socialist opposition party was not so much questioning the far right government for its rampant demolition of Roma neighbourhoods as much as arguing that the government was not doing enough to "resolve the Roma aggression problem" as it came to be known. Ivo Hristov, then an MP of Socialist Party (now MP with the Group of the Progressive Alliance of Socialists and Democrats in the European Parliament) commented in a plenary session of the Bulgarian Parliament that, like the Albanians in Yugoslavia, Roma's demographic growth and demand for rights were the "capsule detonator that is going to blow Bulgaria up".[9] Meanwhile, 2017 being an election year, the head of the socialist party Korneliya Ninova had announced several times that Margaret Thatcher and Theresa May had been an inspiration for her political career. Despite this virtuous signalling to the right, the socialists lost the 2017 elections, and I remember that the victory of Boyko Borisov and his coalition with the far-right United Patriots – some of whom had direct ties to the vigilante groups that abused and pushed back migrants at the Bulgarian/EU-Turkish border – around Europe was framed as Bulgaria's "pro-EU" forces beating socialists. In many ways, this anchoring of post-socialist politics onto the EU have today refashioned far right and fascist groups like Boyko Borisov's coalition government in Bulgaria into "centrist" blocks.

I think here we need to turn to the EU and the role it has played in solidifying far right regimes across post-socialist spaces because Brexit, in all its racist revanchism, also served to redeem EU's structural racism both at its borders and in its interior. Far from articulating a different approach to migration from Brexit, the EU used the Brexit moment to increase its spending towards a new carceral bordering conglomerate which went from €5.6 billion Euros for 2014–2020 to €21.3 billion for 2021–2027 (European Commission undated) with a "new standing corps of 10,000 border guards – to be rolled out until 2027" (European Commission 2019). A great deal of these funds have also been allocated to the Greek and Libyan coast guards who are now routinely engaged in push-backs that result in unaccounted deaths of migrants at sea (Felden and Jawad undated). Unsurprisingly, when the EU parliament issued a statement in support of Black Lives Matter in June 2020,[10] many African migrants on social media asked if that included Black lives on the Mediterranean that the EU is actively involved in shooting, push-backs, and covering up information on violence at its borders.

Much of the debate around Europhiles vs. Eurosceptics, as Fatima El-Tayeb (2020) has recently pointed out, reproduces Europe's internalist story, a colonial amnesia whereby the EU generates its supposed anti-racist stance by suggesting that is the Eurosceptics who are anti-migrant. In reality, however, the far right has converged with the EU in the border security across the region where anti-refugee rhetoric and racism merge in keeping Europe's "eastern gates" safe. A July 2020 promotional electoral video for Croatia's ruling nationalist party, HDZ, for instance, features the EU Commission President Ursula von der Leyen alongside Ireland's former prime minister Leo Varadkar, ex-European Council president Donald Tusk, the German Defence Minister Annegret Kramp-Karrenbauer, and Austrian Chancellor Sebastian Kurz all promoting HDZ to keep a "Safe Croatia".[11] The video is, among other things, a response to the critique that the ruling party has received for beating and pushing migrants back into Bosnia with shaved heads in the shape of a red cross. That the EU also actively sought to cover up Croatia's violence towards migrants is illustrative of how entrenched these relations have become (Tondo and Boffey 2020). HDZ's attempt in May 2020 to sponsor a commemorative mass for its Nazi-allied soldiers in Bosnia, for instance, all the while presiding over the Council of Europe, also shows how these racist and reactionary returns in the region are not in contrast but in collusion with the Europeanness and all that EU integration really stands for, but also how Europe continues to cover up the coloniality of migration (Gutiérrez Rodríguez 2018) by projecting itself as a victim under attack by migrants from its southern and eastern borders. I want to quote Fatima El-Tayeb's recent work at length here because it illustrates this manoeuvring brilliantly:

> Absent from the concerted rewriting of European twentieth-century history after the end of the Cold War, which combined postfascist and postsocialist narratives into a Western capitalist success story, was a third factor in dire need of reassessment: Europe's colonial past. The refusal to engage with this past as internal to Europe's history also shaped the continent's vision of its future, manifest in a steadily growing postcolonial population that remains "un-European" and in futile attempts to once and for all define and fortify Europe's physical, political, and identitarian borders. . . . This malleability is particularly obvious in the perception of refugees and undocumented migrants, especially those classified as "economic migrants" (primarily North and West African Muslims and East European Roma) whose death by the thousands at Europe's southern (and increasingly eastern) border is willingly accepted.
>
> (2020, 76)

Returning to your point about what occludes and to an extent makes impermissible "a transnational analysis of racism, fascism, and anti-communism/anti-socialism" as you put it: I think part of the problem is that we continue to think of colonialism in the third world, socialism in the second, and racism in the first along those spatial and temporal coordinates of Cold War area studies. This broad categorisation still dictates our analysis, which is why for instance we still can't think of Algeria, Angola, Egypt, Ethiopia, Mozambique, or South Yemen as postsocialist but only postcolonial. That countries of the global south rarely make it into postsocialist analysis is illustrative of the eurocentrism with which we continue to think about postsocialism, but also because this convenient division exposes coloniality which Europe refuses to reckon with. Similarly, how can we address Chechnya, Dagestan, or Kosovo today but as postsocialist or post-Soviet or post-conflict but rarely post-colonial? In this sense, this is another reason why the former second world is nearly absent in critical race and decolonial scholarship, as I have argued in examining the colonial entailments in postsocialist projects of "Europeanization" (Rexhepi 2018a).

Madina Tlostanova's work, for some time now, has brought into question this absence by considering the ways in which being postsocialist and postcolonial are neither contradictory nor exceptional political positions but mutually constitutive ones in the larger context of coloniality/modernity. What the implementation of racial capitalism has done across postsocialist spaces since the 1990s is to inscribe those racial hierarchies in the context of labour exploitation and postsocialist capital accumulation through oligarch privatisation of public wealth. In this sense, the post-socialist Chechen migrant in Moscow is the cheap post-colonial labour resource in much the same way that postsocialist and postcolonial migrants are exploited in the context of racial capitalism in Western Europe. Tlostanova's

A Janus Faced Empire: Notes on the Russian Empire in Modernity Written from the Border (2003) is important because she points out how we still lack a political vocabulary, much less a political project to discuss these complex and sometimes contradictory processes of postsocialist coloniality and racial capitalism.

One way to think through a "transnational analysis of racism, fascism, and anti-communism/anti-socialism" as you say, might also be to consider what socialism and postsocialism look like if we were to place the histories and lived experiences of colonised and racialised communities, queer and trans folks at the forefront of post-socialist analysis rather than the footnotes of larger (post) Cold War colour-blind and colonial-less politics. I am thinking here along Ann Stoler's work in general and her *Imperial Durabilities in our Times* (2016) in particular as a significant intervention that calls for attention to the afterlife of empires and their durabilities that hide in plain sight or "go by different names". When Stoler argues that "the geopolitical and spatial distribution of inequalities cast across our world today are not simply mimetic versions of earlier imperial incarnations but refashioned and sometimes opaque and oblique reworkings of them" (2016, 5), she calls for a deeper excavation and exposure of the connectives and continuities between the past and present forms of geopolitical colonial and racial capitalist constellations of power.

So when I try to think how racial capitalism has reworked and refashioned postsocialist racial hierarchies, we come across the dilemma that we addressed earlier in this piece; on the one hand, we have the impoverished position of labour relations of the post-socialist migrants in the West, and on the other hand, racial hierarchies of labour within socialist/post-socialist spaces. While I think they are equally important and inter-related questions, I want to focus on the reworked racial hierarchies in postsocialist spaces specifically and the kind of politics that they propel today. The solidification of far-right politics across the postsocialist spaces has politicised racist anxieties about refugees, impoverishment, security, and demographics by projecting Roma and migrant communities as co-conspirators with "gender ideologies" and queer and trans communities, both conspiring against the racial purity of the nation and its reproduction. In the case of Bulgaria or Hungary, for instance, as in the case of Romania that you have raised, the attack by the far right on racialised and impoverished communities has gone hand in hand with the attack on "gender ideologies". The merging of liberal and right wing with the EU bordering and securitisation platforms in post-socialist spaces has managed to create serious divisions in forging intersectional and international solidarities (Rexhepi 2018b). This is not to say they don't exist. Some of the most crucial solidarity networks between refugees and people living along the Balkan refugee route today have been undertaken by queer and feminist communities such as the Anti-Racist network based out of Thessaloniki or the Transbalkan Solidarity network that recently ran a 48-hour "return-the-bullets-back protest campaign directed at the European Union".[12]

One question that postsocialist scholars need to address is the extent to which socialism was a decolonising project not just in terms of self-determination but more broadly as a process of reparations and redistribution, not just "socialism" as it was segmented into "second world" brackets but socialism more broadly as a decolonising undertaking across the world. Here, we will find more complex histories that can widen solidarity beyond our postsocialist purgatorial position; as I've argued before in conversation with Marina Gržinić and Tjaša Kancler, "the (post) socialist world still cannot resolve its (geo)political position of being in pact and proximity of Euro-American coloniality or its product and defying periphery" (Gržinić, Kancler, and Rexhepi 2020).

AT: We have discussed so many strands here, ever-shifting conjunctures – cross-fadings, as I like to call them – of regimes and ideologies like colonialism, Eurocentrism, fascism, nationalism; of power relations like anti-Semitism, racism, and anti-Romaism; and of their gendered and sexualised aspects. What you point out for Bulgaria and Macedonia, that " 'socialists' . . . frequently merge with nationalists on political questions regarding refugees and particularly racism against Roma communities" is also true for Romania, and indeed it can be extended to the treatment of queer and trans people and feminist, gender, queer, and trans theories. The recent attempted ban of gender studies in Romania and the predecessor referendum in 2018 that attempted to change the constitution to make gay marriage constitutionally impossible have both been driven by the conservatives and the far right and backed by the socialists (Ciocian-Ardeleanu 2018). Aptly the referendum – that failed due to low voter turnout – was called "Referendum for Romania" and advertised with the Romanian national colours. Citing El-Tayeb, you pointed out that debates on Europhiles vs. Eurosceptics reproduce a colonial amnesia in which pro-European appears suddenly to be pro-immigrant and anti-racist. We both have come up with quite a few of these seemingly paradoxical examples in which the socialist left is backing traditionally far-right politics like anti-immigration and homophobia. This left-right convergence is a transnational phenomenon, as shown for example in the US in January 2019, when a group of transphobic feminists held a panel against trans equality and rights under the title: "Concerns From the Left" at an event hosted by the conservative, right-wing Heritage Foundation which has a long history of opposing LGBTQ rights, feminism, and immigration (see Tudor 2021). We could ask what makes left-wing politics left, if not the commitment to oppose hatred? Is it then only economic questions? Of course, these conjunctures do not come as a surprise as we know: socialists backing far-right queer and transphobic legislations and state racism, feminists joining right-wing anti-trans propaganda, or gay people reproducing Islamophobic ideas of emancipation, migrants turning against other migrants as the "new" unwelcome newcomers, etc. You urge us to explore the ways in which "post-Cold War politics of 'Euro-American progress'" have produced "far-right regimes across postsocialist spaces whose primary targets have been Roma people, refugees, trans, and queer communities" and at the same time, all our examples show that there is no easy ascription of any ideology as Western or Eastern, capitalist or socialist, etc. There is no authenticity in either of the terms. What I always get back to then is anti-fascism, anti-nationalism, and anti-racism as terms of political alignment. As we both have shown, these terms only make sense in transnational analysis that opposes epistemological nationalism, as we cannot make sense of racism, nationalism, and fascism if we keep it in the realm of the uncontested national.

PR: I couldn't agree more, in as much as coloniality isn't just about regional repertoires of denial and ignorance over fascism but also how they are attached to larger transnational racist visions of a post-Cold War global colour line. Where we locate ourselves in terms of "anti-fascism, anti-nationalism, and anti-racism as terms of political alignment", as you say, becomes an important question about decolonial praxis and solidarity. If we locate racism, nationalism, and fascism as the workings of coloniality/modernity, we are then called to examine the continuities of Eurocentric epistemologies and histories and their connectivities to racial capitalism not only as "the mere reconstruction of the past", as David Scott argues, but also as "critical appraisal of the present itself" (2004, 41). In this sense, we can only confront postsocialist fascism by aligning ourselves with the "green, red and internationalist" (Afary and Al-Kateb 2020) movements for abolition of oppressive systems of racialised, gendered, and classed relations of coloniality/modernity. Whatever our embodied or embedded position is in working to expose, fight, or abolish postsocialist or postcolonial fascism and however big or small our contributions, we should make sure that the fall of colonial statues across Europe and the United States today is just the beginning of a decolonial insurrection.

Notes

1 https://sexualityandborders.wordpress.com/
2 https://openuniversity.al/index.php/2018/12/13/foto-nga-protesta-9-ditore-e-studenteve/ (accessed August 9, 2020).
3 www.youtube.com/watch?v=T8KWcCUrFDQ (accessed August 9, 2020).
4 www.selmanselma.com/nospace (accessed August 9, 2020).
5 www.channel4.com/programmes/the-romanians-are-coming/videos/all/florins-story/4077544429001 (accessed March 5, 2020).
6 www.youtube.com/watch?v=Yb1AkaKJL08 (accessed March 5, 2020).
7 See the full statement here: https://3minute.net/black-lives-matter-bucuresti/
8 www.youtube.com/watch?v=-pyYoL9ngtE (accessed July 23, 2020).
9 National Assembly of the Republic of Bulgaria, "ТРИДЕСЕТ И ТРЕТО ЗАСЕ-ДАНИЕ," София, сряда, 5 юли 2017 г. Открито в 9,01 ч. www.parliament.bg/bg/plenaryst/ns/52/ID/5785 (accessed July 24, 2020).
10 www.europarl.europa.eu/news/en/press-room/20200615IPR81223/parliament-condemns-all-forms-of-racism-hate-and-violence-and-calls-for-action (accessed July 24, 2020).
11 www.youtube.com/watch?v=GKugC9nemaA (accessed July 24, 2020).
12 https://transbalkanskasolidarnost.home.blog/stop-funding-violence-now (accessed July 24, 2020).

References

Afary, Frieda, and Lara Al-Kateb. 2020. *What Is Holding Back the Formation of a Global Prison Abolitionist Movement to Fight COVID-19 and Capitalism?* Alliance of Middle Eastern and North African Socialists. https://allianceofmesocialists.org/what-is-holding-back-the-formation-of-a-global-prison-abolitionist-movement-to-fight-covid-19-and-capitalism/ [accessed 26 November, 2020].

Anthias, Floya, and Nira Yuval-Davis. 1983. "Contextualizing Feminism: Gender, Ethnic and Class Divisions." *Feminist Review* 15: 62–75. https://doi.org/10.1057/fr.1983.33.

Appiah, Kwame A. 1991. "Is the Post-in Postmodernism the Post-in Postcolonial?" *Critical Inquiry*: 336–357. https://doi.org/10.1086/448586.

Atanasoski, Neda. 2013. *Humanitarian Violence: The U.S. Deployment of Diversity*. Minneapolis, MN: University of Minnesota.

Atanasoski, Neda, and Kalindi Vora. 2018. "Postsocialist Politics and the Ends of Revolution." *Social Identities* 24, no. 2: 139–154. doi:10.1080/13504630.2017.1321712.

Bhambra, Gurminder. 2009. "Postcolonial Europe, or Understanding Europe in Times of the Postcolonial." In *Sage Handbook of European Studies*, 69–85. London: Sage.

Brah, Avtar. 1996. *Cartographies of Diaspora: Contesting Identities*. London: Routledge.

Cercel, Cristian. 2020. "No Politics, No Society: The Unbearable Lightness in Interpreting Romania." *openDemocracy*. www.opendemocracy.net/en/can-europe-make-it/no-politics-no-society-unbearable-lightness-interpreting-romania/ (accessed March 31, 2020).

Cervinkova, Hana. 2012. "Postcolonialism, Postsocialism and the Anthropology of East-Central Europe." *Journal of Postcolonial Writing* 48, no. 2: 155–163. doi:10.1080/174 49855.2012.658246.

Chari, Sharad, and Katherine Verdery. 2009. "Thinking Between the Posts: Postcolonialism, Postsocialism, and Ethnography After the Cold War." *Comparative Studies in Society and History* 51, no. 1: 6–34. doi:10.1017/S0010417509000024.

Ciocian-Ardeleanu, Raluca. 2018. *When Politics Overwrite Values: Romania's Homophobic Referendum*. European Humanist Federation. https://humanistfederation.eu/romania-homophobic-referendum/ [accessed November 26, 2020].

El-Tayeb, Fatima. 2011. *European Others: Queering Ethnicity in Postnational Europe*. Minneapolis, MN: University of Minnesota Press.

El-Tayeb, Fatima. 2020. "The Universal Museum: How the New Germany Built Its Future on Colonial Amnesia." *NKA: Journal of Contemporary African Art* 46, no. 1: 72–82. https://doi.org/10.1215/10757163-8308198.

European Commission. 2019. "A Reinforced European Border and Coast Guard." https://ec.europa.eu/home-affairs/sites/homeaffairs/files/what-we-do/policies/european-agenda-migration/20190401_managing-migration-factsheet-european-border-and-coast-guard_en.pdf (accessed July 24, 2020).

European Commission, undated. "A Step-Change in Migration Management and Border Security." https://ec.europa.eu/home-affairs/sites/homeaffairs/files/what-we-do/policies/european-agenda-migration/20190306_managing-migration-factsheet-step-change-migration-management-border-security-timeline_en.pdf (accessed November 26, 2020).

Felden, Easter, and Amanullah Jawad. undated. "*Deutsche Welle*. Greece: Refugees Attacked and Pushed Back in the Aegean." www.dw.com/en/greece-refugees-attacked-and-pushed-back-in-the-aegean/a-53977151 (accessed July 24, 2020).

Freeman, Elizabeth. 2010. *Time Binds: Queer Temporalities, Queer Histories*. Durham, NC: Duke University Press.

Gilmore, Ruth Wilson. 2007. *Golden Gulag: Prisons, Surplus, Crisis, and Opposition in Globalizing California*. Berkeley, CA: University of California Press.

Griffin, Gabriele, and Rosi Braidotti. 2002. "Whiteness and European Situatedness." In *Thinking Differently: A Reader in European Women's Studies*, edited by Gabriele Griffin and Rosi Braidotti. Chicago: University of Chicago Press.

Gržinić, Marina, Tjaša Kancler, and Piro Rexhepi. 2020. "Decolonial Encounters and the Geopolitics of Racial Capitalism." *Feminist Critique* 3: 13–38. https://feminist.kry-tyka.com/en/articles/decolonial-encounters-and-geopolitics-racial-capitalism (accessed July 24, 2020).

Gutiérrez Rodríguez, Encarnación. 2018. "The Coloniality of Migration and the 'Refugee Crisis': On the Asylum-Migration Nexus, the Transatlantic White European Settler Colonialism-Migration and Racial Capitalism." *Refuge: Canada's Journal on Refugees/Refuge: revue canadienne sur les réfugiés* 34, no. 1. https://doi.org/10.7202/1050851ar.

Hemmings, Clare. 2020. "Revisiting Virality (After Eve Sedgwick)." *The Feminist Review Blog*. https://femrev.wordpress.com/2020/05/26/revisiting-virality-after-eve-sedgwick (accessed July 24, 2020).

Koobak, Redi. 2013. *Whirling Stories: Postsocialist Feminist Imaginaries and the Visual Arts*. Linköping: Linköping University Press.

Mills, Charles W. 2007. "White Ignorance." *Race and Epistemologies of Ignorance* 247: 26–31.

Mills, Charles W. 2015. "Race and Global Justice." *Domination and Global Political Justice: Conceptual, Historical and Institutional Perspectives*: 181–205.

Morse, Felicity. 2013. "Half Our Women 'Look Like Kate Middleton' Romanian Newspaper Says in 'Anti-Britain' Ads." *The Huffington Post*. www.huffpost.com (accessed March 5, 2020).

Nowicka, Magdalena. 2018. "'I Don't Mean to Sound Racist but . . .' Transforming Racism in Transnational Europe." *Ethnic and Racial Studies* 41, no. 5: 824–841. https://doi.org/10.1080/01419870.2017.1302093.

Oprea, Alexandra. 2012. "Romani Feminism in Reactionary Times." *Signs: Journal of Women in Culture and Society* 38, no. 1: 11–21. https://doi.org/10.1086/665945.

Popa, Bogdan. 2018. "Trans* and Legacies of Socialism: Reading Queer Postsocialism in 'Tangerine'." *The Undecidable Unconscious: A Journal of Deconstruction and Psychoanalysis* 5: 27–53. doi:10.1353/ujd.2018.0002.

Rexhepi, Piro. 2018a. "The Politics of Postcolonial Erasure in Sarajevo." *Interventions* 20, no. 6: 930–945. https://doi.org/10.1080/1369801X.2018.1487320.

Rexhepi, Piro. 2018b. "Arab Others at European Borders: Racializing Religion and Refugees Along the Balkan Route." *Ethnic and Racial Studies* 41, no. 12: 2215–2234. https://doi.org/10.1080/01419870.2017.1415455.

Rzepnikowska, Alina. 2019. "Racism and Xenophobia Experienced by Polish Migrants in the UK Before and After Brexit Vote." *Journal of Ethnic and Migration Studies* 45, no. 1: 61–77. https://doi.org/10.1080/1369183X.2018.1451308.

Scott, David. 2004. *Conscripts of Modernity: The Tragedy of Colonial Enlightenment*. Durham, NC: Duke University Press.

Shohat, Ella. 1992. "Notes on the 'Post-Colonial'." *Social Text* nos. 31-32: 99–113. doi:10.2307/466220.

Stoler, Ann Laura. 2016. *Duress: Imperial Durabilities in Our Times*. Durham, NC: Duke University Press.

Suchland, Jennifer. 2011. "Is Postsocialism Transnational?" *Signs* 36, no. 4: 837–862. doi:10.1086/658899.

Tinsley, Omise'eke. 2008. "BLACK ATLANTIC, QUEER ATLANTIC: Queer Imaginings of the Middle Passage." *GLQ: A Journal of Lesbian and Gay Studies* 14, nos. 2–3: 191–215. doi:10.1215/10642684-2007-030.

Tlostanova, Madina. 2003. "A Janus-Faced Empire." In *Notes on the Russian Empire in Modernity, Written from the Border*. Moscow: Block.

Tlostanova, Madina. 2012. "Postsocialist ≠ Postcolonial? On Post-Soviet Imaginary and Global Coloniality." *Journal of Postcolonial Writing* 48, no. 2: 130–142. https://doi.org/10.1080/17449855.2012.658244.

Tondo, Lorenzo, and Daniel Boffey. 2020. "EU 'covered up' Croatia's Failure to Protect Migrants from Border Brutality." *The Guardian.* www.theguardian.com/global-development/2020/jun/15/eu-covered-up-croatias-failure-to-protect-migrants-from-border-brutality (accessed July 24, 2020).

Tudor, Alyosxa. 2017a. "Queering Migration Discourse: Differentiating Racism and Migratism in Postcolonial Europe." *lambda nordica* 22, nos. 2–3: 21–40.

Tudor, Alyosxa. 2017b. "Dimensions of Transnationalism." *Feminist Review* 117, no. 1: 20–40. https://doi.org/10.1057/s41305-017-0092-5.

Tudor, Alyosxa. 2018. "Cross-Fadings of Racialisation and Migratisation: The Postcolonial Turn in Western European Gender and Migration Studies." *Gender, Place and Culture* 25, no. 7: 1057–1072. https://doi.org/10.1080/0966369X.2018.1441141.

Tudor, Alyosxa. 2019. "Im/Possibilities of Refusing and Choosing Gender." *Feminist Theory* 20, no. 4: 361–380. https://doi.org/10.1177/1464700119870640.

Tudor, Alyosxa. 2021. "Decolonising Trans/Gender Studies: Teaching Race, Sexuality and Migration in Times of the Rise of the Global Right." *TSQ: Transgender Studies Quarterly* 8, no. 2.

Chapter 15

"We need to learn about each other and unlearn patterns of racism"

A conversation with Angéla Kóczé

Angéla Kóczé and Petra Bakos

From the point of view of state legislation, East Central European Roma communities were practically invisible during state socialism. Anti-Gypsyism permeated all strata of societies to become a rampant phenomenon after 1989. Anti-Roma racism has been built on old colonial notions – including the "biological" interpretation of race – although its roots run deeper than the Second World War or even the colonial times. Therefore, understanding the historical trajectory, current situation, and future possibilities of Eastern European Roma communities necessitates a dialogue between postcolonial and postsocialist lived experiences and scholarly toolkits. As a scholar, writer, teacher, and cultural and community organiser, Angéla Kóczé has been invested for decades in developing a critical race feminist agenda sensitive to the specific characteristics and needs of East Central European Roma communities. Zooming in and out between personal motivations and wider observations about academic and social patterns, this conversation aims to contribute to feminist scholarship on race and Roma in Eastern Europe.

Petra Bakos: Anti-Roma racism is one of the unifying and persistent characteristics of various East Central European societies that outlasted two world wars and several changes of borders and regimes. Despite Eastern European anti-Gypsyism's historical, geographical, and cultural expansiveness, racism is still only sporadically discussed in East Central Europe.

Angéla Kóczé: There is a certain history in Europe in general of avoiding race as an analytical category. When I am talking about race, I am talking about inferiorisation in the political and social sense, I am not referring to the "biological" concept of race, although the "biological" interpretation also gets mobilised when it comes to the Roma. And I am deliberately using the term inferiorisation as something that happens to groups of people under systematic structural racism. However, in Hungary and in East Central Europe in general we have a particular excuse for not dealing with race, and the argument goes like this: we did not have any colonies therefore we did not have to and do not have to deal with race. Accordingly we talk about race and racialisation exclusively in historical terms (i.e. in connection with colonialism) and we conveniently forget that there were and are also internal forms of colonialisation and inferiorisation within Eastern Europe.

PB: Yes, it is the internal forms of racism, as you call it, that I referred to in my question. As you said, racism often gets swept under the rug by fake excuses that are based on East Central European countries' alleged non-involvement in the colonial enterprise. On the one hand, many Eastern European nations were involved in colonisation through business and military ventures, and basically all Eastern European countries benefitted indirectly from colonisation through the flow of goods and wealth that reached this side of Europe. On the other hand, East Central European states and Hungary in particular are notorious for their avoidance of coming to terms with their involvement in the extermination of their own racialised citizens during Second World War (see e.g. Pető 2019). This wilful ignorance and the accompanying hiatus in social remembrance are further exacerbated by Eastern European academia's unwillingness to engage with race.

AK: That's right. Importantly though there are also scholars who wrote about the historical roots of this unwillingness, for instance, Mathias Möschel (2014) who holds that European academia has refused to use the term "race" and "racialisation" because of the Holocaust – as if not using the concept would somehow make the whole phenomenon disappear. Yes, we are not talking about it, or if we do talk about it we do not name it, or if we name it, we name it in a different way; for instance, in Europe for a while the preferred word has become "ethnicity". The term ethnicity has been applied mostly in a cultural sense, but in particular in the Roma case the cultural focus intersects with racialisation, since, as Ethel C. Brooks (2012) succinctly argues, Roma culture is generally perceived as submissive to the so-called European higher cultures. I should add that European academia as well as the mainstream media tend to only react to discrimination and violence committed by outright racists and rather conveniently overlook that racism is not simply a problem of a bunch of morally wayward extreme right people, as is often depicted, but is a structural phenomenon deeply embedded in our social texture. If we are not conceptualising race and racialisation, we are denying the fact that there is structural discrimination and violence.

PB: I also consider that it is urgent to talk about race in East Central Europe and in Hungary in particular, and not only when discussing issues of the Roma but also when it comes to white communities. In Eastern Europe, whiteness entails invisibility, which translates into privileges such as better chances in the labour market or more credibility in front of state authorities, to name but a few. This holds true in certain Western contexts as well since white Eastern Europeans are generally more welcomed as migrant workers in some Western countries. At the same time, the anti-Eastern European immigrant attitude is tangibly present in the social media discourse surrounding Brexit, for instance, which had racist undertones and made many Eastern Europeans face, for the first time, the fact that there is a perceived racial hierarchy among whites too. East Central European populist governments quickly and effectively instrumentalised this internal white hierarchy for further fuelling of anti-EU sentiments in their countries. This, I fear, has made the public discourse about racial relations in East Europe, including the involvement of East Central European governments in white supremacist projects, once again incapacitated. Which brings us back to your earlier side comment, which in my opinion deserves more attention. You said that racism is not located where most Europeans think it is located (i.e. in the far-right thinking) but permeates all of our power structures.

AK: Absolutely. When I was talking about racism and the racial logic, I said that we, especially in East Central Europe, are so ready to claim that we have nothing to do with racism as it relates to the European colonial past; at the same time we readily use the term racism when talking about people affiliated with far-right ideologies. So, we manage to talk about racism without talking about race! We talk about race as if it were a kind of an attitude, as if it were a moral failure or a psychological issue, when it is, in fact, a social, political, and economic problem manifested in our legislation, in policies, and various social mechanisms. This is what gets denied when we do not focus on the structural embeddedness of race. Let us just take the educational system as an example. Why is that that there are hardly any Roma students in the Hungarian higher education? Only one percent of Hungarian Roma have acquired a degree! There are so many structural obstacles that Roma people cannot overcome individually as they belong to an under-privileged and stigmatised family. Therefore there is a great chance to be disempowered and marginalised. This is why I firmly believe in affirmative action, because otherwise people who arrive in the system with structural disadvantages cannot possibly make it. If we think about the Roma as a group that has been deprived and oppressed for centuries, it is evident that they will not be able to pull themselves up by their bootstraps. Therefore, when thinking about race, we cannot avoid the analysis of power, how power shapes the conditions and the relations among people.

PB: And it has been shaping these for centuries. Is there a historical overview of how through the history of Roma in Europe the concept of race was constructed and manipulated in this region?

AK: There is an emerging scholarship. For instance, Geraldine Heng's recent book (2018) about the Middle Ages has a chapter on the Roma, which proves that, contrary to public belief, anti-Roma racism started much earlier than the Second World War or even the colonial times. But as I see it, there is a lot of resistance in academia against such diachronic overviews. Instead, many researchers choose to focus on the Roma culture, on how fantastic it is, and how amazingly it remained isolated from other social structures; that is, they posit the Roma as Europe's internal, oriental, exotic other. During the past decades, lots of people have built their scholarship in Romani studies on emphasising the distinctive features of Roma, with which they further contributed to the racialisation of the Roma population. Presently, there is a clash within Romani studies: the old school still focuses on the Romani language and culture as distinct from other European languages and cultures, while progressive scholarship aims to introduce a new paradigm, which has integrated critical race studies, postcolonial studies, and feminist critique to challenge the epistemologies of othering (see e.g. Kóczé 2018). Furthermore, in the social sciences there is a trend to work intersectionally, and in these works the Roma often play the role of the token racialised group. I think that is a wrong move again, as it fails to acknowledge that everyone, not only the minorities, are intersectionally positioned. In other words, instead of further focusing on the specificities of the Roma, I believe that the way forward would be for each discipline to critically reconsider what they produced on Roma – if they produced anything at all – and through which lens. The list includes sociology, anthropology, political science, economy, gender studies and, importantly, education studies.

PB: It is telling that in East Central European elementary and secondary school textbooks there is hardly any mention of the Roma, or of the Jewish population for that matter, or if there is, it is in relation to the Holocaust; the discourse within which these minorities are presented is that of lack or loss, while their cultural and other achievements are regularly omitted (see e.g. Spielhaus et al. 2020). This means that the majority of East Central European youth leave school without knowing anything about groups of people that they coexist with, and this ignorance might shape their perspective for a lifetime.

AK: That is why I think it is important to mainstream Roma issues. Then we can think about racialisation within academia and interrogate the racialising features of the academic and educational environment.

PB: Is there a toolkit available that can address race in the specific context of post-socialist East Central European societies? Critical race studies were developed in the US: are they, or rather in what way are they applicable in Eastern Europe?

AK: It is certainly not straightforwardly applicable, but it provides a theoretical basis and framework. There is a perceivable resistance against the import of concepts and theoretical framework of critical race studies as they are considered a "US thing". In my view, this critique is another way to shoo away issues surrounding the conceptualisation of race. For instance, feminism is also a Western concept. But it is seldom asked how feminism could be applicable in Eastern Europe where the context is completely different. The way I see it, feminism provided a very important language and framework that we can use after having carefully contextualised it to see how it is manifested in specific geopolitical locations and socio-political situations. Critical race studies provided a theoretical lens that is similarly applicable.

PB: And what are the stakes for an Eastern European Roma feminist scholar who attempts to navigate the generally Roma-blind US academia and the Hungarian and Eastern European academic and social environment in parallel? Some Roma scholars with whom I talked mentioned the stark contrast between being invisible as Roma in the US, as they were taken as Latino/as or sometimes as Pakistani or Indian, and being in many ways overly visible in the Hungarian/ Eastern European environment, especially as educated Roma.

AK: My experience in North Carolina, where I arrived as a Fulbright Scholar in 2013, is comparable to the experience of W.E.B. Du Bois who arrived in Berlin in the late 1890s. The US academic environment was a revelation for me much like the German academia was for Du Bois. Late 19th century Germany was a racist society, but its targets were not Blacks. Therefore, Du Bois was perceived as a bourgeois Harvard-educated guy. No wonder for Du Bois, as he put it, Berlin was a revelation and the place of his intellectual coming of age (Lewering-Lewis 1993). Similarly, people were certainly put off by my accent in North Carolina, but as I was a Fulbright Fellow from Europe I was simply treated as another European scholar with a strange accent. I was also read as a Latina, for instance, in the YMCA, but altogether I can say that in the US, I was able to step out of my Roma "box". Here in Budapest people quickly "identify" and categorise me, and basically no one cares that I have a PhD, I remain "the" Romani woman at CEU. This condition is certainly limiting, and I have invested many years in subverting my token Roma position in academia. If you are a woman of colour at the university sometimes even your colleagues consider you incompetent because they believe you got your position through some affirmative action. On top of that, they regularly make you feel that you should be grateful to them because they "tolerate" you. This is patronising and certainly racist. So, there you are, you come from a racially stigmatised underprivileged family with low level of education. First you need to fight to get into a university, then to get a PhD, then to publish, then to exist in the academic context where 80% of your colleagues come from white upper middle-class families. In other words, there is a huge gap that you feel you will never ever fill and therefore there is the pressure to prove yourself a hundred times. It is truly exhausting and there are no institutional mechanisms to help you deal with this burden. In fact, the institutional setting adds to your burden because, as a token Roma, you are expected to deal with all Roma-related issues, you are the one on call. Therefore you carry much more responsibility. At the same time, you are the one who is immediately judged because of implicit biases. These mechanisms are very much internal to the system, and these negative stereotypes and prejudices are intrinsically a part of people's thinking in the culture that is racist by default. I should also add that Roma men in academia are more supported than Roma women, because the patriarchal structure of our society is reproduced within academia and among the Roma as well. Unfortunately, there is not much discussion about race or racialisation within Eastern European feminist academic or activist circles either. Nevertheless, I firmly believe in building bridges, and I am trying to step out and find connections and build coalitions. As I have become older, I am much more aware of the importance of investing in alliance building rather than in clashes.

PB: Who would you see as potential allies?

AK: Despite my critique I also see many feminists who are really open to collaboration, and I certainly see other racialised groups and mainly women of other racialised or minority groups as potential allies. Last spring, I participated in a panel held at Harvard together with Patricia Hill Collins, activist women from the Dalit community, and Latina scholars. This brings us back to your earlier question, whether the conceptual language of US critical race studies is applicable or useful.

At that panel, the fact that we were all using the same theoretical language created an epistemic link among us, which came with a crucial sense of solidarity that was denied for people of colour for so long. These kinds of theoretical interrelations and exchanges should be encouraged, supported, and sustained because in the past we did not have dialogues with members of other racialised groups. Instead each of us were confined to their own academic boxes. We have allies among white people too; there are many open minded, self-critical, and reflexive people who have the humbleness that it takes to approach another group, particularly a group that has been racialised and oppressed for centuries. Without humbleness, one cannot build partnerships. We need to learn about each other and at the same time, unlearn patterns of racism. Roma issues were discussed and theorised by white people for too long without acknowledging our lived experience.

PB: You have talked about being exposed to stigmatisation and having to prove yourself as a scholar. How did these experiences influence your management of CEU's Roma Graduate Preparation Program (RGPP)?[1] I refer to the very caring and supportive environment that has been created in the RGPP under your guidance. For instance, there are monthly psychological counselling sessions offered to the students; you also invited me to teach embodied writing in order to build academic resilience and enhance creativity. I see your efforts as pioneering attempts at the institutionalisation of the feminist ethic of care as well as an investment into decolonising teaching practices, both of which are unique in the East Central European academic environment.

AK: This would be exactly the purpose. I think that working as a scholar entails working with the psyche too. I myself studied psychodrama in parallel with my PhD studies to become an assistant facilitator, and I plan to become a fully accredited psychodrama trainer in the future. I am trying to apply a holistic approach, at the RGPP and at the Romaversitas[2] as well. Creating a sound and supportive environment is especially important in our program as our students come from various Eastern European countries from Ukraine to Macedonia with very different experiences. Their entering the US academic context is challenging enough, plus they have to deal with the effects of dislocation from their communities. So, it is definitely the feminist ethics of care and self-care that is at work here – self-care too because one has to be well to be able to help, one has to find her own path as a scholar, as an educator, as a woman, and as a Roma.

Notes

1   The Roma Graduate Preparation Program (RGPP) is an intensive ten-month program at the Central European University in Budapest-Vienna that prepares outstanding Roma graduates with an interest in social sciences and humanities to compete for places on Master's-level courses at internationally recognised universities. The program prepares students for further studies in their chosen field through intensive academic tutoring and helps to raise their level of English to a level necessary for post-graduate study. Students are also engaged in critical debates regarding the political, economic, and social condition and status of Roma through seminars that combine the study of history and

identity with recent developments in the politics of governing Roma communities in the region.

2   The Romaversitas Foundation offers the first comprehensive support and training program for talented Roma youngsters in Hungary. Established in 1996, Romaversitas has supported over 300 Roma students throughout their academic studies in the past 20 years, so that they can successfully graduate and become highly skilled professionals in their chosen field.

References

Brooks, Ethel C. 2012. "The Possibilities of Romani Feminism." *Signs* 38, no. 1: 1–11. doi:10.1086/665947.

Heng, Geraldine. 2018. *The Invention of Race in the European Middle Ages*. Cambridge: Cambridge University Press. doi:10.1017/9781108381710.

Kóczé, Angéla. 2018. "Transgressing Borders: Challenging Racist and Sexist Epistemology." In *Roma Activism: Reimagining Power and Knowledge*, edited by Sam Beck and Ana Ivasiuc, 111–129. Oxford: Berghahn Books.

Lewering-Lewis, David. 1993. *W.E.B. Du Bois: Biography of a Race, 1868–1919*. New York: Henry Holt and Company.

Möschel, Mathias. 2014. *Law, Lawyers and Race: Critical Race Theory from the United States to Europe*. London: Routledge.

Pető, Andrea. 2019. "Non-Remembering the Holocaust in Hungary and Poland." In *Polin Studies in Polish Jewry, Vol. 31: Poland and Hungary, Jewish Realities Compared*, edited by Francois Guesnet, Howard Lupovitch, and Antony Polonsky, 471–480. Liverpool: The Littman Library of Jewish Civilization in association with Liverpool University Press. doi:10.2307/j.ctv1198sv9.

Spielhaus, Riem, Simona Szakács-Behling, Aurora Ailincai, Victoria Hopson, and Marko Pecak. 2020. "The Representation of Roma in European Curricula and Textbooks – Analytical Report." The Roma Education Fund. www.coe.int/en/web/roma-and-travellers/-/publication-of-the-analytical-report-on-the-representation-of-roma-in-european-curricula-and-textbooks.

Chapter 16

Cripping postsocialist chronicity

A conversation with Kateřina Kolářová

Kateřina Kolářová and Redi Koobak

Redi Koobak: As a feminist, queer and crip studies scholar, whose work is located at the intersections of sexuality and gender, critical disability and race/ethnic studies, you have demonstrated a continuous investment in taking up the call for new conceptualisations of the processes of racialisation, ableism, and functioning of the heteronormative gender order in the context of social shifts that mark postsocialism expressed in this call. How do you understand postsocialism in your work?

Kateřina Kolářová: My take on postsocialism is indebted to many feminist and queer scholars who have reframed the persistent understanding of postsocialism as a term used to reference a specific region (as in "area studies") and/or the specific temporal and developmental condition of that region. Needless to say, in such a framing, postsocialism is understood as a term with limited scope and reach; as a term of temporary relevance, that is until the "post" is overcome. My work aligns itself with the archive of critical work that argues that "postsocialism ought to be considered as a condition affecting the entire world" (Shih 2012, 28), and thus a condition entering a world deeply affected by legacies of imperialism and coloniality. In this sense, we can understand postsocialism as an analytical lens.

I like to remind myself that my book *Rehabilitative Postsocialism* has originated from a point of naïveté and an unreflected positionality of a postsocialist subject (Kolářová forthcoming). Getting acquainted with the "Western" disability theory, I was curious about how and why some disability epistemologies get picked up in the Czech postsocialist context, while others do not. For instance, what does it mean that critiques of (more or less merely) physical barriers or theory emphasising positive and "enabling" understandings of disability identity have become intelligible and have been embraced by disability activism and NGOs where work that is more deeply invested in structural critique of able-bodiedness or the racialised nature of ableism – or critiques of liberal disability identity politics – remain perceived as unintelligible or at worst as fancy over-theoretical avant-garde experiments with no real import on the everyday lives of people with disabilities.

At the same time, once I began researching the materials from post-1989, I was struck by how persistently the visions of "transition(ing)" out of the socialist past were coupled with, even overdetermined by, visions of moral rehabilitation and recovery. Being in the postsocialist transition effectively meant being in a period of painful yet necessary rehabilitation that should lead to a cure, understood as capitalism with free market and (neo)liberal democracy. The normative framing of postsocialism that persists till this day is simply an "ideology of cure" (Clare 2017).

Yet, even though the field of (feminist) postsocialist studies has become more diverse and intersectional, analyses of disability or the critical perspectives for which Alison Kafer coined the name "feminist queer crip" (2013) are still largely missing. Coming from feminist queer disability studies myself, I wanted my book to imagine what this perspective would look like when brought into dialogue with the concept of postsocialism. I wanted the views and experiences of disabled/crip people, specifically of crip people of colour, and people considered as dysfunctional, abnormal, and generally not fit enough to cope with life independently, to guide my analysis. Not only because, similarly to postcolonial countries, the postsocialist countries have been seen as crip – as dysfunctional, abnormal, and not fit enough to cope without transnational supervision, help, and surveillance – but primarily because the economic, structural, and ideological changes brought about by postsocialism in Eastern Europe often fall on the lives of people with disabilities with brutal force: people with disabilities, and in particular disabled people of colour are chronically neglected, and their voices and their experiences are never foregrounded.

In short, my work intervenes in several paradoxes defining the predominant understanding of postsocialism. Firstly, despite its intense global impacts, conventionally, postsocialism is an extremely "localised" and "timed" concept. Forgetting about the transnational dimensions of postsocialism contributes to the contemporary revival of the Cold War East/West binary logic. It also feeds the xenophobic and nationalist backlash "culture wars" that we see across Eastern Europe that then, in circular logic, cement the perception of postsocialist Europe as failing in the civilising liberal programme.

Another paradoxical dynamic of postsocialism relates to the fact that the postsocialist transformation (and this is very prominent in the Czech Republic) was conceived of as a moral project. The transformation proposed a nation-wide rehabilitative and healing politics of belonging, constructed through the rehabilitative labour of conditionally included minority subjects. These subjects became locations through which the nation marked its past "ills" and invested in its future promise, all while reinforcing the exclusionary nature of the nation's minoritizing impulse. The book thus maps out the very tangible and very cruel material effects of the moral scripts of postsocialist citizenship across disability, race, class, and sexuality.

Drawing out these paradoxes also accentuates synergies between the postcolonial and postsocialist theories that focus on structural neglect. The dominant ideological interpretations of postsocialism accentuate truncated temporality for which feminist crip of colour scholar Eunjung Kim offers a brilliant term "folded time". She proposes this concept in her study of postcolonial Korea to refer to a particular temporal framework in which only "nondisabled past and [the] cured future become meaningful" (Kim 2018, 1). In such a framework, temporality and morality are superimposed over each other. I follow similar temporal folding in the postsocialist context of the Czech Republic and show how it dominates social imagination to make the logic of sacrifice acceptable, even necessary for the nation to be "cured". The required sacrifice then – as if by nature – legitimises losses of lives that have been always already seen as less valued.

RK: Could you elaborate more specifically on how crip theory informs your work on postsocialism and how might it resonate with postcolonial theory?

KK: Articulated by the disabled community reclaiming their lives that were labelled as twisted, crippled, freak, and generally not worth living, crip theory is a gesture of defiance to normalcy and regimes of compulsory abledness. As such, it provides a rich analytical archive to put pressure on all the metaphors of "catching up", lagging behind, "return", or deviance/sickness of the socialist past, and on the normative expectation that the postsocialist states in Europe "rehabilitate" (themselves) out of postsocialism. To me, crip theory provides a "disorientation device" (Ahmed 2006, 171–172) that allows to unsettle such framings and allows for opening possibilities to imagine the present otherwise. To imagine "crip horizons" – where *crip* is understood as a positionality, an orientation formed through intersections of disability, race, gender/sexuality, and as materialised through (proximity) to experiences of vulnerability, precarity, and abandonment.

One of the beneficial moments of "disorientation" that crip theory prompts is rethinking temporality and the temporal horizons of conditions determined by the ambivalent "post" suffixes (i.e. postsocialism, postcoloniality). In particular, rethinking chronicity via crip theory is crucial for conceptualising the impacts of compulsory development (in the postsocialist context often termed as "transition" or "transformation") to which both postcolonial and postsocialist countries have been subjected. In both contexts, as I have argued elsewhere, "[t]he development fantasy continues to colonise the lives of disabled and racialised communities" (Kolářová and Wiedlack 2016, 125).

Undoubtedly, chronicity has recently obtained a lot of interest, particularly in the context of critiques of the present global neoliberal economy. As a temporal concept that acknowledges stasis, absence of change, and the long duration of the present, chronicity offers conceptual language for thinking about aspirations, promises of social mobility, and hopes for the future as well as ways to think about exploitation, tiredness, exhaustion, and other modes of debility that underwrite the conditions and structures of present lives. Yet again, even the new and exciting scholarship on chronicity has not – similarly to theorisations of neoliberalism and late capitalism – engaged with postsocialism. This is a great hindrance to such debates for many reasons. Obviously, the fall of the socialist states and thus the fall of the socialist "Bloc" as a power centre reinvigorated the neoliberal doctrine, even – as many argued – allowed for its global success. The postsocialist Eastern Europe has thus become a reservoir of the cheap and expendable labour force caught up in the "durational now" and the exhaustingly chronic moment of "living on, not getting better" (Shildrick 2015). And finally, ascriptions of chronic incapacity to change (i.e. become same as the West/North) are one of the most important stigmatising and pathologising narratives about the postsocialist Eastern Europe.

Thus, in *Rehabilitative Postsocialism*, I propose to "crip postsocialist chronicity" (i.e. to think chronicity together and through disability and cripness) and make note of forms of protracted and invisible violence, archive the hurt, and stand witness to the fact that, under the curative times of postsocialism, some bodies and lives cannot be embraced by the rehabilitative, affirmative, and positive promises of future. Thinking about these forms of violence, you cannot but arrive at intersectional analysis, and especially analysis foregrounding the ways in which race and disability interconnect and depend upon each other. For instance, pointing towards the Roma (and more recently also towards the religiously othered refugees) as the embodiment of "mal-" or even "inadaptability" to new conditions of life (i.e. the utter and chronic inability to change) has come to constitute a very powerful category of postsocialist citizenship and its "rehabilitative" morality. In reality, it is their lives that are dominated by the various forms of "slow violence" of postsocialism most drastically. Furthermore, the effects of structural racism and colonial exhaustion are truly chronic – they sediment across generations and across the collective bodies of the racialised communities. The disabling effects of such violence materialise in very varied ways, many of which, again, defy the notion of disability that the "charitable" society is willing to tolerate and deem as deserving of social provision and attention.

"Cripping postsocialist chronicity" thus has to mean to push against and reject the negative pathology ascribed to chronicity that is rooted in the curative logic of postsocialism. I am therefore proposing to reimagine chronicity as a part of our critical vocabulary for analysis of postsocialism. Embracing the chronic, the apparent moments of stagnation and non-progress, allows us to move away from the fantastic frames that foreground and emphasise development, quick transitions, and instead ground our analysis and understanding of postsocialism in frames that acknowledge the complexity and ambiguities of that "which lingers", is experienced as "being stuck" in protracted and not changing moment, or feels "inveterate". Leaning into and embracing chronicity unsettles the normative time of progress, an intervention crucial – as I have noted above – for thinking about how disability, race, sexuality, and gender intersect in the global postsocialist and postcolonial contexts.

Therefore, "cripping postsocialist chronicity" is, finally, also an epistemological intervention as it challenges the category of disability itself and puts pressure on "what" we recognise as disability, or "who" is recognised and embraced by the idea of "person with disability"/ "disabled person". And this is again where inspiration from postcolonial theories is crucial. Many theorists have pointed out that the category of disability articulated in the Western/Northern contexts does not translate well outside of the West/global North, precisely because it cannot encompass the disabling effects of coloniality and the various ways in which disability materialises in the postcolonial and also – as I argue – postsocialist realities. To talk about the ways in which colonial economies build on the extraction of vitality and produce "disabled" bodies that are not recognisable through the identity lens of disability in postcolonial settings, Julie Livingstone coined the term "debility" (2005) that is now explored as an addition to critical repertoire of disability theory.

Similarly, I strive to expand the understanding of cripness and disability through thinking about how the effects of postsocialist "transformation", and of the neoliberal restructuring of postsocialist "transition" are written onto bodies that are not included in the disability identity politics – sex workers, people with HIV, people using substances, Roma living in ghetto-like excluded spaces. . .

RK: At the *Postcolonial and Postsocialist Dialogues* conference, you gave a talk on the "strange affinities" (Hong and Ferguson 2011) between the postcolonial, which is often connected to discussions of race, and the postsocialist which is usually not, in order to imagine how these interstices might play out in thinking about race and forms of racialisation in the context of Eastern Europe. Where do you see tensions between the two frameworks, and where might there be useful convergences?

KK: You are absolutely right to note that the debates in postsocialist scholarship as well as scholarship on postsocialism have not concerned themselves with race to any degree comparable with postcolonial and decolonial studies. In some sense, it is the circular effect of the narrow and limited ways of understanding postsocialism as only pertinent to regions of East, Central, South-East Europe, where (Eastern) Europe nearly automatically means "white". The conceptualisations of Europe generally omit race and modes of racialisation from their analytical and critical register. Furthermore, the post-WWII attempts to make the states ethnically homogenous and nationally defined (efforts that were intensified by the socialist states) deliver on their legacy: diversity – and especially ethnic diversity – is seen as a foreign notion (mostly as an import from the West) that inevitably constitutes a threat to the local national cultures. The fact that ethnic and religious diversity in Western Europe is viewed as a source of social antagonism and a cause of violent clashes cannot be seen only as a manifestation of the recent rise of xenophobic nationalism across the Eastern Europe. As I show in my book, already in the early 1990s, multiculturalism was viewed with distrust and the urban racial segregation (with simplification called ghettos) was seen as a logical and natural result of impossible connection of several ethnic/religious/social groups even by some of the then proponents of liberal civil society.

Bringing postcolonialism and postsocialism together to re-think race and processes of racialisation in the context of postsocialist Europe is thus indeed very necessary. But it might raise some difficult and potentially conflicted questions. For instance, how does race and racialised differentiations manifest and matter "here"? Can we work with the concepts developed in the fields of critical race, ethnic, and indigenous studies to fit the ways in which race and ethnicity matter in the very different Eastern European/postsocialist environments?

To open the discussion about how race and ethnicity materialise in the postsocialist context, we first need to look at how the notion of the Eastern Europe reverberates with racialised concepts in myriad ways. As you yourself pointed out in our previous conversations, the constructions of Eastern Europe have a long and complicated racialised history. The "East" is invoked as and turned into a marker of temporal, cultural, and political distinctions that grow out of a long legacy of associating the East and Eastern Europe with backwardness and primitivity. The constructions of the *postsocialist* Eastern Europe only intensified such orientalist fantasies. The exoticisation and oversexualisation of the *Eastern* women and men is one specific way in which these racialised fantasies manifest. For instance, the development of the gay sex and porn industry in the post-1989 Prague catered predominantly to foreigners. These forms of exploitation (of mostly underage and often times substance-using men) relied on racialised constructions of Eastern Europe. Interestingly, the intense moral panic with which the public responded to the growth of the male-porn and sex industry not only failed to see these forms of transaction as linked to larger forms of labour extraction (Kolářová 2019), but it also utilised the pathologising portrayals of the foreign "homosexuals" to whitewash and cover over other racialised conflicts – namely the violent attacks against the Roma people and Roma communities that spiked across the 1990s.

To draw a full circle here, the anti-Roma violence is part and parcel of the constructions of Eastern Europe and its socialist "deviance" from the natural path of history and modern development. As I pointed out above, the exaggerated stress on overcoming, rehabilitating, functioning and proving one's capacity to adjust to the new path of history produced its others – the Roma who were then ostracised and punished for their presumed "inadaptability" and incompatibility with the national project of catching up.

But then of course, and this point might be too obvious, the distinctions grounded in discourses of race and ethnicity are not exclusive to the West-East axis. They are called upon to articulate complex hierarchies of economic, social, national status within the "East". Precisely because postsocialist spaces are understood as simply forever and "permanently transitional" (Kulpa and Mizielińska 2011, 3), the discourses of transition carry a strong ideological and moral interpellation, provoke and uphold hierarchies of imaginable achievements in development and maturing into a "western type" (Dahrendorf 1991) of liberal democracy and liberal economy.

Against this background of scales of postsocialist success/failure, whiteness has become scaled into newly ethnicised categories. For instance, there might not be a better example of how the category of the East is associated with othered difference than the insistence with which Czechs point out that Czech Republic does not belong to the East/ern but Central Europe, and that Prague is in fact "the heart of Europe". This is not a geographical argument. It is an argument to frame the Czech history as different from the East and as either a part of the story of the West, or alternatively as a bridge between the East and the West.

As to the ethnicisation of whiteness and racialising Eastern Europeans within Eastern Europe, I remember very vividly how in the early 1990s our small town in South Bohemia was worried about the male workers coming from Poland to work at the construction of the local nuclear power plant. I was not allowed outside in late evenings because these workers were seen as uncivilised sexual predators. Again, discourses of sexuality were instrumentalised as a vector of racialisation of these workers. Othered through discourses of sexual danger and as "unskilled" labourers, the workers embodied "East" and its "lower" developmental achievement. Later, the Ukrainians replaced the Poles in this mythology of Czech success and whiteness. Even Slovaks living in the Czech Republic are customarily subjected to discourses of exoticisation and othering. Despite the closeness and mutual understandability of both languages (before their split in 1993, Czech and Slovak republics formed a bilingual federation), Slovaks are customarily forced to speak Czech if they want to "fit in".

These are only some of the complex ways in which racialisation works in the postsocialist Czech Republic and that might not be captured in the concept of race as a white/black binary. Anca Parvulescu (2015) has adapted Claire Jean Kim's concept of "triangulation of race" to describe the mechanics of layered racialisations and the ways in which Eastern European subjects figure in relation to other racialised/postcolonial subjects in the European centres/metropoles. When moved outside of the metropolis and outside of the "centre"/West into the Eastern European context – say Prague or Warsaw – the model gets even more complicated. Then, even the presumably "white" centre – Prague or Warsaw – is always already only temporarily "white" and only provisionally sheltered from the question of "where are you from". The privilege of whiteness scales down as soon as the previously "white" subjects want to cross borders; in the moment, they become "Eastern European" and their whiteness is conditioned by how strong their passport is (Parvulescu 2014), how well they speak the language of one of the "Western" centres (though admittedly "West" too has its own scales and hierarchisations, compare London to Milan, or Berlin to Lisbon, for instance), how well they adapt and perform their closeness to the citizenship of "Western type".

RK: Turning to feminism, while the discursive erasure of the so-called "second world" is rigorously examined by scholarship that is specifically invested in theorising postsocialism as a global condition, it is left unexamined by much of the foundational scholarship in the field of transnational feminist studies. Most transnational feminist analyses do not account for the historical and cultural legacies of state socialism. In your view, how might taking postsocialism seriously, as a global condition, unsettle existing transnational feminist epistemologies?

KK: If transnational feminism is to do justice to its aim to disturb global hierarchies and nationalist paradigms, and to challenge the uneven ways of knowledge (re)production, then it cannot ignore and exclude voices from the postsocialist spaces, and it cannot ignore the ways in which the global power reconfiguration after the fall of socialist states impacted lives of women* globally. It is simply not transnational feminism if it does not include and learn also from feminisms growing from and reflecting on the experiences of state socialism and the postsocialist neoliberal rush. Asking to pay attention to feminisms articulated from the state socialist and postsocialist experiences does not mean anything more but also nothing less than, as you said elsewhere, to ask "for the diversification of frames of reference" (Koobak and Marling 2014, 332).

To unpack this, we can start the diversification of frames of reference by diversifying the histories of transnational feminism itself. When we erase the former socialist space out of the map of relevant feminisms, a hugely important history of transnational solidarity is lost; solidarity that existed before the imperial redrafting of world order at the end of the Cold War made one section of the world into a "non-region" (Nowicka cited in Suchland 2011, 837). It is indeed deeply paradoxical that the histories of women's organisations under state socialism are largely forgotten and neglected in the current transnational feminisms, while transnational networking belonged to the ideological work of the socialist states. For instance, Kristen Ghodsee's *Second World* (2019) shows a fundamental role the socialist states played in supporting the transnational feminist networks of solidarity and how crucial these global networks of political support were for many feminist interventions on global scale. These transnational ties were not only pertinent for women's organising but spanned across other emancipatory projects of socialism. To bring another example, Claire Shaw's study of the (Soviet) formation of "deaf socialist subject" suggests that the socialist utopian promise to achieve social equality for deaf/disabled people embraced transnational deaf networks (Shaw forthcoming). Similarly, Tereza Stejskalová's *Filmmakers of the World, Unite!* (2017) illustrates how important the networks between the socialist states and the post-colonial countries have been for fostering social imaginations of equality, emancipation, and networks of camaraderie. The biggest danger that lies in losing these histories is that in this way we waste very rich archives that could drive our imaginations of *what could be*.

Even more importantly, Ghodsee's work reveals how devastating the demise of socialist states across Eastern Europe and the subsequent decline in the political force of the voices of the former socialist women's organisations was for transnational solidarity and for the position of women in both postsocialist and postcolonial spaces. Thus, one of the ideological complication that these alternative histories of transnational feminisms offer is that the dynamics of the Cold War might have paradoxically proven fortuitous for global solidarity along the East-South, socialist-postcolonial axes, simply because it unsettled the global dominance of the "North/West".

Obviously, the socialist states themselves were not feminist havens nor did they actually hold to fulfilling the promise of gender and sexual equality, but their need for legitimisation and international connections allowed a push for transnational feminist initiatives. Further, we do need to reckon with what it means for the ethical commitments of transnational feminism to point out that the much-celebrated arrival of democracy and liberalism into formerly socialist states might have also lead to much less varied and less rich array of women*'s voices on the global (and national) platforms. Losing sight of the global nature of postsocialism, we are losing sight of the multilateral and multidirectional interconnectedness of global histories; histories that cannot be exhausted by either of the West/East, North/South dyads.

RK: The continued predominance of Western feminist frameworks as a yardstick against which other locations are measured has been critiqued by postcolonial and postsocialist feminist scholars alike. When producing feminist knowledge, how do we move beyond the mere critique of the hegemony of Western epistemological frameworks?

KK: I really like this question because it challenges us to think about the knowledge production and makes us reckon with the fact that no epistemological framework is "innocent", free of ideological commitments, agendas, aspirations, and its own limitations. Academia itself, at least as we know/inhabit it now, is not only a place structured by various forms of global inequalities and power imbalance, it is deeply invested in and even powered by them. At the same time, we all teach and work with epistemologies articulated "outside" the local contexts and in the "West" (I, for one, certainly could be critiqued for using "crip theory" developed in the US context when looking at the postsocialist Czechoslovakia/Czech Republic). So, indeed, what creative strategies can we develop here?

Crip theory is actually a good example for complicating the notion of "Western theory". Even if tied to the US, or Anglo-American context, the political/analytical practice of crip theory has been articulated by subaltern voices of disabled and crip of colour activists and academics. So, despite the fact that it is now arriving from the West/North, it has not been a dominant/dominating epistemological framework. Further, in many ways, using crip theory in the postsocialist context allows for unsettling other forms of epistemologies that have also travelled here from the West/North but whose legitimation is often built on the rejection of the now forgotten and skewed legacies of socialist knowledges. As an example of "travelling theory", crip theory illustrates how such "travel" and translation affects both the context into which it "travels" as well as changes the theory itself by the dialogue with the new contexts.

Thus, rethinking postsocialism with crip theory accentuates the queer "time of coincidence" (Kulpa and Mizielińska 2011) of different epistemologies, different legacies, and different, even contradictory political positions as well as synergies between them. In this sense, it offers an alternative to liberal models focusing on individual self-actualisation, identity, or visions of cultural inclusion that do not speak of economic structures of disadvantage, neoliberal imperatives to abledness, and individualised responsibilisation. So, one of the promises crip theory holds for me is that it pushes against the models of identity that are defined (solely) by affirmation, positivity, and by rejection of any complex relationality to stigma, or "bad feelings". And, as I argued above, actually expansively redraws the boundaries of the category of disability itself.

I wanted to write a book that would imagine and help to articulate "strange affinities", or connections between political positions and struggles that are only rarely seen as interconnected, and sometimes are even imagined to be mutually exclusive, and stand in necessary conflict. I believe, for its embedded attention to how various forms of classification, differentiation, and hierarchisation coproduce each other, crip theory helps me do this. For instance, when several years ago the Czech queer film festival Mezipatra drew attention to the intersectional complexity of queer identities with a trailer that featured people with disabilities, illnesses, and chronically compromised health, part of the queer community rejected any relation to cripness out of fear that acknowledging close proximity to cripness and disability would revive the pathologising theories of homosexuality as deviance and sickness. Such stigmaphobic reactions are part of the hurt caused by the dictates of normality – in its core also intersectional – it requires compulsory able-bodiedness and able-mindedness, as much as whiteness, as much as living up to the requirements of the hetero-cis-gender order. The dictate of normality is also all the more pronounced and all the more powerful in the postsocialist context, where the whole "nation" needs to prove itself and needs to attest to its capacities to rehabilitate. Framing the historical period of state socialism as a deviation from the normative history puts pressure on the performatives of normalcy of the nation. Recognising such interconnectedness across different (or apparently different) positions and political fights draws on the legacy of multiple subaltern resistance projects and, in this sense, revives legacies of transnational feminisms.

Acknowledgements

This text has been facilitated by a research grant, *Post-Socialist Modernity and Social and Cultural Politics of Disability and Disablement* (17–12454J), awarded jointly by the Czech Science Foundation and Deutsche Forschungsgemeinschaft.

References

Ahmed, Sara. 2006. *Queer Phenomenology: Orientations, Objects, Others*. Durham, NC: Duke University Press.
Clare, Eli. 2017. *Brilliant Imperfection: Grappling with Cure*. Durham, NC: Duke University Press.
Dahrendorf, Ralf. 1991. *Úvahy o revoluci v Evropě v dopise, který měl být zaslán jistému pánovi ve Varšavě*. Praha: Evropský kulturní klub.
Ghodsee, Kristen. 2019. *Second World, Second Sex: Socialist Women's Activism and Global Solidarity During the Cold War*. Durham, NC: Duke University Press.
Hong, Grace Kyungwon, and Roderick Ferguson. 2011. *Strange Affinities: The Gender and Sexual Politics of Comparative Racialization*. Durham, NC: Duke University Press.
Kafer, Alison. 2013. *Feminist, Queer, Crip*. Bloomington: Indiana University Press.
Kim, Eunjung. 2018. *Curative Violence: Rehabilitating Disability, Gender, and Sexuality in Modern Korea*. Durham, NC: Duke University Press.

Kolářová, Kateřina. 2019. "Mediating Syndromes of Postcommunism: Disability, Sex, Race, and Labor." *JCMS: Journal of Cinema and Media Studies* 58, no. 4: 156–162. https://doi.org/ 10.1353/cj.2019.0046.

Kolářová, Kateřina. Forthcoming. *Rehabilitative Postsocialism: Disability, Race, Gender and Sexuality and the Limits of National Belonging.* Ann Arbor: Michigan University Press.

Kolářová, Kateřina, and Katharina M. Wiedlack. 2016. "Crip Notes on the Idea of Development." *Somatechnics* 6, no. 2: 125–141. https://doi.org/10.3366/soma.2016.0187.

Koobak, Redi, and Raili Marling. 2014. "The Decolonial Challenge: Framing Post-socialist Central and Eastern Europe Within Transnational Feminist Studies." *European Journal of Women's Studies* 21, no. 4: 330–343. https://doi.org/10.1177/1350506814542882.

Kulpa, Robert, and Joanna Mizielińska. 2011. *De-centring Western Sexualities: Central and Eastern European Perspectives.* Farnham: Ashgate.

Parvulescu, Anca. 2014. *The Traffic in Women's Work: East European Migration and the Making of Europe.* Chicago: University of Chicago Press.

Parvulescu, Anca. 2015. "European Racial Triangulation." In *Postcolonial Transitions in Europe*, edited by Sandra Ponzanesi and Gianmaria Colpani, 25–45. London: Rowman and Littlefield Publishers.

Shaw, Claire. Forthcoming. "'Just Like It Is at Home!' Deafness and Socialist Internationalism During the Cold War." In *Re/imaginations of Disability in State Socialism: Visions, Promises, Frustrations*, edited by Kateřina Kolářová and Martina Winkler. Frankfurt am Main: Campus Verlag.

Shih, Shu-Mei. 2012. "Is the Post in Postsocialism the Post in Posthumanism?" *Social Text* 30: 27–50. https://doi.org/10.1215/01642472-1468308.

Shildrick, Margrit. 2015. "Living on; Not Getting Better." *Feminist Review* 111, no. 1: 10–24. https://doi.org/10.1057/fr.2015.22.

Stejskalová, Tereza, ed. 2017. *Filmmakers of the World, Unite!* Prague: Tranzit.

Suchland, Jennifer. 2011. "Is Postsocialism Transnational?" *Signs* 36, no. 4: 837–862. https://doi.org/10.1086/658899.

Chapter 17

Grappling with the "China crisis"

Positionality, impasse, and potential breakthrough of Chinese feminist diaspora in post-Cold War North America

Weiling Deng

Introduction

This chapter attempts to show how the experience of being feminist and Chinese in the North American academia can be in dialogue with the recent discussions on possible intersections between the postcolonial and postsocialist feminist frameworks (Chari and Verdery 2009; Suchland 2011; Tlostanova 2012). The major argument is that for Chinese feminists in North America, the post-Cold War geopolitical reality is drawn across the Pacific Ocean. In addition, there has been a century-long history of Asian Americans being brutally incorporated into the US imperialist economy that is in stark contrast with the middle-class, urban, cosmopolitan, and liberal stance of the latest generation of diasporic Chinese feminists in the US with their specific subjectivity, visions, and comradeship. I base my analysis of how "Chinese feminism" presents a distinct site of postsocialist-postcolonial feminist knowledge production in the transpacific context, with North American racial politics in the background.

The "Chinese perspective" on seeing postsocialist and postcolonial feminisms in dialogue with each other stretches this productive conversation to engage with what has happened over the Asia-Pacific region since the fall of the Communist world. By focusing on the positionality from which contemporary Chinese feminists cultivate their agency of translation, networking, visibility, and mobility, this chapter draws attention to the racial and class hierarchies perpetuated in the deployment of "gender" as a universal analytical tool.

A brief background: which "Chinese feminism"?

To give a clearer picture of the diasporic Chinese feminists, the earliest of all cohorts that travelled to attend women's studies programs in the West (primarily the US) took place in the late 1980s and early 1990s. Funded by different fellowships, corporate foundations, and increasingly by the combination of these two resources and family assets – a sign of successful postsocialist economic gain on the individual scale – the flow westward has steadily grown since then. This picture is increasingly tainted on both the Chinese and the Western side by the Cold War narrative of authoritarian state versus oppressed women and sexually nonconforming people longing for the transnational recognition of, and support for, their resistance. The Western university represents a portal to the knowledge necessary for a cognitive "awakening" to happen. This adds the value of being with, and included by, the world's progressive minds to the path to neoliberal, elite, and meritocratic education, but does not subvert it.

What this chapter examines, then, is the most recent phase (2015–present) of this continuous flow and network-building of urban, middle-class, highly educated, and "progressive" Chinese youths toward the Western university as a special manifestation of Chinese feminism. The specialness has to do with the politicisation of feminist street performance within China. In March 2015, the sudden arrest of five young Chinese feminist activists, known as the "Feminist Five" incident, ostensibly linked Chinese feminist activism to international human rights discourses that target Third and Second World countries (Suchland 2011). The singular importance of this incident is achieved partly through its reappearance in virtually every public talk of "Chinese feminism" in the Global North that presumably reinforces feminism's plight in China as "as an aberration of capitalist systems" (Suchland 2011, 1). This has led to an interlocking relationship between diasporic Chinese feminism and Cold War ideology: the narrative of Chinese feminist experiences is permitted wider circulation only when it satisfies the appetite for a crisis of state socialism. The enthusiastic search for Chinese women's agency within an oppressive (post-) socialist state serves not only the purpose of recognising women's resistance and wisdom within lived patriarchal structure, but also, perhaps more implicitly, the purpose of testifying before a global audience on China's own political failure as a violator of human rights. This human rights crisis response approach characterises the agenda and everyday work of most feminist non-governmental organisations (NGOs) that have become social hubs of progressive Chinese students who would later apply with their NGO experience to overseas graduate programs. The politicisation of feminist representation merges into the pursuit of meritocratic education and symbolic productivity. Relocated to the proximity of North American universities, this merging contours the activity range of diasporic Chinese feminists.

Chinese feminism's post-2015 development has seen a quick conglomeration of new and continuing Chinese graduate students who were/are based in North America. Unsurprisingly, the recent activities of Chinese feminists are more readily located in places outside the Chinese government's immediate surveillance and also more engaged in the established contradiction between the Communist Party-led China, as a crisis of human rights and humanity, and its politically disobedient diasporic scholars and activists. The term "North American academia" is used as a signifier of elite positions and locations embedded in the colonial history and institutional expansion of Western knowledge. This term also broadly includes the experiences of studying in Western Europe and those about returning to China but working within the interest of "China watch" by people assuming Western liberal positions. Precisely because of the intricate personal and professional feminist networks built against the background of the dominant, colonialist knowledge production of the Western university, I situate my discussion of the positionality and location of diasporic Chinese feminist speeches and acts in the proximity of the North American academia. Here, "North America" holds both Cold War and colonial relations with postsocialist China while engaging in complicit collaboration with the latter to strengthen global capitalism.

Where is Chinese feminism in relation to the "posts"?

Locating Chinese feminism within the parameters of the "posts", one needs to go beyond the emergent scholarship that integrates the ethnographic studies of Chinese women (and queer people) with China's postsocialist development in culture and the economy (Bao 2018; Rofel 2007). In addition, one cannot be settled with the current interest of Chinese feminist activists and scholars in North American multicultural feminist practice that increasingly features immigrants from former Third World countries, feminists, and queers of colour. The focus on "parameters" enables us to draw attention to the underexplored matrix of post-Cold War geopolitical tensions that conditioned and shaped the formation and readjustment of what we consider the contours of Chinese feminism in the 21st century. I attempt to map Chinese feminism in the geographical ties between the (problematically) designated First, Second, and Third Worlds and the ideology of such division (Chari and Verdery 2009, 18–19). While the idea is to reflect on the contested positionality of Chinese feminism in general, I also pay special attention to this chapter's protagonists, the more politicised Chinese "students" of feminism in North America, to demonstrate the interwoven dynamics of capitalist and colonial intervention in the process of forming temporal, spatial, and structural relations between Western and Chinese feminisms.

Temporal marks

Starting from the late 20th century, the manifestations of Chinese feminism, whether in the form of scholarly reasoning, artistic work, or activism, are stories of myriad intersected "afterlives". To begin with the most broadly accepted idea, these stories appear after the end of China's high socialist era where Maoist feminism championed "women hold up half the sky", a hallmark slogan of Chinese women's singular legitimate representative: All China Women's Federation. These manifestations are also after the last nationwide popular protest against the imposition of neoliberalism that ended up in military suppression at Tiananmen Square, an important event contemporaneous with the turmoil that led to the end of the Cold War and to the universalised belief that democracy and capitalism would rule the world.

Another temporal designation of Chinese feminism is the Fourth World Conference on Women in 1995. Held in Beijing six years after the military suppression of citizens, students, and workers' protests against enlarged social stratification, the conference established the concept of "gender" as the dominant rhetoric and yardstick of Chinese women's studies and feminist social work (Spakowski 2011; Min 2014). Chinese women and Chinese feminism(s) have since then been admitted to the global (i.e. liberal democratic) temporality of women's movement, though critical reflections of this act of "connecting track", as is popularly versed, would continue to ebb and flow (Dong 2005; Li 2000; Zhu 2011). Unsurprisingly, there is a major epistemological divide running through those who actively practice feminist research and/or service in China. This disparity, set upon whether there needs to be an alert to the colonialist nature of Western feminist theory, drives serious debates over the identity of Chinese feminism against the understudied geopolitical background of the post-Cold War world.

Yet, one more "after" is often overlooked: China's (semi-)colonial past. Though short, the history of being partially colonised along the country's east coast still haunts. It seeded the idea of eugenics and the anxiety of being weak and defeated by foreign forces within the modern Chinese nationalist discourse. The liberation of the Chinese nation from colonial power did not end racial anxiety, but rather vacuumed the ground in which race could be critically discussed. Racial weakness was symbolically attached to the "backwardness" and vulnerability of Chinese women's bodies, particularly the impoverished and illiterate prostitutes who became the target of modernist public health reform and mandatory re-education in both the Nationalist and Communist regimes (Hershatter 1999). Subsequently, the liberation of all Chinese women, as a paralleling accomplishment of the liberation of the nation, gave rise not only to the victorious assumption of the overcoming of national uncertainty but also to a universal belief that the Chinese race is at once homogeneous and independent and reserves the right to reclaim its subaltern trauma to justify its growing hegemony. Thus, by "assigning race to 'others'" (Tlostanova, Thapar-Björkert and Koobak 2019), China enacts "a series of structured remembrances and forgettings . . . to reinvent a past [it] could leave behind" (Rofel 2007, 198). This enactment is most symbolically encapsulated in the process in which, as Lisa Rofel illustrated in *Desiring China*, urban professional young Chinese women (and gay people) come to embody cosmopolitanism through transcultural desire. What is left behind is not only a socialist economy and aesthetics of life, but also the representation of "Chinese women" as the fundamental victim of colonialism and imperialism.

Transpacific encounters: a Chinese feminist diaspora

The separation between China's past(s) and its present is spatialised in North America where striking spatial and ideological disparities exist between the remnants of old Chinatowns and the new Chinese suburbs. If one tries to locate Chinese feminists in North America today, most of them are outside of both spaces. Indeed, they have created a new diaspora with special identification and rejection of narratives and theories. They are likely to be critical of, and distance themselves from, the new People's Republic of China (PRC) immigrants in the rich suburbs who represent the ideology of the Chinese Communist Party (CCP). At the same time, it is always a delayed realisation, if ever happening, that the time-space of Chinatowns may offer counterhegemonic inspiration to the suggestion that contemporary Chinese feminism may have some historical connections to the anti-racist and anti-colonial struggles within and beyond the United States, because the primary (for some, the only) focus is on "gender". But this postcolonial critique of Western hegemony complicates the postsocialist desire to be dissociated from the "backward" time and space in need of modernisation. Also, it is often mistaken for the nationalist anti-American propaganda in the PRC. At other times, it is accused of deliberately understating and compromising the multicultural nature of feminism (i.e. feminism is universal and *inclusive of* Chinese experiences) and the activist work of Chinese feminists in North America, a negligence out of dogmatic reading of postcolonialism.

This diaspora, which is based on empirical knowledge of what it means to be feminist and Chinese in a global/Western context, explicates the indeterminacy of Chinese feminism's temporo-political framing. There is no singular framing, but multiple ones that are interconnected. In this light, Sharad Chari and Katherine Verdery's (2009) practice of "thinking between the posts" provides a useful platform for theorising Chinese feminism. Countering the convention of thinking of the globe in terms of "three worlds", this integrative vision, termed "post-Cold War", addresses the configuration of "race" and "enemy" – the differentiated and othered – in the technologies that invented and consolidated empires: the socialist and colonial empires. While the overt forms of colonialism and state socialism may discontinue, and this opened the intellectual fields of postcolonialism and postsocialism at different conjunctures, the expertise of "[differentiating] spaces and populations through their contrasting propensities to life and death" (Chari and Verdery 2009, 27) persists in the ceaseless efforts to designate enemies.

The focus on the *expertise of differentiation* is to break with the interest in knowing how a political entity, whether authoritarian or liberal, maintains itself, reproduces its own faults, or is compromised by external forces; and instead, to explore the changing geography of power and privilege. This geopolitical perspective dissolves the illusion that the agency of moving from one sovereign power to another in pursuit of a *role* in cosmopolitan critical thinking is one solid step toward rejecting the structural oppression of the former. What actually happens, if one does not omit the material and geopolitical condition in which the move is made possible at the very beginning, is the redrawing of a map of privilege within the largest geography of post-Cold War power relations, grounded prominently in the identity-based representations of knowledge that include some roles and exclude others. The "identity" here is not merely labelled with class, race, gender, nationality, and so on, but also by the classification of the three worlds – First, Second, and Third – that undergirds the division of intellectual labour along the arbitrary communist/free and traditional/modern binaries (Chari and Verdery 2009).

On this ground, the connection between skills/knowledge and presence/visibility is not politically and economically neutral. Rather, in the post-Cold War world, this connection serves particular rules by which people are relocated and regrouped, convened and divided. The relocation of Chinese feminists to North America, for instance, has much to do with the post-industrial and postsocialist social divisions that have emerged in China since the 1990s and that have convinced them to feel more connected with people similarly well-versed in gender and global feminism than those who are not in line with these vocabularies and the related politics of representation. The criticism of an authoritarian postsocialist government as oppressor of feminist activism is particularly appealing for the cause of gender mainstreaming in this context, as it lends convenient rooting for keeping the world classified as unfree and free along the socialist/capitalist binary. It also strengthens the argument that feminism should have been a universal ideal if not for those in postsocialist states who intend to keep feminism a "Western" thing (Li 2000), which plays right into the inevitability of establishing a universal progressive taskforce consisting of awakened feminists.

The question is not that the authoritarian states, such as China, are mistaken for the brutality that they impose on their own people – women, minorities, critical scholars, political dissidents, and so on. Instead, what should be questioned is how gender, as the central concept of global feminism, became "a new tool to push a neoliberal agenda for development" through training (Min 2014, 587). How, then, is training – representing a thinly veiled hierarchical relationship between the professional and the unprofessional – equal to emancipating? In other words, how has gender become a discipline and how does it discipline? These questions should be thought of in tandem with the understanding that China did not just passively wait to be judged and transformed by these new homogenising development agendas that represent the geopolitical interests of global capitalism. China's active engagement and leadership in global capitalism since the 1990s has made a strong case of countering Western dominance outside the narrative of "transition" (Tlostanova, Thapar-Björkert, and Koobak 2019, 121) or "transitology" (Chari and Verdery 2009, 19). As the "gender turn" (Spakowski 2018, 566) in feminist theorising and practice plays a critical role in the post-Cold War geopolitical rivalry, the agency of presenting oneself in the Chinese feminist diaspora – and more broadly, the transpacific transaction of feminist knowledge and experience as a Chinese national – is complicated with novel powers and privileges that beg for a critical analysis of such diasporic positionality.

The disciplining of "gender" feminism

At least three strands of transnational scholarship focused on gender and women in China were blooming by the time gender began to take over the stage. All of them were shaped by the transforming post-Cold War time and space. One strand is led by anthropologists and historians of Chinese women in North American universities. Inspired by postcolonialism to decentre "western women as the standard" womanhood, these Western academics tried to understand how Chinese women made sense of the country's socialist past while repositioning themselves in the rapidly privatising society (Gilmartin et al. 1994, 7). The second strand, partly joining the first in academic publication, cast a sceptical eye on Western feminism as a tool for analysing Chinese women while giving credit to the Marxist path that brought Chinese women to the present (Li 2000). This second view, according to Li Xiaojiang, was not forgetful of the CCP's tight control of women's sexuality. Rather, it took Marxism as a historical reality that had inscribed in the lives and subjectivities of Chinese women a vision of state-individual relationship that could not be articulated by Western liberal feminism. The last strand was represented by overseas Chinese feminist students who embraced "gender" as an enlightening instrument to help Chinese women see and articulate the discriminations against them. The Ford Foundation played a pivotal role at the turn of the 21st century to support the work of translating gender into China by Chinese NGOs and members of the Chinese Society for Women's Studies (CSWS) in the US (Wang 2004; Min 2014; Spakowski 2018).

Translation: a positionality in a nutshell

Over the next 20 years, the first strand became more of a disciplinary specialty of historians of China who wanted to revisit and unsettle the dominant modernist ideology of liberation and enlightenment that originated in China's New Culture Movement (1915–1925) (Ko 2007; Hershatter 1999). It is more akin to Chinese studies than to gender and feminist studies in the North American academia: the Cold War-instigated area studies took a gender turn (thanks to the impact that the post-civil rights and postcolonial movements have on US-based academics) rather than the Eurocentric construction of "gender" taking a decolonial turn. But it is the latter field that has attracted more contemporary Chinese students. A de-historicising tendency is subsequently formed in the study of the relationship between Chinese women, the state, and modernisation. This change is influenced by the politics of translation within the post-1980s Chinese women's studies.

Between the second and third strands there is an argument of the politics behind translating "gender", because this key term, to a large extent, determines the epistemological choice and positionality of speech or act in the processes of post-Cold War knowledge transaction between China and the West. On a related note, between the two translations of "feminism" in Chinese, *nüxing zhuyi* ("ism" of womanhood and femininity) and *nüquan zhuyi* ("ism" of women's rights and power), the epistemological differences that rest heavily on one character point to the disparate ways in which scholars treat "Chinese" in relation to "feminism". While the latter – more commonly seen on social media today in politicised form – is worried that a falsely essentialised Chinese-versus-Western differentiation may slow down the delivery of Western feminist theories to China and subsequently impede the progress in which Chinese women are granted the right words to voice their oppression, the former warns of the subjugation of the historical specificity of Chinese women's lives to a hegemonic, albeit useful, theoretical reference that is mistaken (by some Chinese feminists themselves) for universal truth (Dong 2005, 9).

Ingrained in these continued arguments are varied anxieties of "the construction, examination, and . . . institutionalization of difference *within* feminist discourses" (Mohanty 1995, 68, original emphasis). Increasingly and involuntarily, Chinese students of feminism – my emphasis on "students" will be explained below – are summoned by "gender feminism" (Spakowski 2018, 566) to seek international sisterhood, commend multiculturalism, and celebrate cross-national solidarity. But all these new exciting developments take place on the ground that "historical interconnection[s]" between peoples subordinated to imperialist oppressions are disintegrated into "discrete and separate histories (or even herstories) and into questions of identity politics" (Mohanty 1995, 69). A typical scene would be an Asian graduate student with an immigrant visa who participated in the 2017 Women's March in Washington and was overwhelmed by the view and sound of a convivially chanting crowd that consisted of feminists of different skin colours. The march was a make-believe gathering via the authenticity of multiculturalism, which convinced her, the student witness, that feminism proved capable of crossing the racial line, now that all races stood together in the United States' capital, and white women willingly and urgently shared stage with Black and Brown feminists to unburden themselves from the guilt of white feminism. While Asians were still too few and dispersed to be spotted in the large marching crowd, the student and her other Chinese colleagues were present. Feminism lifted them up to be in this transnational, multi-thematic, multigenerational, multicultural, and multiracial progressive force. This experience of being present and overwhelmed defined her *authentic* relation to feminist discourse.[1]

Network, experience, and discourse

The word "authentic", as it has reoccurred in Chinese feminist narratives of activism, reiterates that "experience" functions "as an unexamined, catch-all category" (Mohanty 1995, 70), an "ontological given" (Moore 1994, 2). The politics of being, or positionality, as Henrietta Moore argued, "is too often reduced to individual experience and/or to representation: 'I know because I've been there' and 'I know because I am one'" (ibid., 2). An idea that emerged among the debating diasporic Chinese feminists who participated (some physically, others virtually) in the Women's March in the US stressed that Washington, DC, was the main arena and therefore best reflected what the march organisers wanted feminism to look like. It was unfortunate, those who held this idea thought, that not every Chinese feminist who supposedly shared one radical sisterhood with them was able to personally experience the march in DC.

Before long, the Chinese social media saw numerous writings that tried to "debunk the rumours" (Laoqingbiaomei 2017) that came from partial observation from the US West Coast and from the judgment of colleagues in China manipulated by the biased, white-women-focused mainstream news presses. This cluster of essays was but one example of synchronous and intensive productions that strengthen the network of Chinese feminist diaspora in North America. Using a hybridity of media, accessible or inaccessible from mainland China, these productions not only serve the purpose of remaining connected and visible as "Chinese feminists", but they also unify those who wish to be entitled as such. The ability to "actively 'produce' oneself and to present oneself at information exchanges", Elena Gapova argued, is key to building a sense of belonging within the network (Gapova 2015, 26). Altogether, the experience of learning, networking, and regulating a discourse is what I call the "disciplining" of gender, as both the construction of a field or paradigm of study (i.e. gender and feminist studies) and as the act of implicit correction and regulation to unify people around a central ideation.

"Students" of feminism

Many of those who form the Chinese feminist diaspora in North America are "students" of feminism, not simply because they have enrolled in classes that teach gender and feminism and they have been sociologically categorised as students. A more important reason to call them "students" is their submission to the explicit and implicit disciplining of "gender" feminism. But rather than passivity, submission yields a sense of agency that identifies who is a purer feminist. This "student" status will perpetuate until feminism is taken off its shrine (Dong 2005, 8; Zhu 2011, 151) and the students put down their duty of indiscriminately judging the ethical ground of critics of feminism.

Here, feminism does not specifically refer to a given feminist theory or activist guidebook. It does not even specify Western or non-Western, white or Black feminisms. Rather, it is a constructed doctrine by which those who defend its universality are entitled to discipline other takes on feminism. The reason why a number of Chinese feminists abroad (and at home) would go to great lengths to defend feminism's universality has its root in the postcolonial and post-civil rights condition in the United States that prides its achievement in multiculturalism. Multiculturalism has provided them a foothold to be globally connected and recognisable (if not already recognised) feminists. In other words, it is the racial condition and policy in the US academia – both its achievements of self-readjustment and its persistent racial profiling – that brought them to the rank of global feminists.

The promotion of multiculturalism, particularly through the marketing of international higher education, is not simply a domestic solution to reducing inequality. It matters also as a Cold War instrument devised to conceptualise "an economically, politically, and militarily integrated 'free world'" by easing Asian immigrants' entry and naturalisation (Klein 2003, 16). With this instrument, the US has aimed to consolidate capitalism's, and especially its own, legitimacy of representing the future of human civilisation. In the continuum of what Christina Klein called "Cold War Orientalism", the highly educated, progressive Chinese students who are vocal critics of the CCP's authoritarian politics are scooped from their home context and relocated to the benign "middlebrow American" intellectual context, which is "a structure of feeling that privilege[s] precisely the values of interdependence, sympathy, and hybridity" and that fosters the Americans' sentimental and intellectual affiliation with Asia (ibid., 16). Non-communist Asian or Chinese students, in this light, must be understood as a political and economic category to open up the educational "way for the gradual integration of Asian Americans into the social and political mainstream" (ibid., 16).

The transpacific project of progressive integration of Asians resonates with Jennifer Suchland's concept of "feminist homogeneous empty time" (Suchland 2015, 86) which critiques the integration of socialist women's movement into the standard of liberal feminism. These two dimensions of integration – one on race, the other on political time-space – put together a critical understanding of post-Cold War geopolitical map on which I have grounded the analytical category of Chinese "students" of feminism. These Chinese students became a part of what James Kyung-Jin Lee called "the dream of multicultural promise" at the time (the 1980s) when it began to be shattered by urban racial confrontations that soon led to the awakening of progressive American academics and other cultural workers (Lee 2004, XIX). Living up to that dream has since become a part of diasporic Chinese feminists' identity negotiation as they navigate through the imagined and actual spaces of living and working. The American multicultural dream is their accomplishment and constraint at once. The proliferation of Chinese feminist (and queer) writings in the Western university dominated by white males fosters the spectacle of multicultural feminist scholarship. But meanwhile, it suppresses the view of how symbolic production of multiculturalism may paralyse radical, counter-hegemonic diversity that is materially based in living spaces and leaves unquestioned what is really going on in capitalism's racial politics. Therefore, the hailing of multiculturalism is both a tool with which Chinese feminists in North America justify individual and collective gains in the politics of representation, and an impasse for diasporic Chinese feminists that prevents further theoretical and political breakthroughs.

Possible breakthroughs

In light of the disciplining of "gender feminism" and the Cold War motives of American multiculturalism, what may have seemed an apparent individual struggle – self-directed educational aspiration and career planning, an individual's "feminist awakening", or an ordinary citizen's disobedience – is imbricated with the post-Cold War production of knowledge economy that draws heavily on the discourse of human rights. What may have seemed a strategic obsession of equating visibility with activism, while the authoritarian state implements sweeping censorship and threatens to jail dissenting citizens, can leave unchecked how the politics of visibility is woven into broader hegemonic institutions that do not recognise national and ideological borders.

The visibility bar

The broader institution concerned here has two interrelated aspects. First, the "Cold War representations of space and time have shaped knowledge and practice" (Chari and Verdery 2009, 12), which was discussed in the previous section. Second, global capitalism, which is premised on the surrogacy of human labour that spares the "(already) human subjects" the humanitarian freedom to be visible and to prosper upon their creative capacities (Atanasoski and Vora 2019, 4). China's huge pool of "surplus humans", created as the country of 1.4 billion people transformed within just three decades from the most equal to the most unequal economy, is the steadiest base for its own and the world's transnational creative economy (Heinrich 2018, 2). Being the advantaged ones in the new social and class divisions arising after high socialism (Gapova 2015), rather than on the lower rung of the capitalising economy, is an essential, if not the only, ticket to the highly visible international network of cosmopolitan and multicultural progressives aggregated in and around Western universities.

The internationally highlighted, and internet-mediated, representation of "Chinese feminists" as a collective identity results from the intersection between a comparative socio-material advantage in the new lines of inclusion and exclusion in postsocialist Chinese economy and a cultural edge in being nonconforming, which is sometimes politicised along the line of human rights violation. With multiple types of inclusion/exclusion intersected, there is no definitive boundary between the neoliberal use of feminist knowledge and an otherwise anti-capitalist use. In fact, in the diverse engagements of Chinese feminism as a whole, one will often detect both uses in the same activity.

Yet, at the same time those feminist practices seem to cross the class line in Marxist definition, another underdefined "class" arises based on similarity in *expressed* lifestyle, taste, and political view, and on the capability of maneuvering social media and, when necessary, circumventing censorship to remain alerted and expressive of politics. The last facet is what Margaret Roberts (2018) called a "tax on information" paid in monetary, temporal, social, and intellectual forms. I coin the term "visibility bar" to visualise these material and immaterial costs to work as a cosmopolitan (counter-)cultural content producer from an authoritarian state (see Figure 17.1).

The bar is both imagined and real. It is both speculations of what content will be censored and a lived privilege of belonging to the included segments in China's neoliberalisation, which further connects the Chinese professionals to the track of

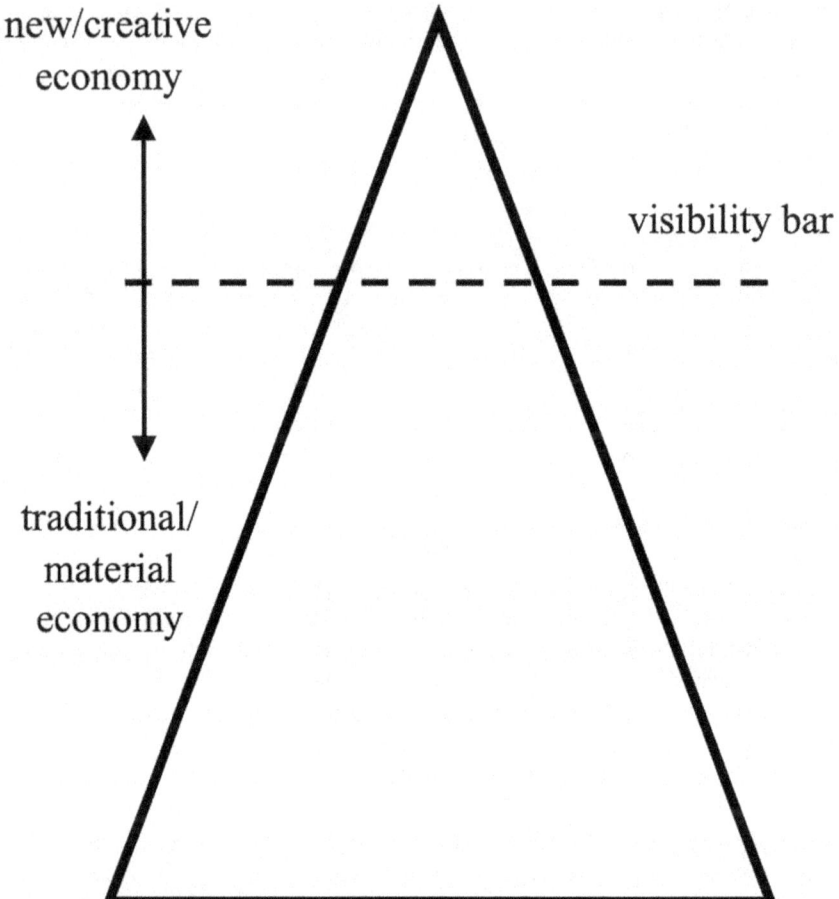

new/creative
economy

traditional/
material
economy

visibility bar

Figure 17.1 A diagram illustrating the "visibility bar". The words "visibility bar"
appear close to the apex of the triangle above the dotted line crossing the apex. On the left side, there is an up-down arrow, with the
words "new/creative economy" appearing above the arrow pointing
up and the words "traditional/material economy" appearing below
the arrow pointing down

international talents (Hoffman 2010, 16). The division between new or creative
economy and traditional or material economy is a universal cause of intensified
class inequality in the post-industrial age. As wealth is accumulated much faster
in the upper part, which is what neoliberalism is about, diversity that is based in
the lower part and that actually challenges neoliberal life planning becomes more
susceptible to appropriation. While the socially constructed "lines" of differentiation are crossed with courage and hard work in the business of representation,

the economically and materially constructed "walls" grow taller paradoxically as more intellectuals of colour and from former Third World countries join the mainstream(ing) of North American multicultural production (Lee 2004). On this note, the role that gender plays in the knowledge-driven global capitalism, and the way in which the universalisation of gender smoothed the path for China to become involved in global capitalism, are serious issues to reconsider.

Get over the "China crisis"

The world has witnessed China raising the visibility bar over the last decade or so, after a brief period of relative freedom. More political dissidents have been jailed and more critical social media accounts censored and eliminated. The Chinese feminist activism's recent hardship manifests this broad crackdown on China's civil society. The opportunity to remain visible either becomes individualised – reliance on family assets increases and international human rights and/or NGO funding goes to the most recognised of all feminist practitioners – or simply collapses for the more vulnerable members. Chinese feminism's attachment to the international human rights discourse may help keep visible and audible the media-savvy activists, many of whom are either physically present in North America or maintain consistent access to mainstream Western media platforms from within mainland China. But it does not help with what may have existed as a common ground of the overall Chinese feminist practice that gets thinned out in the polarisation of distribution of resources for visibility. As a relatively new outcry of China's reputation of a top violator of human rights, "gender", as an analytical category, can become incapacitated when it comes to an unfolding human rights crisis in China, missing out the larger political economic context of global capitalism and the representation of it.

As Rey Chow recalled, a feminist in the West asked after the Tiananmen massacre in 1989: "How should we read what is going on in China in terms of gender?" Chow replied: "We do not, because at the moment of shock Chinese people are degendered and become simply 'Chinese'" (Chow 1991, 82). In this brief moment of question and answer, "gender", deployed as an "established but ill-fitting template" to run a familiar program (Heinrich 2018, 3), can only reach so far as to bracket China's crisis from the rest of the world and attribute it to the country's own historical-cultural deficiency. "Gender" represents the benevolent "multicultural" intervention that is prepared to set off on a humanitarian mission to save lives from the authoritarian government (Melamed 2006). Under the interrogation of "gender", China is not only a political body where human rights crisis prevails, but itself symbolises a crisis of humanity and governance, in opposition of which liberal states define themselves (Chow 1991). The latter interpretation raises the "stake in a critical understanding of the PRC [higher] than the fate of the PRC itself" (Dirlik 2017, 1). In other words, getting trained to use the "gendered" lens to look for/at women in China does not necessarily lead to a better understanding of how its history plays into contemporary life and politics. It may deliver an ahistorical view of the history of the modern Chinese nation: the invisible histories become visible against an abstract, static backdrop. The misrecognition that returning "women" and feminism to patriarchal history means the ultimate failure of feminists' training is what I have referred to as the current impasse of Chinese feminism.

To break through this impasse, one needs to get over the "China crisis". This is not to overlook the actually existing crises – far from it. Rather, it is the way in which we look at those crises that need to be critically examined and readjusted. The kind of breakthrough in need is a methodological one that should do two things. One, it should engage the gendered interrogation of crises and inequalities in China to the critical understanding that China's crisis is an integral part of the world's crisis – that crises are the normalcy of global capitalism sustained by continuous colonialist projects, including the universalisation of progressive ideas over the former Second and Third worlds. Two, it should prompt more proactive contemplations on race among Chinese feminists who tend to find race irrelevant until relocated to a predominantly white environment in the West. The racialisation of Chinese citizens in the wake of dramatic political plight is the immediate and main production of "gendered" investigation that takes the crisis-drawn approach. By trivialising the complexities of "China" to a racial designation, the "gender" tool consolidates the liberal Western institution's authority to assign worthiness to certain experiences and narratives and sideline others according to the communist/free and traditional/modern binaries. To undo this mechanism of knowledge production, critical historiography of the underlying colonial project in Cold War Asia-Pacific should take a more central place in the prospect of expanding Chinese feminism's transnational engagement.

Conclusion

To conclude, the focus on diasporic Chinese feminists in North American academia helps link this emergent community to diaspora studies' commitment to theorising the past, the present, and the future that is not in a simplified chronical order or linear and neutral geographical movement, but with a destabilised and porous national border kept in mind. It also helps make the study of gender a contribution to a historicised understanding of China not as an exceptional developmental model, but as a nation-state in motion from the early stage of the history of colonialism through global late capitalism.

Today we are seeing more threats to sustainable community life from the heightened exploitation of capitalism and thus hearing more calls for socialist feminism. But again, seen from the perspective of the diasporic feminist, more work needs to be done to bridge the gap between postcolonial critique of race and postsocialist class divisions, not simply to make a forgotten past known, but to see contemporary connections between the countries in light of how that past became forgotten.

Note

1   The portrayal of a Chinese graduate student attending the Women's March on Washington is an assemblage of different personal experiences that had been self-published as memoirs on the internet.

References

Atanasoski, Neda, and Kalindi Vora. 2019. *Surrogate Humanity: Race, Robots, and the Politics of Technological Futures*. Durham, NC: Duke University Press.

Bao, Hongwei. 2018. *Queer Comrades: Gay Identity and Tongzhi Activism in Postsocialist China*. Copenhagen: Nordic Institute of Asian Studies Press.

Chari, Sharad, and Katherine Verdery. 2009. "Thinking Between the Posts: Postcolonialism, Postsocialism, and Ethnography After the Cold War." *Comparative Studies in Society and History* 51, no. 1: 6–34.

Chow, Rey. 1991. "Violence in the Other Country: China as Crisis, Spectacle, and Woman." In *Third World Women and the Politics of Feminism*, edited by Chandra Talpade Mohanty, Ann Russo, and Lourdes Torres, 81–100. Bloomington and Indianapolis: Indiana University Press.

Dirlik, Arif. 2017. *Complicities: The People's Republic of China in Global Capitalism*. Chicago: Prickly Paradigm Press.

Dong, Limin. 2005. "Nüxingzhuyi: bentuhua jiqi weidu" [Feminism: Indigenisation and Its Degrees]. *Nankai xuebao* no. 2: 7–12.

Gapova, Elena. 2015. "Becoming Visible in the Digital Age." *Feminist Media Studies* 15, no. 1, 18–35. https://doi.org/10.1080/14680777.2015.988390.

Gilmartin, Christina K. et al. 1994. "Introduction." In *Engendering China: Women, Culture, and the State*, edited by Christina K. Gilmartin et al., 1–24. Cambridge: Harvard University Press.

Heinrich, Ari Larissa. 2018. *Chinese Surplus: Biopolitical Aesthetics and the Medically Commodified Body*. Durham, NC: Duke University Press.

Hershatter, Gail. 1999. *Dangerous Pleasure: Prostitution and Modernity in Twentieth-century Shanghai*. Berkeley, CA: University of California Press.

Hoffman, Lisa. 2010. *Patriotic Professionalism in Urban China: Fostering Talent*. Philadelphia, PA: Temple University Press.

Klein, Christina. 2003. *Cold War Orientalism: Asia in the Middlebrow Imagination, 1945–1961*. Berkeley, CA: University of California Press.

Ko, Dorothy. 2007. *Cinderella's Sisters: A Revisionist History of Footbinding*. Berkeley, CA: University of California Press.

Laoqingbiaomei. 2017. "Fanji yaoyan – Funü youxing qinli zhe: Lishi buhui ru wangye bei xiaoshi" [Debunk the Rumors – Witness of the Women's March: History Will Not Be Made Disappeared Like a Webpage]. *Xin Meiti Nüxing*. www.weibo.com/ttarticle/p/show?id=2309404067496280858008.

Lee, James Kyung-Jin. 2004. *Urban Triage: Race and the Fictions of Multiculturalism*. Minneapolis, MN: University of Minnesota Press.

Li, Xiaojiang. 2000. *Nüxing?zhuyi [Feminine?ism]*. Nanjing: Jiangsu People's Publishing House.

Melamed, Jodi. 2006. "The Spirit of Neoliberalism: From Racial Liberalism to Neoliberal Multiculturalism." *Social Text* 24, no. 4 (Winter): 1–24. https://doi.org/10.1215/01642472-2006-009.

Min, Dongchao. 2014. "Toward an Alternative Traveling Theory." *Signs: Journal of Women in Culture and Society* 39, no. 3 (Spring): 584–592. https://doi.org/10.1086/674323.

Mohanty, Chandra Talpade. 1995. "Feminist Encounters: Locating the Politics of Experience." In *Social Postmodernism: Beyond Identity Politics*, edited by Linda Nicholson and Steven Seidman, 68–86. Cambridge: Cambridge University Press.

Moore, Henrietta. 1994. *A Passion for Difference: Essays in Anthropology and Gender*. Bloomington and Indianapolis: Indiana University Press.

Roberts, Margaret E. 2018. *Censored: Distraction and Diversion Inside China's Great Firewall*. Princeton: Princeton University Press.

Rofel, Lisa. 2007. *Desiring China: Experiments in Neoliberalism, Sexuality, and Public Culture*. Durham, NC: Duke University Press.

Spakowski, Nicola. 2011. "'Gender' Trouble: Feminism in China Under the Impact of Western Theory and the Spatialization of Identity." *positions: east asia cultures critiques* 19, no. 1 (Spring): 31–54. https://doi.org/10.1215/10679847-2010-023.

Spakowski, Nicola. 2018. "Socialist Feminism in Postsocialist China." *positions: east asia cultures critique* 26, no. 4 (November): 561–592. https://doi.org/10.1215/10679847-7050478.

Suchland, Jennifer. 2011. "Is Postsocialism Transnational?" *Signs* 36, no. 4 (Summer): 837–862. https://doi.org/10.1086/658899.

Suchland, Jennifer. 2015. *Economies of Violence: Transnational Feminism, Postsocialism, and the Politics of Sex Trafficking*. Durham, NC: Duke University Press.

Tlostanova, Madina. 2012. "Postsocialist ≠ Postcolonial? On Post-Soviet Imaginary and Global Coloniality." *Journal of Postcolonial Writing* 48, no. 2 (May): 130–142. https://doi.org/10.1080/17449855.2012.658244.

Tlostanova, Madina, Suruchi Thapar-Björkert, and Redi Koobak. 2019. "The Postsocialist 'Missing Other' of Transnational Feminism?" *Feminist Review* no. 121 (March): 81–87. https://doi.org/10.1177/0141778918816946.

Wang, Zheng. 2004. *Yuejie: Kuawenhua Nüquan Shijian [Crossing Borders: Transcultural Feminist Practices]*. Tianjin: Tianjin Renmin Publishing House.

Zhu, Shanjie. 2011. "'Yazhou de zuoyi sixiang yu nüxingzhuyi: Huigu yu zhanwang' gongzuofang zongshu" [Summary of the Workshop on 'Asian Left-Wing Thought and Feminism: Retrospect and Prospect']. *Shanxi Shifan Daxue xuebao* no. 4 (July): 150–154.

Chapter 18

Gendered nationalism in India and Poland

Postcolonial and postsocialist conditions in times of populism

Kasia Narkowicz and Mithilesh Kumar

Introduction

All intellectual collaborations have an autobiography. Similarly, all knowledge productions are embedded within a given time and space. This particular essay has been challenging in the sense that it was written when the phenomenon it seeks to study was still evolving and remains so as well as the advent of pandemic of Covid-19 globally, which has forced us to rethink some of the basic assumptions of contemporary social sciences. This is true especially in the case of analysis of nation-states and their relevance in the period of globalisation. The pandemic brought the nation-state, already in ascendance on the back of conservative nationalism, firmly at the centre of analysis as a primary locus of political power. The impulse of this chapter and the authors was the conviction that the experiences of postcolonial and postsocialist nation-states around the issues of citizenship, nationalism, and emergence of majoritarian identity politics provides a vantage point for an analysis that reveals the conjunctures of political power and praxis in the Global South and Eastern Europe. This conjuncture has the potential to create the possibility for a spread of decolonial politics which was essentially seen as a movement restricted to erstwhile colonies and rarely Europe not too long ago.

This chapter is about nationalist politics aimed at excluding the nations' Others in India and Poland. The choice of studying the political conjunctures of these two countries is not merely idiosyncratic depended on the putative nationalities of the authors of this chapter. The historical experience of both Central Eastern Europe and the Indian Subcontinent point towards definite processes of colonisation, partition, war, and nation-state formation. The contemporary experiences with relation to the question of refugees, immigration, gender rights, and religious identities especially in case of religious minorities have interesting points of convergence.

In this chapter, through the study of a nationwide popular protest against amendment to citizen laws in India primarily led by Muslim women and the political discourse around refugees, immigrants and Muslims in Poland, we discuss how the bodies of the "alien" and the "foreigner" are rendered dangerous and malignant to the nation's body politic. The chapter is based on a critical discourse analysis of media coverage, policy- and public documents, such as the Polish migration policy and the Indian Citizenship (Amendment) Act. Also, we trace the genealogy of right-wing populism to understand its emergence in the foundational moments of the nation-state. A particular focus is directed at how women's bodies become central to these mobilisations, adding to the already existing work on gender and the global right (Graff, Kapur, and Walters 2019). Our contribution seeks to tease out how the internal terrors of each nation-state take centre stage under populist right-wing political regimes and what role gender plays in the control and exclusion of bodies through sexual-racial biopolitical management of lives and deaths.

Postcolonial and postsocialist dialogues and the re-entrance of populist right-wing nationalism

> *How might thinking between the posts clarify the biopolitics of modern racisms in various contexts, and what possibilities might such analysis suggest for anti-racist and democratic political imaginings in the present?*
>
> (Chari and Verdery 2009, 25)

In this section we briefly sketch out the historical contexts of India and Poland and discuss the recent shift in political rule in both countries following the 2014 and 2015 electoral victories of populist right wing parties: Bharatiya Janata Party (BJP) in India and Prawo i Sprawiedliwość (PiS) in Poland.

India

The foundational moment in India's emergence as a nation-state is unequivocally the partition of the Indian Subcontinent into two nation-states of India and Pakistan in 1947. It should be remembered that this partition and massive forced migration occurred against the backdrop of unprecedented communal violence (Butalia 1998). The constitutional promise of secularism, socialism, justice, and equality emerged from this foundational postcolonial political moment. The argument we are making here is that it is possible to trace the contours of popular politics in India in this moment in the nation-state when communalism, communism, nationalism, and secessionism were in a relationship of overdetermination. It is from these overdetermined relations of mutually contradictory and even hostile political forces and formations that it is possible to trace the two strands of populism – left populism and right populism – that have animated Indian politics from the time of India's independence. We argue that it is possible to divide the political chronology of India into four phases where we can look at four distinct movements in competition between left-wing populism and right-wing populism: the first phase (1947–1975), second phase (1977–1992), third phase (1992–2014), and fourth phase (2014–2020).

The first phase immediately after independence was a period of decolonisation which saw an intense ideological struggle between constituent political currents within the Congress Party. This period saw the version of Nehruvian socialism based on non-alignment in foreign policy, state-led mixed economy with the Indian version of five-year plans in political economy, and secularism based on religious tolerance in social relations as forming the dominant ideology around which the political and intellectual elites of the postcolonial state coalesced (Das 2001). However, there were two major currents which went against this elite consensus. One was the extreme left-wing that proclaimed that independence was counterfeit as the ruling elites were still under the dual dominance of foreign capital and native feudal powers (Ghosh 2013). The culmination of this political current reaches in 1967 in Naxalbari Movement which galvanised a large section of peasants and lower middle-class intellectuals. This current exists as the Maoist Movement under various political formations and is now under tremendous decline. The other current was the Hindutva nationalist political current which saw independence as betrayal too because *Akhand Bharat* (United India) was not attained and the ruling elite was seen to have compromised by agreeing to the partition of India. It is this current which culminates in the formation of the Bharatiya Janata Party (BJP). It does so on the social and cultural level through the Rashtriya Swayamsevak Sangh (RSS) which remains the parent organisation and operates in the field of electoral politics through the BJP (Andersen and Damle 2018). It is as a result of this dynamic and evolving relationship between institutional social activism of RSS through a massive network of several grassroot organisations and electoral politics through the BJP that right-wing populism of Hindutva in India appears to be more stable, deeply entrenched, and hugely legitimate in the polity than other right-wing counterparts elsewhere around the globe. This first phase lasts until the declaration of emergency in 1975, which remains in Indian political history a singular political event of state oppression and suppression of opposition.

The second phase and the third phase are marked by a continuation of identity politics separated by a radical shift in political economy with the advent of globalisation in 1991. Of course, it is an extremely schematic and stylised account of vast vicissitudes in politics and social movement. However, there is also more than just a grain of truth when we say that these phases were marked by assertion of dignity and identity in terms of caste, gender, ethnicity, language, and even ecological movements finding articulation largely within the vocabulary of identity movements. These phases also were similar in the sense that the dominant mode of popular movement was based on the vocabulary of rights. This period also saw a gradual and incessant decline of working-class politics with only a few and sporadic movements breaking through onto the political centre stage. The culmination of the second phase is the demolition of the Babri mosque in 1992 (Singh 2018). In this phase, the BJP enters into various electoral alliances increasing its political footprint across the country but really embraces populist politics with the movement against the mosque, which was at once a social, cultural, and political movement. The third phase is marked by some of the boldest innovations in neo-liberal governmentality under the Congress regime (1999–2014), where rights-based discourse propelled by market economy became the elite consensus. This phase ended with coming into power of the BJP under the leadership of the Prime Minister Narendra Modi.

There are two reasons why the fourth phase is shown to be ending abruptly after the relatively short period of six years in 2020. The first one is the Shaheen Bagh Movement discussed in detail below. The second is the laying of the foundation stone of the Ram Temple at the site where Babri mosque stood till 1992. During this period, the political arrangement in Jammu and Kashmir has been changed irretrievably, and triple *talaq* has been abolished and the act made a criminal offense. These two issues also found resonance in the Shaheen Bagh Movement. We discuss both issues in relation to gendered nationalism below.

The point we are trying to make through this rather, admittedly, quaint chronology is to demonstrate how right-wing Hindutva nationalism is not an aberration but something that is foundational to the way in which nation-state has evolved and politics and governance conducted. Similarly, in Poland, the right-wing nationalism that has now truly established itself across political and public discourse has roots that go back to the formation of the Polish state. We focus next on the period of the Partitions in the CEE region and subsequent state formation to point to how colonial and exclusionary ideas of Polish nationalism were formed and have now resurfaced.

Poland

Central and Eastern Europe has always had a precarious relationship with Euro-peanness and the West (Buchowski 2006). This will be discussed through a focus on four phases; Partitions (1772–1918), Communism (1945–1989), EU accession (2004), and the aftermath of the 2015 electoral victory of PiS. The region has historically been imagined as lesser Europe, including by prominent thinkers such as Hegel who have narrated Eastern Europe as subordinate, backward, and irrational and as contributing little to world history and Enlightenment (Tibebu 2011). Ideas around "catching up" with the West were already being formulated during Partition and, together with themes of colonisation, remained central in the formation of a Polish national identity that reverberates today.

The Partition of Poland (then the Polish-Lithuanian Commonwealth) lasted over a century from the end of 18th century, when the country was split between Russia, Prussia and Austria, until 1918 when Poland regained independence as a state. The ambition among Polish nationalists who formed the National Demo-cratic Movement (Endecja) was partly to resist a colonial overtake of Polish territory and partly to find a place for Poland in the global capitalist economy (Snochowska-Gonzales 2020). During this period, the movement for Polish sovereignty against Russian and German colonisation of Poland as well as plans of colonisation of overseas territories were formed. The leader of Endecja, nationalist Roman Dmowski, set out to unite "the Polish body and soul" by uniting Poles in partitioned Poland with the masses that had already emigrated (Snochowska-Gonzales 2020, 112). As Claudia Snochowska-Gonzales (2020) shows through analysis of the early writings of the Endecja movement, Polish colonialism was more a fantasy than an actual plan of overtaking other countries militarily, economically, and culturally (Snochowska-Gonzales 2020; Ureña Valerio 2019). Even after Poland regained independence and made moves towards establishing colonies in Africa in the 1930, it was unsuccessful (Balogun 2018). Instead, as Snochowska-Gonzales argues (2020, 128), what became central to the nationalist movement was the manufacturing of "a dynamic, masculine subject proudly entering the world of modernity". Racial thinking was also central to the early nationalist thought in Poland, focusing on establishing racial hierarchies between the Poles and the Polish Jews who were Othered and described as "mould" and "parasite" that was polluting the Polish body. These themes are returning today in the racial Othering of Muslims. Muslims in India comprise around 14% of the population, while in Poland it is less than 0.1%, although Poles believe that the number is closer to 10% and growing (Narkowicz and Pędziwiatr 2017c).

From 1945 to 1989, the Polish People's Republic (PRL) was a satellite of Soviet Russia. This period has been recognised as another colonisation, with Soviet Russia acting as a coloniser, or as a semi-coloniser since Poland was officially an independent state, but its internal and international politics were profoundly controlled by the leaders of the Soviet bloc countries (Mayblin, Piekut, and Valentine 2016). As Chari and Verdery (2009, 15) argue, the incorporation of countries in Central Europe into the Soviet empire was aimed to create a "buffer zone" that separated the Soviet imperial territory from Western Europe and the "polluting effects" of capitalism. The creation of Central Europe as a distinctive entity also allowed Poland and its neighbours to construct distance from a Slavdom that was less desirable than the West which Poland aspired to be closer to, thus rejecting its position in the European East (Todorova 1997; Janion 2006; Hagen 2003).

The European Union accession in 2004 is another significant point when Poland's position in Europe shifted and impacted its sense of national identity. Leaving its fellow ex-Soviet neighbours behind and making what seemed to be a long sought-after step towards the West, this journey was already predicated on an uneven hierarchical relationship. Debates around EU accession were split between liberals, who couldn't wait to become Europeans and rid themselves of their Polishness, and right-wing conservatives who with equal passion wanted to defend the national identity against foreign threat. As Maria Janion (2011, 2) describes the process, joining the EU was imagining as "defending another Ordon's Redoubt". "Ordon's Redoubt" (Reduta Ordona) is a name of a poem about the last line of defence against the Russian Empire during the Polish uprising by Romantic poet Adam Mickiewicz. Interestingly, the very same redoubt became one of the reasons for opposition to a mosque in a Warsaw neighbourhood in 2010 where the redoubt apparently was stationed – again, serving as a symbol of defending Polishness against foreign threat, whether European or Muslim. The parallel discourses of Poland as on the one hand always lagging behind the West but on the other hand being morally superior and, in contrast to Western countries, able to resist "Islamisation" of their country have gathered strength since 2015. The election that saw the populist right come to power was largely underpinned by exclusionary ideas of strengthening Polish Catholic identity, building borders, and keeping out (Muslim) immigrants. Such visible tensions around Muslims in Poland started around the mosque conflict and has since intensified. This marked a sudden shift from a long history of predominantly peaceful relationships between the Christian and Muslim communities stretching back to the 14th century to a climate in which Muslim presence is considered with increased suspicion, mirroring the global intensification of Islamophobic discourse (Narkowicz and Pędziwiatr 2017c).

The 2015 election victory of the PiS meant a shift to right-wing politics in the country and further deepening of anti-Muslim rhetoric. Like the Indian case, the new ruling party promoted a nationalist politics that aimed to cleanse itself of unwanted foreign intervention. The enemy here was partly the liberal elite of Brussels (EU) and its Western-gazing allies, and partly the refugees hovering at European borders. While Poland needed both, the government took drastic steps to assert its anti-colonial stance through refusing the previously agreed EU quota on the number of refugees to be accepted into Poland and, what is more, banned all Muslim refugees from entering the country (Narkowicz 2018). The justification used was fear of a terrorist attack posed by Muslims if they were welcomed to Poland. The security arguments were frequently weaved in with more openly racialised comments about refugees. For example, the leader of the Law and Justice party, Jarosław Kaczyński, issued a statement in which he warned of the danger of disease that could be brought in with the refugees (Rettman 2015). This of course echoes the earlier Endecja's anti-Semitic rhetoric that has now shifted focus. In 2016, a year after the Polish election, the Endecja movement made a re-entrance to Polish politics with the aim of re-invigorating the core ideas of nationalist Roman Dmowski. Even today colonial rhetoric is central to the movement that fights against Polish subordination and colonial condition and continues to evoke biopolitics by re-focusing on building a strong national body, cleansed of those considered to be polluting it. While the 19th century Endecja excluded Jews as un-assimilable and parasitical, the Endecja of the 21st century focuses on the exclusion of Muslims from its body politic. One of the leaders of the movement, also the President of the far-right nationalist All-Polish Youth organisation, spoke about Islam as civilisationally different and in conflict with "our European civilisation". The central justifications for Islam's perceived backwardness were gender and the rights of women. This discourse gathers prominence among the populist right-wing in the midst of the country's withdrawal (at the time of writing) from the Istanbul Convention on preventing and combating violence against women and domestic violence. Women's rights being invoked like this by the patriarchal right-wing in Poland is a prime example of femonationalism, where gender is strategically evoked for racist purposes (Farris 2017).

The increasing popularity of right-wing nationalism with its focus to reimagine the nation as purely Hindu and Catholic, respectively, cleansed of "foreign invasion", is part of a broader "anti-colonial" movement in the sense that they lay a claim on an imagined pristine and glorious past of sovereign nationhood based on religious and racial identity, which has taken centre stage in right-wing politics of both the BJP and the PiS but that, as we observed earlier, harkens back to the colonial history of each context. These discourses, noticeable in both India and Poland, while remaining Western-oriented, simultaneously resist Western imposition in their anti-colonial politics, viewed as EU paternalism, often by restricting the role of foreign-funded NGOs. Below, we explore the ways that each nations' Others are excluded through gendered techniques.

Femonationalism in Poland and India

In this chapter, we draw on the concept of "femonationalism" developed by Sara Farris (2017) and inspired by Jasbir Puar's (2007) term "homonationalism" to make sense of the role that feminist discourses play in anti-immigration/refugee/Muslim political discourses in Poland and India. Femonationalism encompass processes whereby women's rights are invoked in order to further nationalist, racist, anti-immigration politics. The relationship between women's rights and racist discourses is a complex web of collusions that has a long history, prominent not least within the early women's movement in the context of slavery (Davis 2011). Femonationalism has the support of distinctive and often politically and ideologically opposed groups, such as the nationalist far-right and the liberals, who reproduce colonial rhetoric of saving women from brown men (Spivak 1988; Abu-Lughod 2002; Bhattacharyya 2008; Bracke 2012; Thapar-Björkert and Tlostanova 2018). In this chapter we focus primarily on groups that are not the likely champions of women's rights and who, on the contrary, often lobby against what they call a "gender ideology" that according to them undermines traditional (religious) values (Korolczuk 2020; Verloo 2018). This is part of a wider trend of "global antifeminism" that feminist scholars have already observed in the United States, Brazil, and across Europe (Graff, Kapur, and Walters 2019). Despite being opposed to feminism, the global political right invokes women's rights discourses, particularly in their opposition to immigration and to Muslim migrants. As such, the tired discourses of saving (brown) women from brown men are recycled.

Anti-refugee and anti-immigrant discourses more generally, and security and gender more specifically, feature heavily in both countries' exclusion practices, representing ideas about threat to women's safety and by extension, the safety of the nation. It also reinforces control over women's bodies by positing Muslim refugees as threats to the respectability and security of Polish Catholic and Indian Hindu women. In both countries, it works at the dual rhetorical level of liberating Muslim women from Islamic patriarchy and protecting the honour of the Hindu/

Catholic women who are lured by Muslim men through what is in India termed "Love-Jihad". The focus is on the control and protection of women's bodies as reproducers of the Polish (Catholic) and Indian (Hindu) nation. Both countries place strong emphasis on idealised motherhood (Hill Collins 2005; Yuval-Davis 1997) with Mother Poland and Mother India framing national identity of each country (Janion 2006; Dasgupta 2019). Patriarchal ideas about the centrality of women's role in the reproduction and maintenance of borders is part of efforts to re-build the nation in its purer form, reconstructing an idea of what it once was (Mostov 2012), or imagined to be. Historically, efforts to maintain boundaries that relied on the mobilisation of gendered narratives were prominent already in the post-Civil War Reconstruction era in the United States when former slaves were making claims to the public sphere as citizens, yet their attempts at suffrage were increasingly challenged with racist ideas of black criminality (Davis 2011). The myth of the "black peril" was constructed around ideas of white female vulnerability as well as her purity which translated to the responsibility of keeping the nation white (Ware 2015). Today in India and Poland, the myth of the black rapist is resurfacing with the Muslim male body posing as primary threat to women's purity and the nation. In this way we situate the engagement with women's rights discourses on the side of the populist nationalists in both Poland and India as a continuation of racial exclusions justified in threat of violence against women (Graff, Kapur, and Walters 2019).

Patriarchal nations saving women from Muslim men

The manner in which femonationalism plays itself in the Indian context under the Hindutva rule is two-fold. There is the rising and awakening of the Hindu women embodied in the discourse of the *Bharat Mata* (Mother India) rising to claim her rightful place after the "centuries of cultural oppression" by Muslim and British rule, both identified as foreign. This rhetoric is evident in the case of the Ram Temple Movement. Yet this awakening is within the rule set up by the patriarchal nation-state. In the case of Central and Eastern Europe, feminist scholars have argued that the "anti-colonial" move by right-wing parties has little to do with colonialism and simply opposes what it refers to as arrogance of liberal elites (Korolczuk and Graff 2018). Yet there is more to the popularity of anti-colonial rhetoric in postsocialist countries than simply an appropriation of anti-colonialism. Almost three decades after postsocialist countries underwent Western-imposed shock therapy with neoliberal policies aimed to transform the economy, those groups that did not benefit from the transformation have become increasingly critical of the continuous catching-up rhetoric that they see dictated by the West, and particularly the EU. A symbolic tipping point seems to have been the EU quotas on refugee reception that the 2015 election campaign monopolised on. Growing numbers of people found themselves supporting a nationalist agenda promoted by the ruling party and its far-right allies that had as goal closing off borders to Muslim refugees and reasserting a patriarchal order amidst growing calls for gender equality. In Poland, the debates around Muslims as ultimate Others and the justification of these discourses in narratives of women's rights became more pronounced in the simultaneous context of the refugee crisis and the victory of the right-wing nationalist party PiS in 2015. In India, the victory of the BJP in 2014 ushered in a more directed campaign at curbing the rights of Muslims within the nation as well as Muslim refugees as was seen in the case of Rohingyas. Contemporary nationalistic politics of the two parties, PiS and BJP, invoke women's rights in order to further their political goal towards Catholic and Hindu nations respectively. The connecting elements, also visible in other national contexts, is a focus on violence or the potential of violence to women of the country (Polish Catholic women and Indian Hindu women) where the perpetrator is racialised and Othered. In the cases of India and Poland, the threat to women's safety is posed by the Muslim man. In this set up, both the Polish and Indian right are able to construct traditional religious patriarchal masculinity as the ultimate protectors of "their" women and thus undermine feminist work towards greater gender equality between the sexes. We draw next on examples from Poland's migration policy and its response to the refugee crisis, and India's Citizenship Amendment Act (CAA), the events that unfolded in Shaheen Bagh in response to the CAA.

Poland

"The reception of Muslim immigrants is a greater security threat in Poland, especially for women." (Anna Maria Siarkowska, member of conservative movement Kukiz'15 in 2016).

Femonationalistic narratives run through policy, media, and popular culture in Poland. Gendered narratives, doing the work of justifying Poland's role in criminalising migrants' bodies and passing it off as equality work, point to an inherent tension to the nationalist "anti-colonial" project currently promoted by the PiS government. On the one hand, Euroscepticism and a distaste of liberal Western values is core to the state project of taking back control from what is perceived as foreign interference in a country that has always been narrated as in, but not quite part of, Europe (Hall 1992). On the other hand, and in order to justify the criminalisation of racialised migrant bodies as threat to the nation, the government embraces as its own the European civilisational rhetoric of women's liberation. A shift in right-wing discourse from religious language of morality to one of human rights has been understood by feminist scholars as a strategic move (Korolczuk 2020). Gender and sexual politics are central themes in the current government's nationalist project, usually as part of a mission to resist progressive politics on abortion and gay rights, also understood by the right as threat to children, women, and "traditional values" (Korolczuk 2020). Yet when the threat is an ultimate racialised outsider, gender equality is also evoked as a moral justification of the exclusion of the Other.

Discourses of danger attached to bodies of migrants, refugees, and Muslims (often considered as interchangeable and homogenous) run through the Polish society, from public attitudes to media stories and government policy. In the media, migrant/refugee/Muslim Others are frequently represented through orientalised discourses of invasion of Poland and Europe (Kotras 2017), often and paradoxically treated as one and the same by the Euro-sceptic government. In the context of the "refugee crisis" in 2015, right-wing magazines *wSieci* and *DoRzeczy* published stories with headlines such as: "They are invaders not refugees" (Pędziwiatr 2017). Within these racialised representations there is a link to gender and the subtext is that the migrants will pollute the white Catholic nation. The 2016 sexual assaults on New Year's Eve in Germany's public spaces served as a convenient trigger to populist right-wing debates on the assimilability and commitment to gender equality of the new migrants (Vieten 2018). One of the right-wing magazines published a story that made global headlines called the "Islamic Rape of Europe" [*Islamski Gwałt na Europe*]. On the cover was a white, blond-haired woman dressed in an EU flag, screaming, because hands of brown men were assaulting her by ripping apart the EU flag. Such representations of threat to white women by "dangerous brown men" (Bhattacharyya 2008) are familiar to the Western European vocabulary and have long been an important component of Western imperialism (Kuntsman, Haritaworn, and Petzen 2010). In 2014, the right-wing Catholic magazine *Fronda*, known for their anti-feminist politics, ran a section on Islam and gender which has become a common feature of both right-wing and liberal groups in Poland since the early 2010s. On the cover was a woman covered in a black burqa holding a gun (echoing narratives of threat) and inside the magazine were stories about women's liberation evoking the familiar saving narratives. The magazine argued that "Arab girls . . . know that it is only in Europe that they will be respected" (Narkowicz and Pędziwiatr 2017a). Similarly, orientalised narratives of Muslim women's journeys from oppression to freedom, or from Islamic culture to Western culture, are popular bestsellers in Polish bookshops. These themes are now creeping into official government legislation.

Polish migration policy has in recent years increasingly focussed on securitisation of borders, immigration, and Islamic radicalisation. Despite the very small numbers of Muslims living in Poland, public attitudes towards them are generally hostile, which maps on to the extremely exaggerated sense among the Polish public of the numbers of Muslims in the country (Narkowicz and Pędziwiatr 2017b). In June 2019, a draft of the PiS government's new migration policy was published with a disproportionate attention focussed on safety concerns around immigration and Islam (Pedziwiatr 2019). A particular focus was placed on perceived cultural differences of Muslims and ways in which this poses a threat to gender equality in Poland and Europe. Again, a commitment to women's rights imagined to be enshrined in Polish/European/Western culture is interesting here considering the aforementioned Polish resistance to an international convention on the prevention of violence against women. The migration policy refers to the need for control of migrant inflow from "Africa and some Asian countries" and of migrant assimilation, portraying Muslim migrants as culturally alien and incapable of integration. The document reads: "It seems that there are particular difficulties associated with the admission and integration of the followers of Islam" (MSWiA 2019, 48). Even here gender is brought in to make sense of the ambition to limit the presence of Muslim bodies in Poland. The policy reads, for example, that the "different culture" of potential migrants is a factor of concern, particularly in connection to the impact of "traditional gender roles" on labour participation which is inconsistent with the nationalist politics that the PiS government has led since 2015 that have focussed on attacking what is seen as a "gender ideology". As part of the increased anti-gender agenda the ruling party has emphasised traditional family values of the heterosexual family and has heavily critiqued feminist politics (Korolczuk and Graff 2018). As Vieten (2018) has argued in the case of Germany, violence against women becomes problematised when the perpetrator is non-white and non-Christian. Considering the ongoing government onslaught on gender equality in Poland, the co-optation of feminist vocabulary might seem contradictory, yet is consistent with the broader ways in which femonationalism functions on a global scale.

India

In India, an interesting political move, which has elements of similarity and distinctiveness from the Polish case, is an attempt to provide and create a gendered and segregated space for women of the Muslim community within the body politic. This is evident in the so-called "triple *talaq*" issue, where the incumbent nationalist government, following the judgment by the Supreme Court of India, declared a criminal offence the customary practice of divorce by Muslims in India through three utterances of *talaq* (divorce) by men. The government introduced the Muslim Women (Protection of Rights on Marriage) Bill in 2019. The Act not only deemed the practice illegal in keeping with the judgment of the Supreme Court but also criminalised the practice in which legal provisions were made to prosecute the erring husband with an imprisonment of up to three years. This was widely critiqued as a malevolent attempt to render criminal Muslim men for what was simply a civil offense. The government on the other hand claimed that there has been a decrease of 82% in the cases of triple *talaq* (The Hindu 2020). Triple *talaq* was done deploying a strident rhetoric of gender justice in a religious community that was portrayed as deeply orthodox if not fundamentalist. At once, this move made clear the distinction between women belonging to majority Hindu community with putative legal rights and the Muslim women who were devoid of such rights and must be protected by the state against the orthodoxies of their community. Even with rights, there is a differential relation between the state and Muslim women in this case. Also, in this move, the implicit assumption is that of a religiously aggressive and pathologically fundamentalist men of Muslim community that need to be kept at bay in much the same way as infiltrators and illegal immigrants at the border. Muslim patriarchy becomes, in this state-sponsored gender justice discourse, an insider-infiltrator of the body politic of the nation. The similarity between the illegal immigrant as a parasite and termite with the citizen-Muslim is complete. The Shaheen Bagh Movement turns this discourse on its head by making the claim that the way the BJP-led Indian government has defined illegal immigrant exclusively in terms of her identity as a Muslim bearing the scars of the political and territorial partition of India, actually is the first illegal act, morally and constitutionally mala fide. The Shaheen Bagh Movement then sees itself as foundational in a sense that it radically wants to break the aporia that underscored the overdetermined relations of political forces at the moment of political freedom of India, which we alluded to in the beginning. When the protest against the Citizenship Law began the implementation of triple *talaq* was constantly invoked by the protesters as a proof that the government at the centre is threatening Muslim identity. It is clear that gender especially the discourse on women's rights have found qualified acceptance in the larger Hindutva ideology as it simultaneously can control the extent of Hindu women's participation in the public sphere and can through state action intervene in the "personal laws" of the minority community, a practice that is embedded in Indian politics.

The movement against CAA at Shaheen Bagh, a neighbourhood in Delhi, started on 14 December 2019 immediately after clashes between students of Jamia Milia Islamia, a university in Delhi, and the Delhi police over the passing of the Citizenship (Amendment) Act, 2019, in the parliament. According to this amendment:

> Any person belonging to Hindu, Sikh, Buddhist, Jain, Parsi or Christian community from Afghanistan, Bangladesh or Pakistan, who entered into India on or before the 31st day of December, 2014 and who has been exempted by the Central Government by or under clause (c) of sub-section (2) of section 3 of the Passport (Entry into India) Act, 1920 or from the application of the provisions of the Foreigners Act, 1946 or any rule or order made thereunder, shall not be treated as illegal migrant for the purposes of this Act.

This amendment also mentioned that these immigrants "shall be deemed to be a citizen of India from the date of his entry into India". This was a momentous decision that sought to radically challenge the political consensus, explicit and implicit, around the issues of granting citizenship. India is not a signatory of the 1951 Refugee Convention and has exercised autonomy in providing asylum, care, and citizenship. These have been informed by complex calculation of politics and governmentality (Samaddar 2003) giving the regime of citizenship a degree of flexibility in the Indian context. This stance is also a result of the peculiar condition of the Indian Subcontinent where creation of nation-states following a partition has been witnessed twice and borders between nation-states for all purposes are increasingly porous.

The protest at Shaheen Bagh should be seen as the culmination of the contradictions of nation, citizenship, and gender in the biography of the Indian Nation (Samaddar 2001). The immediate reason for the protest was the Citizenship Law but a closer look at the composition of the protesters makes it clear that it not only brought together at a given space several strands of established oppositional politics but also indicated towards some emerging trends in the formation of oppositional politics. The fact that this movement was constituted mainly by the presence of Muslim women added to the radical nature of the political movement. The Shaheen Bagh Movement and its replication across India should be seen as the claim on constitution, citizenship, and politics by a group that has increasingly been made redundant in the arena of electoral politics. Abhay Kumar Dubey, in his work *Hindu-Ekta Banam Gyan ki Rajneeti* (2019), has made a powerful claim that the social engineering done by the Hindutva forces that is in power today in India, where it has been successful in combining disparate identities under the larger Hindu umbrella, has led to such a large-scale consolidation of Hindu votes that it is no longer important for them to take into account the demands of the Muslim communities. In a way, this is disenfranchisement of an entire community through a precise calculation. In other words, the politics of election has been turned deftly into a politics of population and governmentality. It was this political calculation that Shaheen Bagh Movement challenged. The fact that Shaheen Bagh Movement to a great degree was against this disenfranchisement and the fact of being pushed away from the electoral arena that the claim on Constitution of India by the protesters took on an immediate and urgent articulation. Ranabir Samaddar has powerfully argued about this movement as the fifth moment of insurgent constitutionalism in India starting from the First War of Indian Independence in 1857 (Samaddar 2020). Also, unlike other insurgent movements either Maoist or Sub-nationalist, the women protesters of Shaheen Bagh firmly located their struggle within the constitutional fold, thereby making the movement within the "prescribed" and "tolerated" forms of claim-making (Tilly 2006). The fact that the government could not find a solution to the impasse and it took an organised communal riot and the pandemic to remove the protesters from the site is a clear indication that the Hindutva government was unable to resolve the political dilemmas for the state inherent in the movement. It is for this reason we are calling the movement an unfinished challenge.

Conclusion

This chapter explored postcolonial and postsocialist conjunctures by exploring contemporary expressions of gendered nationalism and femonationalism in India and Poland. Through the analysis of media coverage, policy- and public documents focusing on cases of triple *talaq*, CAA, and Shaheen Bagh (India) and the refugee ban and the new migration policy (Poland), we teased out the anti-Muslim sentiments at the centre of exclusionary politics of current-day populist governments. By tracing the genealogies of right-wing thinking and evolution of national identity in the two countries, we are able to find convergences between postcolonial and postsocialist countries under study, particularly in the ways that they make use of gendered techniques. This chapter contributes to existing work on dialogues across the postcolonial and postsocialist world by bringing together two seemingly different national contexts in dialogue, connecting both their colonial histories and their current gendered mobilisations. Going forward the challenge is to explore resistance to these overlapping right-wing developments and forge meaningful decolonial global politics across postcolonial and postsocialist conditions.

References

Abu-Lughod, L. 2002. "Do Muslim Women Really Need Saving? Anthropological Reflections on Cultural Relativism and Its Others." *American Anthropologist* 104, no. 3: 783–790.

Andersen, W., and S. Damle. 2018. *RSS: A View to the Inside*. Gurgaon: Penguin Viking.

Balogun, B. 2018. "Polish Lebensraum: The Colonial Ambition to Expand on Racial Terms." *Ethnic and Racial Studies* 41, no. 14: 2561–2579.

Bhattacharyya, G. 2008. *Dangerous Brown Men: Exploiting Sex, Violence and Feminism in the War on Terror*. London: Zed Books.

Bracke, S. 2012. "From 'Saving Women' to 'Saving Gays': Rescue Narratives and Their Dis/continuities." *European Journal of Women's Studies* 19, no. 2: 237–252.

Buchowski, M. 2006. "The Specter of Orientalism in Europe: From Exotic Other to Stigmatized Brother." *Anthropological Quarterly* 79, no. 3: 463–482.

Butalia, U. 1998. *The Other Side of Silence: Voices from the Partition of India*. Delhi: Viking.

Chari, S., and K. Verdery. 2009. "Thinking Between the Posts: Postcolonialism, Postsocialism, and Ethnography After the Cold War." *Comparative Studies in Society and History* 51, no. 1: 6–34.

Das, S. 2001. "The Nehru Years in Indian Politics." *Edinburgh Papers in South Asian Studies* no. 16.

Dasgupta, S. 2019. *Awakening Bharat Mata: The Political Beliefs of the Indian Right*. Gurgaon: Penguin Viking.

Davis, A. Y. 2011. *Women, Race, & Class*. New York: Vintage Books.

Dubey, A. K. 2019. *Hind-Ekta Banam Gyan Ki Rajneeti*. New Delhi: Vani Prakshan.

Farris, S. 2017. *In the Name of Women's Rights: The Rise of Femonationalism*. Durham, NC: Duke University Press.

Ghosh, S. 2013. *The Indian Big Bourgeoisie: Its Genesis, Growth, and Character*. Kolkata: Radical Impression.

Graff, A., R. Kapur, and S. Walters. 2019. "Introduction: Gender and the Rise of the Global Right." *Signs: Journal of Women in Culture and Society* 44, no. 3: 541–560.

Hagen, J. 2003. "Redrawing the Imagined Map of Europe: The Rise and Fall of the 'Center'." *Political Geography* 22, no. 5: 489–517.

Hall, S. 1992. "The West and the Rest: Discourse and Power." In *Formations of Modernity*, edited by Stuart Hall and Bram Gieben, 275–331. Oxford: Polity Press and Blackwell.

Hill Collins, P. 2005. "Producing the Mothers of the Nation: Race, Class and Contemporary US Population Policies." In *Women, Citizenship and Difference*, edited by N. Yuval-Davis and P. Werbner, 118–129. New Delhi: Zubaan.

The Hindu. 2020. "About 82% Decline in Triple Talaq Cases Since Law Enacted by Modi Govt: Naqvi," July 22, 2020. www.thehindu.com/news/national/about-82-decline-in-triple-talaq-cases-since-law-enacted-by-modi-govt-naqvi/article32160348.ece.

Janion, M. 2006. *Niesamowita Słowiańszczyzna*. Kraków: Wydawnictwo Literackie.

Janion, M. 2011. "Farewell to Poland? The Uprising of a Nation." *Baltic Worlds*, 4: 4–14.

Korolczuk, E. 2020. "Counteracting Challenges to Gender Equality in the Era of Anti-Gender Campaigns: Competing Gender Knowledges and Affective Solidarity." *Social Politics: International Studies in Gender, State & Society*, 1–24.

Korolczuk, E., and A. Graff. 2018. "Gender as 'Ebola from Brussels': The Anticolonial Frame and the Rise of Illiberal Populism." *Signs: Journal of Women in Culture and Society* 43, no. 4: 797–821.

Kotras, M. 2017. "Dyskurs o imigrantach: Strategie argumentacyjne w polskich tygodnikach opinii." *Folia Sociologica* 59: 59–80.

Kuntsman, A., J. Haritaworn, and J. Petzen. 2010. "Sexualising the 'War on Terror'." In *Thinking Through Islamophobia: Global Perspectives*, edited by S. Sayyid and A. K. Vakil. London: Hurst & Co Publishers.

Mayblin, L., A. Piekut, and G. Valentine. 2016. "'Other' Posts in 'Other' Places: Poland Through a Postcolonial Lens?" *Sociology* 50, no. 1: 60–76.

Mostov, J. 2012. "Sexing the Nation/Desexing the Body: Politics of National Identity in the Former Yugoslavia." In *Gender Ironies of Nationalism*, edited by T. Mayer, 103–126. London: Routledge.

MSWiA. 2019. *Polityka Migracyjna Polski*. Zespół do Spraw Migracji. Redakcja: Departament Analiz i Polityki Migracyjnej MSWiA.

Narkowicz, K. 2018. "'Refugees Not Welcome Here': State, Church and Civil Society Responses to the Refugee Crisis in Poland." *International Journal of Politics, Culture, and Society* 31, no. 4: 357–373.

Narkowicz, K., and K. Pędziwiatr. 2017a. "Saving and Fearing Muslim Women in 'Post-Communist' Poland: Troubling Catholic and Secular Islamophobia." *Gender, Place & Culture* 24, no. 2: 288–299.

Narkowicz, K., and K. Pędziwiatr. 2017b. "Why Are Polish People So Wrong About Muslims in Their Country?" *openDemocracy*. www.opendemocracy.net/en/can-europe-make-it/why-are-polish-people-so-wrong-about-muslims-in.

Narkowicz, K., and K. Pędziwiatr. 2017c. "From Unproblematic to Contentious: Mosques in Poland." *Journal of Ethnic and Migration Studies* 43, no. 3: 441–457.

Pędziwiatr, K. 2017. "Islamophobia in Poland. National Report 2016." In *European Islamophobia Report 2016*, edited by Enes Bayrakli and Farid Hafez. Istanbul: SETA.

Pędziwiatr, K. 2019. "The New Polish Migration Policy – False Start." *openDemocracy*. www.opendemocracy.net/en/can-europe-make-it/the-new-polish-migration-policy-false-start/ (accessed October 30, 2019).

Puar, J. 2007. *Terrorist Assemblages: Homonationalism in Queer Times*. Durham, NC: Duke University Press.

Rettman, A. 2015. "Poland: Election Talk on Migrant 'Protozoas' Gets Ugly." *EU Observer*. https://euobserver.com/political/130672 (accessed October 30, 2019).

Samaddar, R. 2001. *A Biography of the Indian Nation, 1947–1997*. New Delhi: Sage.

Samaddar, R., ed. 2003. *Refugees and the State: Practices of Asylum and Care in India, 1947–2000*. New Delhi: Sage.

Samaddar, R. 2020. "An Insurgent Constitutionalism Is Driving Popular Politics in India Today," January 26, 2020. https://thewire.in/politics/an-insurgent-constitutionalism-is-driving-popular-politics-in-india-today.

Singh, V. 2018. *Ayodhya: City of Faith, City of Discord*. New Delhi: Aleph.

Snochowska-Gonzales, C. 2020. "Exercises in Expansion: Colonial Threads in the National Democracy's Turn Toward Discipline." *Praktyka Teoretyczna* 2, no. 36: 105–135.

Spivak, G. C. 1988. "Can the Subaltern Speak?" In *Marxism and the Interpretation of Culture*, edited by C. Nelson and L. Grossberg, 271–313. Urbana and Chicago: University of Illinois Press.

Thapar-Björkert, S., and M. Tlostanova. 2018. "Identifying to Dis-Identify: Occidentalist Feminism, the Delhi Gang Rape Case and Its Internal Others." *Gender, Place & Culture* 25, no. 7: 1025–1040.

Tibebu, T. 2011. *Hegel and the Third World: The Making of Eurocentrism in World History*. Syracuse, NY: Syracuse University Press.

Tilly, C. 2006. *Regimes and Repertoires*. Chicago: University of Chicago Press.

Todorova, M. 1997. *Imagining the Balkans*. Oxford: Oxford University Press.

Ureña, Valerio L. 2019. *Colonial Fantasies, Imperial Realities: Race Science and the Making of Polishness on the Fringes of the German Empire, 1840–1920*. Athens: Ohio University Press.

Verloo, M. 2018. *Varieties of Opposition to Gender Equality in Europe*. New York and London: Routledge.

Vieten, U. M. 2018. "The New Year's 2015/ 2016 Public Sexual Violence Debate in Germany: Media Discourse, Gendered Anti-Muslim Racism and Criminal Law." In *Media, Crime and Racism*, edited by M. Bhatia, S. Poynting, and W. Tufail, 73–92. London: Palgrave Macmillan.

Ware, V. 2015. *Beyond the Pale: White Women, Racism, and History*. London: Verso Books.

Yuval-Davis, N. 1997. *Gender and Nation*. Cambridge: Cambridge University Press.

Index

For Product Safety Concerns and Information please contact our EU
representative GPSR@taylorandfrancis.com
Taylor & Francis Verlag GmbH, Kaufingerstraße 24, 80331 München, Germany